A PRIVATE WAR FOR LOVE AND MONEY

FATHER MATT BOWLES—An American priest sent to the Vatican, not for his piety, but because the war had taught him how to fight. Now a woman might teach him how to love.

LUCIANA SPOLETO—The beautiful blond contessa who had given her life to her cause. But it was time she gave her heart to a man, even one wearing the collar of a priest.

GARARDO SPINA—A ruthless Sicilian assassin known as "Cornos." Everyone feared him—both the men he hunted and the men he worked for.

FATHER WILLIAM MANKOWSKY—So big a man, he was called "the gorilla"; so gentle a priest, he couldn't hurt a lamb; but was he so good a friend that he'd defy his Church and carry out a daring plan?

THE RED WOMAN—Code name for a secret Communist agent placed high in the Vatican itself. His sins were worse than treason, and his treachery the kiss of death for Father Matt Bowles.

VATICAN GOLD

VATICAN GOLD

John Rester Zodrow

A DELL BOOK

Published by
Dell Publishing Co., Inc.
1 Dag Hammarskjold Plaza
New York, New York 10017

Dell ® TM 681510, Dell Publishing Co., Inc.

ISBN: 0-440-19192-0

Printed in the United States of America
First printing—September 1983

*This book is for
John and Leona,
my mother and father,
who gave values to John,
Mary, David, Michael, Ann, Steven,
Marcia, Michele, and Anthony.*

I wish to acknowledge Jeanne Bernkopf, my editor, who endured this novel's every tortuous phase.

And Gina, my wife, from Aspen and Hawaii to Rome and Palos Verdes.

IN MORALS, WHAT BEGINS IN FEAR
USUALLY ENDS IN WICKEDNESS.
FEAR, AS A PRINCIPLE OR AS A
MOTIVE, IS THE BEGINNING OF ALL EVIL.

Mrs. Jameson

THIS IS THE ROOT OF ALL EVIL.

*Motto on
a Vatican coin*

1.

November 29, 1947

The albino drove the white-sidewalled Packard down the West Side Highway, then zoomed past the Statue of Liberty in the harbor.

"Can I see my mother before I go?" Matt Bowles asked him.

"*Nein*, Father," Hans Fullmer answered. He glanced in the rearview at Father Bowles, who was dressed in clerical suit and Roman collar, his athletic body hunched forward on the back seat where he had been told to sit. "The plane is already waiting!"

"I'll go see her." Father William Mankowsky, known as "the gorilla" because of his six feet nine inches and size 22 shoes, was sitting beside Matt. "Don't worry about Agnes, Matthew."

They ran across Schiff Parkway, then over the Williamsburg Bridge to La Guardia Airport. Its sprawling, half-used airfields were the butt of jokes. In 1947 La Guardia was so rarely used it was known as the "millionaires' club" and "Rockefeller's train station." And though he had seen plenty of foreign service as a chaplain, Matt had never flown before. As they passed the series of unused gates and adjoining empty hangars, dirty banks of snow piled against their sides, Matt felt the hair on his arms stand up.

At gate fourteen, at the end of the horseshoe-shaped airport, Fullmer stopped the car at an aluminum hangar. Through its gate, on the brand-new-looking asphalt, stood a four-engine plane, its rear door open, AIR ITALIA printed in red letters on the white and green fuselage, scrapes and dents on its sides; it had seen a lot of service.

Workers in new dark green overalls were handing wood crates from a large truck onto dollies, pushing them toward the boarding stairs, then lifting them up into the plane. Matt thought he recognized several of them as government agents he had seen that morning at the Cardinal's chancery.

The albino jacked open the door and climbed out. Matt and Mankowsky took the cue and followed him. They approached a La Guardia Airport security guard who stood in front of the gate watching the crates move past him. He was a skinny man, a platform shoe on his short right leg. In his hands, he held a clipboard. Fullmer flashed his badge at him.

"Yes, sir!" the guard said. "Now, I just need the signature of a Matthew Bowles and we're set!"

Matt took the proffered pen and signed the guard's clipboard. The guard eyed the priest's wavy brown hair, his light green eyes, square jawline, and muscled hands and thought the man should have been a boxer, a baseball player, something besides a priest. He didn't fit in that black suit.

"Go wait inside if you wish," Fullmer said to Mankowsky, who nodded and went through the gate.

Fullmer turned to Matt. "I ordered a small bag packed for you. A passport is inside the suitcase beneath your seat. Please board the plane now!" He scanned the area quickly, then walked along the Cyclone fence that surrounded gate fourteen, pulling on a pair of black leather gloves.

"Boy, that guy's in a hurry," the guard said to Matt as he took back the clipboard and checked the signature. He motioned with his head toward the DC-6 that was being loaded. "First time in all my years here I don't know what a rig's carryin'. And that's an Italian plane, our enemy, to boot!"

"I don't know much more than you do," Matt answered as he entered the gate.

It had been an incredible day altogether, starting with the

fight he had had with his pastor, Monsignor MacWarten, because Matt had told Mrs. Rymer that she could still love her husband without having another child, especially now that her husband was out of work. MacWarten had weeks before forbidden Matt to preach from the pulpit because of his unorthodox views; now he was threatening to take away Matt's special work with the children of the parish, as well as Matt's discussion groups with adults. The war, MacWarten told him, had made him into a good soldier, but a lousy priest. The Army might have been a place for heroes, but not the priesthood!

Matt had told himself he had to get out of that parish somehow—either that or leave the priesthood entirely. Everything he stood for seemed to be questioned. But he never hoped for this method: a trip to the Vatican as a special emissary from Cardinal Spellman! And all, it seemed, because the Cardinal wanted a couple of strong priests. Matt's Congressional Medal of Honor had won the duty for him: it certainly hadn't come from any other recommendation.

Two hours ago, they had been in the Cardinal's chancery behind St. Patrick's Cathedral, sitting in the two red leather chairs that always faced Cardinal Spellman's altar-sized desk. The "hot seats," they were called. Matt had expected the worst as they waited for the round-faced prelate to finish studying a sheaf of pages before him. Monsignor James Hare, his assistant, was standing behind him, not giving anything away with his faraway Irish eyes.

"Okay, good," Spellman said suddenly. And Matt thought, here it comes. MacWarten's revenge. The Cardinal folded his hands on top of the sheaf of papers and fixed Matt and Father Mankowsky with his piercing blue eyes.

"Let me be quick about it," Spellman said, checking his watch. "There's a shipment of money that has to be delivered to the Vatican. You know our motherland, the holy Vatican, sits squarely inside Italy. In a little more than a month, on January 1, 1948, to be precise, Italy will have its first free elections. The Communists have put together a powerful party. If they win those elections, they get Italy, and control of the Vatican."

He looked over their heads to the albino, Hans Fullmer, who was standing behind them. "Your immediate superior after you leave this room will be Hans Fullmer. Fullmer is head of Vatican Intelligence, which is known as The Special Office for Public Relations. Obey him as you would me.''

The Cardinal picked up the pages filled with figures and banged them straight on the desk. ''Now, Pope Pius XII awaits our help. Fortunately, our government of the United States of America also wishes to see Italy remain a free country. President Truman and Secretary of State George C. Marshall have supplemented our donations from American Catholics. The Holy Father will use all this to aid the Christian Democrats and turn the tide in the elections.''

''Eminence.'' Father Mankowsky frowned. ''I thought Pope Pius's policy was to remain neutral in politics.''

Spellman leaned across the wide desk, his little white hands splayed on its polished surface. ''Father Mankowsky, Pope Pius is a saint, a living saint! He knows what he is doing!''

Mankowsky bowed his head, reproved.

Monsignor Hare said quickly, ''No one must ever know about this shipment.''

''How much are we carrying over to the Holy Father?'' Matt asked him.

''A little over six hundred million dollars,'' Hare said, glancing quickly for approval to Cardinal Spellman, who nodded proudly.

The gorilla whistled in amazement. Matt frowned.

''Against Monsignor MacWarten's better judgment,'' Spellman now intoned as if he were beginning his morning Mass, ''I decided to pick you for this mission, Father Bowles. I picked you, not because you are an exemplary priest, but because you served in the war. You won a Medal of Honor for killing twenty-two Germans. So, if there's any trouble, you'll have to handle it. You know how to fight. If necessary, you can kill a man with your bare hands. You were trained for it.''

An icelike terror lay suddenly in Matt's stomach. It was June 6, 1944, Vierville sur Mer. The cliffs of Colleville. Dog, Easy, Fox and George companies. He was on Omaha Beach again.

The Cardinal leaned slightly forward. ''This will be your last chance to exonerate yourself after your disobedient attitude to Monsignor MacWarten. Do we understand one another?"

"Yes, Eminence," Matt stammered. "It's just . . . I don't seem to fit sometimes . . . anymore."

"You'll find the priest that's in you. You'll make that transition and knuckle under, won't you, Father?"

"Yes, Your Eminence . . . I'm trying."

"Good!" Spellman said, but let a beat intervene before he went on. "And as for you, Father Mankowsky, I chose you because you are the biggest priest we have. After Father Bowles takes the shipment of money to Rome, you will go over on a separate plane for security's sake. We want you to take these sheets listing every serial number of every bill we sent. The Vatican bank will need these ledgers to verify the shipment, necessary for tax credits to our donors."

"When do I go?" Father Mankowsky inquired politely.

" 'Bout a week from now. That will give the Vatican time to tabulate everything and have it ready for the arrival of our records."

The gorilla nodded, his lanky black hair tumbling down over his deep-set eyes.

Monsignor Hare bent quickly and whispered into the Cardinal's ear. Then he straightened and put his hands inside both of his black cassock sleeves.

"One last thing," Spellman said in a voice so low that Matt and Mankowsky had to concentrate to hear him. "This morning I received an urgent phone call from Rabbi Wolf. He informed me there are a number of Jewish refugees starving and stranded in Rome. They are trying to get home to Palestine. Rabbi Wolf has raised a million dollars for their voyage. You, Father Bowles, will carry the money to them in the pouch we will be given."

Spellman stood up as Monsignor Hare pulled out his chair. Matt and the gorilla rose.

"Rabbi Wolf is my good friend," Spellman warned. "Because of that I am helping him out. But if anything happens, I told him . . . anything"—he paused, peering over his round, frameless glasses—"I will swear I have never heard of their money!"

He raised his hands in blessing, and both Matt and the gorilla dropped to their knees.

"*In nomine Patris, Filii et Spiritus Sanctus*," the Cardinal blessed them in a strong voice that filled the mansion's wood-paneled room. "Your plane leaves at four for Rome. Don't fail me. The very life of our Holy Mother Church is at stake!"

The gorilla was standing near the plane with two dark-haired Italians, both in dark green uniforms.

"*Buon giorno, Padre* Bowles," the pilot greeted Matt as he drew near. "I am Genovese." He was about forty, waist thickening toward middle age. "I hear you are the only passenger. Is it first time you fly? Well, not to worry, *Padre*." The pilot expansively swept his arm toward the big aircraft. "This plane can carry seventy passengers, cruise at three hundred miles per hour. The only one of its kind in all Italy!"

"This is Calamari," Genovese said after he had admired his plane a moment longer. "He is copilot. I am Catholic, he is Mason. We argue all the time. But don't worry, we both work for Vatican, fly all the time too."

Calamari was well named. He looked like a string of fried squid. His muscles were thin on his bones, hands skinny. He didn't seem to have the power to control the four brute engines on the massive DC-6. Matt breathed a prayer of thanksgiving that Genovese was in command.

Shouting erupted outside gate fourteen. The entire group turned, and Matt saw two elderly gentlemen in black overcoats arguing with Hans Fullmer. One wore a homburg, the other was bareheaded, hair white. The white-haired one was refusing to hand over a large leather pouch. The F.B.I. workers were standing around, puzzled, trying to make out what was happening.

"You want me to come with you, Matthew?" Mankowsky offered.

"No, stay here."

Matt walked toward the gate. As he approached, he heard the bareheaded old man protest, "But I am Abraham Hamilburg. This is Harry Smirnoff!"

"We know everything," the albino said.

"Then you must give us receipt."

"No receipt! Spellman does you favor, that is all!"

"Please," Abraham Hamilburg said, "we appreciate what you do. Just sign this paper so we may show we ship it?"

"*Bitte*, give the money to me!" Fullmer exploded. He caught hold of the leather pouch and tried to rip it from the old man's arms. Hamilburg's eyes grew wild as he held on.

Matt stepped forward and squeezed the albino's arm.

Fullmer glared, but slowly pulled his hand away. "You should be on the plane already," he said bitterly, his white eyelashes narrowing.

"I'll sign your receipt," Matt said to Hamilburg. "I'm the one taking it over."

"You'll see it gets to L. Spoleto? The address is on this paper," Smirnoff said, holding out a small slip.

Matt borrowed the pen from the crippled guard and signed Hamilburg's receipt pad. Hamilburg handed the pouch to Matt and bowed deeply. "May God protect you," he said.

"*Shalom*," Smirnoff wished Matt, tipping his homburg.

The two old men shuffled to their waiting slate-gray Hudson and climbed in.

Matt walked through the gate, holding the briefcase.

"You are stupid," Fullmer said, catching up to him. "You sign, is legal. The Jewish money exists. You are responsible, remember that! Not me! Not the Vatican!"

Matt stopped at Mankowsky's side. The pilot and copilot had already gone inside the plane.

"Everything okay?" the gorilla asked.

"Fine," Matt said. "This is the money for those people."

The two outboard engines started up. A spume of grayish-blue smoke wafted from both motors, then the propellers churned up the wind. Both priests' black trousers whipped in the backwash.

"Get on *now*!" Fullmer yelled at Matt.

"Good luck, Matthew," the gorilla said, holding out his hand. "Seems like we did this before."

"It's not the same. It was the war then."

For an instant, the two of them were back at New York Harbor where there was a troop steamer waiting instead of an airplane. It was 1942 and the United States had been losing the war. Matt had come to Mankowsky's Upstate New York parish, suitcase in hand. Gorilla Mankowsky was just finishing a baptism, folding his white stole inside St. Christopher's small baptistry. Matt had greeted the big man, laying two fingers on his forehead. It had been their joke for years.

"Hello, Matthew." Mankowsky was chuckling.

In their early seminary days, a Spanish priest from Catalonia, an exchange teacher, full of his own specious analyses of mankind, had stated no one could possibly become a priest unless he could fit at least three fingers on his forehead. Four was best, signifying highest intelligence. The gorilla couldn't fit two.

Matt began flicking his fingers in the baptistry font, stirring the cold, blessed water. "I signed up," he said.

"You're crazy. Why?"

"I don't know. I can't sleep or do anything but worry about us losing."

After Matthew's basic training, the gorilla had taken the train down from Kingston. They met on the dock with thousands of wives and girl friends sending off their men.

Matthew told the gorilla not to worry. "Chaplains don't get killed. This thing won't change me a bit. I'll be the same mug when I get back."

But after the war, he *had* changed. Not imperceptibly. But majorly. No longer the idealistic, energetic young priest. Something, some part of him had drained out on the ground with all the blood he had left on Omaha Beach.

"Hey," Mankowsky yelled over the noise of the airplane engines, shaking his friend's hand and squeezing it tighter, "don't change anymore!"

"What?"

"I mean it!"

Matt stared at him a moment, then turned without looking back and climbed the boarding stairs.

"See you in a week or so, Matthew!" the gorilla shouted hopefully.

The albino bellowed something to the workers near the stairs and made a pushing motion with his gloved hands.

Matt went into the long fuselage, past the rows of stacked wooden crates held against the plane's sides by belts. He put the leather pouch down and sat in the only seat that remained in the plane, to the left and immediately behind the cockpit. Under the seat, he found his bag.

Calamari slid out of his chair and came back to Matt. "Flotation cushion is under seat in case we ditch in ocean. The captain says it is fine you come up to cockpit and take navigator's chair after takeoff." Calamari cleared his throat. "Even though we often fly for the Vatican, no one tells us much. I am very curious with all this security." He nodded his head at the crates after checking to make sure Captain Genovese wasn't paying attention.

"It's lettuce," Matt grinned.

"It must be special," Calamari joked, "our ship is not even refrigerated." He went back to help the workers close the rear door.

Through his little port window, Matt saw Fullmer walking beside the plane, hand inside his coat, as though he were ready for any last-minute attempt by Communists to stop the flight. The back door slammed shut and Calamari hurried up to his chair in the cockpit.

The plane bumped across the taxiways and swung onto runway number three. Snow flurries skittered across its surface.

Genovese yoked back on his wheel and the DC-6's front tires lifted off the cement runway. The ship angled up, breaking free from the earth, heading upward into the wintery gray sky.

Matt felt a moment of pure exhilaration as he flew up over the skyscrapers of the city he knew so well. From up here, it's changed. Simplified and clean. As God must see us.

Then, remembering the slip of paper he had signed, he felt in his trouser pocket. The refugee money was for "L. Spoleto, 114 Via Rigosa."

2.

Out over the Atlantic, darkness came quickly. Matt was watching Mars and Venus below the half-moon when he thought of his mother. What would she think when the gorilla told her where he had gone? He attempted to console himself with the thought that, once in Rome, he would try to find out what had happened to the annulment he had been trying to obtain for her. The poor woman was living in a constantly tortured state, institutionalized and excommunicated, damned because his father had divorced her and she had remarried, thus violating the laws of the Church.

How she clung to Matt, to the idea that he was a priest, to the hope that somehow, through him, she could at last be saved from her terrible sin. And how that burden of her made him feel imprisoned and helpless, angry at himself. Was that why he allowed her to abuse him on their visits? To punish himself?

Forcing his thoughts from her, he turned, checking the six-hundred-million-dollar cargo that was to be used by a saintly pope to save his Church. Nearby lay the pouch containing the one million for Mr. Spoleto and his Jewish refugees. Why did it always seem that just when you least wanted responsibility, you got it? Christ, he thought, I'm having enough trouble keeping my own life together without this. Do you really want a basket case doing something this important? God had a sense of humor.

He unbuckled his seat belt, stepped over the doorjamb of the cockpit and slipped into the empty navigator's chair behind the two pilots. It was noisier up here, the huge engine props turning, seemingly only inches from the windows. In the moon's glow, the hubs on the props glittered like diamonds.

Calamari turned and waved. "Hello, *Padre* Bowles!"

"Easy to fly this thing?" Matt asked conversationally.

Calamari said, "So you want to be a pilot and stop being a priest, huh?"

Matt tried to smile.

"Don't let him tease you, *Padre*," Genovese said, turning. "This is big plane, but it flies itself if all the engines are running and maybe even if they are not. Here, you just pull up on this wheel to bring up her nose, push down to dive. Then, these pedals on the floor, push left to go left, right for the other way. Simple, huh? Now, you want to fly us to Rome?"

Matt laughed.

Calamari handed him a Thermos of coffee, dug into a nearby sack and offered him a sandwich with a few yellow peppers.

"Thanks," Matt said, taking the coffee. "I'm not hungry."

"You should eat," Calamari shrugged. "Then everything up here would not be so complicated!" The bony man laughed at his own joke.

He finished his coffee. Calamari was busy with the duty of navigating, and Genovese was guiding them through the puffy white clouds, which were illuminated by the moonlight. Matt eased back in his chair. The droning of the four engines' single heartbeat lulled him. And giving in to the obsession he had fought earlier, he began for the thousandth time to think about his mother.

On his last visit, she was sitting in a lawn chair, wearing a lavender and green dress with a frilly white collar, staring up at the oak tree as he strode across the spacious lawn of Blue Oaks Sanitarium on Staten Island. He sat quietly on the grass beside her.

"I don't want any supper," Agnes said, her small mouth

pursing. "I don't care what you say, I won't eat. I've told you that again and again and you won't believe me." She brushed back the black hair that had once been silky from careful brushings and that was now coarse and streaked with gray.

"You don't have to eat if you don't want to," he said, laying his hand on her arm.

Agnes turned, hearing the sound of a familiar voice. She smiled and the smokiness left her eyes.

"How long you been here, Matty?" she asked, stroking his hand.

"Not long."

"Did you come to kiss your poor mother?" She leaned out her cheek, pressing her tongue inside so it bulged at the targeted spot, and cocked her head charmingly. She received his kiss in a way that spoke somehow of how she once had been. Vivacious. Witty. A man-drawing, energetic young woman. Then she pulled away and her mouth resumed its hard, thin line.

Agnes Bowles was an alcoholic. She had been a closet drinker most of her life, keeping it tactfully under control until Robert C. Bowles, Matt's father, had used her drinking to divorce her. Matt had been thirteen at the time. He had entered the seminary that same year—to atone, Agnes always said.

Agnes had managed to marry a second time: Howard Bekins, a good, if unimaginative, husband. But that marriage was accompanied by an announcement by the priest in her home parish in Tarrytown. She had officially been excommunicated from Holy Mother Church.

When Howard drowned in a fishing accident, Matt had committed her to a sanitarium for the purpose of drying her out. She hated what she called "this common place." But most of the time she was mentally not in residence there anyway. Somehow, she still got more than her share of liquor.

"How've you been?"

"Oh, I sit here with nothing to do. Nobody misses me. I don't know why they don't just shoot me."

"You ought to play cards and have some fun. There are lots of people here. Some, I bet, are good dancers."

"How can I have fun when I can't even receive the Sacraments, Matty?"

"Nobody says you can't go to church," he offered lamely.

"But I can't go to Confession or Holy Communion! And my son a priest. For what? When am I going to get my annulment, Matty? I can't wait much longer!"

"Annulments take time. The only place they give them is Rome. And the sacred Rota has to do lots of research to see if a marriage ever took place."

"But it's been years since we filed, Matty. And we've heard nothing! And what if I die?"

"Isn't this a fine, sunny day, Mother? Look down there at the lake. There're ducks on it."

"Some mallards, coupla pintails. I see 'em."

"Look, they're taking off."

She lowered her head and mumbled, "I never wanted that silly divorce in the first place. He put that mortal sin on my soul. I'm damned because of your father."

"The ducks are nearly gone, Mother. Look, see them swoop toward that cornfield? I'll bet they're hungry."

"I never needed that. Never did. Every time he put that filthy man-thing in me and tried to get me pregnant! I didn't want to be swollen up anymore! Why did I have to suffer like that, Matty?"

"It's all over now, Mom," Matt said. He was watching the ducks' flight, which took them over the wide, browning lawns and off toward New York City in the distance.

"Dirty Eddy," Agnes said in a low voice, "dirty, dirty." She shot her gaze up into the tree above them. "Have you come to take me? Who did the dishes this morning? Who mopped the room with her dress? Ugh! He's got his man-thing out. Keep it away! I never need that! NEVVVVER!"

"Mom . . . Agnes?"

"Dirty Eddy! Filthy, filthy!"

Matt sprang up and wrapped his arms around her, holding her.

She buried her face in his shoulder, staining his black clerical coat with her tears.

An attendant in whites came down from the big house. Matt motioned that all was okay, and he went back inside, waving to the young priest.

"It's true." Agnes was weeping softly. "All of it. Why is it we Irish have to suffer so?" She began drying her eyes with her knuckles, then pushed against his chest and he released her. She sat up very straight and began to arrange and rearrange her dress so the creases lay perfectly parallel to her knees. "You know, Matty, I once had a dress with so many polka dots it'd make a schizo puke."

Matt sat back on the grass.

"Of course, I'm not a schizo. I just got some other problems."

She settled back in the wooden lawn chair, easing her spine between a crack of the design. "We always had separate beds. You know that? Had separate bedrooms with Howard too. But I never liked that man. Not really. Always smelled like battery acid, you know?"

"No, I didn't know, Mom. Tell me about Dad." Matt had only dim memories about the father who had left him nearly twenty years ago to live in South America.

"Your father," she said, considering it carefully, "hated that I couldn't bear to be touched while I slept. Did you know that? Slightest jar, I would startle awake. It was me who insisted on separate beds. But I used to climb into his bed every morning. He had a wonderful feel to his skin. Soft for a man. I used to climb in, in the morning, and cuddle my head on his hairy chest. It had to be that way. I couldn't be touched at night, see?"

"Yes, Mom."

"How I loved to kiss him in the mornings. I used to lie full out on top of him, you know. Robert was so big and me small and delicate. He used to call me his little blanket. But when he tried to start that way we had you, Matty, I'd stop him, see? He never liked the vow of chastity I took after you came or that I joined the Little Order of St. Francis for lay people. Did you know that?"

Matt was silent. He could imagine his father's reaction when he first heard about the vow.

"Just you and me now, huh, Matty?"

"You and me."

"Yes, you and me." She was silent a moment. "Did you know I have colitis now? What else do old people with bad consciences have to do but get sick anyway?"

"You and me, Mom."

"That's right. You and me, Matty." Again she grew quiet, and he knew it was coming. She began suddenly, the words spilling like hot coals from her mouth. "You just think I don't know why you left me. Why you went into that seminary. It's because you couldn't stand that your father divorced me. So you punished yourself by denying yourself everything. You were only thirteen! What could you know at that age? Just an innocent, Matty! How could you know you wanted to be a priest?"

"I made my choice. Let's leave it alone. C'mon, Mom."

"I know I'm to blame. You worked thirteen long years to join a new family. You gave up your roots! All to make up for what I did. You should never have been a priest, Matty. You only became a priest because you were ashamed of my divorce! You should have been nothing but a man. But no! You hid. You were too proud!"

"Mom," he begged.

She began to wring her hands, working herself up to the finale he knew was inevitable. It always happened in the same way. Their formula for a visit. Did he somehow, secretly, enjoy this?

"I see right through you!" Agnes was shrieking. "It's the same reason you went to that war too!"

"That's not true," Matt said lightly, trying to shake it off, keep it at arm's length a little longer. But he felt the .45 in his hand, the bone chips sting his face. The thump of his grenade exploding. Had he gone to war to die and ironically returned a hero?

"You know I'm right!" Agnes cried, watching him with a sudden, vicious lucidity. "Look at yourself! Take a good long look! You're a killer! You punished yourself good for me that time, Matty!"

He had been the only man of the cloth ever to receive the Medal of Honor, highest U.S military decoration. The only day he wore it, with its ribbon of light blue silk and thirteen embroidered white stars, was the day Franklin Delano Roosevelt had awarded it. How he had envied the Unknown Soldier as he lay nearby in his decorated coffin! He wished he could have traded places with him.

"You should have been nothing but a man!" his mother was

chanting. "A regular, no-good, ordinary man! A man filled with sin like the rest of us, but no! Well, now you are, Matty! Now, you sinned over there! You're a killer!"

"It's what I had to do . . . ." he mumbled. But her cries overrode his words.

Four other chaplains—two Protestant, one Catholic and one Jewish—posthumously received honorable mention that day he had been awarded the Medal of Honor in Washington, D.C. They had given their life jackets to others when the Army transport ship *Dorchester* was torpedoed and sunk in the North Atlantic in February 1943. But George L. Fox and Clark V. Poling, Protestants; John P. Washington, Roman Catholic; and Alexander D. Goode, Jew, did not receive the Medal of Honor. Instead, they were pictured on a stamp. How he envied their pure brand of heroism. They had killed no one. Or was it that they had died?

In October of 1945, he rode a ticker-tape parade down Madison Avenue with other war heroes, Audie Murphy and David McCampbell. Cardinal Spellman had been in the car behind them. Matt left the city before the dinner in his honor began, retreating to his quiet parish of St. Anselm's on Long Island.

But even there, he was made to be a hero a hundred times a day. In Porter's Quarter, people shook his hand, kids wanted his autograph, his picture kept popping up on the front of every paper in the United States. He hid his medal and, when the subject came up, avoided it like a cancer.

"You're a bad priest!" Agnes was closing in for the kill. "You were never a good *boy*! Killer! Murderer!"

He covered his face with his hands.

"Killer! Murderer!"

"No," he shouted. "Lies! Not true! Yes! Yes!"

He was glad for the noise of the plane's engines, sure that he had cried out. But neither pilot had heard him. He rubbed his face, wiping away the perspiration, trying to slow his breathing. The dawn was seeping through the DC-6's cockpit windows. God, how he needed a drink. He thought of his bottle in the dresser.

As a thin-lipped sun rose on the horizon, they landed at Shannon Airport in Ireland. Workers scrambled over the DC-6, refueling it, checking tire pressures, oil lines and levels. Matt watched Genovese accept the requisition papers through his front cockpit window and sign them. The cargo doors were never opened.

The takeoff from Shannon was uneventful, as was the flight over London. Then, turning over the English Channel, they flew past the French countryside of Bourges over the city of Marseille, then out across the Ligurian Sea. Elba passed beneath them, its dark volcanic soil glistening from a recent rainfall. Looking up, Matt saw a city on rolling hills in the distance.

"Rome?" he asked Genovese.

"*Sí, Padre,*" he said. "We rendezvous forty kilometers north, near Lake Bracciano. It is where all Rome and the Vatican get its water."

"Why are we going there?"

"It's deserted airfield, used sometimes to race bicycles. Swiss Guards from our Vatican are waiting there." Calamari smiled. "They will unload your lettuce!"

A huge reflection of sunlight appeared ahead. Lake Bracciano filled the windshield with its blue expanse.

"You want to sit up here, *Padre*, fasten your seat belt tight," Captain Genovese said over his shoulder. "This landing will be very rough!"

3.

Giuseppe Ferragamo, Communist candidate in the upcoming Italian elections, stepped from his battered white Fiat. He stretched his short legs, stiff after the ride from Rome, and scanned the expanse of unfinished cement runways. Jimson tumbleweeds grew along their length now. The Germans had planned to use the airfield during the war to refuel bombers to protect Rome and southern Italy. But it had never been needed. At Hitler's command, the Germans had retreated from Rome, the result of the deal struck between Hitler and Pope Pius. Rome, the ''open'' city, had fallen without a battle.

The sharp-featured little man buttoned his cream twill suit jacket and checked his watch. It had been nearly fifteen hours since the Red Woman had notified them about the plane leaving New York. And he had spent every second of that time trying to decide how to prevent the money from being delivered to the Vatican.

Ferragamo walked toward the first building and stuck his head inside. Traces of sand, gravel and pieces of reinforcing iron were scattered across the dirt floor—materials once used for the construction of the runways. At the rear, through a cracked window, sunlight filtered down through the dust.

He brushed off his hands, keeping them away from his white trousers, and carefully picked his way through the weeds toward the second building, which looked like a barracks. Testing the ragged screen door, he found it unlocked. He stepped inside and was startled to see what looked like two Swiss Guards standing at the windows. Their disguise had been good enough to fool him. The yellow, red and blue fatigues seemed genuine.

Both men held machine guns and gazed intently at the sky. He recognized Garardo Spina, the one so aptly called Cornos, "the horned one." His head was freshly shaved, leaving his trademark of two hairy valleys at the sides. He claimed always to shave his head this way on the eve of a "battle" so that his appearance alone would rattle the enemy.

"*Buon giorno,*" Ferragamo said to him, smiling uneasily.

Cornos turned, spat on the floor. "Ah, if it is not the next *Presidente* of Italy. Or has your campaign ended now that the money comes?"

"Cardinal Spellman himself will help us," Ferragamo said. "We shall succeed with his money, no?" He laughed in his best velvety chuckle.

"You won't do it with speeches," the horned one growled. "Today ends it! From now on I do things the way I was taught in Sicily. We burn that worthless money!"

It was the first Ferragamo had heard about the money being destroyed. He reached up, smoothed back his rose-scented hair, tried not to look surprised and walked over to the Russian seated at a makeshift table, playing solitaire. Almost immediately he gagged at Nerechenko's body odor.

In his gray suit, white shirt and gray tie, Igor Nerechenko was most proper in his attire, but he refused to bathe. "Catch the pneumonia," he would explain. Concentrating on his solitaire, the Russian absently reached out and poured himself a shot glass of aquavit.

"I tell you to stay away," the Russian grunted, recognizing Ferragamo's presence.

"It's been hours. I was worried."

"The plane comes. Red Woman would not lie to me."

"Where are the Swiss Guards who were supposed to be here?" Ferragamo asked.

"Are there." Nerechenko pointed with his chin to a corner behind himself.

Ferragamo saw four bare feet protruding from beneath a

piece of canvas. He took a quick breath. Gently, gently, he thought. But now he *had* to know!

"Why did you bring only two men with you? We'll need more than that to unload the money from the plane!"

"No need American money! Moscow take care of you!" Nerechenko punctuated the word *Moscow* with a soft slap. "Can take care of Italy too."

"*Faccia presto!*" the horned one cried out suddenly from his lookout at the broken windows. "I hear it!"

Nerechenko lumbered heavily to the window. He thrust his leonine head out and listened. Then he caught sight of something and jerked back outside.

"Fool!" he roared, "your car!"

"I'll move it!" Ferragamo apologized, seeing his Fiat in plain view.

Nerechenko stopped Ferragamo as he made for the door.

"You stay. Now, little politician, you see everything."

The horned one threw back his head and laughed heartily at that.

They were descending, sliding barely over brown hills covered with wild grasses and an occasional brilliant green fir. Captain Genovese was furiously pumping the footpedals, jacking the wheel back and forth, revving the engines, literally diving in for the landing. Ahead, less than a mile, lay the unfinished airport. Even from that distance, Matt could see the overgrown runways, one nearly completed in gray cement, the other only partially bedrocked with black-specked gravel.

There were two buildings near the runways and a small white car near one of the buildings, but no sign of the Swiss Guards.

The plane hovered a moment above the runway because of the heat rising from its surface. Then its tires slapped down with a screech. Genovese reversed the engines and hit the hydraulic brakes. Matt was pitched forward, restrained only by his seat harness. The plane shuddered, skidded and swerved. Less than fifty feet before the runway ended in dirt, Captain Genovese halted the DC-6. He swung the nose around so the plane was again facing the expanse of the runway.

Leaning back in his seat, Calamari wiped perspiration from

his forehead. "Short," he said, worried. "Very short for such a big plane."

Genovese said, "It was never meant to land anything here." He turned and looked out his side window. "That is odd. I thought this was all very secret."

"*Sì*," Calamari agreed. "That white car is where anybody can see it."

Matt leaned forward. Two Mercedes-Benz trucks, their cabs a light yellow with black striping, rolled out from beside the other shack and started toward them.

"Those are Vatican trucks," Captain Genovese said. He reached forward and shut off all four engine switches on the panel. The new silence was eerie. The trucks approached, dust flying up beneath their tires. The white car had not moved.

The first truck parked near the nose. There was only one guard in the cab. The second truck near the loading door held two figures. The man on the passenger side wore a gray suit. The two Swiss Guards walked to the plane.

"Funny they didn't bring more help to unload this stuff," Captain Genovese said, disappointed. "We'll be here all day!"

Someone banged on the rear door.

"Maybe we should give them a hand?" Matt asked.

Genovese nodded, stood up with the copilot and left the cockpit. Matt followed.

The hammering on the rear door grew louder. It sounded like the butt of a gun.

"*Bene, bene!*" Genovese shouted. "You will ruin my airplane!" He put his hand on the release lever to open the door, but through the small window caught sight of the Swiss Guard outside. The man in the gray suit had remained inside the truck.

"Something wrong," Captain Genovese said, turning to Calamari and Matt. "They do not have proper weapons. The guards in the Vatican carry Italian arms. These are too big!"

Stepping forward, Matt peered out the window. He saw an almost bald man spot him and swing up his machine gun. As Matt ducked in disbelief, the first burst slammed through the door. Genovese crumpled. In horror, Matt watched as the captain's head banged against a crate and blood gushed from his belly.

"No!" he heard himself cry. But the war had come again.

Soldiers lay on the sloping beach of Omaha unable to move or crawl. Pinned down by fire from the cliffs above. The flood of faces, always the faces, rose and he was swept away with them. Cordite and splattered flesh in the sand; cries of agony: "Help me, Father. I'm dying!" "Father . . . I . . . I pissed myself!" "I'm blind, I can't see! Medic? Is that you, Father?"

"*Ego te absolvo . . .*"

Faces lit up by incoming shells. Tracing holy oil on stumps, torsos, whatever remained in the thick, sticky splotches of blood. Once, dripping his bottle of Extreme Unction oil into a gaping hole that had been a mouth, the voice still somehow screaming. American boys dying so fast he couldn't anoint them in time.

At Pointe du Hoe, a promontory down the beach, he started climbing. Up the cliffs on ropes the Rangers had hung. Hit seven times. Never slowing until he gained the shell-pitted summit. Then grenading the pillboxes and nests of machine guns. And before returning to his own ministrations of dying Allied below, he had entered the concrete boxes and foxholes and blessed the Germans he had killed.

He bent over Genovese's body and recited Absolution, tracing a cross on his forehead.

"*Ego te absolvo . . .* I absolve you of your sins in the name of the Father, the Son and the Holy Spirit. Amen!"

The words sounded strange, yet automatic, worn. Calamari was face down, unmoving. Suddenly another blast ripped off the door handle. Like a hysterical cat, Calamari jerked up and clawed his way forward. Laying Genovese's lifeless head down, Matt rolled away.

As he arrived at the cockpit, he saw that Calamari was cranking the engines. They were refusing to engage, popping in protest. Matt threw himself in Genovese's chair, staying below the windows.

"Who are they?" Calamari screamed in terror. "Why are they shooting at us?"

"I don't know," Matt said. "Someone has obviously found out about this shipment. Maybe the Communists the Cardinal warned me about." He reached out and pushed Calamari down. "Stay low!"

The closest engine on the starboard wing caught, its propeller spinning. A spray of bullets smashed Calamari's front windshield. He ducked but kept trying to start the other motors.

"Can you make this go with one engine?" Matt asked, crouching as low as he could in the pilot's chair.

"*Si*, but not on takeoff!"

"Maybe the others'll start before we have to."

"And if they don't?"

A burst of shells ripped through the roof of the cockpit. Calamari released the brakes. The DC-6 rolled sluggishly forward.

The outboard engine on the starboard wing coughed and started. The plane picked up speed.

Outside, the horned one began to fire at the tires. Clumps of black latex peeled off the left pair. There was a loud pop, followed by a rush of air. The DC-6 tilted crazily to the left. Gararado Spina reloaded and continued to blast at the fuel tanks in the wings.

In the cockpit, Calamari pumped the rudders desperately. "The tires!" he moaned. "Oh, mama!" He kept cranking the two other engines.

The port inboard started. The DC-6 hobbled down the runway.

"Speed? What is speed?" Calamari screamed, his eyes focused on the lessening stretch of cement ahead. He was fighting without success to keep the plane from bouncing all over the runway.

"Sixty!" Matt shouted. "Sixty-eight!"

Outside, the man in the gray suit slid behind the wheel of his Mercedes. Cornos and the other Communist leaped onto the truck's running boards as it roared after the limping plane.

"Seventy-nine, eighty-one! Try it!"

"We cannot! We will crash! We need one hundred!"

Matt grabbed the pilot's wheel in front of him and pulled. The DC-6's front tires lifted off the pavement. Then banged down.

"Stop it!" Calamari shouted. The dirt field rushed at them.

Matt yanked on the wheel again. The plane's nose rose, then the DC-6 rattled off the end of the cement runway and jolted across the dirt. It fishtailed, skidding out of control.

"We are dead!" Calamari shrieked. He yanked his wheel back. The plane's port wing dipped and smashed against the dirt. Its outboard engine exploded into shrapnel. Calamari yoked the wheel clear back into his stomach.

The plane left the ground like some great heavy bird, three feet above the earth.

"Landing gear!" Calamari shrilled, motioning to a red lever on the panel.

Matt threw it. The wheels folded into the belly. The lack of drag showed. The plane rose slightly. Straight ahead were the brown hills. Calamari banked the craft to the right, circling in a desperate attempt to gain altitude.

At the end of the runway, Garardo Spina hopped off the still-moving truck. The horned one knelt and shot. His bullets stitched the plane's starboard wing. The outermost engine caught fire.

Cornos reloaded and fired another clip. He showed his marksmanship: the bullet blew out Calamari's small side window, two pieces of the steel frame driving into his ribs.

The young pilot's face convulsed as he clutched his side with one hand. He fought to keep the other on the wheel.

"How fast?" he gasped.

"A hundred, no—hundred and three!" Matt replied.

The hills were rushing at the cockpit. "You've got to pull up!" he yelled to Calamari.

There was no reply.

Matt turned. Alfonso Calamari was slumped, unmoving, in his chair, his eyes rolled upward.

4.

The brown hill filled the cockpit's front windows. He could make out the clumps of yellow grass on its side. Desperately, he tried to remember Genovese's teasing instructions on how to fly the plane. What had he said? He pulled the wheel back into his stomach as he had seen Genovese do, but the plane's engines only made a strained whine. The nose was not rising! His hands felt as though he were clutching a jackhammer instead of a wheel!

As the mountain rushed at him, Matt saw that its crest sloped away to the left. He jammed his foot down on the left pedal. He felt the plane lurch sluggishly, then bank. The wheel in his hands wanted to go in that direction, so he turned that too. The hump of the hill slid barely beneath him. Then the blue Ligurian Sea appeared off to his right.

Amazed at what he had done, he let off the pressure on the rudder and the plane righted itself. The equally spaced engines on either wing were having a balancing effect. Leaning forward, he could see that outside Calamari's window, the starboard engine had settled into a billowing ball of smoke. The vibrations in the plane made his teeth chatter. The wind rushing through the shattered windshield made it hard for him to get his breath.

"Holy Mother of God!" he muttered. "What am I going to do?"

Below him now, the terrain changed. Sweeping vistas of green cultivated vineyards dotted with small stone farmhouses rushed beneath him. Workers were pruning the vines, so that the rows behind them were straggly and brown, the earth showing between. The workers shaded their eyes and pointed up as he passed over. He thought about putting on a parachute and leaping from the rear door. But what about Calamari? He might not be dead. And then there was the cargo that he had to deliver. There was no other way than to ride the DC-6 down. But where? He peered through the shattered windshield, searching for the other airport Calamari had mentioned. But he could not spot it.

He was sweating from nervousness now. He pulled off his Roman collar and laid it aside. Reaching out, he lifted the radio microphone free and pressed the button as he had seen Genovese and Calamari do.

"Mayday, Mayday, this is an emergency!" he shouted.

"This is Ciampino Airport. I speak English. Identify yourself," a calm voice said.

"I'm Father Matt Bowles from the United States. I'm flying a DC-6 and I don't know how to fly!"

He let out the button on the mike. "God, do I need a belt!" he muttered.

"You are a priest from America, flying an airplane that you don't know how to fly? Over."

"You got it. What do I do? Over!"

"Do not panic," the voice said. "We need to know where you are, exactly. Over."

"I'm in the air over a bunch of fields."

"Fields?"

"You know, the *fields* where you grow grapes!"

"Ah, *un momento*," the voice crackled. Then after a beat, it came back on the air. "We think you northeast of Roma. Is that possible? Over."

"Anything's possible!" Matt said, his words garbling because his cheeks were shaking so much. The wind was rushing in through the glassless windows.

"Ah, *corretto*. Can you see Roma? Over."

"No, there's nothing but farms out here. Wait, there's a town off to my left."

"Ah, *bene*," the voice said, "that is most likely Isola Farnese. Any moment now you will see The Eternal City. Over."

Ahead, what looked like a bank of earth approached. He pulled back on the wheel, fighting its stronger resistance now, coaxing the plane upward.

The plane wavered, rose at the last second and hopped it. As he passed over the small bank, Matt saw it was a highway. Then, looking up, he spotted Rome.

"I got it!" Matt cried into the microphone. "Rome!"

To the left in the distance, he saw a large white ring that encircled a portion of the city. Directly leading into it was a long and wide chalk-white stretch of concrete.

"I see you!" Matt shouted. "I can see your airport!"

"Impossible," the voice said. "We think not, *signore*."

"It's a runway!" Matt screamed. "There's even a big white circle around your airport!"

"*Un momento*," the voice said. "We must confer. Over."

A blinking radio tower loomed up ahead. Matt frantically pumped the right rudder. The plane banked and slid around it. He felt urine seep down his trouser leg.

The voice came back on the air. "Is not Ciampino you see, but the Vatican."

Now the whole thing made sense to him. The familiar sight, pictured on a thousand tourist postcards. On covers of parochial-school books. Plastic dinner mats. Even an actual aerial photo on the back wall of Monsignor MacWarten's office. The Vatican!

Perched at the back edge of Rome, with green fields leading to its walls, stood the smallest sovereign state in the world. One hundred nine acres surrounded by a tall, castlelike wall. Outside that wall, in a welcoming posture, stood St. Peter's Piazza, its enormity enfolded by Bernini's massive colonnades. The 141 saints on top of its arms. The extreme expanse of the piazza easily held 250,000 people and looked a half mile wide.

"What's that long street leading into it?" Matt asked. He was puzzled yet by the street's resemblance to a runway.

"Via della Conciliazione. It sets off Rome from the Vatican.

Now," the Italian voice crackled, "we wish you to turn away from the city. Please depress the right floor pedal and turn the wheel. . . ."

The lone port engine sputtered, backfired and stopped. The plane tilted awesomely. The DC-6's nose dropped and the plane began to fly sideways through the air. Matt twisted the wheel. But it was like trying to guide an inner tube in a straight line down a snowbank. He remembered the mike in his hand, depressed the button and screamed, "Mayday, Mayday! The left engine's gone. I'm going down!"

But the radio had become a mass of unintelligible static.

The DC-6 dove steeply into Rome. The winds buffeted the cockpit, making Matt's hair stand on end. The plane was shaking so badly he was sure it would come apart.

"Dove sono?" Calamari whimpered, coming to. "Where am I?" He attempted to sit up. He looked where the windshield should have been. What he saw made him scream in terror.

"Ehhhhh! *Sono malato!* I am sick!"

Despite the pain in his side, he grabbed the wheel and threw several switches on the panel. Hydraulic pumps lowered port flaps, compensating somewhat for the single engine running on the starboard wing. Still the plane crabbed in midair, descending in a side-to-side sliding motion.

They were hurtling down at St. Peter's Square. Via della Conciliazione was directly ahead of them. The plane was rolling so badly both men were in danger of being thrown out the windows.

"Impossible!" Calamari was muttering, his eyes wide in disbelief at this thing he was doing. Pedestrians and drivers had spotted the approaching aircraft. Some were waving him off, motioning the plane to go away. Others were running for cover.

The DC-6 shuddered down through the sky.

"You want the landing gear?" Matt asked.

"No wheels!"

The plane violently plummeted another hundred feet. There was pandemonium on the wide avenue below. People were crossing themselves, fleeing, covering their heads. Cars raced along, jumped the curbs onto sidewalks. Kiosk owners were deserting their souvenir stands.

Matt could see the tops of the streetlamps on granite columns.

He saw an outdoor restaurant flash past with diners hiding under tables. Ahead, St. Peter's Square rushed at them.

"*Sono malato, sono malato!*" Calamari was bellowing. The nose of the plane was bucking violently side to side, defying his control.

The DC-6 crashed down on its belly in a shower of sparks. The huge plane skidded down Via della Conciliazione, bouncing and crackling. Propellers smacked the cobblestones and tore from their engine mounts. One sailed through the front windows of a religious bookstore, scattering several browsing nuns. Another cartwheeled merrily down the opposite side of the street and destroyed an empty tourist carriage behind a startled horse. A green trolley appeared from nowhere, made its regular stop and halted directly in their path. They could see the conductor stare in disbelief out his side window.

"*Senta, senta!*" Calamari cursed. He slammed both feet down on the right rudder.

The right wing smacked down on the cobblestones and ripped completely off the plane, shooting away like an out-of-control rocket. The impact torqued the DC-6 around. Its thirty-foot tail snagged the trolley as it passed and tipped it over, hurtling its passengers through its windows.

Sparks flying, the plane scooted backwards at the priceless six-story stone obelisk of the ancient Roman Circus. At the last moment, the fuselage caught one of the protective cement bumpers set up to guard against cars. The plane crumpled around it and stopped.

Smoking, a pile of piecemeal junk, the DC-6 sat less than one hundred feet from the official white line of marble that marked the border of the Vatican State.

Up the street, the tanks in the right wing had begun to burn furiously.

Matt squinted out the pilot's window and saw *carabinieri* rushing toward the plane. Smoke was everywhere, making it hard to see. Swiss Guards in full Renaissance regalia were also surrounding the plane. Tourists in *Lederhosen* stood in stunned little clumps. Some were crossing themselves. Matt turned and looked at Calamari, who popped open one eye, then the other. The copilot seemed catatonic.

A sudden stab of pain made Matt examine his right leg. When he looked at his fingers, they were dripping with blood.

He forced himself to lie back and tried to relax to avoid
sinking into shock.

There were shouts from the back door. Matt felt himself
being lifted from the pilot's chair onto a stretcher. He could
not tell how long he had been waiting. Minutes or moments.
He remembered smelling heavier smoke as he was carried
outside the plane, then he knew he was being handed down
and carried away. A woman ran alongside, yelling to him. He
managed to open his eyes. Above him floated a finely
chiseled face, framed by Dutchboy length, blond hair.

"Is this a DC-6?" the face was asking in English. It was a
very lovely face. Later, Matt would wonder if he had given in
to the impulse to reach up to touch it.

"Did you bring money for us?" The face was fighting off
police officers who were attempting to pull her away.

Matt tried to raise himself on his elbow, but fell back
dizzily. "Who . . . who are . . ."

He was lifted into an ambulance. Four Swiss Guards were
holding her and the entire gathering crowd back. The wreckage of the smoldering plane framed the blond woman as the
ambulance doors were closed.

5.

With a construction crane borrowed from the Allied pro tem
Christian Democratic government of Alcide de Gasperi, Vatican workers lifted the wreckage of the DC-6 from the stones
near St. Peter's Square. The plane's cargo of wooden crates
was long gone. It had been quietly, unceremoniously taken
through the Arco delle Campane gate and stored within the
Vatican walls. The oil, fire and scrape marks on the cobblestones of Via della Conciliazione were sanded off. Streetlamps,
windows and a kiosk were replaced. Store fronts repaired.
Vatican lawyers began negotiating out-of-court settlements on
the No. 8 trolley.

Three days later, the Via della Conciliazione and the piazza
appeared normal again. Life resumed its pleasant, sightseeing
pace.

Articles had appeared in the *Messaggero*, *Tempo* and
Giornale d'Italia newspapers of Rome, detailing the crash-
landing by an Air Italia cargo plane. But since most were
controlled by American Occupational censorship, there was
no question of what the plane carried, nor was there any
investigation by the various reporters.

L'Unità, the Communist paper in Rome, and its Red cousin,
the *Corriere della sera* in Milan, trumpeted word of a planeload
of money received by the Vatican. But the denizens of Rome

were so accustomed to the Red newspapers' rhetoric that most paid no attention to the allegations. Much to Giuseppe Ferragamo's disappointment, nothing at all came of those exposés.

Meanwhile, *l'Osservatore Romano*, the official instrument of the Vatican, ran a series of articles by Pope Pius detailing his own scientific conclusions on the immensity of astronomical space in relation to our known universe. The paper also praised Pope Pius for his continuing mission of speaking to the common people. His subjects for that week included lectures on natural gas (to the gas producers of Italy), newspaper production, cinema techniques, nuclear physics and the most modern ways to slaughter animals. No mention whatsoever was made of a plane landing in the Vatican.

Only after two days passed did there appear a small item on the last page of the Vatican paper. It read:

> An errant airliner sought
> space near St. Peter's Basilica
> after an international flight.

To insure the secrecy of the arrival of six hundred million dollars, the Vatican had arranged for the two survivors of the plane crash to be sequestered in a hospital that stood on an island in the middle of the Tiber River. The ancient hospital, run by the Hospitaller Brothers of St. John, was a perfect place to prevent the curious from coming. Swiss Guards surrounded the boat-shaped island, guarding the two bridges that led down to it.

Inside a large, airy room filled with patients, a small locked cubicle had been erected near the altar on which a priest said daily Mass. Two blue-uniformed Palatine Vatican Guards stood outside the doors of the wooden-walled ceilingless partitions, eyes alert and watchful.

Matt lay on his back, leg throbbing, staring up at the two ancient murals painted on the white, vaulted, curved ceiling: the Good Samaritan assisting a wounded man and Martha serving Jesus in her house. But he could not appreciate them. He closed his eyes and longed for the hot, numbing taste of a whiskey.

The pain from the thirty-stitch gash in his leg made him

restless. The doctors had said the plane's mid-console levers had shattered, cutting a jagged slit above his right knee. But he was chafing to get moving, complete his mission, then immerse himself in the holiness of this city, see the Vatican up close, hopefully experience his religion as the priest he once was.

When he opened his eyes again, above him was a white habit, framed by the high ceiling. He did not look at the face. If he had, he would have seen the nun's lips trembling, her chin stuck out defiantly. In her hands, she held a basin of warm water with a sponge floating in it.

"Time for your . . . bath," she said.

Matt rubbed his perspiring face, closed his eyes again in resignation.

The young nun in the habit of St. Clotilde wrung out the sponge and gently mopped his brow. She dried his face and neck, then began to wash his naked, furred chest, rinsing out the sponge occasionally.

"I speak English," she said. "Do you mind if I talk? I like to practice."

He nodded, his eyes closed.

"You were in that plane that crashed."

He nodded.

"And the other one? There, in the other bed?"

"Copilot."

"All he does is sleep?"

"He was half-dead when he landed the plane, Sister."

"Ah," she said, "then *you* are Matthew Bowles."

"Who wants to know?" he asked, opening one eye slightly.

"Lie quiet. Just rest."

He closed his eye.

She dried his arms and hands. He sighed and seemed to be relaxing now.

"You're new," he said. "You give baths differently."

"Differently?"

"Mmmmm."

"That's part of my job," she said. "I know how to give baths."

She finished his stomach, then lowered the sheet. "You don't wear pajamas?" she asked.

"I'm sorry," Matt said, pulling up the sheet.

"It does not bother me," the young nun said with bravado. "It is my job to wash the bodies of patients."

She pried the sheet from his hands but blushed uncontrollably. Hands shaking, she wrung out the warm sponge, then asked, "Did you have money on board for Jews?"

Matt snapped open both eyes, looked fully at her. Then he yanked the sheet to his chin. "You! You were at the wreck! Who are you?"

The nun tossed the sponge in the water, dried her hands on a towel and stuck out her right one for shaking. "My name is Luciana Spoleto," she said.

"L. Spoleto? I thought you'd be . . . . a man!"

"I'm not," Luciana said, "and you, *Signore* Bowles, owe me one million U.S. dollars! Here's the receipt you signed." She waved it at him. "It arrived by wire yesterday."

"I don't have your money, Sister."

"*Signore*, I am neither a man nor a nun. I borrowed these clothes so I could get into the hospital to see you."

"*Miss* Spoleto, I don't have your money. The Vatican does."

"But I have no way of getting it from the Vatican, Mr. Bowles," she protested. "I've called Prince Milagro, Governor of the Vatican. He does not return my calls."

Matt grinned. She had called him *Mr.* Bowles. He had signed the receipt simply Matthew Bowles. Should he tell her? No, later, if it became necessary. Necessary for what?

"Look," he said, "I've heard things go slow there. Vatican machinery. That's probably what's happening. . . ."

"What is happening," Luciana spat, her eyes flashing, "is that I have thirty Jewish families in my own house, two hundred and seventy-three more billeted across Rome and more arriving every day! I have no money left to feed them! And they all want to go somewhere safe like Palestine to start a new life, and I have no money for that either! It's been nearly a week since you arrived. But you tell me to be patient because the Vatican moves slowly?"

She drew in a deep breath and huffed it out.

Suddenly, the door opened. The guards outside clicked their heels, and blond-haired Monsignor Helmut Kass entered, clad in his black and purple robes. Matt recognized him immediately. The Pope's personal secretary, the most influential churchman in the Vatican.

Matt knew that in 1933, Helmut Kass had headed the powerful political organization in Germany known as the German Catholic Party, and had allied himself closely with Adolf Hitler. But later, he had rejected Hitler's platforms and joined his old friend Cardinal Eugenio Pacelli, then Secretary of State to Pius XI, in arranging the "Third Reich Concordat." In this agreement, Hitler guaranteed the Pope's personal safety and that of the Vatican State and promised to respect the rights of the Church and all Catholics in Germany. In return, Pius XI took a stance of neutrality toward the Nazis.

Somehow, even though Matt knew it was practical for his Church to remain neutral, he had always wondered how a Pope, as God's representative on earth, could take that position of neutrality against such a horror as Nazism.

"Father Matthew Bowles," the Monsignor said, "how are you feeling?"

Luciana grabbed up the water pan. Then she froze. She peeked over her shoulder at Matt. "A priest?" she mouthed silently. Matt winked at her. She scurried to the sink and busied herself dumping out the bathwater.

"Monsignor Kass." Matt kissed Kass's proffered ring. "I've heard a lot about you."

"All good, I hope, Father."

"All smart anyway."

The two churchmen laughed pleasantly. But there had been a barb in Matt's answer, and Kass had caught it. His blue eyes narrowed almost imperceptibly.

"I'm terribly sorry about all this inconvenience, Father. But you see, it would not do to broadcast our little . . . shipment. So you must stay here."

Matt's gaze rose to Luciana at the sink, then he lowered his eyes. He had wondered why she had bolted at Kass's entrance. If Kass had noticed it, he was not revealing anything. "Monsignor, you didn't by any chance find a leather pouch on the plane? It wasn't part of the cargo."

"A pouch . . . ?" Kass asked, cautiously lowering his voice.

"Filled with money."

"Whose?"

"For Jewish refugees—from other Jews in the United States."

An expression, as though his tongue had touched alum, wrinkled Kass's face. "Jews," he said. "Always the Jews. How did it get on board in the first place?"

"Cardinal Spellman included it."

"Well, I know nothing about it." He sighed. "It may be there. We have not tabulated the total shipment yet."

"Please tell them to find it. It's important."

"I will," Kass said. "We wish no trouble with Jews." He smiled now and raised his voice. "In a short while, you must come and sign the records that will arrive with your Father Mankowsky. Then, after that, *Pabst* Pius wishes to reward you by personally creating you Monsignor."

"For what?"

"Because you are a hero."

"I'm no hero," Matt said, thinking of his Medal of Honor, which lay gathering dust in his room. He had never opened its case after bringing it home.

"Well," Kass said, smiling, "call yourself what you want. But *Pabst* Pius wishes to thank you for bringing in the . . . help." He shot a look at the nun who was still busy at the sink.

"Speaking of that," Matt said, "who tipped off the Commies about your rendezvous place at Lake Bracciano?"

Kass again lowered his voice to a whisper. "We are working to find out. He reached out and shook Matt's hand once again. "I would appreciate it if you stayed here a few more days until your injury heals. After that, I will arrange a room for you inside the Vatican for the duration of your stay." He walked to the door, pulled it open. "Goodbye, Monsignor. And *danke*." He exited.

"You should have told me you were a priest!" Luciana accused him as soon as the door closed.

"What difference would it have made? You'd still have barged in here!"

"What was it on that airplane that made you such a hero to them? It must have been something very important!" Luciana was half thinking out loud, watching the door Kass had exited.

"Nothing that concerns you," Matt told her. "And as for your pouch, the Vatican's a big place. It just takes time."

"I don't think you realize my families are hanging on with their fingernails!" She sat down on the edge of Matt's bed, folded her arms across her nun's starched breastplate and stared at him.

"I'll see you get your money."

"Promise?"

He nodded.

"Swear on a Bible?"

"Yes, Luciana!" he smiled, exasperated.

She returned his smile, yet searched his green eyes to make sure he was serious.

"What's it like outside?" he asked. "I don't even have a window in here."

"The sun is shining. But aren't you hurt?"

"My leg wound is bothering me and I'm pretty sore all over. But being out would be good medicine."

"What about Monsignor Kass?" Luciana's eyes widened in dread. "He wanted you in here!"

"I'm sure he wouldn't try to stop a fellow monsignor from taking a walk." Matt grinned at her. "Besides, I need a belt."

"A belt? You need something to hold up your pants?"

"Coffee," Matt lied. "I . . . uh, want some real coffee. Not the hospital kind."

"A belt is coffee? I spent two years at your Georgetown in Washington and I don't know *belt*. But you must be dressed to obtain a . . . belt." She went to the foot of his bed and opened his valise. She laid a pair of black slacks on the bed, then his shoes and a clean pair of socks.

"Where is the, you know?" she gestured at her chest.

"Oh, I only brought one clerical outfit. I guess it was ruined in the crash." He peered down into the opened suitcase on the floor. "That T-shirt will have to do."

She pulled out a folded red cotton shirt and opened it. On the front it said NIAGARA FALLS in black lettering. She looked at it in amazement. "I thought people went there for honeymoons."

"A young pupil gave it to me on my last birthday. I've never had the chance to wear it."

"You sure you are a priest?" she asked suspiciously, as she handed him the gaudy shirt.

"Mostly sure."

She walked to the door and threw it open. One of the Palatine Guards leaned in. In Italian, Luciana barked, "Monsignor Kass wants a cane for this patient. He needs some fresh air. Now!" And she slammed the door.

6.

When they came up from the island, Matt was using the wooden cane the Palatines had given him. He gingerly hobbled up the left connecting bridge that spanned the Tiber, past the Swiss Guards. Luciana, in full nun's regalia, explained she was taking her patient for a little exercise. The guards seemed confused but did nothing to stop them. They stared as the nun swung onto a Vespa she had parked earlier near their post and kicked it into life.

"What do you call this thing?" Matt yelled over the engine's rattling noise.

"A motorcycle, of course! Can you ride all right?"

"Better than walking. I think." He gingerly climbed on behind her.

She drove among hurtling small cars, parked cars, trolleys, buses, trucks, other motorbikes, whistling something as she weaved effortlessly, avoiding collisions.

Matt noticed that on most narrow streets there did not seem enough room for two cars to pass. Yet there were no accidents. Other drivers whizzed by one another within inches and sometimes Luciana squeezed through the middle of them. It was as if every driver on the streets of Rome possessed knowledge of where the other would go at the last moment.

Luciana turned her scooter onto Via della Conciliazione, and the Vatican came into view. It looked different at ground level. The expanse of St. Peter's Square floated toward them. When she was in front of the outdoor Trattoria di San Tomas, Luciana shut off the machine's motor and coasted the bike to its black, wrought-iron railing. It could have been the restaurant he had flown over a few days before. Several diners at nearby tables looked up at the white-habited nun parking the motorbike and the jaunty tourist from Niagara Falls.

"Nothing like your last arrival," Luciana said to Matt.

"Oh, no." Matt breathed his first real breath since they started. "This time I came in on wheels."

Stepping off, he felt as though he were home. In the near distance, the majesty of the piazza's encircling colonnades reached out above him like welcoming arms. Atop them, twenty-foot saints carved in travertine marble stared down imposingly at him.

"Do you miss the pigeons?" Luciana brought him back to earth.

"What?" Matt's gaze swept the air above the piazza, then scanned the niches in the colonnades. Pigeons?

"Not much food here during the war," Luciana grinned mischievously. "So we Romans ate them!" She threw back her head and laughed a tinkling, musical laugh. But he was mildly appalled by such humor in this sacred place.

Luciana insisted on sitting close to her motor scooter, since she said the streets were filled with thieves. Some American and Australian soldiers were seated among the tourists at the other side of the alfresco restaurant, dropping scraps to the cats prowling beneath the tables. Other tourists continued past on the sidewalk, down Via della Conciliazione, heading for St. Peter's Square. Matt was amazed that the street looked perfectly normal. There wasn't one sign of a plane having crashed a few days ago.

A sullen waiter stepped near their table. Matt waited for Luciana to order in Italian.

"Two belts," Luciana said quickly in English, looking up at the waiter's morose face.

"*Che?*" he asked, confused, not understanding.

"Coffees," she said, knowingly. "Isn't that right," she asked Matt.

"Coffee," he frowned. He could taste bourbon.

The waiter shuffled off, turning once to eye the English-speaking nun.

"Have you ever been in the Vatican?" Matt asked, his eyes feasting on the immense piazza and basilica beyond.

"I hid American soldiers inside during the war. I know every inch."

"But I thought . . ."

"I'm a Jewish Catholic," Luciana said. "My family was converted by St. Francis of Assisi in the thirteenth century."

"But why did you hide Allies? Weren't you on Italy's side?"

"At the beginning. My husband Rocco, a colonel in the Fascist regime, used to have German officers to our house to entertain them. One night several of them began to make jokes about Jews. I told them what I thought and threw them out of my house. Rocco and I were never the same after that. Later, my father, a general, was killed, and Rocco died in a plane crash. And I was alone."

"So, you got even by helping us?"

"By chance, I met a group of POWs looking for a place to hide. I gave them shelter. If I hadn't met them, I probably would have killed myself, I was so unhappy. But since I found a way to work out my poison, I lived."

The waiter brought coffees in two demitasse cups on saucers. Matt watched absently as he set them on the table.

"You have money?" Luciana asked.

"Dollars."

"He'll take that. Give him one."

Matt put down a dollar. The waiter took it, sniffed at it and shuffled away. He took up his stance near the door of the trattoria, his arms folded, watching the nun and the tourist.

"Do you mind?" Luciana asked Matt. "This outfit is driving me crazy."

Before he could say anything, she unbuttoned the white bonnet of the nun's habit, pulled it off her head and shook her short blond hair in the sunlight. Several soldiers gaped openly. The waiter threw up his hands in horror and went inside, unwilling to witness any more sacrileges that day.

"That's better." Luciana smiled.

To hide his embarrassment, Matt tasted the coffee. It turned out to be a mistake. "What is this?" He grimaced. "I could chew it!"

"Oh," Luciana giggled, lovely sounds breaking forth, "it's espresso. You wanted American coffee?"

Now Matt began to laugh.

"You are happy," she asked, "because your coffee is disappointing?"

He couldn't get control of himself. "It's . . . it's a joke on me!" He managed to catch his breath. "You see, I really wanted . . . a drink of whiskey. That's what a belt is . . . but I was too ashamed to tell you. So, I said a belt was coffee!"

"Ahhhh!" Luciana laughed, understanding, "you got a good joke played on you!"

The other occupants of the restaurant stared at them.

"You should laugh more," Luciana chuckled.

"I will . . . whenever I order a belt!" He started laughing again.

"Do you wish a belt now?" Luciana asked. "I don't mind."

"No, I don't need one," Matt said, wiping his eyes. "I feel pretty good." He settled back in his chair and sipped his espresso. "Eccch," he said, which made Luciana laugh again.

When she stopped, he realized he did not want to lose the moment. It felt good to be with her.

"Tell me more about what you did in the war," he urged.

"Oh, the rest is simple. I took my revenge on the Axis. I found a new family. I hid escaped POWs in my magnificent house. When the Germans finally raided us, I fled. Monsignor Hugh O'Flaherty, that wonderful 'neutral-neutral' Irishman, as he called himself, gave us shelter in the Vatican, disguising us as priests and nuns and even Swiss Guards. I later joined him in his work of sheltering escaped POWs and Jews for the rest of the war, disguised most of the time as a nun!"

She laughed, then sipped her coffee.

"I sometimes think that the purpose of my whole life is to open my eyes. To see myself as I am. To see the world as it is too. Not as I'd like to be or it to be. And all the while not to grow cynical. All the while, be happy and not to punish myself too much."

"And if we can do that, then what?"

"Well, we die and go to our reward." She caught herself. "But who am I to tell you? You're the priest. You should be guiding me."

"I'm afraid I'm in need of guidance myself these days."

"And what are you looking for?" she asked.

At first, he thought she was toying with him, but then he saw she was serious, eager to find out all about him. So, he said honestly, "I'm not sure of my role as a priest." He looked off at the piazza to break the sudden embarrassment of his revelations. "Before the war, I served one quiet year in a parish. I was happy. Did my duties. Said Mass. Really felt the presence of God. Then I enlisted, wound up in the invasion on Normandy. After I came home, nothing seemed the same."

"That must have been a horrible experience for a priest. How did you feel when you did it?"

"The Army trained us not to feel."

"Like the seminary did too, I suppose."

"Yes. Trust your head, not your heart, was a popular saying."

"What was more terrible to you?" Luciana asked interestedly. "Killing Germans or feeling out of control?"

"What are you getting at?" The aura of warmth was suddenly evaporating between them. He was feeling naked.

"You were trained to be perfect. The perfect priest, perfect priest-soldier. Always in control. But then something unexpected happened, like it happens to all of us. You saw another side of yourself. Rocco's death brought out things in me I never knew existed. Made me dislike myself. Doubt myself."

"I don't doubt I need to be a priest."

"Maybe. Or maybe you need to be a priest because it's safe and you can stay in control?"

"Your face is red," she said. "Have I angered you? Ah, my big mouth."

He stood up. "I'm going now."

"Where?"

"To get your pouch. Isn't that what you want?"

"I'm sorry I made you angry." She bit her lip.

She watched him go across the smaller piazza that fed into St. Peter's Square. His body at least did not suppress what he was feeling. He banged his cane along, disappearing finally among the throngs of pilgrims in the square.

Don't let his appearance deceive you, she told herself. Despite his bright, gray-green eyes and his square shoulders and the boyishness when he jokes, he is a priest. Still, she had not enjoyed being with anyone so much since Rocco. That's only because you've been as good as a nun for five years, she told herself. A virgin by time!

She looked around and saw that the soldiers at the other table were throwing bold glances, eyeing her. Reaching haughtily to where she had laid the nun's cowl, she swept it up, spread its starched sides and pulled it down on her head.

"Back to being a nun!" she murmured. Then she stared defiantly at the soldiers, who looked away, embarrassed.

As Matt painfully hobbled toward the imposing tri-arch face of the basilica, he climbed a smooth, domelike knob of granite, which he supposed had been put there to symbolize the "rock" the church had been founded on. Ahead, at the basilica's entrances, were clumps of tourists. When he arrived at the forefront of the gathering, he saw a purple velvet restraining rope strung between gold poles.

"What's happening?" Matt asked several tourists.

The first replied in Spanish, the next in French. Matt gave up. Over the pilgrims' heads, he spotted a Vatican gate off to the left of the basilica. He excused his way back through the crowd and approached the yellow and black striped guardhouse. A Swiss Guard, with a 270 Beretta rifle, eyed him as he approached.

"You speak English?" Matt asked him.

"*Ja.*"

"I have to see Monsignor Kass."

"Kass?" the guard asked, his face blanching at the name.

"That's right," Matt said, seeing his reaction. "He knows me."

The guard considered him. "Go inside here, in this side door," he motioned. "The captain is there. You tell him, *ja*?"

Matt walked through the gate and entered the portico of St. Peter's Basilica. He limped up the main steps, and, once inside in the dimmer light, he found he was standing in a side aisle near La Pietà.

As he approached the creation in white marble, he could see the veins in the dead Christ's arms. The sagging muscles in his crucified legs. The anguish in Jesus's mother's eyes. It was the most awesomely beautiful work Matt Bowles had ever encountered.

"Who are you?"

Matt turned. A Swiss Guard was standing near him.

"I'm Father Bowles. Please tell Monsignor Kass I must see him. It's urgent!"

"Now?" the guard asked. He looked up toward the front. "Wait here, please." He started off, marching up the main aisle.

Matt looked again at the Pietà, then started to walk down the side aisle. He had heard that it was the largest basilica in the world—that a hundred thousand people could fit into it. Now he believed it.

Slowly, he made his way past the mammoth support columns in the side aisle. There were innumerable chapels, each big enough to be a church by itself. Their altars were encrusted with gold and rubies, amethysts and sapphires, their crucifixes inlaid with emeralds. Chalices were of silver, diamond-studded. He passed black marble sarcophagi. Bronze body castings of former popes. Statues of famous saints, surrounded by cherubic angels. Priceless oils by Raphael, Titian, Poussin, Valentin. Above him, from the golden mosaic roof streamed pink pastel light.

He paused; he could walk no farther as his eyes took in one richness after another. And then he spied the ten-foot-high golden letters that formed the motto of the Catholic Church. The words spoken by Christ to Peter, the first Pope, thousands of years before. The quote ran along each wall and completed itself where it began, above the Papal altar. "You are Peter and upon this rock I will build my Church and the gates of hell shall not prevail against it!" The promise from Jesus himself. His Church to last forever. Through good popes and bad. Through no efforts of man. Through times of peace and war. Forever.

He heard a faint, polite sound of applause. He took several

more steps forward, then looked out into the main, middle aisle.

There, lining either side, were bleachers on which sat the hierarchy of the Church. From their photos in the *National Catholic Register*, Matt recognized Cardinal Domenico Tardini, head of the Section for Extraordinary Ecclesiastical Affairs; Monsignor Giovanni Batista Montini, Under Secretary of State; Cardinal Tisserant, the sharp-tongued Frenchman; Suhard of Paris; Mooney and Cardinal Stritch from the U.S. There were several Eastern Orthodox in black headdress. They were all gazing up in amusement at three men in black leotards who were performing an aerial act over the main aisle, their silver swings attached to two side walls of the basilica, forty feet above the floor. There was no net beneath them. Cages, filled with pacing African lions and Bengal tigers, stood on both sides of the gathering. It looked like a circus performance!

And then as he took another step forward, he was amazed again. For there, framed beneath the forward confessional altar of Bernini sat the leader of his faith, Pope Pius XII! The four twisted black bronze columns surrounded the Pontiff as though guarding him from the gaze of mere mortals. Here was the holiest living man in the world. The churchman with the perfect career. Pacelli admitted into the Secretariat of State at an early age, the "sign" already on him. Appointed nuncio in Munich, Germany, then Secretary of State to Pius XI. A man predestined.

Near Pope Pius, but below him, stood Monsignor Helmut Kass, who led the applause after every catch, turning as he did to encourage two other roped-off sections below the Pontiff. These were filled with diplomats, movie stars and bejeweled royalty in formal attire.

Matt recognized Myron Taylor, the American Ambassador to the Holy See. Seated also in that section were Clark Gable, Gary Cooper, Alan Ladd, Bing Crosby with Joseph Kennedy, and their wives. Near them was an intense young man who looked like a Kennedy. He wore a naval officer's uniform but was not watching the performance. Instead, he seemed to be studying Pope Pius.

Behind the Pope were representatives of the world press. Every once in a while, one of them would stand up and take a picture.

There was a sudden gasp from the assembled crowd as the smallest of the three fliers did a triple roll in the air and was caught at the last second before he fell to the floor. Even some of the journalists clapped. Pope Pius nodded.

The Swiss Guard captain who had stopped Matt waited at the bottom of the main altar steps. He stood very still until Monsignor Kass noticed him. The prelate left his Pontiff's side and went quickly down the sixteen steps of the altar and bent over to listen to the guard. Then he cocked his head up the main aisle. Matt eased back behind the nearest pillar.

Why am I ashamed of being seen? he thought. I feel like a schoolboy caught in the girls' lavatory.

Summoning his courage, he stepped back into the main aisle in time to face the approaching Monsignor.

Kass grimaced, frowning at the Niagara Falls shirt. "You should dress properly, Father Bowles. And besides, I did not say to leave the hospital!"

"What's going on?" Matt asked, watching two male aerialists fly through the air in tandem and catch a swinging bar.

"*Pabst* Pius is entertaining," Kass said.

"Inside a church?"

Kass smiled at his naiveté. "We do things differently here in Italy," he said. "Churches are used for everything. In this case, Pius is reminding the world how lucky it is the Vatican survived the Second World War."

"By staging this?"

"*Pabst* Pius," Kass sighed impatiently, "believes that the Church must maintain good relations with the world. A respected Church is a powerful one. It was only a hundred years ago, we owned most of Italy. We lost it through isolating ourselves. Now we are forced to live within these walls. And during the recent war, we came very close to being exterminated totally. *Pabst* Pius understands these lessons well. The Church must have power!"

"I'm just a priest," Matt said doubtfully. He turned once again and made sure the bizarre event was really taking place here. "I guess I just don't understand. . . ."

"Precisely," Kass said. "What the Catholic Church must always have is power. Power to do God's will. And these acres with all their treasures are the base of our power. Pius knows we would be impotent without our wealth. Who would listen to a poor pope?'' He took a deep breath as if to relieve himself of the burden of explaining such obvious premises. "Now, what are you doing here, Father?"

"It's about that money," Matt said. "The Jews need it right away."

"Can't you see I don't have time now?"

"It's got to be there," Matt said. "I put it on board myself. Maybe it got misplaced in one of the crates. Shouldn't we take a look?"

There was a tremendous round of applause. Kass turned back toward the festivities. He clearly did not want to break away.

"Oh, very well," he agreed reluctantly. "But, *sofort*, quickly, quickly!"

He walked toward the rear of the basilica, then out into the square. Matt followed, trying to keep up, his cane slipping on the smooth marble and getting caught in the cracks of the ancient stones outside. Tourists waiting behind the velvet rope watched the strange procession of the red-sashed, dignified Monsignor and the limping man in a red T-shirt.

To the left of the basilica, at the nearby heavily guarded gate of Arco delle Campane, Kass paused. "You realize," he said to Matt, "you have upset all my elaborate security measures. But now that you are here, you will follow my instructions implicitly. When you return from the bank, speak to this guard." He gestured to a young Swiss with a stiff movement that told of his suppressed anger. "He will show you your room. And you will stay within these Vatican walls until you sign the documents arriving from the United States. Then after you see the Holy Father, you will go home!"

Kass pronounced "go home" with a certain relish.

Now inside the Vatican walls, they made their way through the Piazza del Forno—the Square of the Oven, built in ancient times to bake the Vatican's bread—and up the steps of the Salita della Zecca. Ahead, surrounded by park-size lawns, stood the elegant Casina of Pius IV, which had for centuries served as a private house for popes who wanted to be alone.

They ascended now past the loggia fountain and water-filled moat, up the first flight of gray marble stairs and crossed the black and white marble courtyard. Two Swiss

Guards with semiautomatic Berettas admitted them into the Casina proper.

Inside, Kass led the way up another flight of green marble steps, touched previously, Matt thought, only by the velvet slippers of popes. At that landing, the albino, Hans Fullmer, was supervising the installation of a modern time-lock on a large entryway. The workmen were torching through sculpted bronze doors created by Pollaiuolo in the sixteenth century.

"Monsignor." Fullmer bowed when he saw Kass. He genuflected and kissed his ring. Then he straightened and coldly offered his hand to Matt. "Father Bowles. Congratulations on your successful flight. I hope you are healing well."

"Hi, Fullmer," Matt said. "We've come about that Jewish money."

"The bag *you* signed for."

"Then you saw what he is speaking about?" Monsignor Kass seemed amazed.

"*Ja*, it was loaded in New York."

"We need to check the arrival lists then," Kass sighed. "May we enter?"

Fullmer nodded to the two guards, who pulled the workmen away from the lock they were installing.

"*Rauchen verboten*," the albino announced, warning them not to smoke.

The doors were swung open, and Matt was surprised to see an elegant ballroom with golden chandeliers in the forms of angels holding light bulbs. The wall to his left was broken by large, floor-to-ceiling windows. On the opposite side, a newly installed stainless-steel counter with eight tellers' windows stood in front of a gleaming new thirty-foot safe.

Scattered against the far wall were an extraordinary number of desks with as many as twenty telephones on each. Signs on each of the desks announced their categories: SWISS ARBITRAGE, FRENCH ARBITRAGE, etc. Priests were talking excitedly into their phones, making deals. Above and behind them on the side wall were clocks registering the time in the world's financial capitals: Paris, New York, Bonn, London, Zurich, Rome, Tokyo, Madrid. Matt could hear the priests shouting about money: "*Trenta milioni di yen, sì!*" and "One hundred million dollars to Swiss francs, the rate, please?"

"Marks, Marks, Marks!" another kept repeating into his telephone, his face red and angry.

In the area around the safe, there were more priests, these in black cassocks, with green aprons wrapped around their middles and visors over their foreheads. They were bent over tables, counting stacks of money. Others were wheeling carts full of money into the safe for storing. In front of the counter stood several dignified old men completing their transactions. And above them all, hanging from a wall near the safe, was a single large crucifix.

"Speed is important here," Kass observed, his close-cropped blond head bobbing in approval. "The world outside moves very fast. We must keep up." He turned and smiled expansively and proudly at Matt. "*Tempus fugit*, you see?"

"Or *sic transit gloria mundi*," Matt said. "All depends on your perspective, I guess."

Kass's mouth pursed as if he had just tasted something sour. He spun. "Guido! A moment, Guido!" He beckoned to a tall, balding prelate who was circling among the arbitrage desks, bending over to check tabulations, offer advice.

The prelate laid down the papers he was holding and stood erect. As he approached, Kass whispered to Matt, "We are lucky to get him. He retired at age forty-six. Through shrewd investments, he amassed nearly all the farmland around Rome. But he came out of retirement at *Pabst* Pius's request to run the bank of our little kingdom. We are very lucky!"

"Guido Offeri, please meet Father Bowles," Kass introduced them.

The Monsignor silently stuck out limp fingers. Matt squeezed them quickly and drew away.

"What may I do for you?" the horse-faced, stooped prelate asked in a deep, lugubrious voice. He spoke very, very slowly, giving the illusion he was still counting.

"We are searching for a bag that may have arrived with the shipment," Monsignor Kass explained.

"A pouch," Matt added quickly. "About this big." He shaped it with his hands.

Monsignor Guido Offeri stared impassively. "I have not seen such a thing," he said with absolutely no interest.

"It was on the airplane," Matt said. "I put it there myself."

"Did you crash that plane in the piazza?" Offeri asked, his

dead shark eyes widening but showing no life. "I should have thought you would try Ciampino." He turned and snapped his fingers. "Palmo?"

A little man in a black suit, white shirt and tie looked up from his desk and hurried toward them. He wore an undersized pince-nez that stretched uncomfortably across his wide nose, looking as though it would spring off into the air at any moment.

"The *Segretario* of the Chamber," Offeri said. "He is in charge of passes and accounting. He knows everything." He turned to him. "Palmo, check to see if we received a leather . . . what?"

"Pouch. Here's the receipt for the million." Matt unfolded the crumpled paper. "The serial numbers of the bills are listed there also."

"This should be simple," the *Segretario* said, adjusting his pince-nez glasses farther down his nose. "We have tabulated nearly all the bills already." He went off.

One of the men finished his business at the stainless-steel counter and, pocketing his papers, turned to walk away. Then he saw Monsignor Kass. He came over to him, his arms outstretched in greeting.

"*Monsignore!*" he announced effusively. He kissed his ring, then embraced him.

"Has Guido taken good care of you?" Kass asked in Italian.

"Oh, by all means," the man with the thin, pomaded hair answered. "Everything is going to go just as you want it." He patted the papers inside his coat pocket, affectionately turning to smile at the tall, bent Offeri.

In English, Kass said, "Here is the man responsible for your good fortune. Father Matthew Bowles, I am pleased to introduce *Signore* Rappalo Perfette, former Vice-President and new President of the Banco di Santo Spirito."

"A pleasure," the dignified little man announced, shaking Matt's hand. "You have helped save both Italy and the Catholic Church. I congratulate you, *Padre. Scusi*"—he bowed to the two Monsignors—"but I must hurry back to my bank now."

"*Certo*," Kass said, reassured. He extended his hand again, smiling amiably.

Signore Perfette kissed it quickly, then hurriedly walked toward the door.

Kass turned to Offeri. "Is our little deal completed?"

"*Sì,*" Guido Offeri said, shaking his head up and down. "The Banco di Spirito is ours now."

"You bought a bank?" Matt asked.

"Banks," Offeri corrected him. "All you see here is only temporary. These tellers are on loan from our smaller bank of the Institute of Religious Works in the nearby Holy Office. In a few weeks this money will gradually be transferred to half a dozen civilian-run banks which we own now. The Vatican does not wish to be in the business of banking."

"Only to control it," Kass added with a broad smile.

"But I thought the money Spellman sent over was to be used to beat the Communists in the elections," Matt protested in amazement. "Not to buy up banks!"

Monsignor Offeri laughed. "Only a certain amount goes to the Christian Democrats, Father. The rest will be invested—in Italian manufacturing, banking and agriculture. *Pabst* Pius knows if there is enough coal, wheat, wine, water and electricity, Communism will never be a serious threat here."

"In short," Monsignor Kass added, "the Holy Father has decided the best way to beat Communism is by buying Italy. Very clever, we feel."

"*Sì, sì, sì,*" Offeri said, agreeing sagaciously.

Matt felt all the more disoriented by what he was witnessing. But who was he to question? Whatever the Pope did was for the good of the Church somehow. Besides, these were underlings, not the Holy Father, running the business end.

The *Segretario* crossed the marble floor, scanning a long sheet of figures as he walked. When he came near them, he shook his head. "We have no serial numbers that correspond to your receipt."

"Well, that settles it," Kass said. "Perhaps something happened to your pouch in that crash."

"*Segretario!*" someone called from the tellers' cages. The group spun and a young priest emerged through the electrically locked gate of the stainless-steel counter and came toward them, his black cassock skirts too high above his brown shoes. He was clearly a poor Italian priest. In his hands, he held a leather pouch with steel rivets.

"That's it!" Matt said, grabbing it from him. He turned it over and saw that its back had been slashed open.

"I found it inside a trash can," the young priest said.

"Are you absolutely sure the bills on his receipt are not in our bank?" Monsignor Guido Offeri asked his *Segretario*.

"Most certain," Palmo said, adjusting the pince-nez that was too tight on his bulbous nose. "Nearly all the bills that arrived in the shipment have been registered and verified. The ones that remain are in denominations of under twenty dollars. We have missed nothing!"

"Thank you, *Monsignore*," Kass said, shaking the chicken-wing hand of Offeri. "You also, *Segretario*."

"You didn't see or count the money in New York," Fullmer said to Matt as they passed through the twenty-foot-high bronze doors. "Those Jews are tricky. Maybe there was none. Just newspaper or something."

"You have all the answers, don't you?" Matt said.

The albino took a deep breath, bowed and, motioning for the doors to be closed, turned his back on Matt, busying himself with overseeing the installation of the time lock.

Matt turned to Kass. "Look," he said, "I have to clear this thing up. You have to let me see Pope Pius."

"I cannot."

"You mean you won't."

"Have it your way," the Monsignor said impatiently. He glanced at his watch, eager to return to the festivities taking place in St. Peter's.

"Isn't it apparent somebody around here did this?" Matt asked, holding up the ruined pouch.

"That is a serious allegation," Kass protested. "You had better be sure of your facts, Father."

"I'm sure it *arrived* here."

"Father, I assure you, we do not have thieves inside the Vatican!"

"Look, Monsignor," Matt said in a conciliatory tone, "there was a million dollars in here. The Vatican has many times that. Until we find out what happened, why don't you just replace their money? It'd be an act of charity."

"We could not do that. It would be an admission that the Vatican is wealthy. Very bad publicity to flash our money around."

"Look, Monsignor," Matt tried a new tack. "I'm responsible to a certain Luciana Spoleto and her refugees for their money that's missing. You have to understand my position."

"I know this woman Spoleto. She was a troublemaker during the war and she is a troublemaker now. I advise you not to get mixed up with her and her latest cause, that band of Jews. Besides," the Monsignor added slyly, "the Vatican is not legally liable for their missing money anyway. And neither are you."

"You sound like a lawyer, Monsignor."

"I am a Jesuit lawyer. And if you were my client, Father Bowles, I would advise you to forget this whole matter."

"Thank you for your advice," Matt said, his voice hard. "But while Pope Pius may agree the Vatican is not *legally* responsible, he might wonder whatever happened to *morally*."

He dropped the empty pouch at Kass's feet and went down the steps. Kass watched him, his temples throbbing beneath his close-cropped blond hair.

Hans Fullmer stooped and picked up the pouch. "Do you wish me to investigate about their money?" he asked Kass.

"Look into it quietly," Kass said. "Then report to me." He looked down at the pouch Fullmer held. "In the meantime, dispose of that. It only reminds me of trouble."

7.

Limping his way toward the gate of the bells, at Arco delle Campane, he saw Luciana out in the square, sitting atop her Vespa. She waved to him from the open piazza.

"Do you wish to see your room now?" the young Swiss Guard asked as he passed beneath the arch's checkpoint.

"Not yet," Matt told him. He was not looking forward to dealing with Luciana. What could he tell her?

"You may not leave the Vatican," the guard told him as he saw Matt continuing onward toward the piazza.

"Be just a minute," Matt said over his shoulder without stopping.

The guard watched as the American priest in the T-shirt headed toward what appeared to be a perfectly dressed nun in white, squatted cross-legged on the seat of a Vespa.

"You have our money?" she asked before he could say anything.

"Not yet." No reason to alarm her. It all had to be a mistake. "There's been a . . . mix-up. I plan on seeing Pope Pius. He'll straighten it out."

"How will you do that?"

"I have that appointment with him, remember?"

"That's not for a week, maybe more!"

"I'll manage to see him sooner."

"How?"

He turned away from her as much to avoid her eyes as to think. As he did, he faced the basilica. The crowd that had massed in front of it was gone. That probably meant the circus act inside was over.

"You're looking in the wrong place," Luciana said. She got off the Vespa and stood close to his shoulder. "Up there," she pointed. "That's the Apostolic Palace. Pius's room is on the fourth floor, second window from the right."

"I know that," Matt said. "Any schoolboy does." The Swiss Guard was staring at them. Matt turned and glared up at the dull-orange Apostolic Palace.

Luciana shrugged, went back to her Vespa and sat on it.

"Any ideas yet?" she asked after a while.

"I'm thinking," Matt said.

"Well, while you think, let me tell you something. There are only five gates into the Vatican. The Arco delle Campane on the left of the basilica that you came out of; another to its far left over this colonnade, which is the Sant' Uffizio; then to the right, there's St. Anne's Gate, which is reserved for all business; and farther to the right, the Ingrèsso al musei, entrance to the Vatican museums. None of those will do you any good."

Matt continued to gaze stubbornly up at the palace.

"Finally, there's the fifth. It's called the Portone di Bronzo. Heavily guarded. It leads to Pope Pius."

"Oh? And where might that be?"

"There," Luciana gestured to beneath the nearby right Bernini colonnade. "Right next to the Vatican police station."

A double set of marble stairs led up to two massive Bronze Doors. At the top of the stairs stood six Swiss Guards, physically blocking the wide entrance.

"Even if you got past them, you'd never make it to the Pope. He's got twelve rooms of bodyguards."

"What about a back way? I could go through that Arco delle Campane gate I just came out, circle around back of the basilica to the Apostolic Palace."

"You'd get as far as the Courtyard of the Oven," she said. "There are Swiss there too."

He remembered seeing them. "How about *through* the

basilica?'' he asked, turning toward its granite front, which loomed above them.

"You can't get *out* of the back of the basilica into the Vatican proper.''

Matt turned and looked longingly up at the Apostolic Palace. ''Somehow I'll see him,'' he said determinedly. ''I have to. He'll straighten all this out.''

''How can you be so sure?''

''There are things wrong with the Church, Luciana. But not with Pope Pius.''

He continued to stare at the palace.

''Why don't you come home with me and have supper with my families? Maybe together we can think of that plan.''

''I'm not hungry. Besides, I can't.'' He checked his Swiss. The young guard was still watching him.

''Too bad. Tonight we have fish soup and *avanzi*.''

''*Avanzi?*'' Matt asked, turning. ''Sounds like marching orders.''

''Leftovers,'' Luciana grinned.

Matt turned once again toward the Apostolic Palace, stopped by the Bronze Doors and the half-dozen Swiss Guards who blocked its entrance.

''The Pope will still be there tomorrow. And we certainly have that long. What do you say?''

Matt hesitated a moment longer, tucked his cane beneath his arm, then swung his stiffened leg over the back of the motorbike. Luciana glided off, zipping in between two groups of African pilgrims. He grabbed on to the handles beside his seat, knowing what was coming once she was in the street.

''Halt!'' he heard his Swiss cry. But he did not turn around.

''Since this is your first time in Roma,'' Luciana shouted over her shoulder, ''I'm going to take the long way home!''

She kept the throttle of the little Vespa cranked open as they roared past stores advertising yellow and black boxes of Kodak film. ''First the Trastevere!'' she shouted over her shoulder at him, whipping through streets even more narrow than he had seen. ''It means 'across the Tiber'! These people think they are the true Romans! They look down at the rest of us!''

The maze of streets was crowded with people hollering at one another. Men with accordions or guitars in hand sang as they walked. Everything seemed louder here. A large stone wall was covered solidly with posters of Alcide de Gasperi, the Christian Democratic candidate, and Giuseppe Ferragamo. "Behind that wall is the Regina Coeli!"

"Oh, a church?" Matt asked, automatically translating the Latin to mean "Queen of Heaven."

"No, our prison!" Luciana was amused.

They flew over a bridge above the Tiber, crisscrossing busy avenues, then finally up Via Veneto. Luciana yelled that this was the fanciest street in Rome. More whores than anywhere else!

Despite the postwar poverty, everyone here seemed fashionably dressed. Women in sable furs, men in three-piece suits with glistening watch-fob chains across their stomachs. All sitting elegantly in glass-covered restaurants.

"The *bella figura*!" Luciana explained. "At home, they are poor. Here, out in public, they look rich!"

Electric-powered green trolley cars clattered past them, bands of street urchins clinging to their rears. Allied soldiers inside whistled at young girls. One street became another with more dizzying displays of architecture.

"The Spanish Steps, my favorite place in Roma!" Luciana shouted gaily as they dodged a furious taxi driver. "Home of pickpockets! The steps were built by the French and Italian, not Spanish!" She laughed at the sight of three landings, covered with pink azaleas, that led up to a twin-belfried church. "The Quirinal Palazzo!" she turned, as they flashed past a magnificent castle on a hill. "Home of Alcide de Gasperi, another kind of pickpocket!"

Sweet scents of orange blossoms hung in the air by the ancient Roman Forum. Clanking traffic dinned their words. Their senses were assaulted by the heavy, overpowering exhaust fumes of the buses, the dusty nostril-filling ruins of bombed-out buildings, bumpy cobblestones, ragged boys and beggars chasing them, dogs fighting, copulating, beggar women baring their breasts hoping for money to feed the babies in their arms—Luciana gave one a little coin saying, "It is bad luck to refuse"—bread baking in *pasticcerias*, the tangy smells of sauces simmering in apartments above them, the sour odors of urine, the sounds of babies crying, someone playing a tambourine on a street corner, people arguing politics, jabbing the air in front of one another's chests. And everywhere a sweet soft light from the sky that removed all edges.

They went past the Palazzo di Venezia's monument to military valor. "That's called the birthday cake because it looks lousy. Mussolini built it!"

"Why is it so old and dirty?"

"Because, as for most new buildings in Rome, they used a poor grade of marble to build it. Very porous! And no matter how they clean it, the fumes from the buses and cars dirty it up again."

They shot up a hill. "You see those steps?" she asked, happy as a child. "There's a church on top. And there's never been a wedding inside it since it was built in 1540!"

"Why?" he asked, seeing the steep steps rise straight up into the sky and thinking of drawings of Jack and his beanstalk.

"Because no bride wants to arrive sweating!"

The Colosseum appeared out of nowhere. One minute, they were on an ordinary-looking street; the next, there it was. It was a pattern of Rome.

The road circled the Colosseum, so Luciana drove around it. Matt could see the dilapidated yet intact shell. Tourists flowed through the arches on ground level and could be seen picking their way upward into the stone bleachers.

"That's where the first Christians were martyred!" Matt reminded her excitedly.

"The Colosseum was not built until 70 A.D. By then a lot of Christians were in power. There were very few of them martyred there!"

"How do you know so much?"

"Every Roman prides himself on the history of his city!"

They zoomed down quieter streets filled with people in coarse wool, simpler clothing. Again, as elsewhere, the streets were immaculate. They rounded a corner, and he saw the reason why. A blue-uniformed army of men and women, long-handled straw brooms in hand, were whisking all refuse into piles.

They halted at the Trevi Fountain, fashioned in the eighteenth century. "It is nothing special, not very old. The whole thing is a front for a water aqueduct built by Marcus Agrippa in 19 B.C."

Matt watched the tumbling waterfalls cascading down past

playful water nymphs, dolphins and imposing statues of Triton and other Roman gods.

"Legend says that if you throw in a coin, you're sure to return to Rome," Luciana told him.

Matt fished in his pocket and pulled out his change. He had a dime and a penny.

"Does the Trevi accept American coins?"

"The city of Rome, which is bankrupt and which collects all coins from this fountain, takes anything!"

Matt turned and threw the penny over his shoulder. It splashed near the lower edge of a waterfall. "Well, that takes care of that," he said. "Looks like I'm coming back." He handed Luciana the dime.

"I'm not leaving, remember?" she objected.

"You can never tell."

She shrugged. Turning her back, she flipped the coin high into the air. Instead of landing in the water, the dime tinkled along the pavement in front of the fountain. Several urchins rushed to pick it up.

"You missed," Matt remarked teasingly.

"It doesn't matter." Luciana was somberly watching the street boys run away with the dime. "I told you I'm not going anywhere."

8.

She started up the Vespa, and they drove slowly now through several side streets, emerging finally on the Tiber. Luciana was strangely quiet. Matt saw that they had circled back to the left bank of the Tiber, near his island hospital of Isola Tiberina, which sat in the middle of the river. They went through a gate in a wrought-iron fence and into a small street with open markets displaying escarole, eggplants, carrots, bell peppers, tomatoes, mushrooms and artichokes.

"You're in the Jewish ghetto now," Luciana told him. "This is where Jews were ordered to live and work, starting in the sixteenth century."

"Who made them live here?" Matt asked, curious.

"Pope Paul IV," Luciana said, spitting on the ground.

Along Via Rigosa, the little naked light bulbs that hung on thin metal arms stretching from sides of buildings sputtered on in anticipation of approaching nightfall. There was a chill in the air that reminded Matt it was winter here in Rome.

Stopping the bike before a two-story pink house, Luciana swung off as a short, heavily muscled man suddenly opened the iron gates and sprinted down to meet her.

"This is Ruffino," she said to Matt. "A bomb killed his family. He was kind enough to allow me to live here after I lost my house."

She said something to Ruffino, and he reached out and shook Matt's hand. "Father Bowles," he said in stilted English. "It's my honor."

He bowed, took the bike and wheeled it up after them, closing the heavy gates and locking them.

"Where is everyone?" Luciana asked.

"Eating, Contessa. The neighbors brought a little meat."

"You're in luck," Luciana said to Matt. "A real feast."

The tone of her voice had changed. Since they had neared this house, traveling from the Trevi Fountain, she had become more grim.

As they entered the warm marble passageway, Matt whispered to Luciana, "Why does he call you Contessa?"

"Part of an old tradition. Everyone in Italy is count, countess, prince or something." She shrugged it off.

He followed Luciana through inner doors. A buxom woman was yelling up the bannister to the second floor. Lines of emaciated children were filing in silence down past her. Adults followed, they too as bony as skeletons.

The strapping, broad-faced woman with a sizeable dark moustache on her upper lip threw a stevedore-sized arm around Luciana and led her away. Matt accompanied them into the large kitchen. The children were seating themselves around a long table. Some of them looked up briefly, then bent to their bowls of soup. Women were policing their eating, making sure the children wasted no food by spilling.

Luciana introduced Father Matt, and Hannah Orteglio shook his hand politely. She was a mammoth woman, fat from many sins of pasta.

"Do you speak English?" he asked, trying to draw her out.

"*Sì, cèrto!*" she said, her brows knitting sternly. "I cook for English family before war. How you say, I was also nanny!"

"Quite a lot of people here speak English," Luciana said to Matt.

"The refugees too?"

"Some of them. Ivan Cohen, our handyman from Graz, for instance. It's a second language here in Europe, you know, used for business mostly. It's how we of different languages communicate in this house."

"Contessa," Hannah said, changing the subject, "will you eat now?"

"Later. I want to see Milko and his two boys first."

"They were moved in this afternoon."

"Do they have enough room?" Luciana seemed concerned. "After Ivan put up the partition in my bedroom, I was afraid their half would be too small."

"It is fine," Hannah said. "Go up and see quickly, then come eat. You are too skinny, Contessa. You too, if you wish," she said halfheartedly to Matt before waddling into the kitchen.

"I don't think she likes me," he said as they started up the staircase together.

"If anything, your shirt helps. Like a lot of other Romans, she mistrusts the Church. It's nothing personal."

At the second-floor landing, Luciana paused at a door that had been newly hung. "Milko and his two boys, Dzido and Milko, Jr., all have fevers. They came to us from Treblinka."

"Treblinka?" Matt wondered. "I thought the concentration camps emptied out a couple of years ago?"

"They did. But what do you think happened to the prisoners of those camps?"

"Well, the papers said they were given medical care, released, taken back to where they lived."

"And what if they had no homes or even businesses to return to? What if their families were gone, brothers and sisters, mothers and fathers gassed? Shattered existences. Their places gone forever, nothing for them anymore. These who come now to Rome are those outcasts. The ones not able to fit anywhere in Europe again. You know what happens when you make a piece of clothing? You cut out your pattern and the remnants drop to the floor. No matter how hard you try to do something with them, they will always be remnants." She knocked on the door. "About six months ago, the word went out from Haganah, the Jewish agency for resettlement, that anyone left in Europe wishing to leave for Palestine could depart from Rome. There had already been massive exoduses from Germany, France, Austria and Poland."

"Then the Haganah will help you in sending these refugees to Palestine?" Matt asked.

"After that announcement, the Haganah ran out of funds. Now they need all the money to finance their War of Liberation in Palestine. The remnants of Treblinka, Auschwitz, Buchenwald are stranded."

She knocked again, this time insistently. "We've located two ships, though. And if we're lucky enough to get our money from the Vatican, we'll buy them and ship these last ones home."

What appeared to be an old woman tentatively cracked open the door and peered out. "Contessa!" she cried, reached for Luciana and tugged her inside. Matt barely had time to enter before she slammed the door. They were standing in a nearly dark room. Only a few stray rays of light pierced the shuttered windows from the outside.

"There is nothing to fear here, Marie," Luciana explained to her in German.

"They do not like the light," the woman reminded her.

Luciana touched her arm in a comforting gesture, then she turned to Matt and explained in English, "This is Marie Schollander. She's also from the concentration camp at Treblinka. Yesterday was her twenty-sixth birthday."

Matt nodded to the young woman who was old beyond her years. Then he heard Luciana speak to someone, and he swung and in the dim light saw that a man and two children were in a small bed. The children were staring pitifully, their eyes too large for their bony, shrunken heads. The man watched him sullenly. Wild-eyed, the man tried to answer the questions Luciana asked him, but appeared close to being out of control. And all the while, his eyes darted to Matt.

"Don't worry about us," Milko told Luciana nervously. "We are enjoying our new quarters."

"Daddy tells us stories," one of the boys announced to her. His eyes were bright with fever. His younger brother, however, seemed exhausted by awakening. He turned his head into Milko's side and dozed off.

"Soon, perhaps next week, Daddy says, we shall go to the land of milk and honey," the older boy, Dzido, told Luciana.

"It's true," she said encouragingly. "We'll take you there on those two ships waiting in Civitavecchia Harbor!"

Suddenly, Milko eased out from between his two boys. He

stood and faced Luciana. It was as if the tension he was feeling because a stranger was in the room had become suddenly too much and he could no longer stay still. He stood up now, popping the waistband on the underwear that was all he was wearing.

"Who is he?" he hissed, pointing to Matt.

"A friend."

"Who?"

"A priest of God. A friend."

Milko looked over his shoulder like a wary animal. He turned back to Luciana. "You won't open the blinds, will you?" he demanded.

"You may keep your part of the room as dark as you like," Luciana said. "It won't bother me."

He stared at her a moment, then his skeleton-shaped body sagged in relief. "Thank you," he murmured. "Thank you . . . for understanding. It's just . . . the light is so . . . and we . . ."

Luciana reached out and hugged him.

"Soon," she whispered, "you will be well, Milko. Your body will heal and inside, you won't be afraid of the light."

"If God wills," he said. He allowed himself to be led back to bed by the young-old woman, Marie Schollander.

"I will have Doctor Fiacci come tomorrow to examine them," Luciana told Marie. Then she pulled Matt from the room.

"What is wrong with him?" he asked once they were outside and the door was closed.

"Milko was a prostitute in the concentration camp."

"And the boys?"

"The same. Used by the guards at night. None of them, including Milko, saw the sun for six years."

During dinner, most of the refugees ate their food quickly, excused themselves and went upstairs to their rooms. Matt learned the names of some from a white-haired old man named Rabbi Meister, who introduced him around. Marie Schollander carried several trays up to Milko and his two sons. In a little while, the long table in the kitchen was deserted.

*   *   *

Luciana had changed into a pair of worn green army trousers and a soft, blue cotton blouse. Along with Hannah and two of the other women, she was stacking and washing dishes, whistling a gay little song. Matt was finishing his coffee at the long table, watching her and the women.

"You know, Contessa," Hannah began scolding her softly in Italian, "you should not have to work so hard!"

"Speak in English," Luciana said. "We have a guest."

Hannah gave Matt a look, shrugged, then without speaking went back to her dishes.

"You work hard, volunteer your time," Luciana told her in English. "I'm no different than you."

"But you are a contessa!" one of the other women answered.

"I do this because I have no regular family. I need to be useful and needed too."

"And if you had a family?" Hannah wanted to know, joining in English.

"Then I would have no time for this, I suppose."

"Ah, we all need families," Hannah bemoaned playfully. "It is a requirement of life."

"And men!" one of the others spoke up.

"Men are like liquor," the remaining woman giggled. "You don't like the way they taste or smell, but you love the way they make you feel!"

Everyone roared at that. Matt grinned. Then there were several whispered sentences between them that he could not hear. The women snickered.

"Soon you should get married," Hannah told Luciana when they had quieted. She rattled the dishes in the dishwater to emphasize her point. "That's healthy. That's what you need!"

"Well, I would, but no one's asked me!" Luciana spun and secretly winked at Matt. He was enjoying this glimpse of intimate women's talk.

"But, Contessa," one of the women said, continuing to regard Matt's presence as unimportant. "You are beautiful! It should be easy. Flies to candy!"

"Italian men are put off by what I do. So, I don't get asked. Maybe they think I'm too bossy."

"Tsk. Tsk. Very sad. How sad!" the women chorused.

"Well, what about you, Hannah? When are you getting married again?" Luciana wanted to know.

"Oh, that is not for me!" The big woman laughed cheerfully. "I wait for my Bosco to return from that Allied POW camp in Africa. You'll see!"

"And when he comes home, you'll start up a family," Luciana pointed out. "But right now, this is what women without men do."

"And there are plenty of us." Hannah dropped more dishes noisily into the water.

"*Sì, sì*, too many. Too many. How sad!" the other women chorused.

A short, professorial-looking man with very thick glasses suddenly rushed into the kitchen. "Both ships are ready!" he shouted, out of breath. "They finished outfitting them this afternoon!"

Luciana and the others wheeled in anticipation, dish towels in hand.

The man slumped exhaustedly beside Matt at the table, taking no notice of him. "But we have less than forty-eight hours to buy them! After that, they are gone!"

"Gone? Where, Ivan?" Luciana asked, sitting also.

"Marcheshi will sell them to someone in Genoa to haul coal."

"Coal? Coal is more important to him than humans?"

"He says he has honored our agreement until now. Our options on those two ships run out day after tomorrow."—

Luciana smacked the table with her open palm. "He will wait! He has to!" she muttered.

"He won't," Ivan said.

Luciana lapsed into a pensive, worried stare. She sat at the table, far off in her thoughts.

Hannah set coffee, hard rolls and a steaming bowl of fish soup before Ivan. "It's from the bottom," she said. "The best. I saved it for you, knowing you would be tired after the long trip to Civitavecchia."

"You're a good woman," he said. "If I walk and hitchhike that seventy-two kilometers one more time, my feet will fall off!"

"Luciana told you to take her motorbike."

"Oh, no! I'm afraid of that thing."

"You're silly. Eat your soup!"

He tasted it. "You're a good cook." He smacked his lips at Hannah. "When are you going to marry me?"

"You behave yourself," Hannah warned him good-naturedly. "My Bosco is working his way back from Africa and he will thrash you good!"

Ivan caught sight of Matt and laid down his spoon.

"Oh, sorry," Luciana said. "I forgot my manners. This is Father Matt Bowles. Ivan Cohen. Ivan can fix anything. He's been a watchmaker, a sailor on ships, even an inventor of a machine that takes salt out of ocean water."

"Pleased to meet someone so talented." Matt stuck out his hand.

"A priest," Ivan said, ignoring it. He went back to eating his soup. "Did you get our money from the Vatican?" he asked Luciana after a couple of mouthfuls.

"Not yet." She looked uncertain and avoided Matt's gaze.

"Don't worry," Matt assured Ivan. "The Vatican's good for it."

"Your Pope does nothing for Jews. If he's so concerned, where's our money? It's been nearly a week!"

"Pius threw open the monasteries and churches all across Europe, gave your people shelter. He established the Vatican Information Service, which dealt with prisoners, refugees, missing persons and orphans. There were letters from Jews all over the world during and after the war that he answered personally."

Ivan Cohen pushed away his soup, no longer hungry. "Forgive me, Father," he said. "I know those stories. I speak from another experience." He got up, put his nearly untouched bowl and coffee cup by the sink and left the kitchen. The two refugee women who had been washing dishes followed, wiping their hands on their long skirts. Hannah rattled the dishes in the sink in approval.

Luciana got up from the table and went to the sink. She picked up a plate to dry it.

"Why are there so few ships around?" Matt asked her. "There must be other ones than this Marcheshi's."

"Toward the end of the war, most of Italy's shipping was

sunk by Mussolini," Luciana explained. "He scuttled our entire merchant fleet to protect our harbors, he said. The few that are around are like Marcheshi's, raised from the bottom of the ocean."

"But what about buying ships from other countries? France, Switzerland, Spain, Portugal? Even England must have ships to sell."

"You forget," Luciana smiled at the irony, "the British who control Palestine have put travel restrictions on Jews and have made it an international crime to sell ships to sail Jews there. Prime Minister Clement Attlee has pressured all of Europe and even the United States not to sell ships to us." She picked up a serving bowl to dry it.

"Don't give up," Matt chided her. "If you don't get these ships, something will turn up."

She slammed the bowl down so hard it startled him. "You don't understand!" she glared at him. "These Jews are the last. For thousands of years, Jews have said, 'Next Year in Jerusalem,' meaning the sacred pilgrimage home. Home, where there will be no more persecution, no anti-Semitism, no gold stars on their chests, no concentration camps, no ghettos, no stigmas for being a Jew! And for many who are too old, too weak, this may be their last chance. Even now, a war is starting in Palestine. Who knows how long that will go on? And these people don't want to die here! They want to do that in Palestine! That concept may seem strange to you, but I tell you as God is my witness, if those two ships now at Civitavecchia sail without them, my families will die here of broken hearts and their souls will burn in a kind of Gehenna. It will be a sign they are lost forever."

Shaking, she turned, picked up the bowl. "I swear we will not lose those ships! Not now!"

The bowl slipped from her fingers and smashed on the floor. "Goddamn everything!" she cried in frustration. She threw down the towel and stalked from the kitchen. Matt could hear her muttering as she took the stairs two at a time.

"Go to her," Hannah said, stooping and picking up the pieces.

"I'll give you a hand first."

"No, she is more important. And for some reason, she values you. Talk to her."

Matt walked up the staircase. At the top of the stairs, to the right, he saw there was a door ajar. He pushed it open and found himself inside a library that was now filled with cots and opened trunks.

The old man whom Matt had met at dinner, Rabbi Meister, with a white beard and a black yarmulke on his stringy salt-and-pepper hair, sat in the only chair. There were many children at his feet. Matt had seen him secretly slipping his food to the kids.

"Who knows Ten?" he asked in Hebrew, acknowledging Matt's presence with a nod.

"I know Ten." A very small, undeveloped little teenager rose to her feet. "Ten Commandments, Nine months to bear, Eighth day to circumcise, Seventh day for Sabbath, Six books of Mishnah, Five books of Torah, Four the Mothers, Three the Fathers, Two the Tablets, One is God in Heaven and Earth."

The old man said, "Very fine, Ruth." Then in English, "And won't you join us, Father Matthew?"

"Go ahead, Rabbi Meister," Matt said. "I can only stay a minute."

"Our little daughter Ruth is from the camp at Theresienstadt. She lost her speech but is now regaining it."

"Sounds like she speaks very well." Matt smiled at the girl, who was in her teens, yet looked perhaps nine. She was very thin in her oversized dress, a waif, but her big brown appealing eyes smiled up at him.

Matt crouched beside her. "Where were you born, honey?" he asked.

"Cremona," she said, her eyes bright.

"I'm from Venice," another child offered. Matt knew him as Klaus. The boy used crutches and had been attracted to him at dinner because of his cane. "I'm from the first-ever ghetto. Did you know that is where the word comes from, Father? *Getar*," the boy pronounced proudly, looking at Meister. "It means to cast in iron. You see there was a foundry in our Venice ghetto!"

Other children told Matt that they were from Firenze (Florence, Meister translated), Isola della Scala, Ventimiglia, Trieste, Ponte nelle Alpi, even Lienz and Amstetten in Austria.

"So you are all from this part of Europe?" Matt asked them.

The children nodded and Rabbi Meister explained: "You see, Father, these here in Luciana's house were the last to be shipped to the concentration camps. In 1938, Benito Mussolini pushed through his racist programs that forced Jews out of their jobs. But it wasn't until the Germans moved into northern Italy that the purge began to sweep Italy and its surrounding borders. The holocaust here began in 1944, very late in the war."

"Near my father and mother's house in the ghetto in Venice," Klaus, the small boy with crutches, said, "there is a plaque which reads: 'And nothing shall purge your deaths from our memories, for our memories are your only grave.' My father, who is still living and here with me, made me memorize that."

Matt reached out and laid a comforting hand on the boy's shoulder.

"Who knows Thirteen?" the old man asked, his dark eyes twinkling. "Klaus?"

"I know!" the small boy levered up on his crutches. Klaus stood up as straight as he could and recited proudly in Yiddish, "Thirteen God's attributes, Twelve the Tribes, Eleven stars for Joseph, Ten Commandments, Nine months to bear, Eighth day to circumcise, Seventh day for Sabbath, Six books of Mishnah, Five books of Torah, Four the Mothers . . ."

Matt silently backed out of the door. He retraced himself through the foyer, then emerged into the hallway.

The door next to that room was Milko's and his two boys'. He stepped down the hallway to an adjacent door, which was larger and more ornate. He knocked and, when there was no answer, opened it. The smell of perfume reached his nostrils. The scent reminded him of a forest after a rain, filled with delicate flowers.

The bedroom's French windows were open and the light from outside bathed the bed, chaise and dressing table in soft evening grays.

"Luciana?" he called.

She answered in a low voice, "Out here. On the balcony."

He crossed the room, feeling the springiness of expensive

rugs beneath his feet. Bright scarves lay on the headboard of the bed, across the back of her dressing chair. There was an open box of white face powder before her makeup mirror. An elegant, polished armoire, its doors spread so that the body-length mirrors reflected each other, stood near the oval-shaped doorways that led out to the balcony.

Too much furniture for this small room, he thought. Almost as if Luciana had relinquished all claim to a former world, except this one small remaining portion of space.

Outside, Luciana was staring forward over a carved marble railing, dabbing at her eyes with a handkerchief. Matt kept his gaze on the city of Rome before them, the Palatine Hill and ancient Forum ruins nearby, the Basilica of St. Peter and Vatican City in the distance.

She blew her nose, then sniffled.

"If it's the money you're worried about," Matt said, breaking the silence, "please believe me. You'll get it. I'll go see Pope Pius. He must know you helped at the Vatican during the war. He'll remember you for that."

"I doubt it. Let's just say he doesn't like troublemakers."

"And when did you make trouble? During the war?"

"Yes, as I told you. I dressed POWs in priests' clothing, snuck them right past the German and Swiss Guards. Along with Father O'Flaherty, I hid them in the deserted embassy buildings inside the Vatican."

"And no one found out?"

"The Vatican never knew a thing. Then someone told Monsignor Kass, who alerted Pope Pius. After that Pius himself gave orders to the guards to chase away the Allied escapees seeking refuge."

"Now you're beginning to sound like your friend Ivan. You know His Holiness couldn't have done that."

Luciana shrugged. "Catholics get shown only what the Vatican wants them to see. I live in this Pope's parish. I see what is happening."

She faced him now, her high cheekbones reflecting the distant lights of St. Peter's Square. "I used to see my Church as holy, even heavenly. Now I see buildings of cold marble, filled with bureaucrats, altars heavy with jewels, museums full of ancient masterpieces. No spirit there. It seems the

Church, instead of reaching out, spreading its arms, is hugging itself, intent only on its own survival."

"We just went through a war, Luciana. Our Church had to protect itself to survive!"

"Survive? What about the three hundred and thirty-two ordinary people who were executed by the Germans right here in Rome? Bakers, lawyers, gardeners, students, bankers, kidnapped off the streets, taken to the Ardeatine caves outside Rome and shot one by one in the back of the head. Did *they* have no right to survive?"

"I don't know what you are talking about," Matt said.

"On March 23, 1944, thirty-two SS police were ambushed by Communists in an alley called Via Rasella. It's near the Vatican. In retaliation, Hitler ordered Colonel Kappler, who was in charge of Rome, to round up three hundred thirty-two Roman men. They were picked up at random off the streets, herded into sealed meat trucks and driven to the Ardeatine caves just south of Rome. The Germans forced their prisoners inside these man-made caves, made them squat and then shot them in the head. It took sixty-seven SS soldiers a complete day to finish their work. When they were done, German engineers dynamited the caves and sealed them off. After the war, we Italians made a monument out of them."

"But what does all this have to do with His Holiness?" Matt asked, trying to keep his voice steady.

"Pope Pius knew beforehand about the executions."

"He couldn't have!" He felt hot blood rising to his face.

"And the day after the executions *l'Osservatore Romano*, the official newspaper of the Vatican, asked all Roman citizens to maintain a spirit of sacrifice. The Pope asked us not to riot!"

"If Pope Pius had known about the massacre, he'd have stopped it! He'd have done something!"

"Only Monsignor Orsenigo, our Roman nuncio, spoke out against the atrocity. When he died, a year later, he was buried as a *persona non grata*, without even an obituary in *l'Osservatore Romano*."

"I don't believe you! You got your facts mixed up or something! If you *are* right, why didn't news of this get out?"

"Because the Vatican controls the press. And because there

was a signed neutrality pact with the Third Reich. Because even during the war, Pope Pius XII continued getting four million marks a year from German Catholics. Because he never said a word when the Nazis rounded up one thousand and seven Jews in Rome to deport them to Auschwitz. Because he never turned away German tanks when they rumbled through the open city of Rome to fight the Allies at nearby Anzio. Because he did nothing about the torture of Allied POWs, partisans and political prisoners in Via Tasso prison and by the Gestapo in Via Principe Amedeo and Pensione Jaccarino. And why? All because he was trying to save a bunch of buildings!''

Now Matt exploded. "Ever since I've met you, you've done nothing but criticize my Church! And yet I, as a member of that Church, am doing my best to help you with your refugees! If we're all as terrible as you make us out, why should I work for your cause?''

"*Matteo*, I am not attacking good Catholics. I like to think of myself as one! But I'm ashamed of what the Church has become! Look around! Really look!'' She spun to the sight outside her balcony. "See it as it is!'' She thrust her finger at the distant vertical dotted glow of lights on the horizon. "That big smokestack? It's the electric company of Rome. The Vatican owns it. Over there, those low buildings are Roman water plants. Vatican owned!'' She swung in an arc, gesturing, her hand sweeping the city. "The telephone company, sewerage facilities, apartments, business buildings. All you see has been owned or controlled by the Vatican for many years. Now I hear the Church is going to build two hundred hydroelectric plants on rivers in northern Italy, buy coalfields in the Pyrenees, make cars in Milan, grow wheat in Brindisi, grapes in Ravenna and here in the Alban hills, can fishes in Palermo. Business will soon be booming in Italy. Someone told me my old friend at Banco di Spirito bank, *Signore* Perfette, is ready to open his doors again. The Vatican bought his bank! Why do they want so much power? And where . . . where do they get such sudden wealth?''

She was silent a moment, then she turned to him, realizing. "That big money came from the United States, didn't it? You brought it in your airplane!''

Matt, completely surprised, glared at her.

"It's true, isn't it?"

"All right!" he shouted. "You guessed, so what? That money's going to be used to save Italy!"

"Save Italy!" It sounded like she wanted to laugh but the sound died in her throat. "From what?"

"Communists! You're supposed to be the one with your eyes open. Are you blind to what's happening?" He turned from the balcony, burst across her bedroom. "Don't bother to show me out! It's been an inspiring evening!"

She pursued him through the hall, down the stairs. "Something has happened to our money, hasn't it! If you brought it on your airplane, where is it?"

"You know so much about my Church's functions, why don't you find out what has happened to it yourself!" He leaned heavily on his cane as he went out the front door.

Hannah came out of the kitchen, a cup of tea in her hand. She watched, astonished, as Luciana flew down the stairs. "What, what is it?"

"Something's happened to our money!" Luciana cried as she ran outside.

"Ah, priests." Hannah shook her head. She hurriedly kissed her thumbnail, then rubbed her eyes with it to rid herself of a priest's evil eye.

Outside, Luciana saw Matt cross the courtyard and stump down the street. She ran after him. Thunder crossed the sky.

"Where is our million for our ships?" she demanded when she caught up with him. "Tell me the truth! It didn't arrive, did it?" She caught hold of his arm and swung him around.

"It came on the plane," he said fiercely. "It just got . . . misplaced." He turned up the street again.

"Misplaced?! You mean *lost*!" She ran alongside him.

"*Mis*-placed! You'll get your money!"

"Will we, Father? Why don't we have it now? Even if it is only *mis*-placed, couldn't the Vatican lend us the money until they locate it?"

"They'll replace it!" Matt screamed. "Or they'll find it! The trouble with you is you have faith in no one."

She stopped, stamped her foot, letting him go on. "Go live in your dream, priest!" Several lights came on in the houses on the street. "Go back and hide in the priesthood, close your eyes to everything! Our money is gone! *Gone!*"

She could hear his cane banging furiously down the narrow, dark ghetto street. She took a deep breath and huffed it out. A woman cursed her from an upper window. Luciana raised her arm, slapped the inside of her elbow in insult. Then she turned back toward home, the rain now starting down.

9.

That night, a Northern Adriatic blew into Rome. It was the first big storm of the winter, a signal for even the hardiest tourists to go home. The cold rain fell thickly from the black sky, whipped about by the northern wind. Small prewar cars, at home in the tight streets, raced down Corso Vittorio Emanuele, the main avenue of Rome. One of those cars, its windshield wipers flicking inadequately at the downpour, was driven by Gararardo Spina. Passing car lights gleamed off the top of his semibald head, the reflections playing through the two parallel rows of hair.

"Slowly, comrade." Igor Nerechenko in his gray baggy suit tried to sound unworried from the other seat. He had spilled aquavit on his woolen trousers. "You drive too fast. You are dangerous!"

Nerechenko knew just how dangerous Spina was. Only recently, the horned one had laid the groundwork for the Communist Party in France by kidnapping the opposition candidate's children and strangling them one by one until the man had dropped out of the race. Finally, after the elections, when the Communist candidate had won a chief post in the National Assembly, Spina had murdered the remaining two little girls. Even children talk, he had said.

This present campaign would make their sixth together.

Since freeing Spina from the gallows where he was to die for having turned traitor during the war, Nerechenko had operated with Spina in Albania, Czechoslovakia, Rumania, Lithuania, Poland and France, each a bright jewel in the crown of Mother Russia. Now would come the supreme prize, the diamond that Master Josef Stalin desired so badly. Italy, the centralized European country from which he could control the Mediterranean, and thereby, as Napoleon had observed so long before, the world. And Nerechenko would need Cornos to help him again. Therefore, he could not have his assassin out of control like this.

But the horned one began muttering, driving faster in the blinding rain. "It's been one big failure, one mistake after another here."

"Don't worry, comrade."

"I am tired of dealing with this ferret, Ferragamo. He should be kept yapping his speeches from wooden stands, not planning stupidities. We have failed to get that money, thanks to him. Your meeting with the Red Woman had better work out. If even a spy from the Vatican cannot help us, I'll take over!"

Igor Nerechenko turned and studied his Sicilian friend. He knew Spina grew in vitality after every killing yet still prayed fervently to the Blessed Virgin. It made him full of tensions that only seemed to quiet after he murdered. But it had been a long time since Cornos had killed.

"Comrade Gararardo Spina," Igor said placatingly, "it is only a little time before you do your work. Then you will feel good again."

Spina grumbled something Nerechenko could not hear, then spotted the Trattoria Candida and stepped on the brakes, skidding the car to the curb.

Nerechenko opened his door. "Go and have supper somewhere," he said.

"Sure, what else to do?" Spina muttered crossly.

Nerechenko slammed the door so hard the small car rocked on its springs. The Russian jumped over the running water at the curb as the horned one drove away. Pushing through the wooden front door with its tiny circular window, he stood in the steamy, overheated restaurant, glanced briefly across the tiny room and saw that, as he had requested, it was empty.

The woman who was the cook and owner was sitting at a rear table, drinking bottled water. She was a trusted member of the Communist Party.

Nerechenko snapped off the two overhead, naked light bulbs. The woman brought a candle to a table. She caught Nerechenko's foul odor as he sat down and coughed politely, then lit a stick of sandalwood incense on a table behind him.

"Do you wish some food now, comrade?" she asked.

"Later," the Russian said. "Lock the front when the one I am expecting arrives. He will use the kitchen to exit."

"*Sí*, comrade," she said. She crossed the room and stood patiently by the door.

Almost immediately, a figure in a long black coat entered the darkened restaurant, turned his face toward the side wall and waited until the owner locked up and ran into a back room.

Nerechenko motioned the Red Woman to his table, then seated himself across from his visitor. The Woman's face was hidden in the shadows. Only his slender hands were visible.

"What do you want with me now?" he demanded. "Haven't I done enough? Didn't I tell you where the plane would land? What more do you want? It isn't my fault you missed destroying the money!"

Nerechenko leaned back in his chair, confidently in control. "Have you succeeded?" he asked in Russian.

The traitor was silent. But his hands twisted in the meager light from the candle. "There was too much security." The Red Woman's voice was a squeak. "Before I could act, the money had been stored in a safe."

Nerechenko thrust his massive torso across the table. "Comrade, I gave specific orders that if the money got past us at Lake Bracciano, you were to destroy it."

The Red Woman quickly lifted a briefcase onto the table. He opened it. Inside was a package, wrapped in Vatican-embossed butcher paper, tied with twine.

"What is this, Red Woman?" Nerechenko snorted.

"A gift." The spy's voice rose too high. "To show my sincerity." He withdrew his hands and put them back in his lap.

Nerechenko ripped away the wax-coated paper of the package. Bills spilled inside the briefcase. "What is this?"

"American money!" the Red Woman said enthusiastically. "For your cause!"

"How much is here?" The Russian did not touch the scattered bills.

"Eight hundred and sixty-three thousand-dollar bills!"

"You stole this, yet you could not destroy the entire amount?"

"No, no!" The Red Woman's voice was confiding, bordering now on a shared joke. "This money was separate. It is Jews' money! No one knew of its existence!"

"Jews?"

"A Father Matthew Bowles, the one who escaped you at Lake Bracciano, brought it over. I could not obtain all of it, you see. A teller, curse him, came into the bank just as I was cutting open the leather pouch. But I was able to smuggle most of it out. I knew it would help your cause. It's perfect, don't you see, because it will never be missed and . . ."

Nerechenko shoved the money back at the Red Woman, who looked startled. "You do not understand! You need lesson, Comrade Red Woman! I do not *need* any American money!"

"But . . . this would finance a great deal. . . ." the Red Woman protested. "Think of all the radio advertising . . . the posters for Ferragamo . . . the goodwill it would buy!"

"Burn it," Nerechenko said.

"What . . . whaaat?" The Red Woman closed the lid of the case. His hands were shaking. "I . . . I refuse! I'm sure it would be . . . of use. Don't you see that?"

"I see only that in your dossier"—Nerechenko leaned back—"there is a description how you sleep in bed. You wear two pairs of pajamas. You wrap your knees, ankles, elbows in bandages because you are afraid your joints will fall apart while you sleep. You are very afraid, Red Woman. Do you want to tell the world you wrap your cock in basil, comrade? Why basil?"

There was no movement from the Red Woman.

"The dossier on you has many interesting facts." In the wavering light from the candle, Nerechenko's eyes were not cruel but weary. This was business. "You do not allow the little boys to see your face. Why is that? Can you not perform if someone stares at you?"

The Red Woman looked around the restaurant to see if the owner was within hearing distance.

"Do you wish the world to know how you make love, Comrade Red Woman? You are a man in appearance, but you are not a man in bed. Shall I inform Pope Pius how in Russia you once raped a four-year-old boy? How you then tortured him to death, using pliers on his body? Strange, Red Woman. You are woman, yet not very motherly to the little boys you choose."

"Enough!" the traitor exploded. "Stop!"

There was a startled movement in the kitchen, where the owner waited.

In the ensuing silence, Nerechenko took a deep breath, then eased forward, resting his hands on the table top. "It is your bad luck, comrade, that I spotted you outside the Vatican. Stalin himself would like to know where you are. He has a few scores to settle. You remember, for instance, how you failed to assassinate Adolf Hitler? A classic case of bungling, comrade."

The Red Woman groaned softly in reply.

"Good. We communicate. So, their money is safe. You are not, Comrade Red Woman. You have failed by not obeying me. Now, you must make a plan, comrade. One that will stop the Vatican from financing De Gasperi's Christian Democrats. One that will persuade Italians to vote for us!"

"You ask too much!" the Red Woman objected. "I . . . I cannot perform miracles!"

"Think! Think hard, comrade! Give me something, or else I will start to leak the dossier I obtained to the newspapers! How would that be, a fine thing, yes? Italians reading about one so high in the Vatican performing such animal acts! And then Master Stalin sending 'mad-dog' Beria and his NKVD butchers for you."

The Red Woman shuddered and lifted his hands onto the table top again. Nerechenko withdrew his. "There will arrive by plane the tally sheets of all the money sent from the United States. The bills will be listed individually."

Nerechenko could not help but grin slightly. But he tried not to react eagerly to this news. "What is that to us? Records! So what?"

"With them," the Red Woman explained patiently, "you

could prove to the Italians there was a vast amount of money that came from the United States. You could show the Italian people that the rich Vatican is backing the Christian Democrats.''

''When do these records arrive in Rome?''

''In a few days. A priest, Father William Mankowsky, will bring them.''

''That is something, Comrade Red Woman. I will let Cornos himself handle this priest personally. He grows stale. Do you have any objections to that?''

The spy shook his head helplessly.

''Now,'' Nerechenko said, ''we will await your final plan. If it is good, it will buy your freedom from me forever.''

The Red Woman rose wearily, pushing back his chair. ''Do you swear it is still true no one but you knows my new identity?'' he asked the Russian.

''That is our deal, comrade.''

The Red Woman nodded. Taking the briefcase, he entered the kitchen, exiting opposite the way he had come in.

In a bit, the owner stuck her head inside.

''Turn on the lights,'' Nerechenko said, extracting the half-empty bottle of aquavit from his coat pocket. ''Bring me ice. I drink, eat too.''

Spina had disobeyed Nerechenko's orders. Instead of driving off to find his supper, he had parked in back of the trattoria knowing this would be where the Red Woman would come out. He was tired of always getting orders that tied his hands. He felt he had a right to know about this Red Woman.

He sat in the little car, hunched down, his stomach grumbling in hunger.

After a long while, the back door of the Trattoria Candida opened, and a slight figure, bent forward in the falling rain, crossed the Piazza Risorgimento and walked toward the towering stone wall that ran around the Vatican State. Spina smeared the front windshield with his hand. He could not make out the face.

Then the angular man walked beneath a lamppost and the horned one drew in his breath sharply, totally surprised.

*   *   *

Entering the Gate of St. Anne, the main business entrance of the Vatican, the Red Woman passed a single guard, bundled against the rain in his black slicker.

The guard saluted properly, recognizing him.

The Red Woman did not acknowledge the greeting. Instead, he scurried past the green copper guardhouse, hunching his shoulders against the driving rain. Nearly running, he wound his way through the narrow streets of Vatican City. Turning at the corner bakery, he passed the butcher shop, then the shoemaker's door, and aimed for the large two-stacked power station.

Pausing momentarily at its side entrance, the Red Woman checked for passersby, then quickly ran down the concrete steps and pulled open the heavy iron door. Inside, the boilers hissed with the rush of natural gas, their flames dancing in stark shadows on the bare basement walls.

In the harsh, orange light from the holes in the boilers' four cast-iron doors, the Red Woman edged across the basement, caught hold of a long steel poker and pulled open the nearest, glowing door.

For a moment, he stood there, making himself realize what he was about to do. What a waste of useful money. Nerechenko was wrong. He was sure of it. But there was nothing he could do. His secrets must be kept safe at all costs. He had come too far in the hierarchy of the Vatican State to relinquish his power now. Someday he would be free of Nerechenko.

He snapped open the briefcase and took out the Jewish money. Then, one by one, he peeled off the eight hundred sixty-three one-thousand-dollar bills and flipped them into the boiler, watching them burst into flames, their ashes disappearing upward in the boiler's draft in stringlike phantoms.

10.

Father Matt Bowles had gone two blocks when he realized he was lost. The rain fell in thick sheets as he limped along favoring his hurt leg, stumbling occasionally in a pot hole in the street or sidewalk. The rain soaked his hair, his T-shirt and ran inside the waistband of his trousers. But he paid little attention to it. His mind was working feverishly, refuting every one of the charges made by Luciana against Pope Pius.

But what about her charges against him? Luciana's words stung him as he wound up one narrow street after another, searching for signs to his hospital.

Was he going through life with his eyes closed? Seeking safety by being a priest? Had being in the war made him feel what all men feel? Out of control, fragmented? Even *mortal*?

"You should never have been a priest. I see right through you!" He could hear his mother.

He was tempted to lose his way. To become totally lost as he was now in this dark city. To wallow in his chaotic emotions. The urge to let go, fall from this cliff he was clinging to. To slip finally, as he thought about it, into a state . . . what did the Eastern religions call it . . . nirvana? Only in his case, a sensual nirvana. Because the truth of it was he had felt like a man and not a priest this afternoon at the restaurant with Luciana. Was that why he had reacted so strongly to what she said afterwards? Was that old temptation, the one with Mimi, really the core of this?

He put his head down into the driving rain and, nearly blind, hobbled around a downhill corner.

As he continued to slog through the streets, he stopped looking at the street signs indented as stone plaques in the sides of the buildings. They made no sense to him anyway. Instead, he turned to the past signs in his heart.

It was the ninth of June, 1944, and he had been taken by ambulance from Normandy on Omaha Beach to St. Croix. There he was lifted off with the others who had survived that trip and taken to a crowded central room with a vaulted ceiling. Mud-free, white and starched nurses changed his bandages and readied him for surgery. He had watched out his window as others from the ambulance were buried in the neat little rows of the military-style cemetery, its crosses forever standing, it seemed, at attention.

When he was finally wheeled into the operating room, an auburn-haired nurse smiled down at him.

"Hi," Matt had mumbled.

The French nurse's hair was naturally curly and showed even beneath her paper stocking-cap. "Don't worry. I'll be here with you," she said in her softly accented way, and she stroked the inside of his wrist with her fingers.

Matt started to ask her name, but before he could make the words come, he fell asleep. When he awoke, the French nurse was sitting beside his bed. She had tawny skin and sleek dark hair and her face was fine-etched, nose pert, cheekbones high. Her cool fingers were long and elegant, her breasts small, her hips almost little-girlish.

"How are you feeling?" she asked.

"Not too good." Matt tried to smile. His buttocks and hipbone ached where they had removed the shattered German slugs. And he had a throb in his bandaged left shoulder. "Who are you?"

"Mimi," she said. And the next thing he remembered was waking up again and her saying, "You have slept a whole day. All the time you were having, how do you say, night . . ."

"Nightmares."

In the following days, between Mimi's visits, some boys in his battalion visited him, said they'd follow him anywhere, thanked him for making them move when they had been pinned down. To them, he was a hero. But it seemed to him they were talking about a priest gone crazy, a maniac. He refused to sign his autograph on the papers they brought him. In the end, he found himself lapsing into long stares out the nearby window that viewed the cemetery. Finally, he rudely had asked that last group to leave. The boys were stunned by their hero's harshness.

"Get out," he had murmured, feeling unwanted tears spring into his eyes. "Get out! Please!"

He ordered the nurses to take away the vases that held cut wild flowers and roses. He lay watching his hands on the white sheets of the hospital, expecting to find bloody imprints whenever they moved.

Mimi soothed him by reading to him, and he would concentrate on her, marveling at her white uniform. Trying to forget the filth and dried blood and saliva on men's faces and the sand and mud that had got into everything, especially during those agonizing times when the bowels became more important than dying and a mad dash to a neutral foxhole ended with a feeling of sand and filth in the rectum.

It was a strange and wonderfully removed world he was in now. The wandering sounds of the ambulatory-wounded talking, visiting one another inside the big, white-ceilinged room. The slowly revolving wooden fans that bathed the room in soft breezes, and Mimi, reading, smiling, caring—not knowing anything about his past.

It was during that time that Matt first admitted he felt something lacking in himself. He was not, as he had always believed and been taught in the seminary, totally complete. Needing no one. And he spent sleepless, tossing nights as he healed, feeling his body grow stronger, trying to stop the thoughts of Mimi Vandereaux, trying to deny the image of her body.

It was during their garden exercises that he first touched her—his elbow brushing her upcurving breast. He had touched only one other girl in his life there. It had been in the eighth grade, shortly before he had entered the seminary. The girl had reported him to Mother Superior. Only after he had made

a devout confession had Mother Mary Theresa been satisfied
and allowed him to resume his classes. But Mimi, beside him
in the garden, did not complain. Instead she turned slightly so
her breast pressed into his elbow, and he could feel her har-
dened nipple.

As they rounded the cement walk with its purple-centered
white pansies, he turned and, looking down, saw her eyes
darting away as if she were ashamed, yet hopeful, of what had
developed between them.

"Do you know where I live?" Mimi asked, her cheeks
flushing.

Matt shook his head.

"Go to the end of the only street in St. Croix, turn right. I
am by the church, in a small house. I will leave a candle
burning."

"Mimi," Matt said, "I . . ."

"I know you are a priest. But I love you."

She walked him back to his bed, caressing his wrist secretly.

Blinded with desire, he convinced himself that this would
be a kind of panacea to all his problems. So he resolved,
despite his vow of priestly chastity, to go to her.

That night, Matt dressed in his tans and tie, leaving off his
captain's bars and chaplain's identification pins. Working his
set of crutches, he made his way awkwardly down the brick
rue de St. Croix. There was a fountain and square in the
center of the town. The fountain had been hit by a howitzer
and lay in rubble. He walked past it and headed toward the
end of the street. The sound of singing drifted out from a
boarded-up building. He paused, hesitated, feeling the need
for fortification. Opening the door, he was greeted by French
peasants celebrating their independence.

Ordering a brandy, Matt sipped it carefully, sitting at a
little table, his crutches against the wall. A chanteuse sang
"Viva France," and the bartender, red-haired and emotional,
eyes filled with tears, refilled his glass four times and each
time refused payment. Upon leaving, Matt was given two
bottles of table Bordeaux.

He wove his way up the street, feeling the effect of the
prewar brandy the bartender had brought out for the victory
celebration. He turned right, as Mimi had instructed him.
Ahead, less than a hundred feet past a crude log-and-stucco

church, was a small, gabled house. A candle was lit, flickering in the window.

He stared at the lighted invitation to a new life, a life he had always denied himself, one which now he felt he needed desperately.

Gripping the bottles tightly, he made himself approach her door, which was discreetly hidden by a hedge. As he reached up to knock, the sound of a man singing came to his ears. Afraid he would be recognized, Matt hid himself. The man passed, weaving drunkenly, then saw him and stopped.

"You are wasting your time," he said in French.

Not understanding, but relaxing because the man was French, Matt eased out, his face half-lit now by the candle shining from Mimi's front window.

"Yank?" the man asked after a bit.

"American. Yes."

"Ah, good. I will speak English then."

Matt could see that the rotund, shadowy figure was barely able to stand. "What is it you have there in your hands, a little wine perhaps?"

The roundish shape approached. The man was a priest. He was wearing the white collar under a black sweater, which was matted as though it had been rained on.

The priest uncorked one of the bottles of Bordeaux, upended it, then wiped his mouth. "So," he said, "are you celebrating the liberation of France or Paris? It is Paris today for me. Are you a soldier from the hospital?" The priest eyed the uniform for rank.

Matt watched with disgust as the priest took another long pull on the bottle.

"So, my soldier," the priest said. "You wish to be nameless, but I am *Père* Flambert. I am an earthy man, if you see what I mean, and I will tell you, you are wasting your time knocking at that one's door."

He raised the bottle of wine and finished it off, then dropped the empty container to the street. It clinked across the worn bricks and rolled into the gutter.

"Do you know this woman?" the priest asked, grinning now.

"She is my friend."

"Ah, she is a friend to all, so long as they are priests." He turned toward the light. "My time is Thursday. So even I am underprivileged tonight. A pity, my young American soldier, that you are not a priest, *oui*?"

He took the other bottle from Matt's limp hand and uncorked it. Then, upending it, he started up the street.

"Come along, soldier," the drunken priest bellowed, waving the bottle over his head. "Let us enjoy ourselves. Tomorrow we may die."

Matt stared for a while at the glowing candle in the leaded-pane window. Then he went up the street with *Père* Flambert. Together, they drank in the bar. Toward dawn, feeling drunk and self-righteous, Matt told *Père* Flambert that he was a Catholic priest, serving as a chaplain in the Army.

Flambert downed his glass of Burgundy and thoughtfully said, "So we are both priests. But you see, I am vulnerable. You are not. And tomorrow, I will confess my sins to my bishop and struggle to be a priest. I will fall again, I imagine. But my weakness is my salvation. God loves a sinner. But for you, you who are on the razor's edge of perfection, every step is precarious. If you had lain with Mimi tonight, you would have felt beyond the reach of God, unforgivable. I do not. Sin is part of my existence. And with the help of God, I recover from it."

Matt could not tell if the priest was joking. What he was saying sounded so absurd.

"You Yanks," Flambert was continuing, red wine spittle on his lips, "live with scorecards. You keep close count on everything. Very efficient! Forty-two sins, you deserve hell. Why not laugh and enjoy it? Don't be like some little mouse, sneaking around. Laugh loud! And repent with tears! That's the way. Do everything with your whole heart. . . ." He abruptly passed out. The red-haired owner of the bar obligingly picked him up and made him comfortable on a cot in a windowless back room.

"*Père* Flambert is a man too," the owner said as he covered him with a moth-eaten army blanket. "He has his faults like any other." To Matt's surprise, he bent and kissed both of the sleeping priest's cheeks and led Matt out.

The rest of the night, Matt drank slowly, trying to get drunk, but unable. He kept hearing the tavern owner's com-

ments about Flambert being a man. Finally, he fell asleep on
the bar.

When he awoke, he was not in a bed as was *Père* Flambert
but on a bench near the shelled fountain. The sun was up and
the air was hot. Sitting up, he vomited until there was nothing
else left. Then he noticed several women washing clothing at
the fountain. Embarrassed, he searched quickly for his crutches,
but he must have left them in the tavern, which was locked. He
limped back to the hospital.

During the next several days, while he waited for his
medical discharge, he avoided Mimi. Once at his bed, she
asked him why he had not come. But he pretended to be
sleepy and rolled over.

When he received his discharge, he thumbed a ride to the
nearby port of Le Havre and rented a cheap room overlooking
the harbor. Someone told him a troopship was due in the next
few days. And as he waited, he thought about the close call
with Mimi.

It would have been so easy. He could have decided by
never having to make the decision. The act of love would
have resolved everything in his mind. By sinning, he would
have proven he was not worthy of being a priest. But what
had stopped him? Not his high-flown philosophy but a wreck
of a French priest. Or was Flambert the real priest?

As news came that the troopship drew closer, his resolve to
be a holy, perfect as possible priest returned. He begged God
to forgive him for that night he had nearly forsaken his vows.
And he saw clearly that the way to protect himself from
himself was to build a wall. An everyday existence. Coming
and going. Routine and ritualized. No war. No Mimi. No
identity-shaking events. Conceal himself again in a parish.

But it had not worked very successfully, had it? And the
finger of God had plucked him out. And here he was. All
come around again. On the front line. It didn't matter a whit
that he had hidden at St. Anselm's. His own, personal destiny
had continued. Perhaps had been repeated. And again, he was
drawn to a woman and again, he had become responsible for
others.

Near dawn, he was stopped by an American Army patrol of
MPs. In the rising morning light, he saw he was near the

round, bubble-topped Pantheon, where Luciana had said Raphael was buried. After checking his passport to verify he was who he claimed to be, the MPs gave him a ride in their jeep to the hospital, kidding the former chaplain that he had been "close" to his destination, only "three miles as the crow flies!"

In his black mood, Matt had stomped across the Fabricio Bridge, then clattered noisily through the hospital corridors of sleeping patients. He had no wish to rest. He was obsessed only with seeing Pope Pius. Once back inside his makeshift room at the hospital, he quickly gathered up soap and towels and took a hot shower in the baths at the end of the hall. Then he shaved, borrowed a black cassock, white T-shirt and underwear from one of the Hospitaller Brothers and put them on. As he was packing his suitcase, Alfonso Calamari woke up.

"*Scherzo da prete*," he said to Matt. "You made a priest's joke out of me!" He began to chuckle. "That landing you made me do was the best I ever made." He was chortling, shaking his head at the joke, when Matt closed his suitcase and picked it up to depart.

"*Padre?*" Calamari called to him.

"Yes?"

"I forgive you for making me land like that."

Matt forced a smile.

Suitcase in hand, Matt picked his way above the rain-swollen Tiber. The rain had stopped now. But the sun was hidden and the streets were wet. Thousands of new posters on glistening walls, depicting a stern-faced Alcide de Gasperi, the Christian Democratic candidate, stated, ROMA, SÌ! RUSSIA, NO!

He turned down the far end of Via della Conciliazione and noticed for the first time that among the sidewalk restaurants were religious souvenir shops. Plaster statues of the Virgin, Christ, saints and popes stood in their windows. Bundles of rosaries and scapulars hung in every open doorway. Fold-out picture books of the Vatican's eight museums, five galleries and Sistine Chapel were waiting to be purchased. Venus de Milos, centaurs, Bacchuses, and Zeuses dallying with Aphrodites in plaster casts littered the sidewalks in front of the stores. Priests and nuns manned the counters.

Passing the restaurant Luciana had picked yesterday, he saw that where the plane had finally rested, there was an

outdoor marketplace. He had not noticed it yesterday because
he had been so taken with the towering grandeur of St. Peter's
Square. Now an army of hucksters had erected their awnings
on flatbed trucks and spread out their merchandise. They were
eagerly cajoling passersby to buy leather purses, sandals! ("How
can you be a pilgrim unless you come in simple sandals?")
Windup metal toy statues of St. Peter, the saint's right arm
lifting in blessing; embossed letter-openers with Pope Pius's
image on the handles; white and black shawls to cover women's
heads before entering the basilica; pencil sharpeners in the
form of the basilica and a thousand other knickknacks all
produced in cheap fashion.

On one of the trucks Matt spotted a dollar-size silver coin
in a basket. The coin held a handsome likeness of Pope Pius.
When he picked it up, he saw that near its edge were the Latin
words *Hic Est Radix Malorum Omnium*. "This is the root of
all evil."

"You like?" the proprietor asked.

"Is this a medal?" Matt asked him, setting down his
suitcase.

"No, no! Vatican money! You want?"

"I'll buy it as a souvenir for my mother. How much?"

"Fifteen hundred lire. Very cheap."

Matt paid the man without haggling. He pocketed the coin.
"What about all this stuff you sell here? Is it yours?" He
pointed to the man's truck bed full of bins.

"Oh, no!" the vendor said, his brown face crinkling into a
sad smile. "Is Vatican. I get commission from Cardinal
Tardini." A couple called to him. They were holding up a
pair of pilgrim's sandals. He hurried to make the sale.

Disconcerted by the man's answer, Matt crossed over the
white marble line that marked the Vatican's boundary. He
made his way across the shiny, wet cobblestones of St. Peter's
Square toward the Arco delle Campane gate at the left of the
basilica. As he approached, he saw that the Swiss Guard
Monsignor Kass had assigned him yesterday was on duty.

"Monsignor Kass is most angry with you!" the guard
announced. "You have got me into a lot of trouble by leaving,
Father!"

The Swiss looked around, then spun on his heel and headed
inside the Vatican wall.

In less than a hundred yards, they approached the severe Teutonic Institute, to the left of the basilica. Entering through a small arch, Matt found himself in the midst of an ancient cemetery, with tombstones and monuments of all sizes. The resting places of German popes, cardinals, politicians and wealthy German benefactors cluttered the courtyard without design. Some were adorned with statues of a weeping Jesus, surrounded by little angels. Others held a Germanic coat of arms. One sarcophagus in the corner, near the front entrance to the college, depicted death as a skeleton, clad in a black monk's robe, swinging his scythe.

"Why is this called a German Institute?" Matt asked the Swiss Guard as he used his cane on the steps of the building. They were climbing toward its entrance.

"The Teutonic Institute is used to train German priests. It is sanctioned by Pope Pius as the highest order of studies in the world."

"The Vatican runs a German seminary?" Matt asked, trying to keep pace with the swiftly moving guard.

"*Nein,*" he replied. "Germans own this ground and all its buildings. They have since 790."

The guard led the way through wrought-iron doors and a marble foyer, then up three flights of stone steps, finally turning down a long, narrow whitewashed corridor. He unlocked a door and handed Matt the key.

"This is your room," he said.

"Where are all the German students?"

"They have gone home for Christmas holidays."

Matt stood a moment, surveying the student's cubicle. It was whitewashed and severe, with only a bed and a small wooden dresser. In the corner sat a toilet without a seat ring. He tossed his suitcase on the bed, noticing with dismay that it bounced with a heavy thud.

"It's a seminary, all right," he groaned to himself. He turned to the guard. "I have to see Pope Pius."

"Is not possible. Monsignor Kass left specific instructions not to admit you anywhere."

"May I use a telephone, then?" Matt thought quickly. He knew Cardinal Spellman in New York could use his influence to get him an audience with Pius.

"Do you wish to call inside the Vatican?" the guard asked.

"No. The United States."

The guard thought on that a moment, then said, "You will need permission for that. To get it, we must go to the Governor's Palace. But you would need a pass. Besides, that is against my orders."

"This is important. Maybe life and death."

"Very well," the guard said hesitantly. "But you must stay with me all the time."

He led the way back through the cold, stone-floored corridor, then down the foot-worn flights of cut stone, out through the cemetery in the courtyard.

They walked deeper into the Vatican, along the high left nave wall of St. Peter's Basilica, across a little piazza dedicated to the First Roman Martyrs, then under the portico of the basilica's gigantic sacristy, to the long *scala* in front of the Church of St. Stephen. For the first time, as Matt climbed the steps with his cane, he realized that the entire state of the Vatican was built on one big hill. The only flat part was behind him in St. Peter's Square.

They were ascending the *scala* and were now higher than the basilica's dome or even its highest part, the lantern, which sat as a crown on its top. On his right, embedded in the hillside, Matt saw the crossed Papal coat of arms, composed of yellow flowers and sculptured green bushes, and, then gaining the summit of the *scala,* the railroad station with its travertine bas-reliefs depicting the Prophet Elijah on his carriage of fire, and the miraculous draught of fishes. A lone locomotive was chugging idly in the station.

The Swiss Guard headed toward an imposing three-story brown building that Matt had seen yesterday on his way to the bank. A bronze sign over the doors stated, PALAZZO DEL GOVERNATORATO. Matt followed him inside. There under ceilings of gigantic crystal chandeliers were diplomats from every nation, seated outside various cubicles waiting to fulfill their missions of business.

The guard walked up the wide, crescent-shaped gold and marble staircase that led to the mezzanine. Matt trailed after him.

At the top of the stairs, he saw that the guard had stopped and was waiting beside *Segretario* Palmo, the toad-faced little man he had seen in the bank. Palmo was seated behind a small desk, stamping passes for three Irish-looking Cardinals who then filed through the railing past his post and entered the door marked UFFICIO DEL GOVERNATORATO.

The *Segretario* acknowledged the presence of the guard, listened a moment to him, then looked up at Matt. "I am sorry, Father Bowles. But it is not within my power to allow you to call the United States. And Monsignor Kass, whose jurisdiction it is, is presently doing his daily radio show."

"His radio show?"

"*Certo*, Father. The Vatican broadcasts to the entire world."

Suddenly, Matt realized there was another way to reach Cardinal Spellman. The massive Vatican radio network linked the entire Catholic world to Rome. There were operators in every city, manning smaller sets, ready to receive direct instructions from the Holy Father on every subject.

"May I visit Monsignor Kass in the station?" he asked Palmo. "I won't be any bother."

But as if Palmo were reading his mind, the *Segretario* said, "Father, you know, of course, Cardinal Spellman has gone to Japan. He will not return for several weeks. Besides, there is no need to assure him you arrived safely with the shipment. He already knows. Anything else, Father?"

"Yes. Have you found the Jewish money yet?"

"We have almost finished our tabulations. Still no sign of it. But I will tell Monsignor Kass you inquired again. In the meantime, the good Monsignor tells me Father William Mankowsky and the necessary records to verify the shipment will arrive tomorrow."

"Tomorrow?" Matt asked, surprised. He had supposed he would have a week before he was sent home.

"*Sì, sì*, Father," Palmo tried to smile, adjusting the pince-nez perched on his wide proboscis. "We finished our tabulations ahead of schedule. It was Monsignor Kass's idea to send early for Father Mankowsky. Besides, there is no reason to keep you here any longer than necessary, don't you agree? So please make yourself available at exactly 7:30 A.M. tomorrow in the bank. After that, we will put you on a plane and send you both back to your New York."

"I hope that's enough time for the Holy Father to see me," Matt said, thinking quickly. "You haven't forgotten about him making me a Monsignor, have you?"

"I'm really not sure about that." Palmo coughed nervously. "Again, it is not my area. But I believe Monsignor Kass said Pope Pius will bless a hat for you, making you *monsignore in absentia*. I'm sorry, but you understand Pope Pius's schedule is very busy, very crowded. Anything else, Father?"

Matt checked his temper. There was no way he was going away without somehow seeing Pius. But right now he had another important matter to bring up.

"Nearly seven years ago, I applied for a canonical annulment of my mother's marriage. Whom do I see about this?"

"Our Rota is very busy," Palmo protested, removing the iron pince-nez, which left deep imprints on both sides of his nose. "But allow me to do you this favor, Father Bowles. Give me your mother's full name and the date you started the petition. I shall have one of my employees seek out her file."

"Agnes Matilda Bowles. I filed April 11, 1940."

"Was the necessary fee paid?" he asked, writing down the information.

"No, she didn't have the sixteen thousand dollars."

"Ah, pauper classification. Well, that explains it, Father. Those applications get done last. And you can imagine the Holy Rota's case load."

"I can imagine."

"Well, I'll certainly check it for you," Palmo said. "But don't count on too much." And he put on his pince-nez to signal that their business was concluded. Then he noticed that Matt was glaring at him.

"Something wrong, Father?"

"Yes," Matt said. "Could you have the guard show me where I can say Mass before I hurt somebody?"

With Palmo's permission the guard led him to the nearby sacristy of St. Peter's. Inside the octagonally shaped room were fifty-three dressing counters and closetsful of different-colored vestments. There were the traditional liturgical chasuble colors: red for a martyr; white signifying the special purity of a saint; black for requiem masses for the dead; purple for penance; green for joyous occasions. But each here in the sacristy at St. Peter's was inlaid with gold and silver embroidery, with jewels and ancient pieces of art sewn onto the front and back.

The sacristan, a Franciscan monk in worn-out sandals, chose the color gold, which doubled for all colors in a liturgical emergency, and laid out a set of vestments. As Matt dressed, he noticed the ancient reliquaries, dalmatics of deep blue, the bronze tomb of Sixtus IV, gold and silver tabernacles in glass showcases. The art treasures surrounding him gave the dressing room the feeling of a museum. Finishing his vesting prayers, Matt pulled on the chasuble and mentioned the museum-like quality to the guard, who stood politely nearby.

"Pius *has* converted it into a museum," he said. "He has done so so that everyone may see the treasures of our Vatican and realize the value we hold to the world."

Matt draped the golden veil over the chalice and the cardboard pall on its top.

"First altar to your right," the monk told him.

"Shall I wait for you here, Father?" the guard asked Matt, his voice echoing off the fifty-foot ceiling.

"No, I'll check in at your guard post."

The guard hesitated, looked to the Franciscan, who nodded, then left.

Matt went out of the sacristy and found his altar's candles already lit. Several other priests were saying Mass nearby. Above his altar, he noticed an over-sized sculpture of Pope Leo turning Attila the Hun back from Rome.

"Hic est Corpus Meum," he said at the Consecration. *"This is My Body,"* and then, like always, it began. Did he have that power anymore to bring Him physically down from heaven? What was this he held in his hands? Bread . . . or flesh? His heart was filled with sawdust. A wave of despair swept over him. Even the strength he had expected to find here in Rome was nowhere to be found.

The Vatican was full of contradictions. Tainted, earthy, with its crowded stalls of vendors at its walls; Godlike in its intensity of worship. Center of Christianity; headquarters to the Vatican bank. Pool of grace; business as usual. Storehouse of prayer; treasury of priceless masterpieces; worth millions; unwilling to donate a penny to Jewish refugees.

"Hoc est Calix Sanguinis Meum . . ." he forced himself to say over the wine. *"This is My Blood. . . . This IS My Blood!"*

He realized he was sweating. Omitting the rest of the prayers, he bent over suddenly to consume the sacred wine and bread. . . .

"Protect me," he prayed. "Save me from doubting."

Hundreds upon hundreds of voices suddenly filled the basilica. It took him a moment to hear them. He turned his head slightly and saw that a long line of lay people had entered. With joyful voices, they sang at the top of their lungs: "Holy! Holy! Holy, Lord!"

Pure. Sweet. Intense.

He closed his eyes, suddenly immersed in needed emotion. The voices lifted him higher and higher. And he took the Host into his mouth and felt a leap of faith he had not experienced since before the war. And drinking the Blood, he was renewed, reborn, cleansed and strengthened to continue the fight.

Matt made his thanksgiving, then borrowed a breviary from another priest, who was from England, and said his morning Lauds. Seated in the only pews in St. Peter's that stood before the golden altar, Matt read quickly. He was in a hurry. He had not yet thought of a way to get to Pope Pius. And he must! He would! Two ships waited in a harbor. Desperate people's hopes hinged on a pouch of money. Pope Pius's reputation was at stake too. And his own future—intertwined in it all. He would see Pope Pius before the day was finished . . . and find his way back.

On the way out of the basilica, Matt stopped at the famous green statue of the seated St. Peter. The first pope's foot was worn down from so many kisses and strokings by visiting faithful. He reached out and rested his hand on the smooth, melted foot.

"I'm open for suggestions," he whispered. But the statue only stared off, enraptured at some heavenly vision.

He left the sacristy and went down to the gate of Arco delle Campane, gesturing to the same Swiss Guard to let him know his destination was only the nearby expanse of St. Peter's Square. Suspicious, the guard followed him out and kept him in sight.

The sun was out, drying the remaining puddles of rainwater. Matt stepped into the square, using his cane. Near its center, he turned, pausing. To the left, above the piazza itself, he could see the rooftop of the Holy Office, once known as the

"Office of the Inquisition." To his right were the apartments of the Holy Father, the square separating the two.

He was deep in thought when he heard, "Standing in the present spot, one can experience the optical illusion of Bernini's colonnades being supported by a single line of pillars."

Curious, he swung around. Luciana was sitting on her motorbike, wearing baggy pants and a thick Irish sweater. She was smiling, her arms crossed at her chest. "I am sorry," she said contritely.

"And that's it? You come around here, say you're sorry and that's supposed to take care of it?"

"Don't you forgive me?"

"What? No way! And call me Father! That is my correct title!" He glared angrily at several pilgrims who were watching.

"Ah, I see, Father. You wish to keep your anger. Then you can have nothing to do with me!"

In exasperation, Matt folded his arms and turned so he faced the Apostolic Palace. Out of the corner of his eye he noticed the young Swiss begin to wave him back.

Suddenly, he saw three priests in simple black cassocks approach the Bronze Doors and ascend the stairway. They nodded to the Swiss Guards, who admitted them without question. Each of the priests held a bundle of legal-looking papers.

"Where do I go if I get past those guards?" Matt quickly asked Luciana over his shoulder. The young Swiss was now striding determinedly toward him from the Arco delle Campane.

"I've never been inside there before. But after you enter the Portico of Constantine, I've heard there is a staircase to the right. It's called the Stairway of Pius IX. That will take you up into the Apostolic Apartment. But you will never get all the way to Pope Pius. Too many bodyguards."

"Nothing ventured." Matt turned and limped hurriedly toward a nearby kiosk.

Luciana watched with curiosity as Matt bought a thick pile of newspapers from the priest behind the counter, folded them, then limped quickly toward the Bronze Doors. The Swiss now began to run after him across the piazza.

"He'll never make it." But she crossed her fingers.

He went under the right colonnade of Lorenzo Bernini, up the double sets of steps toward the six Swiss Guards. Anxiously,

Luciana slid off the Vespa. Head down, Matt gained the top step and flashed the guards his newspapers. They parted and let him pass.

"I don't believe it!" Luciana cried.

Then the young Swiss ran up the steps and shouted something to the others. The six of them at the Bronze Doors turned and looked over their shoulders. Then they broke.

Standing on her tiptoes, Luciana shuddered as she saw one of the guards grab Matt. Another took the newspapers and began rifling through them. Matt was suddenly wheeled around, his arms pinioned behind him. In a glint of sunlight, Luciana saw a very modern pair of handcuffs clamped on his wrists.

"Gesù, have mercy!" she begged as her heart sank. Matt was led away, inside the gates.

11.

While two of the Swiss Guards returned to their post at the Bronze Doors, the other four led Matt forward beneath the five-story ceiling of the Portico of Constantine. The young Swiss said, "Now you're in trouble. They are taking you to the Vatican jail." He looked vindicated as he went off. Matt watched the nearby marble stairs of Pius IX recede. He had been so close to the living quarters of the Holy Father!

The guards hustled him along the marble floor of the portico toward the opposite end, where a larger staircase fed both up and down. As they pushed him onto the down stairway, a round Archbishop with big hands and feet and a large, hooked nose appeared from below. He stepped aside and watched curiously as Matt was led downward.

"*Che cos' è?*" he pleasantly asked of the guards.

One of them respectfully chattered something back to him in Italian.

"*Lasciatelo andare!*" he heard the Archbishop cry.

The guards halted. A lieutenant jabbered something at the other three, then went up the landing to where the Archbishop was standing. He began explaining the situation to the Archbishop, who listened patiently while eyeing Matt.

"*Lasciatelo a me!*" the Archbishop insisted when the lieutenant had become quiet.

The officer looked worried. Nevertheless, he barked an order to his three subordinates who surrounded Matt. One of them unlocked the handcuffs, hung them back on his belt and handed Matt his cane. Then the three of them went up the stairs with the lieutenant.

Matt made his way up the stairs. The Archbishop was smiling at him.

"Thank you, Excellency," Matt said to him.

"Ah, an American trespasser! No wonder!" the Archbishop began to laugh heartily. "You Americans always disregard the Vatican's rules!" He seemed delighted by his observation.

Matt turned to make sure the guards were really gone. They were nearing the far end of the portico now, about to resume their positions at the Bronze Doors. His eyes swept the stairs of Pius IX.

The Archbishop did not miss the movement.

"You know, Father," he said merrily, "even though I'm Italian, I always watch myself when I come to the Vatican. It's a very tough place. Very strict rules. One false move and pffffft!" He made a motion to slice his throat.

Matt grinned nervously.

"If you go up those other stairs without a pass from the Office of His Excellency, *Segretario* Palmo of the Chamber, the guards there will arrest you again and place you in the Vatican prison."

Matt decided to trust him. "I'm Matt Bowles," he said turning, holding out his hand.

"Angelo Roncalli." The jovial Archbishop shook his hand. "What is it you seek, Father?"

"I've got to see the Pope."

"Well, he's not up those stairs anyway, my son."

"But I have to speak to him! Something terrible has happened."

"Come on," the Archbishop said, starting up the other half of the staircase. "Walk with me."

"But . . ." Matt said, looking longingly down the portico.

"Come, come, tell me about it," Roncalli said, disappearing around the corner. "I have an appointment and I can't be late!"

Matt hesitated a moment longer, then reluctantly followed the Archbishop up the stairs, his cane sounding heavily on each step. As they entered the first of the Vatican museums, he began to relate the entire story, complete with the plane landing, the Jewish refugees needing their money for the ships and how the pouch had mysteriously turned up empty.

Archbishop Roncalli's smile slipped from his face as he listened to the end of Matt's tale.

"In Turkey," Archbishop Roncalli began thoughtfully, "where I was stationed during the war, I once had a thousand stranded Jewish children on my hands. They were in danger of being returned to Nazi Germany. I know your worry, Father, for them and for yourself. For them, because they might perish. For yourself, because if we fail, if we hurt more than help, then our souls will be plunged deeper into hell than any others."

"What did you *do* with your thousand children?" Matt asked.

"*Do* with them?" Roncalli laughed. He seemed to laugh heartily at the slightest provocation. "Why, I did the only thing I could *do* with them! I rented a ship and sent them away to people who would care for them instead of kill them!"

"That's wonderful, Excellency," Matt commented. "Do you think Pope Pius will do the same?"

The Archbishop stopped. His back was to a lower wing of a museum filled with friezes, sarcophagi and thousands of antique white and black marble busts, portraits of famous, powerful men of ancient Rome.

"Pope Pius lives for his Church. Because of that, he has long made decisions that preclude any open commitments." He turned away heavily. Matt trailed him through an outdoor courtyard. "Those days during the war were terrible times. You must understand that, Father. Terrible. The world had gone mad. Even the Vatican, which by tradition stands as a peaceful island amidst the swirling waters of the world, was chaotic within its own walls. Did you know we lost one thousand Polish priests at Dachau? Thousands of Orthodox Serbs in Croatia under Ustashi? Three hundred thousand Catholic Hungarians gassed and cremated at Auschwitz?"

"But surely Pius did what he could," Matt protested. "I've heard about all the churches and monasteries and convents he threw open to refugees."

"He did encourage such a policy. But because he was afraid of angering Adolf Hitler, he did not put that policy into effect in Germany, Poland and other countries where it was needed most." He spoke this sorrowfully, yet without condemnation. The heavyset Archbishop stopped in the middle of the outdoor Belvedere Courtyard and faced Matt momentarily.

"Understand me," he explained. "I am loyal to His Holiness. I have nothing but the deepest sympathy for what he endured during World War Two. His soul has been wracked with the knowledge of what occurred. A lesser man, such as myself, could not have endured what he suffered. So I pray constantly that he may find the peace he seeks now."

Matt accompanied the Archbishop as he entered the adjoining Pinacoteca Museum. "Another thing you should know," Roncalli said abruptly, breaking the silence as they passed Raphael's immense painting, *The Transfiguration,* "His Holiness has received a lot of criticism for being anti-Semitic, for not openly excommunicating Hitler. And to top it all, a lot of key positions in the Vatican are now German held. He is very sensitive to criticism. Very sensitive to the topic of Jews."

"Why does he have Germans around him?" Matt asked.

"It has nothing to do with sympathizing with Nazism, if that's what you're thinking, Father. It's just that His Holiness spent most of his days in Germany before becoming Pontiff. He naturally relates to Germans. Even Sister Pasqualina, his housekeeper, is German. But while he's so careful in most things, in this, he seems naive to the world's reactions."

"Excellency," Matt said, "despite what his accusers say, I know he'll help these Jewish folks. He's got to!"

"I pray he will, Father. But there is a saying, very much observed around here. 'To lift one's finger as Pope causes waves as if a boulder were dropped into a quiet pond.' "

"I'll take my chances," Matt said. "But I've got to see him! Won't you help me?"

"That is why God permitted you and me to meet on the stairs."

"Then you'll get me an audience with him?"

"You've already got one." Roncalli grinned broadly as he stopped before the door to the Egyptian Museum. "Whom do you think my appointment is with?"

12.

His heart pumping wildly, Matt Bowles stepped down into a darkened, sunken hall of the Egyptian Museum with Angelo Roncalli. The only light in the room came from glass cases. As he drew close he saw that they housed mummies. The room reeked with the odor of formaldehyde.

Archbishop Roncalli made his way past the display cases and headed toward a side room. As Matt followed, Roncalli opened that room's door, but stopped respectfully. Looking beyond him, Matt saw Pope Pius XII seated before a small work counter. His eyes were closed behind his round gold-rimmed glasses. His thin lips were tightly compressed. His hands, the long fingers intertwined, rested before him.

A boxy, ruddy-faced nun in gray garb stood to his right. Matt recognized her immediately. It was the legendary Sister Pasqualina, the nun who ran the personal world of Pope Pius and was said to influence even world policy.

On the Pope's other side was a young man with whitish-blond hair. He was bent over a black bag. It took Matt a moment in the dimness of the room to realize that the blond man was preparing an injection.

"We must wait," Roncalli whispered over his shoulder as he half closed the door.

"What is happening?"

"That is the Swiss physician, Dr. Paul Niehans, the Holy Father's personal doctor. He is giving the Pontiff an injection of his 'cellular rejuvenation therapy.' "

"What does it do?" Matt whispered into the Archbishop's ear.

"It gives the Pontiff strength. As I understand it, the formula contains finely chopped pieces of brain, liver, kidneys, thyroid and endocrine glands from the fetus of a sheep. Niehans also adds sexual organs from other young animals."

While Matt watched through the crack of the door, the Swiss doctor quickly drew back the Holy Father's left sleeve of his white cassock. He inserted the needle beneath the skin on the forearm. A red patch, about the size of a half dollar, appeared subcutaneously.

The doctor withdrew the needle, placed a bandage over it and pulled down the Pontiff's sleeve. Pope Pius still did not open his eyes. The young doctor closed his case, bowed respectfully and pushed open the door, exiting past Matt and Archbishop Roncalli.

Sister Pasqualina, who now saw them, bent and whispered something to Pope Pius. The nun's starched cowl rustled softly as she hovered over the Pontiff in the silent room.

The Pontiff listened a moment, then opened his eyes and turned toward the doorway. He smiled. Archbishop Roncalli genuflected, kissed the ring of St. Peter on the Pontiff's hand and received a blessing. Then he spoke privately to the Holy Father.

Pope Pius nodded.

"Father Bowles?" Roncalli beckoned.

Matt made his way into the workroom. In the light from the work lamp, he now saw that the Holy Father wore a white glove on his left hand and had a green apron wrapped around his white soutane at the waist.

Matt knelt and Pius held out his bare right hand. Matt kissed St. Peter's ring, overcome with the emotion of the moment.

"My brother," Pius said in precise English, "how nice it is to greet you. It was you who brought us the beneficence from our brother, Cardinal Spellman in America!"

"Yes, Holiness," Matt stammered, rising. "It was an honor."

"You flatter us, my son. May God bless you for your generosity. You are very kind to God's unworthy servant."

For the first time, Matt was aware of a fluttering, frenzied noise. He looked up and saw two plain brown sparrows in a cage that sat on top of a glass case near the Holy Father. The birds were battering themselves against the bars.

"Ah, do not mind our children," the Pontiff said, seeing Matt stare. "They will quiet when they become tame. We keep our sparrows near our person at all times to remind us we must have humility. God in his wisdom remembers even the sparrow, of which we are one."

The nun interjected, "Holiness, do you wish me to put away the collection? Your time is precious. Don't forget you have an audience with the postal workers of Italy shortly."

"Yes, we must go. But first, allow us to show Archbishop Roncalli and Father Bowles the newest addition to our Egyptian Museum." He pointed to a tray in front of him. "These good luck charms were put in coffins of ancient Egyptians, sometime around the Coptic period. *Signora* Datometti, the wife of our Italian ambassador to Egypt, has just donated these carved talismans to our museum. We love to come and gaze at new artifacts when the museums are closed. They provide us with much pleasure and recreation."

Archbishop Roncalli picked up one of the tiny jackal-like figurines from the tray. "All these were packed in tombs, Holiness?"

"Yes. They serve to remind us how mortal we humans are. They were supposed to have brought luck to the deceased." Pius took the terra-cotta piece from Roncalli and gazed at it a moment. "I may request one for my own coffin," he mused.

"Surely, your place in heaven is assured," Roncalli told him.

"We hope so."

"You have fifteen minutes," Sister Pasqualina checked her pocket watch and informed Roncalli. The stout nun reached past the Pontiff, picked up the tray and waited for him to replace the jackal. *"Danke,"* she told him. She replaced the tray, locked the case. Then she pulled off the white glove the Pontiff had worn and tossed it into a nearby wastebasket. She pulled a bottle of alcohol from her robe pocket.

"This will take a moment," the Holy Father apologized. "Sister Pasqualina does not like germs."

Roncalli walked away diplomatically, making a show of examining other cases full of Egyptian death charms, but Matt could not take his eyes from the Holy Father.

Pasqualina removed the massive gold ring of St. Peter, symbol of the Pope's authority, and disinfected it with her bottle of alcohol. The Holy Father closed his eyes again and seemed removed from what she was doing. She put the ring back on his center finger, wiped one last time at his hands, then finished by packing the bottle of alcohol back inside her gray robe.

"Now, thirteen minutes," Pasqualina warned Roncalli. "You may speak to *Pabst* Pius while we walk, yes?" She took the Holy Father by the arm and, without waiting, guided him through the doorway.

Roncalli caught Matt's worried look. "Don't worry. Just be patient. It's going to happen now." He drew Matt out of the workroom, through the center viewing area of the Egyptian Museum and up the steps into the main connecting hallway of the Vatican museums.

When they were outside, Roncalli caught up with the Holy Father. Pasqualina dropped back to accompany Matt. She seemed to appraise him for the first time as she said, "I am Pasqualina Lenhart, member of the order of St. Anne," and thrust out a chubby hand.

"Pleased to meet you, Sister," Matt managed, shaking it. He had heard a lot of gossip about this famous nun. He knew she had been called such terrible names as "The Popess" and "Virgo Potens." So the humble simplicity with which she had just introduced herself surprised him. For he knew also that she was not just a member of the order of St. Anne, but had founded it.

"The money you brought is for our good cause," Pasqualina continued confidently. She looked straight forward. "Only a strong Vatican can survive this attack by Communism!"

"But is it necessary the Church enter big business to achieve that?" It just came out. Matt was surprised to find himself sounding like Luciana.

"Never question the Holy Father," Pasqualina warned, her

voice suddenly icy. "He knows what is best and will see that nothing shall harm us."

Matt was furious with himself. Why had he asked such a stupid question?

Two Swiss Guards appeared suddenly from niches inset in the walls and opened a set of doors. Matt saw a long set of stairs ahead and realized that below was the Constantine Portico. They had returned to where he had met Roncalli. Time was short. What was taking Roncalli so long? He still seemed to be discussing his own business.

Suddenly, at mid-landing, Roncalli turned and beckoned to him. Matt stepped down quickly so that he faced the Holy Father.

"Angelo, our beloved friend," Pius said to Matt, stopping also on the landing, "has just told us of your emergency. He explained some things, but I need details. Did Cardinal Spellman authorize carrying this pouch for Jews?"

"Yes, Holiness."

"And this money was to help Jewish refugees support themselves and migrate to Palestine?"

"That's correct, Holiness. But I've already asked Monsignor Kass and *Segretario* Palmo about it. They cannot find the money I brought."

"Do you know about this, Pasqualina?" the Holy Father turned momentarily to the box-shaped nun who yet stood on the steps above them.

"I have heard of this complication, but apparently all has been done that could be. We do not have the money."

Pius nodded, thinking. "How much was there?"

"The figure was one million U.S. dollars, Holiness," Matt replied quickly.

"Something should be done," Pius said. "This seems to be a great injustice."

"The Communists must not know of the donations from the U.S." the nun said carefully. "It is advantageous with the coming elections not to reveal our wealth. It could be used against us."

"Holiness," Roncalli countered quickly, "it would be good to demonstrate that the Church and yourself have no anti-Semitic feelings."

Pius nodded, listening.

Pasqualina said, "Archbishop, we, the Church, have always been neutral. And while the Church's priority is to defeat Communists in Italy, we should not further Zionism."

Roncalli was about to protest further when a worker cried out above them. His overalls were filthy and his face was covered with dirt. He waved his hands frantically. *"Sua Santità?"* he shouted down. *"Scusi!"*

Pius looked up, recognized him and gathered up his white skirt. He hurried gingerly up the stairs.

"What's happening?" Matt asked Roncalli.

"I don't know," the Archbishop advised, "but don't worry, we'll get your money."

They hurried to catch up. Led by the worker, Pasqualina and the Holy Father crossed the choir loft above St. Peter's Basilica. Matt and Roncalli pursued them as they entered a secret passageway that ran inside the basilica wall. Finally the small group filed down a winding set of stairs.

At a level beneath the basilica, the Holy Father hurriedly boarded a small elevator. Matt and Roncalli barely had time to jump on before it descended.

When the doors opened again, they were in a cellar with a dirt floor. Striding forcefully, Pius XII left the elevator.

"Where's he going?" Matt asked Roncalli, as they followed more slowly now, ducking naked light bulbs that hung from the ceiling.

"This is His Holiness's pet project," Roncalli whispered to Matt. "He's had men digging down here since 1939."

"For what?"

"The bones of Saint Peter. This is the pre-Constantine necropolis built in the second century." Roncalli smiled in the dark cavelike cellar. "The most promising bones were uncovered here in 1942. Monsignor Kass keeps them locked away in his desk drawer. He is guarding them there until His Holiness can see if they match St. Peter's skull, which is kept in St. John Lateran Church here in Rome."

The Pope stopped ahead and peered down what appeared to be a lighted shaft.

"But why hasn't Pope Pius tried to match the bones already? Why has he waited five years?" Matt wanted to know as they too approached the strong light that shone from beneath the floor.

"Because Kass has always found an excuse not to." Roncalli grinned broadly. "What if these bones don't match the skull? Then what? Which relic would you disqualify? The skull or the bones?"

"Corregio!" the Holy Father was calling down the stone shaft. "Corregio?" Pasqualina was holding the hem of the Pontiff's robe up out of the dirt.

Matt peered down the hole and saw a lighted excavation with crisscrossing walls sunk deep into the earth. The words CAMPO P were stenciled on the nearby wall of the shaft. A tall ladder leaned against the near side.

"Why is His Holiness so obsessed with finding these bones in the first place?" Matt whispered to the Archbishop.

"The Holy Father believes that the bones of St. Peter will prove conclusively there is a direct linkage to Christ, who founded our Church. He believes this would convert the entire world to Catholicism."

"Corregio! Corregio?" Pope Pius was calling impatiently down the hole. The Pontiff's face was eager. The peaceful repose Matt had been so struck by earlier was gone.

A young man in goggles climbed the ladder and stuck his dusty head up over the top of the shaft. "Holiness?" he jabbered in Italian. "We have found a small chest in the correct area!"

A clay casket with hammered metal hinges and no lid was handed up from below. Corregio climbed out and set it down. Inside were three human leg bones.

"It will take time to carbon date them," Corregio said.

"Go now! Do it immediately!" the Holy Father commanded.

Corregio ran toward the elevator, ancient urn held forth in his hands.

"Holiness, no more time. We are late now!" Sister Pasqualina scolded him. She tugged him by the sleeve toward the elevator.

"We had better get your answer quickly!" Roncalli suggested. But as they started once again after Pope Pius, the elevator doors opened and Monsignor Guido Offeri, the prelate who ran the Vatican bank, stepped out. He kissed the Holy Father's ring.

"I was told I might find you here, Holiness," he said in Italian. "May we go upstairs?"

"He is due at an audience with the postal workers of Italy," Pasqualina said. "And I need time to remove the grime from his person."

"What is it?" Pius asked Monsignor Offeri. "Do we have problems with the bank?"

"Some items," Offeri said, opening a ledger he held. "They are all very large. First, we have just learned Standard Oil found new reserves in Texas."

"*Compra*," Pius said.

"Good, I agree, Holiness. Next, as we discussed, clothing is in great demand after the war. I suggest we build that cotton-weaving factory in Milan. You have seen the plans and figures."

Pope Pius nodded.

In the harsh light of the naked light bulbs, Matt was forced to admit the Pontiff knew about everything. Had Luciana been right . . . about everything?

"Bottled water is proving a loser. But perhaps it is a good investment for the future."

"Stay, as I told you, in staples."

Offeri nodded and closed his book. The elevator doors opened. The Pontiff started toward them. Pasqualina picked up the white skirt of his cassock. Roncalli gave Matt a push, and he stumbled forward.

"Holiness?" Matt cried. "Did you forget about the Jews?"

"Oh," the Pope said, seeing him. "You wished us to replace the money for the refugees?"

"Yes, Holiness." Matt felt his voice quaver.

"Guido," the Holy Father addressed the banker, "you know about this situation. What do you say? Shall we help them?"

"Thank God, we do not have to," the horse-faced prelate sighed.

"We don't understand," the Pontiff adjusted his round, gold glasses.

"I was about to notify Father Bowles by messenger," Offeri apologized. "But I see he is here." He turned partly to Matt. "The Jewish money has been located."

"Where?" Matt asked, amazed.

"It was included by mistake in a sum delivered to *Signore* Perfette to purchase his bank. Most regrettable. But when one is dealing with so much . . . and our help is new and relatively untrained . . . well . . ." He bowed in profound apology.

"So they can have their money? Now?" Matt asked anxiously.

"*Signore* Perfette has it waiting at this very moment."

"And with their money take our blessing," Pope Pius raised his hand, making the sign of the cross. "Tell them we send our prayers. And for you, Monsignor Bowles, our congratulations!"

The Holy Father turned and quickly boarded the elevator. Sister Pasqualina pushed a button and the doors closed.

Matt was staring at the elevator, lost in new thought.

"Well, Father," Roncalli beamed happily, "it all turned out for the best."

"Yes, it did, Excellency," Matt said. "I can't tell you how relieved I am. Yet, I wonder . . ."

"Wonder?" Roncalli asked, his face wreathed with his usual wide smile.

"What would have happened if their money hadn't been found? Would the Holy Father have helped them anyway?"

Realizing the implications of the question, Roncalli turned to Offeri. But the banker looked away. He engaged the elevator. When the car arrived, he got on and went up without waiting for Matt or Roncalli.

Roncalli walked to the elevator and pressed the button to call for it. "Come, my brother," he said. "Let's go up out of this place full of shadows."

13.

Matt came rushing up the series of winding steps near the Papal altar. A Swiss Guard seemed startled to see anyone come from below, but only watched as the priest in his black cassock passed by, striding across the basilica floor.

Matt hurried past the side altars, not even noticing the Pietà now. He wanted to find Luciana, tell her how wrong she had been. And yet, somehow, this victory nagged him. It had not been complete. Pius had not *given* this money back himself. At any rate, he assured himself, what was important was that they had it.

Emerging from the basilica onto its front steps, Matt blinked at the bright sunlight and searched the square. Luciana was still standing beside her motorbike, anxiously watching the double Bronze Doors through which he had entered.

As he started down toward her, he heard his name called. He wheeled toward the nearby Arco delle Campane gate and saw the young Swiss Guard who was in charge of him stare at him.

"Father!" he cried. "Wait there! Don't move!" Pilgrims watched as he raced across the short distance to the front steps of the basilica on which Matt stood.

"How did you get away?" the guard demanded. "Didn't they arrest you?"

"I got pardoned." Matt smiled at him. "Don't worry, I saw Pope Pius."

"You saw the Holy Father?"

"Yes, and now I have to go to the Bank of Santo Spirito. Tell Monsignor Kass, the Holy Father allowed me to go."

The guard nodded dumbly, obviously in awe at what had happened. Matt noticed he held a telegram in his hand.

"That for me?" he asked.

"Oh, yes, Father." The guard's tone changed. He seemed overwhelmed by all that had happened this morning. "From a Father Mankowsky in the United States, I was told. I was on my way to give it to you in the jail when . . ." he broke off and instead handed it to Matt, who took the telegram and stuffed it inside his pocket. He started down the steps. Luciana was wheeling her motorbike toward the basilica now, and he had his eyes on her, watching her approach.

"You had better open your telegram," the Swiss Guard told him.

"I know what it's about," Matt said over his shoulder. "Father Mankowsky's coming tomorrow."

The guard, still stunned, went back to his post. Luciana stopped as Matt came down the steps.

"I was worried! I saw you arrested!"

"I'm okay." He grinned expansively, putting his hands on top of her handlebars. "Everything's okay."

"You did it? You got our money?" she gasped.

He nodded happily.

She flew to him, wrapping her arms around his neck. He pulled away, startled, surprised, and shot a quick glance at the Swiss Guard, who was staring.

"Sorry." She grinned. "But I would have hugged the devil for that! Now where's our money?"

"It's waiting with a certain *Signore* Perfette. Is he the one you mentioned last night?"

"That old lecher! Of course, it's him!" She stomped the motorbike into life. It roared up a cloud of blue smoke, which engulfed a group of penguinlike nuns. "Did he have it all along?" she asked, as Matt painfully swung on.

"It was mixed up with Vatican monies."

She gunned the bike, but instead of going, slowly swiveled around to Matt. "I have to say something. I was wrong about

Pope Pius and the Vatican! Now, we can go!'' And as she pulled away, Matt, caught off guard because of her apology, was forced to wrap his arms around her waist to save himself.

At the Santo Spirito bank, they were ushered into *Signore* Perfette's glass-walled office. Outside in the main room, through Perfette's office windows, Matt and Luciana could see lines of Italians queued up, waiting to make transactions.

"Most are seeking loans," the pomaded Perfette confided from behind his desk. "It is nice to be back in business."

"By the grace of the Vatican," Luciana told him.

Perfette's face dropped. He coughed, leaned his small body across the desk and pulled a wooden box toward him. The box was covered with labels of Rossino Vino. "We should let bygones be bygones," he said smilingly to Luciana. "I am sorry I had no money to donate to your cause of the Jewish refugees."

"You are right," she said. "And I am sorry I called you a little mouse."

He bowed at that. "Your apology is accepted."

Luciana stood, opened the top of the rough-sided container and took out a small packet of bills, bound together by the Vatican bank's paper ring. She counted some of it, then raised it limply. "Where is the rest?"

"Rest?" Perfette asked, puzzled. "There are one hundred and thirty-seven one-thousand-dollar bills!"

"Where are the other eight hundred and sixty-three, you little mouse?" Luciana shouted at him. "What have you done, thief? Taken poor refugees' money?"

"I . . . I swear, Luciana. That was all that arrived!"

Luciana slammed the box lid shut and glared at him a moment. Then she whipped around and stared at Matt. "I take it all back! I was right when I said your Vatican doesn't care!"

Matt stood, opened the box and checked its contents. "What happened?" he asked Perfette. "Something *must* have happened!"

"This is what they sent me," the bank president explained. "This is all there is."

"Something's wrong." Matt shook his head in disbelief.

"Yes, our money is gone! That is what's wrong," Luciana cried.

"You don't know that, Luciana."

"Oh? And who's going to give back our eight hundred and sixty-three thousand dollars now? The Vatican? Pope Pius himself?"

He desperately wanted to tell her "Yes!" But all he could do was to take the box and follow her out as she left.

She stopped the Vespa in front of her house in the ghetto and swung off, the box containing the money positioned between her feet on the floorboard of the scooter. A large, red-cabbed city sanitation truck was standing nearby, but she did not even look at it.

"Come inside, Father," she said to Matt. "Everyone must know about this."

He was still sitting forlornly on the back of the bike. He got off, using his cane, and followed her up the main steps.

When the first tiny coffin appeared in the doorway, Luciana froze.

"What has happened?" she demanded of the two garbage men who were carrying the little box. In postwar Italy, there were no proper trucks for the dead. Bodies were put immediately into plain, pinewood boxes and carted off in garbage trucks for burial.

"We don't know, *signora*," one of the sweating men replied. "We come on calls all day long. We don't wait to hear the stories."

She pushed up past them and ran into the open foyer of her house. There, on the floor, were two more coffins, an adult-sized and another child's.

"My God!" she cried, her hands flying to her mouth. She dropped the box of bills on the steps.

Marie Schollander, the young woman who looked old, appeared above on the stairs, weeping.

"What, what, *che e cosa è*," Luciana demanded, rushing to her.

"Milko, his two little boys," Marie sobbed. "They were so happy to be here with you. Then, last night—no, this morning—someone said the ships were gone."

"The ships are not gone!"

"They are! They are!" Marie slumped onto the stairs and

pressed her wrinkled face into the folds of her skirt and sobbed hysterically.

Hannah Orteglio, her eyes puffy from crying, came down the stairs. "Ivan called from Civitavecchia this morning after you left. Marcheshi sold the ships to someone else."

Matt was standing at the foot of the stairs. He looked up and saw a motley gathering of ill-fed children and adults watching from the landing. They looked down impassively, emotionlessly, at the remaining coffins. It was, Matt thought, as if they had witnessed this scene a thousand times before.

"A note," Marie managed between sobs, "I found it. . . . There was blood everywhere!" She reached into her cotton apron and extracted a wadded-up piece of butcher's paper.

Luciana unfolded it. Matt stepped up the stairs and read silently with her:

> For too long, my friends, I have feared the light. My sons are both weak. We will be waiting for you in Jerusalem.

> Shalom.
> Milko Strassberg

"He did it with a razor," Hannah blurted suddenly. "Cut Milko Junior's and Dzido's throats first. I brought him the blade to shave!" She lapsed into fresh tears.

The two sanitation workers appeared, hoisted up the adult coffin and left without a word. Marie wailed louder at the sight. Luciana sat and caressed her hair to comfort her.

The faces at the top of the stairs continued to gaze down. Some of the children were looking at Matt. He felt the same sense of desperation he had had just before he climbed the cliffs at Omaha.

"Hannah," he asked, "where is Ivan Cohen?"

"With Ruffino at Civitavecchia, I suppose," she said, mopping her eyes and moustached face with a flowered red handkerchief.

"Is there a suit here that would fit me? A tie, a pressed white shirt?"

"What are you doing?" Luciana asked, hearing his request. She was still holding Marie's head in her lap.

"It won't work if I go there as a priest," Matt told her. "I need to inspire Marcheshi's confidence. Not come with my hat in my hands. I have to look as though we can afford his ships."

The white-bearded Rabbi Meister stepped forth from the crowd at the top of the stairs. "Father," the old man said, "I couldn't help but overhear. We all want to know, have you . . . found our money?"

"Yes!" Matt told him. He fixed Luciana with a decisive gaze. "The Vatican has returned every last penny!" He bent down and picked up the Rossino Vino box, then held it over his head for all to see.

Luciana stared at Matt, puzzled. But she held her tongue.

"Is this true?" Hannah asked her. Matt held her eyes and nodded to her slowly, grimly.

"True," Luciana whispered.

"Praise Yahweh!" Rabbi Meister shouted from above them. "Oh, if this good news had only come this morning, Milko and his children would be alive! Now, let us hope no one else will die before we board our ships!"

"No one else will die!" Matt shouted up. "I swear to that!"

A silence fell. Little Ruth smiled shyly at him.

"Who's in charge up there?" Matt asked. "You, Rabbi Meister?"

"Yes, Father?" he asked eagerly.

"You know all the houses in the city where the refugees are staying?"

"But, of course!"

"All right, send out messengers. Tell all of the refugees to pack what they can carry. Tomorrow, as soon as it grows dark, they are to walk to the harbor of Civitavecchia!"

"But, Father, what if the ships, as Ivan said, *are* gone?" someone asked.

A hush settled like a thick snow. The children watched Father Matt, waiting.

"I promise you, the ships will be there. I intend to keep them there for you! Now, hurry. Go alert everyone!"

Rabbi Meister called out in a surprisingly booming voice, "Come to the teaching room! All of you! You too, Marie, we need you. Come on, that's right!" He was pushing the children ahead of him. "I will need runners. Who's the fastest here?" Marie got up from the steps and joined the crowd that followed Meister into their nearby room. Some were still looking with disbelief over their shoulders at Matt.

"Father," Hannah said, "you will destroy them if you fail to get back the ships."

"Get me a suit," Matt said, ignoring her. "And while you're at it, a map of the Vatican. One as detailed as possible."

"A map of the Vatican? For what, Father?"

"Never mind!" He whacked her on her broad behind.

She put a hand down, astonished.

"Now!" Matt commanded.

Stunned, Hannah ran up the stairs.

"I don't know what you are planning," Luciana said, when she saw they were alone, "but Hannah was right. You can't toy with these people. Their hopes have been crushed too often."

"Does Marcheshi know you?"

"What?" she asked, confused at his sudden change of subject.

"I want you to dress in your finest."

"Matt, what are you planning? Don't you realize that even if the ships are there, we do not have the money?"

"We'll get it," he said evasively.

"Matt, it's over! Face it, we're finished!"

"That doesn't sound like the Luciana I know."

"I'm tired, damn it! I've tried and tried! Now this happens! You've got to know when to give up, don't you? Go back to the United States. It's too late for us."

"God will help us, Luciana."

"And if He doesn't?"

"He will!" Matt uttered so desperately it shocked her. "He *has* to!"

Suddenly, she understood. This was as much for him as for her refugees. The frightened look in his eyes confirmed that.

Below, the two sanitation workers picked up the final child's coffin and departed. She looked at the sad spectacle and tears flooded her eyes. Impulsively, she turned back to Matt.

"I'll be ready in a minute," she said, avoiding his eyes. She ran up the stairs.

He watched her go, then heard the door slam as she entered her room to dress.

He made himself focus. What was he doing? Pressing God as he had pressed Pope Pius? It was a crazy chance. But for him, the war had started again. Three casualties already on the beach. As he ascended the stairs to find his suit, he prayed the ships would still be there.

14.

At Matt's insistence, Hannah borrowed a 1937 American-made Kaiser-Frazer from Pynchon Nossi, a well-to-do friend who had survived the war in Switzerland and had recently returned to live in Rome. The car was painted candy-apple red and looked, as Matt said, "ritzy enough." He didn't say for what.

Clad in one of Luciana's husband's cream-colored suits with a white shirt and black tie, Matt was at the car, cane in hand, waiting, when Luciana came down the steps. He was awed by her transformation and looked away. It was Hannah who whistled her appreciation. Luciana wore a prewar calf-length mauve skirt from Paris, topped by an expensive silk blouse with purple orchids around the shoulders. A wide school-girl's hat with a broad purple band sat atop her blond head.

She walked quickly toward the car, but stopped suddenly at the door when she saw Matt. The color drained from her face, and she looked as though she would faint.

"What's wrong?" he asked, seeing her.

"Nothing . . . it's just, for a moment . . . I thought you were Rocco!"

He looked away again, embarrassed anew.

She got into the car and asked lightly, "So how do I look?"

"Great," he said truthfully, but did not elaborate. He was fiddling with the keys to the car, concentrating on inserting them into the mechanism. He pushed the little stainless-steel button, and the engine turned over and ran smoothly.

"You mind telling me now why we're dressed up like this?" Luciana asked him as he let out the clutch. She waved to Hannah on the steps.

"I think Mr. Marcheshi will be more impressed with us if we can seem to represent a rich firm that wants his ships."

"But we don't have enough money! And pretending won't help us! What are we doing?"

"Trust me," he said as they drove through the ghetto and glided onto the Lungaretta above the Tiber.

"Okay," she said after a while. "I trust you. Now what?"

"You're a translator who works with multinational corporations. Where do I go?"

"Turn left. And you?"

"Representative of . . . Human Dynamics. A charitable foundation in the United States. We need his two ships."

They crossed the boulevard in front of the Caius Cestius pyramid, brought stone by stone from Egypt to celebrate Rome's conquest. "What makes you think he will sell them to us?"

"Because the United States just defeated Italy," Matt said. "And Marcheshi, as a businessman, fears our power."

"Clever. But all this still depends on the two ships being there."

"They'll be there!" Matt said, as they drove through the outskirts of Rome.

Luciana watched the way he was now handling the car. He looked like a man in charge.

"Rocco's suit fits you!" she told him finally.

"Baggy around the waist," he mumbled, without looking at her. He drove faster.

They followed Via Ostiense out of Rome over green-grassed hills that stood above the blue Tyrrhenian Sea. It was nearly four o'clock when they passed the little chalk-walled town of Fregene on the coast. They had run along the rocky coastline for nearly sixty kilometers, Matt driving quietly. Then suddenly they dropped down into a narrow valley and wound around several sharp curves. Ahead lay the harbor of Civitavecchia.

It was not a wide port, Matt saw, but a deep one, offering shelter for any sized ship in its huge pocket. Its man-made stone seawall stretched from a nearby hillock to the right across its mouth. Its left flank was protected naturally from the sea by a promontory that curved inward like a banana. In the inward curve of the banana lay the twisted remains of rusting steel cranes, one toppled, the other torn in half from a bomb. Anchored near them were two British Navy warships, a light cruiser and a destroyer. The destroyer, with her two 5-inch .38-caliber guns and 40-millimeters, was built for pursuit, her long hull designed for speeds of up to thirty-four knots.

As they descended Matt noted that there was no sign of Marcheshi's ships. But he could not yet see all of the harbor. Peppering the hills above were small shacks, the homes of the once-prosperous dock workers. By the looks of the crumbled docks and the paintless houses on the hills, it had been a long time since Civitavecchia had seen prosperity.

"Turn down to the right, I think," Luciana suggested.

They turned off the potholed highway onto a steep dirt road. Ahead of them, two men were walking. Luciana said, "It's Ivan and Ruffino."

Matt slowed the car, then stopped.

Ivan was startled. "Luciana! What is this? What are you doing here?"

"We've come to see about the ships."

"Didn't you get our message?" Ruffino said, bending down to the window.

"The refugees received it," Luciana said. She decided to finish. "Milko and his two boys are . . . dead."

"Dead?" Ruffino asked, not believing what he had heard.

But Ivan saw the truth in Luciana's sad eyes. "Damn!" he said. He hit his fist against Matt's doorframe.

"Oh, no!" Ruffino said, realizing finally.

The two men stood outside, looking away to hide their tears.

Luciana sat quietly with Matt.

"Are the ships still here?" Matt asked, eyeing the harbor.

"Marcheshi sold both of them to some Greek named Onassis," Ruffino replied.

"Have they sailed?"

"An hour ago, *Father*," Ivan said, inflecting disparagingly.

Luciana looked at Matt. "Maybe there will be another ship available soon," she said hopefully.

"Sure, sure," Ivan said. "And maybe the ocean will part so we can walk home to Palestine."

"Contessa," Ruffino announced hesitantly, "there *is* another ship."

"Where?" Luciana wanted to know.

"Fool," Ivan cursed him. "It is not a ship. It is a ferry. Ferries do not go to sea. They stay in lakes or do short trips hauling cars."

"Ruffino, does Marcheshi have that ferry now?" Matt asked the old man.

"Sì, sì, Padre. A big one!"

"Two fools!" Ivan ranted. "So he has a ferry, so what?"

Matt started the car. He put it into gear and without waiting started down the road. Ruffino jumped on the trunk lid and rode with them. But Ivan stood unmoving in the dirt.

"Idiots!" he called after them. He kicked at the dirt in the road. But when the car was down at the old, rotting docks, he started down himself, cursing beneath his breath.

A large shack badly in need of repair stood beside the softly lapping water. The tide was out and there was only the tiniest curl of a wave falling on the beach.

As they got out of the car, they could hear a baby crying. Matt approached the rickety, unfinished porch, most of which was constructed of cast-off shipping crates. A man pushed through the grease-spotted door and stepped out into the sunlight. He was fat, balding and wore a yellowed, sleeveless tank T-shirt and a pair of pasta-stained pants. The brown belt was undone, giving the impression that he had only recently pulled his trousers on.

"Buon giorno, signore."

Luciana came near the porch now. She explained who the impressive-looking man in the white suit standing beside her was, said that he had come all the way from the United States, that she was his hired interpreter, that he, knowing of the scarcity of ships, was interested in acquiring one of Victor Marcheshi's, whose fame had been heard of even in America.

Marcheshi listened carefully, then spoke to her.

"He wants to know who exactly you work for," she said turning to Matt.

"Tell him a Great Man."

"Who's that?"

Matt shot his eyes upward, signifying it was God.

"He won't believe it." But she told Marcheshi anyway.

Marcheshi looked puzzled a moment, then he brightened. "The Great Man in America? John D. Rockefeller?"

Luciana translated.

Matt shrugged. "Why not?"

Grinning, Luciana confirmed Mr. Marcheshi's guess.

In a solemn voice, Marcheshi now requested something. "He wants to see your card," she explained to Matt.

"My card?"

"Everyone who is important in Italy has his own business card. It's a customary thing. Very impressive. It makes you legitimate."

"I haven't got one!" Matt looked stumped. How far could this charade go? Maybe this was a sign to call a halt to his scheme. Then a new thought hit him. "Wait a minute! Does Marcheshi know English?"

"Not a word."

Matt reached into the back pocket of his elegant white suit and pulled out his wallet. With a flourish, he produced a card. Luciana took it. It read, "Joe Hardy, Plumber. 1427 Magnolia. Porter's Quarter, Long Island. 24 hour service. Reasonable rates."

"Who is this?" Luciana asked him.

"He's fixed the plumbing for St. Anselm's Church. Just tell Marcheshi, Hardy works right under the Great Man himself."

Luciana sighed, then turned to Marcheshi, who was waiting. She explained that this card belonged to Matt Bowles's boss, and the importance attached to it.

Marcheshi accepted the card as if it were an ingot of gold. He read it aloud several times: "HardY. HardY!" Then he shook Matt's hand.

"*Come sta?*" Marcheshi grinned. But then he turned, irritated, and motioned at Ruffino and Ivan who were just arriving. He asked Luciana just what these two "tramp Jews" were doing in the company of such a distinguished businessman.

"We work for him," Ruffino replied before Luciana could get out a word.

"Since when?" Marcheshi squinted. "Two minutes ago you were broke, both sniveling at my feet. Now you tell me you work for this fine gentleman?"

Luciana cleared her throat, got Marcheshi's attention, and explained that this American had come from the Great Man with the express purpose of acquiring a new ship to transport Jewish refugees. It was a matter of a small charity and didn't he, Victor Marcheshi, surely understand what it was like to do something every once in a while for the less fortunate? Surely, great men did not begrudge small kindnesses to the lowly such as these two pitiful Jews.

"Ah, si," Marcheshi said, his chest expanding pridefully. Then to Ruffino and Ivan, "You are most fortunate to have acquired such a *patrono*!"

At last convinced of the nobility of this occasion, Marcheshi buckled his belt. He asked them to please follow him. Leading the way past his shack, Marcheshi guided them up the hillock that hid a small part of the harbor from view. Gaining its summit, they saw Marcheshi's working yard, littered with ropes, cutting torches and bales of creosote.

Situated between two parallel tie-up docks was a three-tiered flat-bottom ferry, its forward half raised in a makeshift dry dock, its stern still wallowing in the sea.

The ferry's sides were rusty and coated with barnacles and seaweed; its superstructure, including the wheelhouse, was smashed flat. There was a large hole in the starboard side and it was obvious from the totally corroded railings, warped decks and capstans that the ferry had been under the ocean most of the war.

"Tell him it's a piece of junk! We don't want it," Matt said. He turned back and started walking down the hill.

Luciana's eyes widened in shock. She started to yell, "Come back!" Instead, she got hold of herself and informed Marcheshi her boss considered his ship worthless.

Marcheshi immediately ran after Matt, drawing pictures of future grandeur with his hands, reminding the representative of the Great Man what it could look like painted and fixed up.

Matt kept on going.

"Grande nave!" Marcheshi was shouting.

"He says it's a huge ship and it'll carry a lot of cargo! Lots and lots of people too!" Luciana shouted hopefully after Matt.

Matt stopped. He turned, reluctantly, came back up the hill, viewed the ferry a moment, then shook his head in disappointment at such a dismal wreck of a ship. "Ask him," he directed Luciana, "how much it would be to"—he sniffed theatrically in disgust—"buy this thing."

Marcheshi listened, then babbled back to her for quite some time.

Leaving them, Matt walked down toward the docks, stopping near the ferry, then stepping across tangled mooring lines. Ruffino and Ivan silently accompanied him. Then Luciana came down, Marcheshi tagging behind her.

"Marcheshi says he knows the British don't want Jews to go to Palestine," she announced to Matt. "He says the British sink all the refugees' boats and that if they sink this ferry, they will know who sold it."

"But you were going to sell those two ships to us before," Ivan shouted angrily at Marcheshi in Italian.

"I change my mind now! Never!" Marcheshi opened his arms to show he was being truthful. He approached the group, who stood on the splintered docks near the prow of the ferry. "Is too dangerous to go to Palestine!"

"You took our option money! And you would have taken more, and never given us the ships! You're a liar and a cheat!" Ivan accused him.

Marcheshi shrugged conclusively.

"You, Marcheshi," Ivan went on, unable to restrain himself, "are a Jew like us! Why don't you act like one and help us instead of trying to cut our throats?"

"I am a Jew, yes," Marcheshi grinned mockingly, "but not Zionist. I do not need a country to call my own. With money comes all my territory."

Ivan spat in the water among several floating dead fish.

"Tell Mr. Marcheshi," Matt said, pretending to look bored, "to give us a price. We will pay him for ruining his good reputation."

"Quanto costa?" Luciana translated.

"Owwwww!" Marcheshi howled, as if suddenly stricken

with pain. He rubbed his fat belly. "I don't know! Too much. Too much!"

"Anything would be too much for that wreck," Ivan said to him. "It's a cinch nobody would ride below, out of the fresh air, in her stinking belly!"

"Quanto costa?" Matt asked quietly, imitating Luciana's phrase.

"Ow, ow!" Marcheshi lifted his leg and farted loudly. "Small ships go for many lire! This one is big, very big! And too much risk! I stick my neck out! Illegal! Ow! Ow!"

"You are slime!" Ivan growled at Marcheshi. "Those other ships were good. This ferry will turn turtle on the ocean and you know it!"

Marcheshi shrugged and moved away from Ivan.

"How much were you paying for the other ships?" Matt asked Luciana as he watched the fat man's antics.

"With option and everything, the scheduled price was nearly a million for both."

"Tell Marcheshi, then, that the Great Man never desires his representatives to dicker. We make one offer and that's it. We will pay him one million U.S. dollars, cash, for this wreck of a ferry."

"Negotiate with him, Matt!"

"Tell him."

Luciana swung on Marcheshi and translated. He listened politely, then said something and folded his arms.

Matt asked Luciana, "Did he agree?"

"No, he wants, let's see, the current exchange rate for lire to dollars is five seventy-five . . . he wants a million, three hundred thousand."

Ivan hawked something up and spat it near Marcheshi's shoes. The ship owner moved delicately away from the spittle on the dock, then continued to watch Matt and Luciana.

"Tell him, we will pay him *exactly* one million dollars. No more. It's what the deal was before."

Luciana turned to Marcheshi. She began in a mellow, soft voice that rose to a near scream as Marcheshi folded his arms tighter around his chest and shook his head repeatedly at her. Finally, she huffed out her breath in exasperation and turned to Matt.

"He won't budge. He says someone else who is law-abiding will come along and buy his ferry."

"He's bluffing."

Luciana shrugged. "I don't think so."

"Then why did he come after me when I walked down that hill?" Matt whispered, shooting a quick camouflage smile at Marcheshi, who was studying him.

"You hurt his pride."

"That's it?"

"He's Italian," Luciana sighed. "He didn't care so much about selling the boat as not giving you the last word."

Matt frowned. He looked at Marcheshi. Marcheshi grinned at him.

"Let's see just how much Italian pride he's got when it comes to old-fashioned greed. Tell Marcheshi we are leaving now."

Luciana translated.

Victor Marcheshi's smile remained, but it appeared strained.

"Tell him also," Matt said, "that every step I take will mean fifty thousand dollars less for his ferry."

Luciana told Marcheshi that.

"Say too, that there are other ships waiting our inspection. Norway, Yugoslavia. Anywhere but Italy."

Luciana spoke to Marcheshi, who began to frown. When she finished, Matt turned on his heel and took one giant step and stopped. Luciana, Ruffino and even Ivan, who spat again, followed.

"Oh!" Marcheshi grunted.

Matt took another step over a water hose.

"Ow, no, oh!" Marcheshi mumbled.

Swinging his cane round once in the air, Matt hopped across the remains of an iron boiler, leaped a sloppily coiled hawser and sprang over a prone acetylene tank.

"Yeow! Ow! OW!" Marcheshi screamed. He rattled off something to Luciana.

Matt froze. "What did he say?" he asked Luciana without turning.

"He agrees to one million!"

"Oh, too late for that," Matt said. "To get a million for the ferry now, he must also agree to contingencies!"

Luciana turned and told Marcheshi that.

Hearing no reply, Matt slowly lifted his right foot.

Marcheshi bellowed, *"Bene! Prego, prego!"*

Matt spun. Marcheshi ran toward him, his hand out to seal the deal. Matt accepted the Italian's hand, gripping it hard. The smile that had graced Marcheshi's face faded totally as Matt began to squeeze.

"The contingencies are," Matt said, "first, your supervisor will be Ivan Cohen. He's familiar with all aspects of shipbuilding."

Ivan looked surprised at that statement.

While Luciana translated to Marcheshi, Matt yet gripped Marcheshi's hand and asked Ivan, "Can you do it?"

"Before the war, I was a merchant marine," he began to protest, "but . . ." he caught himself suddenly. Then he said with determination, "If I can, I will make her run. But I don't see the money."

"It'll be here."

"Okay, okay!" Marcheshi agreed about Ivan, after Luciana had translated.

But when he tried to pull away, Matt squeezed his hand harder. "One more," Matt said. "We need this ship ready by tomorrow night."

"That's not possible!"

"We don't want it painted or all fixed up, you simpleton," Ivan told him. "Maybe the British will leave a scow like this one alone when they see it. We just need her floating and her motors working!"

"But all her housing, even the captain's bridge, is gone," Marcheshi complained, pointing with his free hand at the squashed ferry. "I can't get that ready by tomorrow night!"

"Are there cables connected to the rudder?" Ivan asked him.

"Yes, but . . ."

"We'll steer her from the bottom deck." He was already planning. "Cut that squashed upper housing completely off."

"But the rudder is bent, the rubber hydraulic lines have rotted, the forward bulwark is full of cement, put there by Mussolini to sink her!"

"We don't need pressure lines," Ivan said. "We'll steer her by pulley and levers. As for the cement in the prow, the better to ram the British with!'' He turned and spat at the British ships that guarded the gate of the harbor.

Marcheshi tried to pull his hand away. Matt crunched it tighter. ''Deal?''

''Contratto!'' Marcheshi squealed.

Matt grinned at him and let him go. ''Give him the hundred thirty-seven thousand dollars now,'' he told her as Marcheshi massaged, then blew on, his aching hand.

''All of it?''

''All of it. Tell him we want a receipt for its deposit.''

Luciana hesitated, then opened her purse. She pulled out the bills. Forgetting his hand, Marcheshi grabbed the loose bills and counted them. Satisfied, he licked his lips and spoke to Luciana.

''He wants to know when he will receive the rest,'' she told Matt.

''Tomorrow.''

''Tomorrow? Where are you going to get . . . ?''

''Tell him.''

Luciana translated.

Marcheshi reached to shake Matt's hand once more, thought better of it, bowed instead, then ran down the length of the dock, sail-like pants billowing.

Ivan jumped off the dock onto the ferry's lowest deck and stood shaking his head at the remains of tangled railings, capstans and buckled iron deck slabs.

''Father,'' Ruffino said, his body bent confusedly forward, ''Ivan thinks you are a fool. Marcheshi thinks you a fool. I am trying not to. But where are you going to get such an unearthly sum of money?''

All along, he knew if he got this far, it would have to come out. But for a moment, Matt said nothing, as though not to give his thoughts reality by speaking the words. ''It will come from an unearthly kingdom,'' he admitted finally. ''The Vatican bank.''

''But you said yourself the bank won't . . .'' Luciana stopped mid-sentence and gaped. ''You plan to *rob* the Vatican bank?!''

Ruffino suddenly stiffened as though he were at military attention. ''Father,'' he announced, ''it has always been my fantasy to avenge myself on Mussolini!''

"What does robbing the Vatican have to do with Mussolini?" Matt wanted to know.

"It was he who gave it wealth in the first place. Before 1929, the Vatican was broke. Then Mussolini paid it ninety million dollars. He started your Church's misfortune. I will be proud to take some of that away!"

"Ruffino, wait in the car," Luciana commanded him.

"Right away, Contessa." He bowed and trooped off up the dock.

"What's wrong with you?" Luciana spun on Matt. "I thought you came here putting your trust in God! But all the while you were thinking about stealing that money!"

He looked at her as from a distance.

"This is insane, Matt. Impossible. A gigantic wall surrounds every foot of the Vatican. It's a hundred feet high in parts. There are Swiss everywhere! It's a secured fortress. That's what it was built for!"

"I've already figured out how to get into the bank."

"Getting in is just part of the problem! What about getting out? And even if by some miracle you did make it out, where would you go? Haven't you noticed the Vatican is inside Rome?"

Down at the far end of the pier, Marcheshi started up a small diesel generator. He began to blow an electric whistle that was attached to it.

"Matt," Luciana begged, her voice aching, "you're a priest. You can't do this to your beliefs. What I told you about Pope Pius—what happened during the war—was only to open your eyes. I never intended this!"

"My eyes are wide open." Matt looked solemnly at her. "The Church owes you that money. No matter what, I will see we pay our debt!"

She turned away in despair.

Matt reached out, gripped her arms. "Luciana," he said in a flat, hard tone, "I became a priest because I thought it the best way to save my immortal soul. I do this for that same reason!"

Her blue eyes were glistening with tears. Impulsively, she pulled his head down and kissed his forehead.

Shouts suddenly filled the air above them. From the shanty-town surrounding the harbor of Civitavecchia, workers appeared, pulling on hats, shirts, boots, shoes, streaming down from their little shacks. The men and women cried to one another, eagerly answering the whistled announcements that work was available.

"Let's go," Luciana told Matt. "We've got work to do ourselves!"

15.

In postwar Europe, the Americans and British occupied Rome. England was represented there by her Embassy behind Via Veneto, and there were always a few British Tommies discreetly patrolling their sections of the city. The Jewish ghetto was in American territory. But when Matt pulled up to Ruffino's house, there were nearly twenty British soldiers herding refugees out the front door. A major and his aide stood there on the steps, accepting papers that Luciana knew were passports and visas and tossing them into the box his aide held.

Matt stopped the car.

"I've been expecting this," Luciana told him and Ruffino, who was in the back seat.

"What are they doing?" Matt asked as he peered through the Kaiser's windshield at the refugees filing out and the many friendly neighbors of the ghetto who stood below in the courtyard and on the street silently watching in disapproval. There must have been three hundred Jews there altogether.

"My guess is Prime Minister Attlee is stepping up his operation to keep Jews from emigrating to Palestine," Luciana observed. "They've hassled us before. This is the first time the soldiers have taken their passports!" She jacked open her door and stepped out. "You had better stay here," she said to Matt. "No sense in tipping them off to your presence."

She and Ruffino went up toward the crowd. Matt settled down in his seat and watched as Luciana pushed her way up the steps, then angrily called out and approached the major, who held a riding crop beneath his right arm. The major bowed politely and began listening to Luciana's tirade.

Matt let his eyes rove across the faces. It looked as though the whole ghetto had turned out for this. They were watching with as much concern as the refugees.

At the edge of the crowd, a battered car caught Matt's eye. In the front seat sat the man with two hairy valleys. Next to him, the other one from Lake Bracciano.

Matt stepped from the car and, without closing the door, began excusing himself through the crowd. When he had passed Ruffino's house, he came up on the passenger's side of the beat up car and bent down.

"What are you doing here?" Matt asked.

The hulking man in the gray suit turned, his eyes showing shock and recognition. He recovered quickly, however, and, as a predator might confidently regard his prey, smiled at Matt.

"You're Communists, aren't you!" Matt demanded. "What do you want here?"

The big man turned away, muttered something Matt did not understand to the driver. He half-expected the horned one to rise up out of the car with a gun. Instead he started the car and roared off.

Matt clutched the big man's arm. He did not know what he was trying to accomplish. It seemed the only thing he could do. As the car accelerated crazily through the gathered crowd, Matt pulled himself close to the door, flattening himself as best he could. The horned one drove near the side of a building. Matt's cane struck a wall and flipped away, skittering behind him on the stones. The man in the gray suit stuck his face close and said in a heavily accented Slavic voice, "Stay away, priest!" And he hit him in the face.

The Fiat sped away. Matt rolled and thumped across the stones, clutching his hurt leg, hoping he would not burst open the stitches. When he could stop, he stood and found he was only bruised. One of the women from Luciana's house brought him his cane. He took it and had started to go back to the Kaiser when the British major blocked his way.

"Italian drivers," the major quipped. "Nearly got run over several times myself. You all right, old chap?"

Matt nodded, unwilling to speak and give away his nationality. He bent and brushed off his trousers.

The major slapped his crop against his leg several times, studying him. Luciana came up quickly.

"Major Wingate, how long will you keep these poor Jews' passports?"

"As I said, madam"—the major turned his gaze on her— "you are presently in violation of the Allied Health Code. Too many people in one house for the amount of facilities, if you get my meaning. And there are many other houses like this one across the city." He picked a folded paper from his pocket. "Yes, the total invoiced is over twenty-five hundred Jews. Quite a few, I might say. Gathered for what purpose I do not know, but I can guess, madam."

"And just where do you think they can go without their papers?" Luciana asked pointedly.

"If," the major said, "they go back whence they came, I will return their passports."

"And if not?"

"Madam, I have a job to do. These poor buggers are living in subhuman conditions. I've warned you before about packing them in like this. This was the third and last time. If they are still in the same houses by next week, I will disperse them myself."

"To a camp?"

"Perhaps, madam. But if I were you"—he smiled—"I would not encourage them to disperse to Palestine." He eyed Matt one last time as if memorizing him. He touched the flat, leather bill of his hat, turned and barked an order to his men. They filled the lorry. As he and his aide, box of passports in hand, swung up into the passenger's seat, the truck lurched off.

"Does he suspect about the ship?" Matt asked Luciana.

"Wingate knows something is up. But he doesn't know what, or he would have had us arrested. You can bet he'll be keeping a close eye on us though. He expects with taking our passports, we'll tip our hand." She turned to Matt. "Who were your friends who tried to run you over?"

"Communists. I don't know what they wanted here."

"They're like vultures. They look for trouble. Jews always make good copy for their political machine," Luciana told him. "They're very cozy with some of the British too, probably got tipped off."

They went up through the crowd of concerned neighborhood Jews. Her families began to question her all at once about what was happening.

Halfway up the steps to the house, Luciana turned, raised her hands and shouted to the assemblage, "Don't expect to get your papers back unless you go home."

"We have no homes!" someone yelled. "Where else do they think we can go?"

"The British suspect some of you here are trying to go to Palestine!" Luciana shrugged, a small smile on her face.

"Any fool in his right mind knows we Jews are under restrictions not to travel to Palestine," Rabbi Meister yelled. The crowd laughed and began to relax.

"But they have our passports, all our identity!" a woman near Meister suddenly cried.

Luciana raised her hands again. "We have a ship on which you will need no passports. Your new identities await you in your homeland. Keep your lips sealed. Go about your business and don't look excited. Children, don't talk with any strangers!"

"Next Year in Jerusalem!" someone solemnly intoned. It had been the thought of Jews for nearly two thousand years.

Marie Schollander surprised herself by suddenly shouting, "May this be the last time we ever say 'Next Year in Jerusalem'!"

A sound went up from the crowd like a bellowing roar. A profound emotion from the heart. And Matt thought again of his decision to rob the Vatican. He wanted to do the right thing for his Church and the right thing for these refugees. But he was not a crook, and this crime did not come easily to him.

What if he should fail? If he caused the death and destruction of these innocent people? What was he doing? It was insane, impossible! He had been carried away by a crazy idea!

Then he felt a hand in his. A small hand. And he looked

down and there was Ruth, the little girl from the Theresienstadt concentration camp, gazing up at him. Her brown eyes were too big and luminous for her bony head, her limbs cruelly thin and angular, her chest protruding in the too-large dress she wore. What had she suffered already?

Ashamed, he bent and picked her up in his arms. She was startlingly light, her frame as delicate as a butterfly's. Luciana stood nearby, unseen, tears rolling down her cheeks.

"God forgive me," Matt said to Ruth.

She kissed him, and he carried her up the steps with the others as they entered the house.

During Hannah's supper of gnocchi, refugees continued to straggle in from their tasks of alerting everyone across the city. They came in and, despite having been relieved of their papers, were glowing with new life. They jabbered excitedly as they described the joys of their fellow Jews upon learning that they were sailing tomorrow night. Rabbi Meister led a prayer, thanking God for the beneficence of Pope Pius XII. Then someone started singing "Hava Nagila."

Matt, Luciana and Ruffino trooped to the rear of the kitchen. The refugees noticed them but kept on with their song. Some were even dancing.

Luciana led Matt and Ruffino to the small pantry. "They are singing about a boat they do not have," she said, when she had closed the pantry door and turned on the single light bulb over the chopping-block table. The shelves lining the pantry held beans, garlic, tomatoes, onions and some winter squashes.

Ruffino said, "It *is* an irony that while we plan to rob the Vatican bank, our friends in the kitchen thank God for the imaginary help of Pope Pius."

There was a knock at the door, and Hannah entered, took a folded paper out of her apron and laid it on the butcher block. "Here is the map you requested," she told Matt. "I heard you two talking on the bannister this afternoon. It was then I knew you didn't have the money . . . yet."

"You eavesdropped!" Luciana accused her.

"Of course. Why not? Whatever you're planning, I am part of it!"

Matt and Ruffino looked at Luciana.

Luciana said, "Robbing the Vatican bank will be dangerous, Hannah. Your husband, Bosco, would not want you involved."

"Bosco is probably dead," Hannah said, crossing her fat arms on her chest. "It's time I faced up to that. Anyway, if it's the bank you're after, I'll report all of you unless you let me join you."

"Can you drive a car?" Matt asked, unable to suppress a smile at her nonchalance.

"I was born driving."

He smoothed out the map. "Not a very good one. Looks old." He took off his suit jacket and loosened his tie.

"Made in 1882," Hannah explained. "The priest in the religious souvenir store told me it was the latest. He said the Vatican does not encourage maps and that no one ever asks for one anyway."

Luciana peered at the map. "I can sketch in the twentieth-century buildings." She found a pencil on one of the food shelves. Then she indicated the location of the Historical Museum, the Vatican Pinacoteca with its priceless oils, and the new wing of the Vatican Museum in which Matt had seen Pope Pius enjoying his Egyptian figurines. She outlined the Ethiopian College, the Marconi-designed radio station on the top of Vatican Hill, the power station at the bottom and the Governor's Palace in the middle next to the railway station.

Lastly, she drew in the Swiss Guard barracks, which were behind the Vatican wall.

"How many guards quartered here?" Matt gestured at the barracks.

"Varies. If the Pope is in residence, two hundred."

Hannah let out a little whistle. "Whatever we do, we stay away from there!"

"Don't worry," Luciana told her, "the bank is located in the Casina of Pius IV. That's here." She tapped her pencil on a T-shaped building, surrounded by cement walks. It was toward the rear of the map, halfway up on the Vatican Hill.

"Very open to view," Ruffino submitted.

"I imagine that's why they picked it," Matt said. "Anyone approaching can be identified a long way off. There are Swiss Guards at the front and rear entrances of the bank."

Luciana tossed down the pencil. "Getting in is not the problem. Father Matt has a way."

"We can use the same method Luciana did during the war to sneak in POWs." He pointed at the gate of Arco delle Campane to the left of the basilica. "Is this the gate you want to enter, Luciana?"

"No, the Gate of St. Anne. It's closer to the Casina." She tapped the main entrance to the right of St. Peter's Square. "The busiest of all gates. Easy to get through."

"Good," Matt said. "When do the guards change?"

"Every four hours, starting at eight."

"So eight to noon, twelve to four, four to eight, right?"

"That's it. And they close the gates at midnight, start again the next morning at eight."

"You and Ruffino will enter just before eight A.M.," Matt decided. "That way different guards will let you in and out."

"But Contessa, how will they pass us inside so easily?" Ruffino scratched his head.

"Because you will be a Lord Cardinal of the Catholic Church and I your coadjutor Bishop."

"So I'm to be a cardinal?" Ruffino asked, straightening.

"For a little while," Luciana said. "Then, you're going to become a janitor."

Ruffino sighed playfully. "Back to my station in life. I knew it was too good to be true."

"What is this nonsense?" Hannah interrupted. "From cardinal to janitor and Luciana a bishop? Tell us your plan, Father!"

"Tomorrow at seven thirty A.M.," Matt said, hovering over the map, "I meet my old friend Father Mankowsky at the bank here to sign and verify the tally sheets that he'll bring from the United States. When no one is looking, I'll stuff the money we need into a wastepaper basket and light a match to the basket. Then, before they can call the Vatican Fire Department, you, Ruffino, having changed out of your cardinal's costume, will arrive in a janitor's uniform and take it away."

"But, forgive me, Father," Ruffino apologized, "how can you be so certain they will let a janitor remove the trash can from the bank?"

"Because it will be full of smoke. And they'll want it out.

They're afraid of fire in the bank. They don't even allow smoking there.''

"But if there has been a fire in the can, won't our money burn?''

"Some of it will. But I'll pack it tight so no oxygen can get below. It will be a quick fire with a lot of smoke.''

"That is clever,'' Hannah said in admiration of the plan. "You will make it so *they* rob their own bank. In order to get rid of the stink and smoke of a fire, they order out their own money and give it to us.''

"At least, that's what we hope,'' Matt said. "Now, Ruffino, you arrive at exactly eight thirty, that should give me time, then take that can out to wherever they dump their trash.''

"That would be here, the stone bin behind the Fountain of the Eagle.'' Luciana pointed to a large pool on the map. An eagle with outstretched wings and talons indicated the ancient fountain.

Ruffino nodded as Matt continued, "Leave the money in a sack you will be carrying, then you will go back to being a cardinal again. In a little while, Luciana, disguised as a bishop, will come by, pick up the sack and put it inside one of her large cassock pockets. Hannah, you will be in your car here on Via di Porta Angelica right outside St. Anne's Gate. You'll pick up Luciana and Ruffino, drive to the outside of the left Bernini column, where I'll be waiting. Then we'll all go to Civitavecchia to pay off Marcheshi.''

"So you are counting on nobody even knowing there was a robbery,'' Hannah concluded.

"That's right,'' Matt said. "If everything works, we should be gone before they even discover the money is missing.''

"Will this Father Mankowsky cooperate with you?'' Hannah looked uneasily first at Luciana, then Ruffino.

"If Matt says he'll do it, he will,'' Luciana told her. "But I've got a question. How much does eight hundred sixty-three thousand dollars weigh?''

"Yes, Father.'' Ruffino got worried. "We will need a mule!''

"Can we dress a mule up in bishop's clothing?'' Hannah laughed. But no one shared her mirth.

"I'll try my best to get the biggest bills,'' Matt explained to

Luciana and Ruffino. "If the two of you split it up, there's plenty of room in those deep cassock pockets you'll have."

"*Scusi*, Father." Hannah ran her finger around the clear markings of the high wall on the map. "But what do you do if something goes wrong?"

"The plan," Luciana answered quickly, "is we pick a low section of the Vatican wall and leap over."

"But once over, you would be in Rome. Then the Italian *carabinieri* would pursue you. How could we get to Civitavecchia?"

"It's the best we can do under the circumstances," Matt said.

"*Gesù!*" Hannah moaned. "Bank robberies are supposed to be precise, everything planned down to the last detail! Here you do not even have a good escape plan!" She bent over the map. "Luciana," she said, "what about the Passetto Vaticano?"

"The tunnel? The one beneath the Tiber?"

"Yes, the popes' secret passage to the Castel Sant' Angelo."

"What tunnel are you talking about?" Matt asked with interest, as he studied the map.

"Built by Alexander V in the fifteen hundreds," Ruffino told him. "He and other popes used it to escape into the Castel Sant' Angelo fortress whenever the barbarians attacked."

"Forget about that tunnel!" Luciana ordered them. "It's a death trap. During the war, the Germans never even bothered to seal it off. Some POWs tried to use it to get into the Vatican and drowned!"

"Where's the entrance?" Matt persisted.

"I don't know," Hannah admitted. "You, Ruffino?"

Ruffino hesitated. He was looking at Luciana. "Forgive me, mistress," he apologized and placed a calloused finger on a spot behind a wall.

"But that's by the barracks of the Swiss Guard!" Hannah groaned.

"Makes sense militarily," Matt said. "They could defend the Pontiff up until the last minute. Where does it come out?"

"Here, a half mile away by the Tiber, inside the Castel Sant' Angelo. It's a museum now." Ruffino showed him.

"What time does the museum open and close?"

"Ten in the morning. Closes early, by one, I think."

"If we need this alternative escape route, we'll go through

the tunnel and wait on the other end until the museum closes.''
Matt turned to Hannah. "You keep the car just outside St.
Anne's Gate like we planned. If we don't show up by—say—
nine thirty, then drive across to this fort of Sant' Angelo and
wait for us there.''

"This is insane!" Luciana cried. "From stories I've heard,
it would be like trying to swim under a waterfall! The Tiber
has collapsed the tunnel. Maybe the tunnel's plugged altogether!''

There was nothing anyone could say.

"Tonight," Matt said, folding the map, "I don't think we
should stay here. It's better not to have these people involved.''

"We can use my old house as the base of operations,"
Luciana offered. "It's been empty ever since the Germans
raided it.''

"It will be like going home again, mistress.'' Ruffino
smiled at her.

"Hannah,'' Luciana asked her, "can you get the car
fueled?''

"I'll tell Pynchon Nossi I need to visit a sick relative. He's
got several liters hidden away for just such an emergency.''

Matt yawned suddenly.

"How long has it been since you slept?'' Luciana asked
him.

"Couple of days.'' He yawned again.

"Ruffino,'' Luciana commanded, "go to my friend the
Capo. The one who runs the religious vestment store. Tell
him to prepare a cardinal's outfit and a bishop's for me. He
knows my size.''

"Won't this man Capo wonder about the reasons for these
costumes?'' Matt worried.

"During the war,'' Luciana said, "the Capo was a partisan,
a member of the underground. He will ask no questions.''

She turned back to Ruffino. "Tell the Capo he must also
make a janitor's uniform for you and a soft, cloth bag for the
money. Tell him too the janitor's uniform should be dark blue
for that level of the Vatican. Oh, and have him put a yellow
and blue emblem with Pope Pius's coat of arms above the right
chest pocket.''

Ruffino bowed slightly and went out with Hannah.

"I need to change clothes for tomorrow," Matt sighed. "My cassock is upstairs."

"I'll change too. Then you should get some rest." She cast a last, hopeful look at the map. "Can we do it?"

"God willing." Matt tried to smile hopefully. But he couldn't help but wonder if that was slightly blasphemous. Rather than think about it, he snapped off the light.

16.

For the Communist Party candidate, Giuseppe Ferragamo, it had been a long, difficult day. The little man had on three separate occasions been pelted with rotten eggs while giving a speech from a truck, been jeered at by thugs while standing on the trunk of his Fiat and, finally, been chased by a vicious dog in a field near the Circus Maximus. The dog, a German shepherd, had ripped his right trouser leg.

Now, entering the Communist headquarters on Via delle Botteghe Oscure, Ferragamo did not feel like a worthy candidate at all. He was sweaty, tired and full of despair. Yet, before the day was finished, he had a remaining task to perform. Campaign funds were, as usual, nearly gone. Apparently, Mother Russia, as Nerechenko called her, thought campaigns could be won on a lot of rhetoric and very few rubles. Ferragamo had to finish the day by contacting local Communist supporters once again and begging for their assistance.

He pushed through the front door, past the two empty desks normally filled by secretaries, past the poster slogans on the walls, past the red hammer-and-sickle flags, and walked toward his small office at the rear. It was threadbare: couch, desk, two chairs, one of which was broken. Yet he looked forward to being alone after the day he had had. To his dismay, as he stepped through the open doorway, he saw Igor Nerechenko was behind his desk. And to add to his discomfort, the assassin Cornos was sprawled on the couch, reading an Italian comic book.

"Ah, here is our candidate, working late!" Nerechenko said. He was reading the evening's edition of *L'Unità,* the Communist paper.

"Yes, trying to raise money," Ferragamo countered, pointedly picking up the telephone and opening his small red book.

"Mother Russia takes care of you," Nerechenko recited, without taking his eyes away from the newspaper.

Forced to stand, Ferragamo made several calls. The replies, though sympathetic, offered little help. "Maybe tomorrow, comrade." "Business is not so good yet, comrade."

On the fourth call, however, this one to old friend Victor Marcheshi, Ferragamo thought he found something. Marcheshi, too, begged off donating any money. "It is hard. Everyone is scratching for a living." But he mentioned that there was someone in Italy, "who today saved me from the fate of a pauper!"

"Who?" Ferragamo wanted to know.

"*Signore* Matthew Bowles."

"And what does he do?"

"Oh, donates money to Jews," Marcheshi allowed. "He bought one of my boats."

"Ah, he paid a lot?"

"No, no," Marcheshi poor-mouthed, "just enough to pay the bills. Too bad he is American, this fellow, Bowles. He might have helped our cause, yes, comrade-next-President?"

"Sure, sure." Ferragamo knew he was being palmed off. "I will be in touch. *Ciao*!" And he hung up.

Nerechenko looked up. "News?" he asked, half-interested.

"Someone bought a ship from Victor Marcheshi today. The one in Civitavecchia who raises wrecks from the bottom of the ocean. It's the third he's sold this week, the lying moneymonger."

"Ah, a Communist who supports with his mouth." Nerechenko went back to reading his paper.

"An American bought one of his boats for Jews," Ferragamo said. "Matthew Bowles, I think, was his name. I wish that man was a Communist!"

Nerechenko lowered his paper. He uncorked the bottle of aquavit that sat on Ferragamo's desk and poured himself a shot.

"You are calm, comrade!" Ferragamo said in a rare show of anger in front of his superior. "Very confident! 'Everything just fine!' Do you realize this is December sixth and the elections will take place on January first? Less than a month away!"

"Do not panic," Nerechenko said.

"Buona notte!" Ferragamo said. "I am going to check the receipts on my bakery, and after that, I go home to dream about how Mother Russia will miraculously win this election!" He slammed the door.

The Russian poured himself another glass of aquavit. "Cornos," he said after a bit, "the Red Woman mentioned a Matthew Bowles."

The horned one shrugged. He was interested in his comic.

"He was the priest at the airport and yesterday in the ghetto. Now he goes to Civitavecchia to buy a ship for those Jews," Nerechenko half mused to himself. It had been a fortuitous happening that had drawn him to the ghetto yesterday. After he had received word from his friend Major Wingate that there would be a roust, he had gone, remembering the Red Woman's offer of the Jewish money. He had been mildly curious to view these ragtag Jews. Through his career, he had learned to sniff out and follow trouble. Trouble was better than any spy and could turn up more information. And sometimes, as now, two unrelated events might have a connection. Matthew Bowles. What was he up to?

"Comrade," Nerechenko persisted, still worrying the information, "all this about the Jews is very curious. It intrigues me, comrade. Shall we take a ride to see *Signore* Marcheshi?"

"It won't take long? I don't want to miss this Mankowsky's arrival at the airport."

"You will not," Nerechenko vowed. "I told you, he is yours."

At Civitavecchia, it was nearly dark and Nerechenko had sent Spina down to the lighted dry docks below. His stomach rumbled uncomfortably. This campaign was too long, too

complicated. Not like the others. He longed for his home-
town of Minsk and his wife Natalie's fleshy thighs.

The horned one returned out of breath and slid into the car.
"There are workers repairing an old ferry down there," Spina
said.

"And?"

"That Bowles bought it. The word is he will pay one
million American dollars!"

"So Marcheshi did lie!" Nerechenko mulled over that.

"This whole town is working on that ferry," Cornos
revealed. "Everyone is saying it is a big job, that the ferry
must be ready to sail by tomorrow night."

"Why so soon?"

"No one knows. The owner, Marcheshi, is not talking. Do
you wish me to hold a fire under his balls? Then he will tell
us why!"

"Not yet. Is the British Navy involved in any way? Are
there sailors watching down there?"

"None."

"Where does this priest expect to get a million dollars?"
Nerechenko wondered as Spina started the small car and
revved its worn-out engine. "I know the Jews do not have it.
And how many banks own that kind of money?"

"Pah, they are broke like the rest of Italy."

"I am very curious. Let us quickly visit with the Red Woman.
Perhaps he can tell us more."

The normal procedure for contacting the Red Woman was
complicated and time-consuming. Nerechenko would run an
ad in *Tempo*, a small daily Roman newspaper, stating, "Mr.
Kostelantz requires good Holstein or Brahman steer from
Russia." Since no one seeking to sell cows in Rome had one
from Russia, no one ever answered the ad except the Red
Woman. His reply would arrive via telephone. Then a meeting would be arranged, the spot agreed on by both parties.
But tonight it was crucial that Nerechenko see the Red Woman
immediately. The Red Woman would not be pleased with this
break in procedure, but there was no other way. In the beginning of their association, Nerechenko had forced the Red
Woman to give him a telephone number to be used in case of

such an emergency. Nerechenko had no idea where it was connected.

He instructed Cornos to drop him off at the first kiosk they spotted after entering Rome. Paying the owner of the lighted newspaper stand for the right to use his telephone, Nerechenko dialed the number. In a little bit, to his surprise, a woman answered. She did not have the voice of a nun.

"*Buono?*" she purred in a sultry tone.

Nerechenko explained he was a good friend of a certain man and had been given this number to contact him. Nerechenko gave his fictitious name of Kostelantz and told her that this was a matter of grave import.

The woman asked him to wait a moment. She would see if anyone of that description was there. In less time than it took for the kiosk owner to sell a bottle of shaving lotion, she was back on the line.

"Mr. Kostelantz," she said. "He asks you to come to 311 Via Rustici."

"Is that near the Colosseum?"

"*Si,*" she said. And the line went dead.

At Rustici, which was below the Colosseum but not in view of it, Cornos stopped the car. The night was waning and the moonlight fell on the smooth cobblestones of the street, filling it with broken shadows.

"I am going to Ciampino Airport now," Cornos announced as soon as Nerechenko stepped from the car.

"Is it not too early, comrade? Relax," the Russian said, leaning back inside the door.

"I need to set my plan!" The horned one's voice was elated at what he was being allowed to do. "There will be many Swiss around this priest Mankowsky! And my plan must be set in motion early! The timing of the explosion is important!"

"The explosion? What about the papers?"

"They won't be hurt. My explosion is diversionary. The rest will be personal, up close with this priest!"

"Wait for me here," Nerechenko told him. "There is time for your plan. I will need a ride back to headquarters."

"Hire a taxi!" Spina shouted, starting the car.

"Wait!" Nerechenko bellowed.

Cornos cursed blackly but shut off the motor. He slouched in his seat.

Nerechenko slammed the door and went up to the green-porticoed building and rang the brass bell. In a moment, a boy in jockey's livery opened one of the doors. In the dim red light of the room, Nerechenko saw the boy gesture wearily to a set of stairs. Closing the door, the boy took up his position once again near the front doors, seated on a small divan, his hands folded meekly between his legs as Nerechenko climbed upward.

Upstairs, two fake blondes in filmy pink and white negligees were reading philosophy books by Kant and Heidegger. One of them looked up at the Russian, sniffed at his odor, but stood.

"I am Sophia."

"Where is the proprietor?" Nerechenko demanded, avoiding her. "Tell him Kostelantz is here!"

"Don't you like me?" she asked. "If you want boys, too bad. You can't have the one below. He's the owner's. So I'll make you happy."

A man with a badly pockmarked face stuck his head out from behind a set of velvet curtains. "Kostelantz?" he asked. "I am Principio. Follow me, please."

Nerechenko pushed through the purple curtains, following the man down a smooth, waxed marble passageway that reeked of pine disinfectant, past rooms with their doors closed, then down a short flight of steps. Finally, the owner gestured to a rubber-sealed entrance and went away.

Nerechenko pulled open the heavy, slablike door and stepped inside. It was a steam room, lined with wooden benches. It was empty except for the Red Woman, who was wrapped in a sheet, and a small boy whose head lolled on his knee. The boy appeared to be drugged.

"You violated our confidence," the Red Woman accused Nerechenko, when he had sat opposite him.

"It is an emergency."

"Always an emergency!"

"Comrade Red Woman, this time I come to do you a favor."

The Red Woman reached down and swept the boy's dark

hair off his forehead. "I find your generosity hard to believe. Why should you do me a favor?"

"To help you, comrade!"

The Red Woman snickered derisively.

"What would you say if I told you that this priest, Matthew Bowles, is involved with the Jews? I saw him with them this afternoon."

"That is not news. We know that!"

"But do you know, Comrade Red Woman, that he plans to pay one million dollars to buy a boat for them?" Nerechenko had played his trump card. Now, he leaned back and waited to see if the Red Woman could tell him more than he already knew.

"I burned their money, I swear it!" the Red Woman suddenly gasped. "You must believe that! Only a hundred thirty-seven thousand dollars was returned to them!"

"Help me believe," Nerechenko said. "How do I know you're not double-crossing me and helping this priest yourself?"

"Why would I?" the Red Woman protested.

"Then where is Bowles getting the rest of the money? No bank in Italy could loan it to him. The only big source is the Vatican. Has there been another shipment from the U.S. that you haven't told me about?" Nerechenko's gray suit was seeping now with dark stains. But he ignored the discomfort and the fact that he had to walk out of the steam room in a little while and perhaps catch "the pneumonia."

"I know for certain," the Red Woman spoke in a whisper, "that there was no other shipment. I know too that no one gave Bowles the million."

"Then how, comrade? For as sure as we sit here, he either has it or has found a way to get it."

"Perhaps he *has* borrowed the money from a bank in the United States," the Red Woman said after a moment. "There is no other way he could have it."

"Let us consider this priest's character," Nerechenko said. "What do you know about him?"

"He's a parish priest, that's all."

"Nothing else?"

"Oh, during the war, he fought at Normandy. I heard he won a medal for his bravery."

"Ah," Nerechenko nodded, "a man of action. So he is no

ordinary priest, comrade. This priest may do something, anything at all!''

"Not anything." The Red Woman caressed the head in his lap. "He seems a good priest, after all."

"But what if, comrade," Nerechenko pressed, "what if he was convinced that what he was doing was right? Then it is possible for this unusual priest, Bowles, to do anything. Are you following my logic?"

The Red Woman seemed not to hear. He was gazing down at the boy.

"And let us assume, then," Nerechenko was hurrying forward with his line of reasoning, "that one, he does not have the money. And two, the only place to get it is the Vatican bank. And three . . .''

The traitor suddenly stiffened, his hand tightening in the boy's hair. "Impossible! Our security is the best in the world!"

The Red Woman shoved the boy's head off his knee. It thumped down on the wooden bench. He moved nervously away from the inert form as though he were pulling in to defend himself against this unexpected assault.

Good, Nerechenko thought. I hit a nerve. All this *is* possible, then.

"What audacity!" the Red Woman exclaimed. "Does Bowles think he can rob our bank?"

"He knows your layout. He has seen everything. And he has the motivation that you gave him.''

The Red Woman shifted uncomfortably. "All this is speculation, of course."

"Can you take the chance he will not attempt it?"

"What do you wish from me?" the Red Woman sighed audibly.

"From you? Nothing but to be a hero, comrade. Simply capture this priest if a robbery is attempted."

"And what do you get from all this?"

"When you catch him, you turn him over to the Italian authorities. He will be tried. Perhaps in his trial, not only will the existence of the Vatican's vast wealth be revealed but also that it was to be used to elect a candidate of the Christian Democratic Party. This will cause a very big scandal, comrade. Italians will hear about this, then go to the polls in less than three weeks and vote for the Communist Party. On January first, we will have Italy!''

"And what about the ledger sheets that arrive tomorrow?'' the Red Woman asked carefully after a moment's silence. ''Will you steal those as planned? I would! You could expose them too!''

Something about the eagerness with which the traitor brought up the ledgers made Nerechenko pause. The sweat was dripping uncomfortably from his thick, hooded eyes, and his suit had been transformed into a soggy rag. But his disciplined mind was working, and he saw that the Red Woman might be trying to steer him away from his purpose. What if there were no sheets? Could that in some way affect these plans? He could not fathom how . . . yet the manner in which the Red Woman had changed subjects so quickly alarmed him.

"Your only concern will be to bring this priest Bowles to trial.'' The Russian smiled unblinkingly, seemingly ignoring the Red Woman's suggestion. He stood and pushed open the door. ''And after that, as I promised, I will destroy the file the Master has on you.'' And he left the room.

The Red Woman leaned back, more frightened than he had ever been. He knew useful files were never destroyed. After this, there would be another blackmail and another. He would never be free. And somehow the Russian had smelled the trap of destroying the tally sheets! Had he suspected too that Bowles might use them as his opportunity to get inside the bank?

He forced himself to forget that disappointment and turned his mind instead back to Nerechenko. Only this Russian knew his new identity. That meant if he killed him, the link would be removed. And if he could catch this priest Bowles he might even emerge as a hero within the Vatican. The Cardinals, even the Holy Father, would respect him as the one who saved the Vatican bank. Afterwards, there was no other choice than to erase Nerechenko. Then his future would be bright again. His life would be his own.

The boy stirred and with that movement, the Red Woman felt hope and a longing awaken within his loins. He reached across and threw open the boy's bath sheet and knelt on the floor.

*   *   *

Outside, the night was now moonless. Nerechenko stood shivering in front of 311 Via Rustici and waited for Spina to pick him up. He hoped the assassin had not disobeyed him and gone to Ciampino to kill that priest Mankowsky. If he had, it would be tragic. The perfect opportunity to stop the Christian Democrats and win this election might be lost.

A small car's headlights flashed down the block and the sound of burning rubber told Nerechenko that his plan was yet secure. Now to calm down Cornos.

"We have a problem," he said as he entered the car. "The American priest is going to rob the Vatican bank. But he might not do it without those ledger sheets. So I do not want you to kill that priest Mankowsky."

Cornos let that sink in. He revved the motor slightly as he thought about it, tapping the footfeed gently. Nerechenko braced himself, ready in case the car spurted off. But in the dashboard lights of the car, the horned one's face was that of an expressionless gargoyle. He put the Fiat gently into gear and slowly, very slowly, pulled away from the curb. It was the slowest he had ever driven.

"So, comrade," Nerechenko tried to sound merry, "do we understand one another?"

"Anything you say, comrade." Spina drove so slowly there were cars honking behind him.

Despite the warmth of the car, Nerechenko shuddered. For while he knew Cornos would obey him this time, he knew too that there would soon be a time in which he would indulge himself in a bloodbath. It had happened before. In Rumania, a union officer targeted for assassination by Cornos had died accidentally in an auto accident. The horned one had been so furious he had gone out and killed three innocent people who were having their lunches in Sjotcziz Park.

Nerechenko tried to forget that. He did not like the feeling of being out of control of this killer. His only other option would be to stop Spina himself. But right now he did not want to think about that at all. He wanted to focus on the robbery of the Vatican and the big Communist win afterwards in Italy.

Later that same night, Monsignor Helmut Kass swept through the anteroom of his office, past the lines of cases of ancient tomes, held in place by chicken wire. He hated this part of the trip. Why hadn't he been given offices closer to the Holy Father anyway? After all, he was the Pontiff's personal secretary. He imagined that Sister Pasqualina, that despot, had had something to do with putting him inside the left wing of the Holy Office. It was a cruel joke that his office stood amidst all the books on the Index—the list of those condemned through the ages as heretical or salacious by the Holy Curia.

Glancing at his watch, he saw it was nearly midnight. Well past his bedtime. He pushed through the door at the end of the darkened corridor and immediately his spirits rose. His lovely office, carpeted with a thick, scarlet pile, his desk and appointments of teakwood, silver and gold, never failed to remind him of the power he wielded.

He was pleased to find Monsignor Guido Offeri, Governor Prince Chieti Milagro, and Hans Fullmer waiting as he had requested.

"Gentlemen," he said, "please be seated. This will take just a moment."

He settled himself behind his large desk. "I am sorry for calling this meeting so late," he said, realigning his gold-plated letter opener, "but Pope Pius keeps late hours. He has heard that only part of the Jews' money was recovered."

"That's true," Guido Offeri gravely nodded his condorlike neck. He looked like he had been sleeping. *"Signore* Perfette of the Santo Spirito Bank has sent me a memorandum stating there is eight hundred and sixty-three thousand still missing."

"We must determine what happened," Kass said. "Mr. Fullmer, I asked you to investigate."

"I found no trace of it, Monsignor." The albino blinked his bleached eyes. "In my investigation, I did, however, discover a minor thief. I fired Isto Molinari today for stealing tires from the Vatican garage. Do we wish to press charges?"

"No, no publicity. You know that. Prince Milagro?"

"Assisting Mr. Fullmer"—the Pope's royal nephew spread his hands in helplessness—"I ordered all civil department heads to flush out any gossip, any bragging about knowledge of that money. But I uncovered nothing. Believe me, as in the past, we would have heard something. Some piece of confession, guilt, pride, something. I don't believe anyone in the Vatican had anything to do with this." The Prince had come dressed in a tuxedo, probably straight from an opera. The others were more casual.

"And you, Guido?"

"My tellers, financiers, administratives know nothing. *Segretario* Palmo has grilled all potential weaklings and uncovered not a scrap of wrongdoings. Also, there are positively no miscalculations in our ledgers. I feel we must assume that that portion of the Jews' money never existed."

"That is my conclusion also," the albino spoke up. "I think it was a clever ruse to obtain more funds for their program of Zionism."

Monsignor Helmut Kass picked up the letter opener. A cameo photo of Pius XII was implanted at its head. He tapped it twice, then three times.

"All right," he said, "I will inform Pope Pius that it is our position that no money is missing—that the Jews were given all that was sent to them. We will hear no more of it. Now, I want tomorrow to go very smoothly and quickly. Once those tally sheets arrive with Father Mankowsky from the United States, I want them signed as a mere formality. Then have both of those priests, Bowles and Mankowsky, put on an airplane and shipped back to New York. Do I make myself clear?"

"Very," Hans Fullmer snapped. And at that, the four men went to their beds.

17.

It was a short trip to her former mansion on Via del Corso. But by the time Luciana pulled the bike into the alleylike street in the rear, Matt was nearly asleep. He had changed back into his black trousers and was carrying the borrowed black cassock. Luciana was wearing her loose-fitting army fatigues and a soft man's shirt.

"We're here," she whispered, shutting off the bike's engine.

Matt rubbed his face to clear his head. "Doesn't anybody live here?" he asked, seeing the immense silhouette of the palazzo above him.

"Not since I was caught hiding POWs during the war. And it holds too many memories for me to return." She pushed the bike into an enclosure off the alley and shut an iron gate behind it. "Give me your hand," she said, "we're going through the basement. I don't want anybody to know there's someone here now."

She pulled him down the alley, then stopped and squatted before a dark opening only two by three feet wide. "See you at the bottom," she said. "And watch your leg!" She disappeared.

Matt squeezed himself inside, bending his wounded leg carefully, groped for a hold, found none and shot down a long

steel chute to the bottom. Luciana reached out and found him.
"You okay?" she asked.

He was coughing, spitting out coal dust. "Great," he said.
He took a step and his cane slipped from his hand, rattling
across a floor he could not see.

"Stay put," she warned.

By the sound of her footsteps, Matt knew she was climbing.
In a moment, he heard her open a door and fumble around for
something. Then she struck a match and lit the candle she was
holding.

Matt spotted his cane, fetched it and hobbled up the
basement's staircase. He followed through a large pantry, past
a doorless, vandalized refrigerator and into what was a kitchen.
The windows had been knocked out and the stove and sinks
ripped from the wall. Yet the blue-tiled ceilings and marble
walls recalled the kitchen's era of elegance.

He trailed her through a long passageway lined with peeling
dark wood. She threw open two large sliding doors, and they
entered a living room worthy of a castle.

A carved marble fireplace with a frieze depicting wood
nymphs stood at the far wall. Broken and chipped chandeliers
hung from the water-stained ceilings. There was another water
stain on one wall where the rain had come in from broken
windows. The wooden floor was stripped bare, and in the
flickering candlelight there seemed to be only two pieces of
furniture, both covered by grayish sheets.

"Lots of memories?" he asked.

She nodded.

"We don't have to stay."

"Oh, it's not so bad," she said too gaily. "This was a
happy room, filled with laughing voices, dancing, chamber
music. . . ."

Matt was watching her.

"Look," she said. She walked to a gray sheet and flicked it
off, revealing a couch. She pulled off several of its cushions
and arranged them in front of the cold fireplace. "We can
build a fire. . . . I'm sure there's coal downstairs. . . . Somewhere . . . It's not so bad. . . ."

Matt wanted to wrap his arms around her. She seemed so
small and vulnerable standing in the middle of that big baro-
nial room. He wanted to hug her to himself and say, "It's all

right." But he could not. He was, after all, a priest. A half priest, maybe. But still a priest.

"I'll get some coal," he mumbled. "You need the candle?"

"No," she said, sinking to one of the cushions. "I won't need it to see."

He picked up the candle from the floor. Gripping its hammered, bronze base, he left the room and went back into the basement, filled an old box with coal and carried it upstairs. In the kitchen, he paused to rinse off the coal dust. He turned on the sink spigot. At first it belched out green, but finally cool, clear water appeared. He washed his face. Finally, he withdrew a clean handkerchief from his cassock, dried himself and rinsed it out.

He reentered the living room, the light from the candle preceding him as he limped toward the fireplace. Luciana was where he had left her, staring at the empty hearth, her long legs, clad in her army fatigues, crossed at the ankles.

He handed her the handkerchief. "It's clean," he said. "Wash your face."

She took it, smiling at the gesture of kindness.

He pushed together several small pieces of charred wood that had been left in the fireplace and lit a fire. Then he piled on the coal. The flames brightened the lonely room, and the fire's heat rolled out from beneath the tall, stone mantel. Matt sat on a cushion near Luciana.

"Did you really hide POWs here?" he asked. "It's hard to picture it."

"They used to sit around this very room. I had lots of furniture then. They'd tell me stories about where they came from, talk about their little towns back in the U.S., about drinking beer on Saturday nights and what their girls were like. I traveled from Oregon to Georgia, North Dakota to Texas, right here in this living room."

"And what stories did you tell them?"

"Oh, how I was always the proper little girl growing up. You know, ballet lessons, piano, singing, going to the opera. 'Hotsy-totsy,' the Americans used to tease me, 'but look how you turned out! Sheltering the enemy!' "

The fire crackled in the big room, echoing off the bare walls. She saw that Matt was staring wearily into the fire, caught by something in the flames.

"You should go to bed."

"In a minute."

"What are you seeing in there?"

"How we turn out. It's funny, isn't it? You and me. We did everything right, but tomorrow we're going to rob our Church's bank. Hotsy-totsy. You never know."

She got up and led the way out of the warm living room and up a creaking wooden staircase. Matt carried his folded cassock.

At the landing on the second floor, she stopped before one of the dusty doors. "There are no sheets, but there were some blankets last time I looked." She opened the door and the candlelight filled the room. A double bed sat in the middle of the floor, its mattress bare.

Luciana crossed the room, went into a walk-in cedar-lined closet and returned with several blankets. She handed one to him, and they were both standing in the doorway. He caught the heady scent of her, which reminded him again of a forest after a rain. He was looking down at her face. She parted her lips slightly as though to ask a question.

"What?" when she didn't say it.

"Thank you."

"For what?"

"I don't feel lonely tonight." She looked like she wanted to say more, but bit her lip.

Matt nervously crushed the bundle of his cassock in his hands and seemed to welcome the rustling of paper that they both heard.

"Oh, the telegram." He yanked it out of a pocket.

"The one from the Swiss Guard this morning?"

He tore it open and read it silently. For a moment, he did not react, then he balled it up angrily in his fist.

"What is it?" she asked anxiously.

"Nothing," he said, shoving it back into his pocket. He threw his cassock into his room and pulled the door shut. "I . . . have to go out."

"Where?"

"Out! Just out!"

"I'll go with you."

"No!" His face and neck muscles were corded with an unbearable tension. "I . . . want to be alone." He thrust the candle out to her. She took it and he went down the stairs. She heard the front bolt shoved back, then the door slammed behind him.

Luciana hesitated, then crossed the corridor and entered her own room, busying herself by spreading out a blanket for her bed. Then she stopped, took in a deep breath and blew it out.

"Ahhh! What have I become? The great charity worker and afraid to be a woman?"

She caught up the candle, went to her door and threw it open. Then she hurried down the stairs, blew out the candle at the front door and went out into the street.

She found him at the Assyriano-Barra. He was sitting inside the smoky tavern at a rear table. Two empty glasses already sat by his outstretched hand, which clutched a third. She entered, ignoring the whistles and lecherous appraisals of the men who were standing at the iron bar.

The telegram was lying on the table next to the glasses. Sitting, she watched him a moment, his eyes far off, then she took the telegram, straightened it out and saw that it had come from Father William Mankowsky.

REGRET TO INFORM YOU YOUR MOTHER DIED 5:43 A.M. N. Y. TIME STOP FUNERAL AWAITS YOUR RETURN STOP REQUIESCAT STOP YOUR FRIEND MANKOWSKY.

"Oh, no," Luciana cried out softly.

"She was waiting for an annulment from the Church," Matt said in a strangled voice. "But it cost too much!" He slammed the table with his fist. "If I had any doubts before about what I'm doing tomorrow . . . !" He let it go, downed his drink instead.

"Want another?"

"Sure, why not? I want to get drunk!"

"What are you drinking?"

"I ordered whiskey. I don't know what this is."

She sniffed the glass. "It's Scotch. That's whiskey here. You want bourbon?"

He nodded.

Luciana swiveled and yelled something in Italian at the bartender. Two of the five Italians who were gaping at her turned away when they heard the command in her voice. One shoved the sawdust aside on the floor, creating a clean place for his foot.

The bartender brought two glasses of bourbon. He set them down, and Luciana paid for them and the others Matt had drunk. She sipped hers quietly.

"Did you love her a lot?" she asked after a bit.

"I hated her." He took a gulp of the amber liquid. "That's better." He smacked his lips.

"Did you really?"

He looked at her. "No. I used my mother to scourge myself. But in some ways, she was right about me. Oh, she was wrong about a lot of other things, but she was right about my being ashamed of her divorce. She always used to say that was why I became a priest."

"Was it?"

"No. But I was still ashamed of her. And it didn't cause me a lot of pain to move out of the house at thirteen. I badgered her until she gave permission for me to join the seminary. It felt good to be away from her drinking." He rolled the whiskey around in the glass, studying it.

"But I failed in one thing she counted on me for, the one way she knew I could save her soul. She died without receiving her annulment."

"Don't be so hard on yourself. Forgive yourself."

"You know"—Matt raised his eyes in the candlelight as if he had not heard her—"you were right about me too. I was hiding in a parish because I thought that was the only way I could be a perfect priest. The war tore that away. Now this has exposed me again." He took her hand. "You're good, Luciana. God made you good. You're alive, every part of you. You remind me in a way of a French priest, *Père* Flambert. He had great gusto like you."

"Was he a good priest?"

"Terrible! But he was a great sinner, which helped!"

Luciana frowned, not understanding. "Are you getting drunk?" she asked.

He shrugged, upended the rest of his whiskey. Luciana pushed hers over to him.

"Tell me a good thing about your mother."

"What?" His tongue was getting thick.

"A way you'll remember her."

"I don't need it!"

"You need it more than you do that." Luciana touched his full whiskey glass.

In defiance, he picked up the glass, put it to his lips to drain it, but did not. Instead, he set it back down untouched.

"I used to say, 'Mom, you remember the time I hit the tree?' I always brought it up when it got bad between us. 'Of course,' she'd say, 'that other seminarian was crawling into the back seat and kicked your steering wheel with his foot and you ran the car into the tree. You went right through the windshield.'

" 'Remember what happened after that?'

" 'That surgeon wired your mouth shut. Put little stainless wires between your teeth so your jaw would heal.'

" 'And my nose?'

" 'You broke it. He put stuffing in it.'

"We repeated this story many times, but it was always new and special since this was her strongest link to me." He was setting the glass down, making little wet circles that interlinked.

"Then she'd say, 'But then because he wired your mouth shut, it filled with blood and you couldn't breathe. And it was the middle of the night and that surgeon couldn't be reached.'

" 'And what did I ask you to do?'

" 'Help you meditate and not panic so you could breathe. You were only seventeen, for cripes' sake!'

" 'And you read me the Bible. Remember, Mom?'

" 'That's right, Matty. And the way you gagged all night. Oh, it was terrible!'

" 'But you kept me alive, Mom. All through the night!'

" 'I'll never forget,' she'd say. 'Never.' And she'd grip my hand tight. Her eyes would fill with tears, and she'd look at me with love, remembering. Her criticism of me would stop. It was our bond. Our strong pact between us.

"She'd say, 'You and me, Matty. You and me!'

"*You and me, Mom. You and me.* God, I wish it had been better." He looked up suddenly at Luciana. Through the heavy smoke of the bar, he could see she was crying silently with him. He wiped his own tears, then stood up. "Let's go back."

Arm in arm, they left the bar.

They made their way back to the mansion and went up the

front entrance, only to realize the door was locked. Matt reached through a broken window, climbed inside and let Luciana in through the tall oak door. Silently, they climbed the stairs to the second level.

"Good night," he said to her as they again stood between their bedrooms.

She went toward her door.

He turned as if to say something, denied it and entered his room.

She stood in the hallway a moment, then crossed and, without knocking, entered his room. He was lying uncovered on his side, his face away from her.

He did not look up as she threw a blanket over him. Only when she slipped in behind him did he turn at last so she lay on his arm against his chest. Then fully clothed, her head on his chest, her hand caressing him, she stayed with him the entire night, not sleeping, not talking, only comforting him as he mourned.

In the morning, just before dawn, she heard Hannah and Ruffino enter below. Then their voices died down as they went to sleep, probably near the fire, she imagined. Matt stirred. He had dropped off to sleep for an hour or so, but now Luciana felt his hand touch her breast.

"No," she said softly.

She lay still as his hand undid the buttons on her shirt. He raised on one elbow and brought his mouth to hers and kissed her deeply, cupping her breast with his hand.

"Don't," she said, "we can't . . ."

But he stopped her words with another kiss. Then suddenly she found herself kissing him, smothering his face, burying her nose in his neck, hair, inhaling him, her mouth hungry, taking great tastes.

She undressed him, kissing him in all the places she now realized she had wanted to, brushing her lips across the wound in his poor hurt thigh. And then he was within her, and they were one living thing, crying out through one mouth, rising together, suspended, continuing in deep involuntary ecstasies from both throats, yet one throat, thrusting upward, tremoring together, meeting, receiving amidst continuing whimpers.

And afterwards, as they lay together, discovering one another's bodies in quieted caresses, she asked, "Are you sad?"

He knew that she meant the best and worst thing in his whole life had just happened. He had become a man, with no priestly pretenses.

She stroked his hair. "*Matteo, Matteo,*" she murmured, "don't be sad. It's not the end of anything."

"I feel good, alive . . . like any man should feel," he told her, his cheek nestled against her firm breast. "I can't hide from myself anymore, I don't want to."

"But still you belong to God too. I feel it. Don't decide too fast!"

"I feel more weak yet somehow stronger than I've ever felt in my life."

"Oooooo," she keened, cradling his head within her arms, "damn you. I can't help myself. You make me so crazy I don't even know my name."

"I know I'm in love with you."

"I adore you, *caro*! But are we wicked for loving one another? Maybe we shall be punished. Maybe we'll fail at the bank."

He laughed. "We won't! Not if we don't punish ourselves. And God doesn't want us to. And after this, we'll get married. What do you say?"

"Stop it!" she told him. "One night making love and you think you have found all the answers. I'm not a little pill of sugar the doctor gives to sick-in-the-head patients!" she said, trying to hide her pleasure and fear. She had never suspected he would think of marriage. She was drawn to him but afraid for him. It was too much too soon.

He hugged her tighter against himself, his legs entwined in hers, and kissed her. "I want to marry you."

She pushed him away with her fists, putting a distance between them on the bed. "You're not ready for marriage. You're a baby learning how to walk. Take it easy. Don't go too fast, *Matteo*. Don't let your emotions fool you."

"I'm not afraid of what I feel or of problems in the future. We'll solve those. I'll leave the priesthood and we'll get married!"

"No!" she said. "Stop talking like that! Why should I

even want an ex-priest who was a virgin as my husband. Do you think I want to raise a child?''

He studied her a moment, convinced she was only trying to protect him. ''You'll be good for me.'' He smiled. ''I need your strong emotions to keep me from disappearing into my philosophical head. You're exactly what I need, and I know it. So if it takes an eternity, I'll convince you to be my wife! And then you'll see how lucky you are to get me, and how good a husband I'll make!''

She couldn't help but laugh. But she said, ''*Matteo*, why can't you just be satisfied with what we have? You want too much!''

''I want everything!'' he growled playfully, hugging her. ''I've been without *any*thing too long!'' He laughed and kissed her stomach.

She shivered, then realized it had grown cold in the room. The sudden change made her glance at the window above them. Heavy flakes were drifting down.

''It's snowing,'' she cried, ''look!''

He rolled over and looked pleased. ''I didn't think that happened often in Rome.''

''The last time . . . was the day . . . Rocco was killed!''

''This is a good snow. Don't worry like that.''

But she clung to him. They were lying there, gathering strength from one another, when suddenly they heard Ruffino's shouts from below.

18.

Luciana pulled on her fatigue pants and shirt and opened the door. Ruffino was just puffing up the stairway.

"Contessa, it is time to go!" he shouted.

Matt, fearing trouble, had appeared at the door. He was naked except for his shoes and black trousers. He suddenly looked embarrassed and Ruffino caught it.

"Sorry," Ruffino lowered his eyes. "It's nearly six, Contessa."

"Well, where are the bishop's and cardinal's clothing?" Luciana asked, trying to be businesslike. "Did you get my shells? And where is Hannah with the car? Is it fueled?" She kept glancing over at Matt's naked chest in embarrassment.

"The Capo has been sewing for us all night. He said to come first thing this morning and everything would be ready. Hannah got the car and gas. She will be waiting. She left already to cook breakfast for the refugees." He handed Matt a small packet of stick matches.

"Good," Matt said. "Now, will you wait for us downstairs, Ruffino?"

"*Sì, sì!*" Ruffino looked glad to get away. "I am sorry to have disturbed you, Contessa, but it was time. . . ." He shuffled down the steps.

Luciana closed the door. Matt wrapped his arms around her tightly, pulling her into his chest.

"I sleep with a priest and feel more guilty than he does! What a thing! Who could guess it? *Matteo, Matteo,*" Luciana buried her head against him. "I'm very, very scared!"

"I love you, Luciana. Tell me you love me."

"I adore you," she whispered, softening against him in resignation.

"Let the worst come!" Matt told her. "Whatever happens today, it won't stop our love."

Luciana snuggled tighter into him. "I would go to hell for you! But *Matteo,* there's still time to back out. We can, you know!"

Matt squeezed her one last time. Then he said, "Come on, let's get started. We have to get the refugees their money."

He dressed quickly, pulling on Rocco's white T-shirt, then slipping his cassock over his head. When he had finished buttoning it, he felt something, drew it out of a pocket. Luciana, who was pulling on her socks, looked up and saw he held a coin.

"What is it?" she asked.

"Money minted by Pope Pius. I bought it for my mother." He raised his arm to fling it into a corner.

"Don't! I've got a better use for it."

He handed it to her, kissed her lightly and left the room. She lingered a few moments to put on her shoes. By the time she went downstairs he had gone.

Outside, she and Ruffino found the streets covered with patchy snow. A cold wind was blowing in from the north, whipping the snow back and forth in little swirling funnels as Luciana drove Ruffino down Via del Corso, then traveled all the way across Rome, until they were outside the ancient walls.

They parked in front of the San Sebastiano religious vestments store. As they entered it, they saw a small group of nuns trying on new gray habits, parading in front of several floor-length mirrors.

"Luciana!" a tall, bony man called from behind his counter. He was wearing a much-repaired uniform of the Partisan Italian army. During the war, Capo Mario Brindisi had served in the underground, and now, with pride, he continued to wear that tattered uniform. He came forward and kissed Luciana on both cheeks.

"My sweet *Gesù*, it's good to see you." He beamed. "The last time I saw you during the war, you were running from the Germans across Piazza de Montecitorio."

"That's right, I picked up an American POW right in front of the Chamber of the Deputies, while Mussolini was speaking to the legislature!" She laughed in glee. "And two blocks later, the Germans couldn't find us, because I had fitted that American with one of your cassocks and he was a priest! A priest and a nun walking reverently side by side down the street!"

They both laughed, and he hugged her a long time, then held her at arm's length. "And now we work again?" he asked.

"One more time," she said.

"It is not the same as the war," Ruffino, who was standing politely nearby, offered.

"No, my old friend Ruffino," Capo allowed, "this time it is not the Germans, but a new enemy, I suppose. And you were wise not to tell me any more about it. These days I am only a businessman, and I don't want to know much."

The nuns erupted in high-pitched girlish giggles as one of the young ones tried on a white veil, swinging it back and forth, modeling it.

"Women never change," the Capo commented, glancing at them with affection. "Come, both of you, come where it is quieter." He tugged Luciana gently, and Ruffino followed them into the next section, which was filled with black, red and white cassocks on mannequins. There were garments for priests, bishops, archbishops, cardinals, even the Pope. There were also golden monstrances studded with diamonds in glass cases around the walls. Ruffino admired one in the shape of a cross.

"How have you been?" Luciana asked the Capo.

"Oh, you know, I make a killing. And every night I pray none of my customers finds out an infidel Jew sells them their holy accessories."

"It's good to see you. We had some times in the war."

"*Sì*, we beat those Germans, *i tedeschi*, didn't we?"

"I have everything prepared." The Capo dropped his voice. "And I did not hesitate, since even without knowing your cause, I knew instantly I would be on your side!"

Luciana kissed him fondly.

"Just go into that dressing room there and put it all on. Ruffino, your room is on the right."

Luciana stepped quickly inside a small cubicle and drew shut the lush velvet drapes. Without removing her pants or blouse, she put on the black cassock of a bishop, with its red buttons and red piping on the sleeves. She tied the red sash at her waist and hung the gold pectoral cross, complete with a large sapphire in its center, from the third button on her cassock. She picked up the black cape with its inner purple silk lining and thanked God it was part of the costume. With it on, she was sure that no one could tell she was a woman.

Glancing at herself in the full-length mirror, she tried on the *zucchetto*, the small purple skullcap worn by bishops. But no matter how she positioned it, too much of her blond hair showed. Choosing instead a hat called a biretta, which the Capo had also provided, she stuffed her hair up beneath it, pulling it down tight on her head. Under the wide-brimmed hat, she looked like a small, effeminate bishop. Not unusual at all, she decided.

When she emerged from the dressing booth, Ruffino was waiting for her in the voluminous crimson silks of a cardinal. He doffed his red biretta and bowed solemnly.

"How do I look?" he asked.

"Like a cardinal," she said. "So don't bow to a bishop."

"Yes, Contessa!"

"Do you have the janitor's costume on underneath?"

He undid a button to reveal the dark blue shirt of the uniform and the lighter blue and yellow Papal badge on his left chest pocket. Then he reached into a pocket and withdrew two flashlights and handed Luciana one of them. "For the tunnel, in case."

Luciana shuddered as she took hers. She hoped she would not have to use it.

"One more thing." The Capo grinned at his handiwork. "Here is the bag you ordered." He handed it to Ruffino, who tucked it deep inside one of the cassock's side pockets. "And for you." The Capo held out a .25 caliber revolver to Luciana. "Loaded and an extra box of shells. In case."

She took it and the small carton, put them in opposite pockets and turned to go. He caught hold of her sleeve.

"Let me go with you. To hell with all this!" he waved his arms at his establishment. "I can't let you go alone, Luciana!"

"You've done more than enough," she told him. "Now, be a good soldier and follow orders!" She kissed his cheek.

"*Bella paisana*," he whispered.

"*Paisano*," she answered him.

Pulling on black wool overcoats, she and Ruffino went toward the front door. The nuns were startled by the sight of the hierarchy.

"*Buon giorno, Eminenze!*" they cried, stopping their revelry, not understanding how they had missed the entrance of two such high churchmen.

"*Buon giorno, Sorelles*," Ruffino answered them in his best stentorian voice. "You look very pretty this morning." Bowing to the nuns, the Lord Cardinal of the Roman Catholic Church blessed them and swept elegantly through the door. Luciana rolled her eyes and followed him.

"Do we take your Vespa, Contessa?" Ruffino asked once outside.

"No, from here we walk," she said. "And don't call me Contessa. From now on, I am *Vescovo* and you will be addressed as *Cardinale*."

Ruffino nodded and stomped off as pompously as he could manage. Luciana tagged along meekly beside him down the wide Via della Marta. It would be a long walk to the Vatican.

At 7:12, Matt limped across snow-littered St. Peter's Square. The mammoth piazza was nearly deserted. Only a few pilgrims shuffled toward the basilica. A Spanish-sounding woman was halfway across the square, walking on her knees, murmuring loudly her "Ave Marias" to atone for her sins.

He went up to the Arco delle Campane gate that he usually used and saw that he did not know either of the two guards on duty, both carrying Beretta rifles and bayonets.

"I'm Father Matt Bowles," he said to the guard with the two yellow-ribboned gold medals on his chest.

The thin-lipped guard, who was a sergeant, stared at him a moment. Then he said in guttural English, "Follow me. I am to take you to the refectory."

Matt hobbled along beside the Swiss, past the gloomy Teutonic Institute, where only yesterday he had left his suitcase. It seemed like weeks ago.

They came close to a building that was named St. Martha's Hospice, a large straw-colored palazzo with small windows. Matt caned up the granite steps. The guard opened the door. "Do you know how I got my medals, Father?" he asked, pointing to his chest.

Matt paused. Up close now, he saw likenesses of Pope Pius embossed on both. It was the same image as on the coin he had bought.

"The little one here is for my fine marksmanship," the guard announced. "The other for bravery during an attempted assassination on Pope Pius's life."

Matt took in the grim eyes of the guard and nodded as he went through the door. His neck tingled with a sudden rush of adrenaline. Had the guard's words been a warning? Did they *expect* him to rob the bank this morning? Was this a trap? It couldn't be, he told himself.

He went through the foyer. The guard circled in front of him and threw open a second door. Matt stepped inside. They were in a large cafeteria, filled with at least twenty long tables. A white enamel counter ran the length of the room at the far end. Priests, nuns, monsignors and bishops were queued up, trays in hand, getting their breakfasts from Pasqualina's nun-cooks.

"Are you hungry, Father?" the guard with the hard eyes asked.

"Maybe some coffee."

The guard said, "I will get that, Father. Now, seat yourself at the far table." He pointed. "The other American priest is waiting for you there. He arrived an hour ago."

The gorilla, clad in a black traveling suit, stood up and waved. As Matt worked his way through the tables, Mankowsky brought up two thick fingers and covered his forehead. Matt grinned at his antic.

"I missed you," he said.

"Me too, Matthew!"

Then Matt's eyes slid away and he mumbled, "How do you like Rome?"

"I haven't seen much. They brought me straight here."

Matt felt awkward. So much had happened in these past few days, it was like meeting a stranger. He was trying his best not to show the tension he felt, but he knew the gorilla was picking it up.

"Cold here," Mankowsky said, blowing on his hands. "Is it supposed to be this cold in Rome, Matthew?"

"Snowed last night."

The two men were silent again. "You got my telegram?" Mankowsky asked finally as they sat down on the wooden bench at the table.

Matt nodded. "How did she die?"

"Cirrhosis, they think. They wanted to do an autopsy, but I waived it. Was that all right?"

"Sure."

"Remember, Matthew, death is just a passage. Agnes is happy."

"She died excommunicated. She's in hell."

Mankowsky searched for something comforting to say but couldn't manage the words. "That's . . . pretty harsh, Matthew. . . ." he tried finally.

"It's the truth. She was too poor to go to heaven. She couldn't afford an annulment."

The gorilla was studying his friend closely. "We heard you had trouble coming over," he coaxed Matt to talk. "We heard the Communists tried to stop your plane, that you crashed near the Vatican. Are you all right, Matthew?"

Matt grinned for him. "I'm okay," he said.

"It must have been awful, crashing like that," Mankowsky said, sipping his mixture of milk and coffee, trying to find a way to the feelings and familiar ways he had expected from his friend.

But Matt only turned abruptly, the smile vanishing from his lips. The gorilla spun and saw that the Swiss Guard was coming toward them, carrying Matt's coffee.

"You still my friend?" Matt asked quickly, never taking his eyes off the approaching guard.

"You bet, Matthew! You don't have to ask that!"

"Good. I want you to do me a favor today."

"Anything, Matthew. What do you need? How can I help?"

"We're going to rob the bank here," Matt whispered. His expression made clear that he was not fooling. The gorilla was struck dumb. The guard reached the table and set the coffee down.

"Anything else, Father Bowles?" the guard asked.

"No, thank you."

"You, Father Mankowsky?".

"What?" the gorilla blurted.

"More coffee?"

"Uh, oh . . . no, no!"

"Very well, then," the guard said. He checked his watch. "It is seven thirty. By now Monsignor Kass, *Segretario* Palmo, Prince Milagro and Monsignor Offeri are waiting in the bank for the sheets. When you finish your coffee, Father, we should go."

Matt took a swallow of the hot coffee and stood up. "I'm finished."

"Matthew?" the gorilla asked, his eyes panicky, "I . . ."

"What is it, Father Mankowsky?" the guard asked when he saw the big priest upset.

"It's okay, Willie," Matt said, tugging him up by an arm. "It'll be over before you know it."

Uncertainly, Father William Mankowsky rose to his full six feet nine inches. He picked up a large leather briefcase. The guard led the way out of the refectory, which was now filling with ecclesiastics who had finished their morning Masses and were readying for the day's business.

All the way to the concave-shaped Casina of Pius IV, across snow-piled courtyards filled with Swiss Guards, Father Mankowsky said nothing. Several times Matt caught Willie studying him as they walked. Matt knew that all the pleasure Father Mankowsky would have felt at being inside the Vatican was now lost in dread. It was unfair to put his old friend through this. But there was no other way.

They went up the marble steps of the Casina to its Bronze Doors. Hans Fullmer was waiting for them.

"Welcome to the Vatican," he greeted Father Mankowsky.

"Thank you." The gorilla glanced at Matt, then looked away.

Fullmer opened one of the tall doors; it had the newly attached time lock on it.

Inside, the tellers—priests in their green aprons and green visors to shield the glare from the crystal chandeliers above—were signing bank notes, issuing currency and taking deposits at the windows. Well-dressed men wearing London Saville and Pucci suits were at the counters.

The gorilla seemed overwhelmed by the bustle of the atmosphere.

Kass, Offeri, Milagro and Palmo were at a special table that had been set up near the now-empty arbitrage section. Monsignor Kass stood up when he saw them enter.

"Ah, Monsignor Mankowsky!" Monsignor Kass welcomed him. He shook his hand, pointedly ignoring Matt.

"Pleased to meet you," the gorilla said, "but you are mistaken, Monsignor Kass. I'm just a priest."

"Not after today," Kass said. "Pope Pius plans to make you a Monsignor for your special errand of mercy."

Kass introduced "Monsignor" Mankowsky to Prince Milagro, Governor of the Vatican, Guido Offeri and *Segretario* Palmo.

"Shall we get on with it, gentlemen?" Kass then asked. He motioned to the table. "If you, Father Mankowsky, will produce the tally sheets that confirm the amount of the money sent to us, we will show you our tabulation and you can sign it and we'll be finished. This needn't take much time."

The gorilla set the briefcase on the table.

"We can't sign the tally papers without making a count," Matt announced to all.

"A count?" Kass growled. "That would take . . . days!"

"Well, Monsignor, back home we have a government agency called the I.R.S. And if they audit our Catholic donors over their charitable write-offs, I can't testify in their behalf unless I, in good conscience, know all the money arrived. I mean, we've already had some trouble on that point, haven't we?"

Kass turned as purple as an approaching thunderstorm. He wheeled to Monsignor Offeri.

"It *is* normal practice," the prelate-banker shrugged. "The donors should be properly protected." Then he glanced at Matt. "But Monsignor Kass is correct also. A count of the entire amount is a long, time-consuming affair. Would you be satisfied with a spot count? It would be accurate, with only a slight statistical error."

"Of course, Monsignor," Matt said, "we can make a spot count."

"That acceptable to you, Father Mankowsky?" Prince Milagro requested.

"Uh . . . fine," the gorilla coughed.

"Good," Offeri said. "Because not a fifth of the original money from the United States is intact within our vault. A lot has been exchanged, loaned and invested. How much do you wish to check against your serial numbers?"

"Ten million," Matt said offhandedly, as though he were just thinking it all up on the spur of the moment. "Make it all big bills."

"Very well," Offeri said, motioning to *Segretario* Palmo, who adjusted the pince-nez on his nose and went toward the Milano vault.

"Is this table all right to work on?" Guido Offeri asked Matt solicitously.

"Fine."

"Uh . . . yes," Mankowsky managed.

"Please hurry," Kass said, openly annoyed with all these demands. "Pope Pius is most anxious. But he will understand how important it is for the donors to have their contributions verified correctly before 1947 ends." He said something quickly in Italian to Monsignor Offeri, who hurried now to the vault to help Palmo.

"Notify me the moment you finish!" Kass commanded and he left the bank. Prince Milagro, also ignoring Matt, murmured something about being needed elsewhere, nodded pleasantly to Father Mankowsky and left.

Matt walked to the edge of the table and caught hold of a trash can with his foot. He slid it under their counting table. Satisfied that none of the guards or tellers had paid any attention to his action, he sat down.

"You can't be serious, Matthew," the gorilla whispered in a shaky voice.

"Remember the money for the Jewish refugees?"

"Yes, in that pouch."

"It *was* in that pouch. I brought it to Rome, but no one has seen it since my plane was attacked. I begged the Holy Father to replace the money, but he accepts no responsibility for it."

"But it isn't his responsibility, Matthew. Surely he will turn it over as soon as the money is found. Why do you have to commit a crime to get it?"

"Because I'm responsible for that money, and this is the refugees' last chance to buy their passage to Palestine."

"But Matthew, what if . . ." the gorilla started, then swallowed his words. For *Segretario* Palmo was standing right behind them. He had pushed up a wooden cart, its top shelf piled with neatly bound packets of bills on top of which was a thick red ledger.

"Did I interrupt something?" Palmo asked, removing his pince-nez to scrutinize them closely.

"Just talking over old times." Matt smiled up at Palmo.

Palmo handed the ledger to Father Mankowsky, who accepted it with shaking hands. "This cart contains exactly four million in U.S. currency, in fifty-, hundred-, and thousand-dollar notes. You will find our entry of this amount on pages thirty-two to forty-seven of this book."

"Remember, you do not have to count all the bills, Fathers. Just do enough matching to satisfy yourselves. I will be seated nearby in the arbitrage section if you need any assistance."

"That reminds me," Matt said. "The last time I was here, this area was ringing with phones—people selling and buying money all over the world. What happened?"

"Our arbitrage division is now centered in a bank in Turin that we purchased. It will be quieter for you now that they are gone, won't it?"

The *Segretario* walked less than fifteen feet away and placed himself at a desk marked GERMAN ARBITRAGE. He sat facing them.

Matt grinned at him, reached out and filled both hands with packets of bills from the cart. He handed several to Mankowsky.

"Matthew . . ." the gorilla protested, taking them, "I . . ."

"Just check 'em," Matt whispered. "Ignore what I do. That's all I need from you. Just ignore what I do."

Matt glanced at the clock above. It was 7:57. Luciana and Ruffino would be entering the business gate of St. Anne.

19.

Precisely three hundred yards from where Matt sat, two prelates of the Roman Catholic Church were approaching the Swiss Guards at St. Anne's Gate. The two churchmen paused momentarily at the ragged beggar who sat on the sidewalk in front of the high, thick Vatican wall. The guards watched with admiration as the two paid their respects to the beggar.

"Here, woman," Luciana whispered as she held the coin with the likeness of Pope Pius. The woman reached up to snatch it away. But Luciana held on to it, refusing to give it up. "I need your blessing," she insisted.

"*Reverendo*," the woman said humbly, "it is I who should seek yours!"

"I demand a blessing of luck!" Luciana smiled down at her. "You alone possess that."

The woman bowed, taking the coin.

The Swiss Guard watched as the narrow-shouldered Bishop straightened now and, along with the Cardinal, sauntered carefully toward their gate.

"*Eminenze!*" a guard greeted them. "May I be so bold as to ask your names, please?"

Ruffino gaped stupidly. He looked to the coadjutor Bishop who was standing now, biretta down, face hidden from the guard.

"It is just I do not remember you," the young guard apologized, "and I . . . *un momento.*" A truck piled full of sugar beets had pulled up to the gate. Since he was the senior officer on duty, the guard ran over to direct the driver to the Vatican grocery store.

The coadjutor bishop rudely grabbed hold of the Cardinal's sleeve and pulled him through the gate and up the street of the Cancello di Sant'Anna.

"Don't walk fast," Luciana told Ruffino. "Walk with dignity."

"A moment!" the other guard called to them when he saw them moving off.

"Don't turn around, don't stop!" Luciana instructed Ruffino.

"Eminenze!" the guard at the truck hollered when he saw them.

The second guard said to him, "You know these old ones. They have bad hearing!" He laughed.

The first guard shrugged comically and waved through the truck driver, who was laughing also.

Luciana and Ruffino passed the lovely, small church of St. Anne on the right. Behind them the beet truck turned down that street.

"What time do you enter the bank to pick up the wastebasket?" Luciana asked, rehearsing him.

"At exactly eight thirty on the dot!" Ruffino recited.

They skirted the barracks of the Swiss Guards on their left, both of them thinking of the entrance to the dreaded Passetto Vaticano, the popes' secret escape tunnel, which they might have to use. Then they went into shadow beneath the ancient tower of Nicholas V. Across from the tower, Luciana noticed that the sentries of the Ufficio di Vigilanza, the Vatican City's police department, were in their sentry post. The police force was mostly ceremonial, since nothing unlawful ever happened in the Vatican. Nothing until now, Luciana thought.

Far above, from the vantage point of the stone tower of Nicholas V, the Red Woman watched the progress of the two prelates. Like all the rest of the comings and goings through the business gate of St. Anne's that morning, these two looked normal. He lowered the glasses.

Earlier, he had seen the American priest enter at Arco delle

Campane gate. Anxiously, he raised the binoculars again and scanned the gate. No new arrivals. What if Bowles wasn't planning to rob the bank at all? He could not afford to think that way!

Again, he lowered the glasses. His best strategy now would be to surround the bank and wait, hoping he could figure out Bowles's scheme before it succeeded. Any activity around the Casina could easily be spotted in time, he assured himself.

The Red Woman turned to the sergeant of the Swiss Guard, who was standing quietly beside him. The soldier had been handpicked because of the bravery and loyalty he had exhibited in the past. The two medals on his blouse attested to that.

"Go close all the gates now," the Red Woman told him. "Tell the others to surround the bank."

The guard saluted. He hurried down the long, winding corkscrew stone steps, his heavy leather boots thumping a quick rhythm as he descended the tower's seven stories.

Matt checked the clocks above what had been the currency exchange section of the bank. The one over Rome said 8:16. Luciana and Ruffino were getting in position by now. He felt the stick matches in his pocket, then reached out with his toes and scooted the trash can so it rested between his legs. He continued counting bills, cross-checking their serial numbers against tally sheets. Glancing up, he noticed that Palmo was scrutinizing the priest-tellers behind the counters who were paying out notes, conversing with clients. The Swiss Guards who were stationed on the inside of the tall, sculpted doors stared impassively forward, at attention.

"Here goes," Matt whispered to the gorilla.

"Matthew, please! Don't!" Mankowsky begged. He was expecting to see his friend jump up and stick out a pistol. Instead, he saw him lift his cassock skirts, appear to get comfortable, then re-cover his legs. What was he up to?

Matt now unbuttoned the lower half of his cassock and sat back, continuing all the while to count the large bills. But Mankowsky saw that every third or fourth disappeared below the table.

From the park-lined bench on which she sat, in the small grotto high up Vatican Hill, Luciana could see the stone trash bin below. It was a large, rectangularly carved chest, oil-stained and old, nestling within a special three-sided cement wall meant to hide it from view. Ruffino, as cardinal *or* janitor, was nowhere in sight. But she imagined he was changing by now and ready to begin his janitor's act. She checked her watch. 8:22. Eight minutes.

Three Swiss Guards crossed the spacious lawns in front of the Casina and hurried up its checkerboard steps. What were they rushing to? Was there trouble? Oh, hurry up, *Matteo.* God forgive us and bless us! Hurry now. Please hurry!

She was biting her bottom lip so hard she did not notice the salty blood in her mouth. Forcing herself to be calm, she kept trying to convince herself she was only one of the many prelates traversing the gardens of the Vatican, taking a rest, meditating. But inside the purple bishop's soutane, she could feel her heart thud.

Was *Matteo*'s friend, the gorilla, cooperating?

Hurry, *caro*! For God's, Mary's and Joseph's sake, don't get caught! There are thousands of survivors of the holocaust hoping on this! Hurry, my lover! Hurry, hurry, hurry!

Then she saw the figure of Ruffino in his janitor's clothes stroll past the bin below.

From above the bank near his new vantage point at the Monumento di San Pietro, the Red Woman spotted a stoutly built man dressed as a member of the Pontiff's janitorial staff, complete with blue uniform and insignia on his shirt. Curiously, he watched him as he began to pace near the stone trash bin. The janitor glanced at his wristwatch. Was he, like himself, waiting for something to happen inside the bank? The Red Woman continued to observe him.

Inside the bank, the gorilla had frozen. He was sitting staring down at the wooden tabletop, his face paralyzed with fear.

Matt glanced up at the clock. 8:29.

"Willie?" Matt asked, hurriedly smuggling bills into the wastebasket between his legs.

The gorilla did not reply. But Matt heard it clear across the table. From deep inside the huge man's stomach, a sound not unlike rolling thunder emerged.

"Ahhhh! I'm sick!" Mankowsky stood up suddenly. His chair clattered to the floor. He dashed toward the Bronze Doors.

Segretario Palmo rose in alarm. The gorilla, in a steamrolling tackle, burst through the two Swiss, scattering them like yellow-striped bowling pins. Palmo approached Matt in a rush. Matt closed his legs to hide the wastebasket.

"What happened?" Palmo cried in alarm.

"Father Mankowsky's not feeling well. Too much traveling. You better go help him!" Matt quickly pressed Palmo. "He's very sick!"

The *Segretario* hesitated.

"I'll be okay," Matt told him. "I'm nearly finished anyway."

Palmo reluctantly disappeared out the doors.

Matt waited a few moments, then picked up three one-thousand-dollar bills and dropped them between his thighs. The clock said 8:30. More boldly, he grabbed two handfuls of hundreds, hoping it was enough. It had to be! He was running out of time!

He crumpled the tally sheets, shoved them through the opening in his cassock and struck a match. Dropping it into the can, he waited until he could smell the smoke, then gave the can a little shove with his foot so it slid out from beneath his cassock.

Now he picked up a fresh package of money and continued to check the serial numbers. Come on, come on. Somebody see it! He kept hoping. What was wrong? He had the sinking thought the fire had gone out.

A teller behind the long counter began shouting, pointing at the flaming wastebasket beneath the table.

Matt pulled off his borrowed cassock and waved it at the flames a moment, stalling, letting the fire burn well down through the top papers. Then, wadding up his black robe, he stuffed it tight into the trash can and smothered the flames.

Smoke hung everywhere in the bank. Some of the customers were coughing.

Matt saw the clock. 8:31! Where was Ruffino?!

"You speak English?" Matt asked the teller who had spotted the fire first.

"A . . . a little!" the young priest managed. He was shaken.

"Better call somebody to take this out."

"Ah, a custodian." The priest understood. "*Si!*" He went toward the doors, but to his amazement, Ruffino in his janitor's outfit poked his head inside, then ran toward the smoking basket and swooped it up.

"I smelled it!" he called to the priest and carried out the smoldering wastebasket, smoke streaming into his face.

Matt sat down and began to count again. The young priest and the tellers, a little dazed, but taking their cue from the priest who had lost his cassock to a fire and yet was again calmly counting at his table, went back to the business of banking.

Matt sat there, every nerve straining, and tried to appear calm, all the while listening intently for sounds outside the bank.

Suddenly, Palmo appeared in the doorway. He was wiping his face with a handkerchief. He walked swiftly across the floor of the large room and, when he arrived at Matt's table, bent over and said, "Your friend will be all right." Then he sniffed. "Do I smell something burning?"

Rifle shots echoed across the lawns outside, followed by commands of "*Fermo!*" Matt grabbed up his cane, sprang across the floor, ahead of Palmo, hurried down the double stairways and out through the small courtyard. He saw Swiss Guards running everywhere on the lawns below, their Beretta rifles and machine guns held ready.

Leaving a confused Palmo, Matt hobbled past the Fountain of the Mirrors where Ruffino was to have changed. Still no sign of him. The guards were rushing through the portico that led toward the Vatican museums. Something had gone wrong!

Walking as quickly as he could through the passageway, Matt emerged in the massive symmetrical Courtyard of the Belvedere. It was surrounded on all four sides by the wings of the Vatican Museum. To his horror, he saw Luciana and Ruffino run across its loose-pebbled surface, a bag held between them. Luciana was in her bishop's costume. But Ruffino had not had time to change from being a janitor.

A soldier raised his rifle to fire at them. Matt leaped on him. The shot ricocheted off the cobblestones at the guard's feet. Near the far wall, Matt saw Luciana and Ruffino find a doorway and flee through it. A half dozen guards pursued.

The Swiss whom Matt had knocked down scrambled to his feet now. He appeared shocked at Matt's action. But the sergeant with the two medals on his chest suddenly appeared and slung a heavy arm beneath Matt's neck, choking him. The gorilla, adjusting his pants, came into the courtyard, attracted by all the commotion. When he saw Matthew being attacked by the guard, he froze, unable to help him. Then, in his uncertainty, he turned and ran back into the bank.

Matt dropped his cane, got a grip on the sergeant's forearm and threw him over his head. The other guard, forgetting his shyness in attacking a priest, charged him with rifle butt raised. Matt neatly sidestepped him, Army style, and punched him in a kidney.

Hobbling off, Matt heard heavy boots close behind him as he cut beneath the tower of Nicholas V, then turned down the main street by the Farmacia Vaticana. He could not outrun them. His only chance was to hide. Ahead, he saw what looked like a cave.

Veering toward it, he hurled himself inside. It was a car park, a place where the Vatican workers kept their autos. He worked his way through the lines of automobiles, crouching finally beneath a large Mercedes-Benz truck filled with asphalt. Positioning himself beneath its drive shaft, he caught hold and pulled himself up. Then, painfully swinging his bad leg over it, he rolled on top of it, his back wedged against the bed of the truck.

The guards ran by the truck, searching. Several bent and peered beneath the parked vehicles. The one with the medals shouted something from the other side of the underground garage.

Matt waited until he heard their footsteps fade away, then lowered himself onto the cool cement. He looked up and saw light above him from an air shaft. Abandoning his cane, he eased out from beneath the truck, climbed onto the hood of the Mercedes-Benz and crawled out through the cement window. Standing up in the street, he looked quickly around but could see no guards. The landmark tower of Nicholas was above and behind him now. That was good, because it meant he had gone to the east, toward St. Anne's Gate. He put his back to the cement wall of the car park and peered around the corner. Swiss were scattering everywhere. A bell was ringing across the narrow street—in a general alarm, he supposed. If he was right, that bell was attached to the barracks of the guards.

He waited until the next wave of guards passed, then re-crossed the main street of Vatican City. Shopkeepers were standing outside, wiping their hands on aprons as he limped gamely down Via del Pellegrino. From beneath a now de-serted sentry post, he paused and looked down the main street. The huge Gate of St. Anne had been closed! That meant that probably all exits were locked. Nearby, he could see that the guards continued to pour out of two long, low barracks. They were cocking their rifles as they ran to their preset rendezvous points.

Matt crossed himself and dusted off his black trousers and white T-shirt. His only hope was to find the entrance to the Passetto Vaticano. Luciana and Ruffino should be there already. He threw back his shoulders and walked as nonchalantly as he could toward the barracks. The guards rushed past him, fixing bayonets.

He strolled past the first long rectangular building. He was now within twenty-five feet of the outward wall of the Vatican. Damn, why hadn't the map shown exactly where the tunnel began?

Suddenly, he heard gunfire. He wheeled. Ruffino and Luciana were racing down the main street of St. Anne toward him.

"Here! It's here!" Luciana screamed when she saw him. He hurried back toward her. She ducked into a narrow wooden gate that he had not noticed. Ruffino held it open for him as he entered, then barred it with an iron bolt from within. Luciana had continued running down the narrow walkway. She was carrying the sack of money.

The gate splintered as rifle bullets smashed through it. Outside, soldiers were screaming battle cries as they urged each other over the gate. One tried to climb over it, but iron spikes on top pierced his hands. He fell back screaming in pain.

Matt and Ruffino made their way down the ancient winding path, hugging the back of the barracks. Ruffino slipped on the damp, mossy bricks and fell to his knees. Matt stopped, pulled him quickly upright. Behind, he could hear the gate collapse inward and the triumphant cries of the Swiss.

Near the outside towering wall of the Vatican itself, the passage narrowed. Matt had to turn sideways to get through. Ahead, he could see Luciana, standing, stopped before a low iron door. Behind it was the brick entrance to the tunnel. She threw up her hands in frustration.

"Locked!" she groaned. A massive padlock hung on its green-stained entrance.

She reached inside her bishop's black and purple soutane, pulled out the pistol, and fired. The shot missed the padlock entirely, denting the door.

Matt grabbed her hand, pointed the pistol point-blank at the lock. She pulled the trigger. The ancient padlock blew apart. He tugged back the bolt, dug his fingers into the narrow slit between the door and the bricked entrance, and pulled. The door creaked open a half foot.

"Go!" he yelled to Luciana

Luciana ducked into the darkened tunnel. Matt spun. Ruffino was battling a Swiss Guard in the path behind them.

"Ruffino!" Matt cried.

The faithful porter heard and swung around. His face was jubilant. "We are winning!" he cried ecstatically.

The bayonet blade that pierced Ruffino's breastbone surprised both of them. Ruffino lowered his eyes, saw its razor-sharp edges protruding through his chest, reached down to touch it and collapsed in death.

Matt started back to help him. Then he saw the sergeant with the two medals leap over Ruffino.

Matt dove through the small doorway. Seizing the iron ring inside, he pulled the heavy door shut and searched for the inside lock. There had to be one: the tunnel had been designed to allow a pope to retreat safely. He fumbled across the darkened surface, scraping his nails in his desperate attempt. Suddenly, the door lit up. Luciana was standing behind him with a flashlight. Fingers were exploring the door's edge when he found the bolt on the bottom. He slid it into place.

"Ruffino?" Luciana asked as they stood there momentarily, the flashlight between them.

Matt shook his head and took the bag of money. He heard Luciana's whimper of pain.

They headed down a steep ramp, clinging to the algae-ridden sides to keep from slipping.

"Steps!" Luciana announced, lifting her bishop's skirts. Her breath was coming in gasps now. She turned quickly and flashed their only light on Matt so he could find his footing. Then she paused.

"Listen," she said.

A low, rolling rumble filled the tunnel ahead.

"What is it?"

"The river," she cried suddenly. "We're trapped!"

Behind them, there was a muffled explosion followed by the sound of the iron door falling inward off its hinges.

Matt took hold of Luciana's hand and pulled her swiftly forward. The tunnel was so low now that they had to bend over. The smell, which had been dank, turned putrid. The ceiling dripped a mucouslike water on their heads, and the earth beneath their feet thickened into ankle-deep ooze. The tunnel began to twist and change directions, narrowing further, heading downward.

As they skidded around a tight bend, Matt lost his footing. They tumbled down, bumping and scraping themselves against the tunnel's crudely fashioned stone sides. Matt tried to claw for a hold, but each time his fingers slipped off.

They were falling into the darkness. The sound below was a shuddering roar. Luciana's arm struck something. The flashlight flew from her grip. It bounced crazily ahead of them, its beam dancing against the narrow sides of the passage as they hurtled after it. Then ahead, Matt saw the flashlight wedge and stop.

He grabbed for Luciana, braced himself for the crash, pushing out his legs to take the impact. His shoes struck something solid.

In a moment, his head cleared. He reached for the muddied flashlight, shone it on her. She nodded her head to signal that she was okay. Like his, her face and body were covered with muck.

The stitches in his leg had burst. The open wound made him want to cry out. He could feel the warmth of his own blood coursing over his knee and shin as he began to crawl, his head bumping the roof of the tunnel. Water was raining down from the ceiling. He moved forward a few steps and pointed the light to the left wall. It was broken. A great crack ran the length of the right wall too. Rivulets were rising from the floor.

He worked his way down past the seepage. A wave of air struck his face. He swung the flashlight down to a swiftly moving torrent of black water.

Luciana arrived behind him and peered over his shoulder. "We can't make it past that," she screamed over the thunderlike booming. "It's the Tiber!"

"Hold on to me," he said. "I'm a good swimmer. Give me the money, I'll tie it to my belt."

He reached out to take it from her. There was a sudden noise behind them, and the sergeant, his tunic and two medals muddied, slid into view. He pointed his bayoneted rifle at them. "Surrender!" he ordered.

To Luciana's surprise, Matt raised his hands, the money sack over his head.

"It's not worth dying for!" he screamed at her over the roaring noise behind them.

"You have sense," the guard complimented him. "How bad could a life sentence be in Regina Coeli?"

"At least I'll be alive," Matt said.

He tossed the flashlight up to the guard. But as he did, he turned it off.

The sergeant fired three times into the blackness. When he found the flashlight, he turned it onto the boiling mass of dark water. The priest and woman were gone. He played it across the wide hole in the floor of the tunnel until it reached the nearly vertical bank of moss-encased tunnel on the other side. Would it have been possible for them to gain that far bank?

He doubted it. For a moment, he stood listening to the terrible hissing of the water as it surged across the floor of the broken section of tunnel. He held the light on it, waiting to see if anything, even a piece of clothing, surfaced. But nothing did.

He yelled to the soldiers above that he was coming up. On the bare chance that the priest and woman had somehow made it through the water, he would go to the other end of the tunnel at the Castel Sant' Angelo. And there he would wait for them.

20.

Directly across from St. Anne's Gate on Pio Borgo, Hannah
Orteglio sat waiting. For what seemed the fiftieth time, she
checked her watch. 8:56. Where were they? Even though she
had been instructed to wait here until 9:30, she had supposed
that the whole thing would be over and finished before nine.
That was not unreasonable, since Ruffino was supposed to
have been in the bank in his janitor's uniform at precisely
8:30.

Clerics and businessmen came and went through St. Anne's
Gate. Pilgrims brushed against the Kaiser-Frazer, hurrying
toward St. Peter's Square down the street. But two men stood
unmoving beside a battered white Fiat. The huge man in the
lumpy gray suit and the bald man with two rows of hair
seemed also to be watching St. Anne's Gate for some reason.
Were they police?

The two Swiss Guards stationed outside St. Anne's Gate
spun around, as though hearing a command. Then, abruptly,
they began to swing shut the heavy wooden gates.

Hannah started the car and drove in front of the entrance.
Just as the gates eclipsed the inner view, she saw Swiss
swarming everywhere, fixing bayonets. The strident "bleep-
bleep" of an alarm horn was screaming.

Bewildered, frightened, she drove down the street, away

from the Vatican. Should she turn around? Go back and park where she had been? In her rearview mirror, she saw the large man in the gray suit now walk toward St. Anne's Gate. Who *was* he?

She made a right turn, deciding to head back. Again she drove past the Vatican wall. The siren inside was still blaring. The two men from the Fiat were both standing expectantly near the gate. She right-turned again and parked, the nose of the Kaiser headed away from the Vatican.

"God, the Father of Abraham," she prayed, "take us safely through this nightmare!"

She sat there perhaps ten minutes. Her watch moved in agonizing stages to 9:14. It was clear there had been trouble. She would have to proceed across the Tiber to the Castel Sant' Angelo. But it was not 9:30 yet. To hell with that, she decided.

She leaned forward to twist the keys in the ignition. But her fingers were shaking so badly, the keys jangled to the floor.

As she groped for them, there was a series of shouts. She glanced upward and in the rearview saw a contingent of Swiss appear from St. Anne's Gate. The one in the lead was muddied from head to toe. He clumped with his men past her car, marching double time down Via dei Corridori. Ahead, she could see the squat, three-tiered fortress of Castel Sant' Angelo.

Hannah trailed the guards down Via dei Corridori and over Vaticano Lungotevere Castello, the elevated street that ran on both banks above the Tiber River. Shutting off the engine, she glided silently to a halt and watched the Vatican soldiers charge toward the main gate of the Castel Sant' Angelo over a drawbridge that spanned the deep moat.

"Oh, *Dio*!" she prayed. *"Dio, Dio!"*

Unable to sit still any longer, Hannah got out of the car. She knew it was a silly move, that anyone seeing her watch the soldiers disappear inside the castle would know she was somehow involved. But she couldn't help herself. Knees nearly buckling, she waited. To support herself, she leaned against the chest-high stone railing that protected pedestrians from a fall into the Tiber below. As her hand brushed against the snow piled on the cold white travertine rail, she noticed something bobbing along.

At first she ignored it. Then the image repeated itself, pestering her. She leaned over the railing and there in the brown-green water, she saw something. Shoulders. A figure. No, two! The sun's angle was wrong. Sharp rays sheeted the waters. She squinted, raised a hand to shade her eyes, and for a moment, barely an instant, she saw Father Matt holding Luciana's unconscious face above the water. Then he was swept downstream in the wide river, and was gone.

Quickly, she sprinted back toward her car. From behind her, Swiss now disgorged from the drawbridge. They were shouting at one another disgustedly. They hadn't found anyone at that end of the Passetto Vaticano. They began searching the Tiber, scanning its muddy waters.

Gathering her wits, Hannah forced herself to U-turn slowly. She drove across Ponte Vittorio Emanuele, then made a right turn onto Lungotevere Fiorentini d' Altoviti on the opposite side of the river. She drove carefully a few blocks until a check in her mirror showed there were no guards in view. Then, flooring the gas pedal, she sped away.

As Hannah drove, the image of Luciana's lifeless face held above the waters by Father Matt tore at her. What had happened? Something terrible! Through the crowded avenues, she cursed stop lights, running them if there were no *carabinieri* in the intersections in their white gloves. The winding road above the Tiber, planned for idle strollers, seemed interminable to her. Finally, the tight-turned Lungotevere gave way to the Riva Ostiense highway, and she could drive as fast as she liked. She had a spot in mind where she might safely help them out.

At the Ponte Marconi, the last bridge at the edge of Rome, she pulled off and parked. Quickly, she got out. Holding her breath she searched upriver, praying to God that she had not missed them, that they had not drowned. Logically, she told herself, Father Matt would get as far out of town as possible. And there was nowhere that he could have emerged from the river without being seen until now. From here on out, the Tiber would meander peacefully through the green hills of the Roman countryside.

Around the bend appeared two small bobbing heads. She gripped the stone handrail, then checked to see if there were any passersby. No one.

As the figures closed on the bridge, Hannah leaned far over its railing. She could see Father Matt struggling yet to hold Luciana above the waves.

"Father!" she called. "Matt! Matt Bowles!"

Just before he went under the bridge, he looked up. His face appeared exhausted, drawn.

Hannah ran across the bridge to the other side. They were being carried toward some fields of vineyards. "Try to get out! Around the next bend! I'll be waiting!" she screamed.

If he heard, he did not respond.

Putting the car into gear, she continued over the bridge to the right bank of the Tiber, then turned left on Via della Magliana. The Basilica of St. Paul was across the river as she drove.

Parking beside a recently pruned vineyard, she left the car and ran down to the river. Its banks were now dirt; the tall cement and stone walls that had lined it all through Rome had stopped at the Marconi Bridge. She slipped on the muddy bank, fell and scrambled to her feet. At the level of the river, there was no sign of them. Only bulrushes—and a few mud hens cruising the calmer water.

Then she heard the sound of heavy breathing. Turning, she pushed through the cattails and vines, her shoes filling with the cold, soggy mud. There, at the river's edge, was Father Matt bent over Luciana. His pants leg was very bloody.

Hannah knelt beside him. Both Matt and Luciana were covered with greenish muck. Luciana, still in her black-and-red bishop's outfit, lay on her stomach, her feet floating yet in the water. The bag full of money was wound tightly around Father Matt's wrist. He ignored it as he straddled Luciana and pumped her lungs.

"What happened, oh, what happened?" Hannah moaned.

"Someone knew!" Matt said, trying to get his own breath. "Someone was waiting for us!" He was working furiously on Luciana, pumping harder and harder on her back, fighting for any response.

"God," he mumbled, "not now! Not like this! Please, God!"

He would not stop. Occasionally water gurgled from Luciana's mouth. But she did not move.

He began whacking her sharply on the back, hitting her

lifeless body. "Give her back!" he shouted. He looked demonic, with his brown hair plastered across his forehead, mud and pieces of river weed in his clothes. "Let her live! She must live!" He hit Luciana harder and harder with his open hand in the square of her back.

"She's dead!" Hannah could stand it no longer. She lunged and caught his arms, holding them. "She's dead! Let her rest!"

He stopped then, looked up at this stout, matronly woman and sagged in defeat. He began to weep painfully. Deeply wracking sobs tore his chest.

Hannah released him and half fell, half sat back on the muddy bank and lowered her head into her hands.

It was then that they both heard Luciana sneeze.

Matt rolled her over. Luciana's hands fluttered. He kissed her and she coughed, turned on her side and weakly vomited. He hugged her limp form to his chest.

"*Matteo, Matteo,*" she cried feebly. Hannah helped him pull off the ruined bishop's robe. She took the pistol from one of the pockets.

"Praise be to my God and yours," Hannah uttered.

21.

Together, Matt and Hannah fought for their footing on the steep bank as they helped Luciana up to the car. They had just settled into the back seat of the Kaiser when someone upriver shouted.

They looked up and saw a truckload of Swiss parked on the Marconi Bridge. One of them, covered with mud, was standing on the bridge, focusing directly on them with binoculars.

"Get in," Matt said. "They know we're alive!"

He started the car and zoomed off down the little road that ran on that bank above the river. The guards had already boarded their Mercedes-Benz truck and were rolling across the bridge.

"How do I get to the coast?" Matt asked Hannah.

"Turn here, no, the next one. *Sì*, here!"

The red Kaiser skidded off the road, hit a soft shoulder, catty-cornered a plowed field and jumped up onto the main highway.

"Tell me," Hannah begged Matt. "What happened to Ruffino?"

"He died holding off Swiss."

"How awful! Poor Ruffino! And how did you get away, Father?"

"The tunnel was flooded, a dead end. A guard caught up to

us, so I pretended to surrender and then threw him our only flashlight. I tackled Luciana and fell backwards into a whirlpool. We were sucked under. Thank God for that, or we would have been shot." He kicked away the sopping wet bag of money that lay beneath his feet. Then he turned quickly to check Luciana in the back seat. She smiled at him weakly. He turned back and put his foot firmly on the pedal. Hannah watched the speedometer approach eighty.

"We were down under that water for an eternity, banging and bumping against what must have been the outer sides of the tunnel. That's how Luciana got hurt. I know I blacked out. The next thing I remember, light was shining through my closed lids. I opened them and saw the sun above. Somehow, I had managed to hold on to her."

"That was when I spotted you in the river," Hannah said, turning around to draw the coat more snugly beneath Luciana's chin. "Praise the Almighty you are both alive! And miraculously, you got the money, Father! The refugees will have their Promised Land after all!"

"Not unless we get to Civitavecchia first, Hannah!" He was driving very fast along Ostiense, which now forked away from the Tiber and headed toward the open sea. "No one but us knew about the robbery. But whoever was smart enough to have figured it out might know about the ferry in Civitavecchia too!"

"But what about the refugees? They haven't even started out yet! And the Swiss are behind us now!" She cranked around. The truck was not in sight yet.

"There's . . . another harbor," Luciana managed from the back seat. "We'll have to move the ferry there. It's called . . . Capo Linaro."

"Or maybe you could take it to Ladispoli," Hannah offered. "It's closer to Roma. Don't forget the refugees will be walking!"

"Ladispoli is too rocky," Luciana said. "Capo Linaro is farther, but it'll have to do." Then she noticed Matt's leg. It was bleeding through his pants. "You're hurt." She pointed.

"I'll be okay," he said.

As they threaded their way down the steep dirt road toward the harbor floor, they could see workers clambering over the ferry. Its superstructure had been stripped away now so that only two tiers remained. The bridge had been moved from the top third level to the bottom, main deck. Inside a crude wooden frame stood the ferry's large wheel and other gadgets needed to drive her.

The ferry's rear end had been jacked up out of the water, and it now sat entirely in dry dock. The hole in its bow had been patched. But little else had been accomplished. Rusty and twisted, it sat forlornly, sagging above the green water, its bottom flat and exposed.

Luciana took a hard look at it, then lay back down without comment. Her reaction expressed what the others were thinking.

"Well," Matt tried to sound cheerful, "at least no one's here waiting for us!" But he double-checked the British destroyer and cruiser at the other end of the harbor for any signs of activity.

Parking the car near Marcheshi's shack, Matt got out and helped Luciana out of the back seat. Hannah slid under the wheel immediately.

"On your way back, don't forget to avoid the Swiss," he cautioned her. "They can't be too far behind us."

"I'll take another way!" Hannah shouted.

"Tell all the refugees they have to be at Capo Linaro by midnight," Luciana told her. "That's the deadline. We won't be able to wait any longer."

"I'll have them there!" Hannah squeezed her hand. "Good luck, Contessa." She gave Luciana the small pistol. "*Salute*," she said.

Luciana kissed her cheek. The big woman threw the car into gear, turned it around, heading back up the dirt hill, bouncing violently, heedless of the ruts. It was obvious she was on a mission.

"How is your leg?" Luciana asked Matt.

"Better," he said. "The bleeding's stopped." His pants leg was now crusted.

Matt took Luciana's hand, and they hurried as fast as his aching leg would carry him over the hillock, then down onto the docks. Ivan, who was in the new wheelhouse, saw them coming and jumped up from the lower deck at once.

"Did you get the money?" he asked Luciana when he had leaped onto the wooden dock.

Matt raised the filthy, wet bag he carried in his hand. Behind his thick glasses, Ivan's eyes widened first at the sight, then widened even further with a new respect as he stared at the priest.

"You look like you have been through a war!" he told them. "How did you get it?"

"Tell you later," Matt said. "We need to move this boat out of Civitavecchia fast! Where's Marcheshi?"

Several workers with bandanas wrapped over their sweating heads were standing watching the dirty man who had arrived with a sack.

Cohen turned around, whistled. Marcheshi appeared from the hold, beneath the lower deck. He took his time approaching, not recognizing Matt as the representative of the Great Man.

"The ship is not ready to sail," Ivan told Matt as Marcheshi lumbered toward them. "We have only one motor working really well."

"Is she fueled?"

"No, of course not!"

"Do that now!"

"All right! There are some fifty-gallon drums of diesel on the dock."

"Good. Can you steer her?"

"Yes. . . ."

"Is she watertight?"

"All patched up, but . . ."

"We have no choice," Matt said, then he held out his hand: "Hello, Victor."

Marcheshi stopped, thunderstruck. "*Signore* Bowles?" he asked, seeing the man in a torn T-shirt, filthy black trousers and muddy shoes.

"We're in a hurry," Luciana told him. "We'll be taking our boat now."

"Now? Is *not* ready!"

Ivan told him it had to be.

"But the money?" Marcheshi asked suddenly.

Matt held up the dripping cotton sack. Marcheshi looked askance a moment, but reached out, took it, peered inside, then realized he was surrounded by workers and shoved it inside his sleeveless shirt.

"Come, I count it," he said as he started up toward his shack.

"Clear the ferry. Cast off all lines but one," Matt told Ivan. "We're leaving in five minutes." He took Luciana by the arm and pulled her up toward Marcheshi's shack. "Are you okay?" he asked her as they strode up the dock.

"I'm alive." She grinned at him bravely. But he could tell she was in pain.

They pushed open the grease-stained, unfinished front door of the shack to discover a different world inside. Mr. Marcheshi had dumped the soggy mess of bills on an elegant Chippendale desk. Queen Anne chairs and Louis XIV tables filled the shack's main room. A massive blue, gold and red Persian carpet covered the wood floor. Elaborately framed oil paintings hung on the walls. Fortunes were being made in postwar Italy, and Marcheshi bit by bit, it seemed, was beginning to show his.

He was counting the wet bills slowly, straightening each one, making sure it was not counterfeit.

"Tell him to hurry," Matt told Luciana.

Luciana scolded Marcheshi. But he ignored her and continued to take his time.

"Three hundred seventy," he counted the thousands one by one, "three hundred seventy-one . . ."

Matt hobbled across the floor and looked out the window. From here, he had a clear view of the entire dirt road.

"Five hundred! Five hundred one," Marcheshi carefully smoothed the money. "Wet, wet! How could this happen?"

"Mind your own business!" Luciana told him. "It's money, isn't it?"

As Marcheshi saw the pile of bills dwindling, he began to count faster, apparently worried at its decreasing capability to match the agreed-on amount. He snapped the last hundred bills down in a hurry, his worst fears confirmed.

"Eight hundred fifty-four thousand," he told Luciana. "You are missing nine thousand!"

"You counted wrong!"

"What is it?" Matt asked her, turning from his post at the window.

"With the one hundred thirty-seven thousand we already gave him, we still owe nine thousand more."

"I was afraid of that. Things got crazy in the bank!"

Marcheshi saw Matt's expression, folded his arms and leaned back in his office chair. "I want the rest of my money!" he announced.

"Tell him we'll get him the rest later," Matt told her. "We've got to go!" He started toward the door.

Luciana began her sentence, but Marcheshi yanked open a drawer and pulled out a U.S. military .45. *"Fermo!"* he ordered and stood up.

Matt and Luciana wheeled and faced him.

"You are thieves!" Marcheshi berated them. "This money doesn't come wet out of a bank! You are frauds!" But he shoved the money into a desk drawer and locked it.

Luciana started to translate, but Marcheshi cut in again. "I'll show you what we do to thieves out here," he said. "We don't have fancy trials like in Roma. We execute them. That is our justice!" He gestured with the .45 toward the door.

Matt opened it and limped out. At the top of the road, a Mercedes-Benz diesel appeared. It began rolling down toward them.

Marcheshi, seeing the truckload of Swiss, grinned and motioned them off the porch. They started down the steps with Marcheshi's .45 digging into Matt's back. Luciana suddenly groaned, clutched her sides and doubled over in pain. Matt reached for her. In that same instant, there was a muffled "pop" and the sweat-stained boat owner collapsed like a rag doll and rolled down the steps. Luciana stood holding her .25-caliber pistol in a shaking hand. She was staring in horror at what she had done. Matt kicked away Marcheshi's .45 and rolled him over.

"He's not dead," he said, examining the entry of the bullet. It had gone cleanly through his shoulder.

He took the pistol from Luciana, pocketed it and pulled her down the steps.

The Swiss were advancing down the road.

At Ivan's directions, workers were casting off lines, loading the fuel drums, throwing rubber acetylene hoses onto the dock and handing down hammers, chisels, caulking.

Matt lifted Luciana to the deck of the ferry, then, favoring his leg, hopped up also.

"Start the engine!" Matt told Ivan.

"It will do little good!" he shouted. "We are high and dry! It will take hours to lower her into the water!"

Matt peered over the side. The ferry was still ten feet above the water in its dry dock.

"Luciana, get everyone on ropes!"

"What are you going to do?" Ivan asked.

"Pull it off!" Matt told him. "Go start your engine!"

"She will crack in two when she falls!" Ivan wailed fearfully, but scurried down into the engine room.

Luciana ran to the rear of the dilapidated ship and yelled down to the workers what she wanted them to do.

A worker by the name of Marti told Luciana they wouldn't unless they got paid first. He said since the boat was leaving, they might never see their wages.

"Pull us off," Luciana offered, "and I'll tell you where Marcheshi's money is!"

"*Scusi*," Marti said, "but how can we trust you?"

"I am Contessa Luciana Maria Lamberghini Francesca Spoleto! I swear by my royalty, on the grave of my ancestors, I will reveal where the money is! I also swear to you it is stolen and you must be very cautious about it!"

Marti, obviously impressed, turned quickly to several of the elder workers. They nodded.

"It's in Marcheshi's desk!" Luciana shouted as loudly as she could.

A hundred men secured a hawser to the stern of the ferry. A second rope flew up and was wound around the center capstan above the propeller.

"*Uno, duo, TRE!*" Marti commanded,

The hawsers snapped tight as piano wires. The dry dock cracked. The ferry wavered, rocked, but the underpinnings held. Marti shrugged up at Luciana.

Matt saw that the Swiss were already at the end of the docks.

The men prepared to pull on the ropes again. But suddenly a rumbling came from the ferry's belly. The huge ship shook as its motor started. Its propeller spun rapidly in thin air. The entire boat shivered and quaked. The dry dock beneath it began to splinter.

The huge ferry tilted and splashed into the harbor.

The workers were casting off the hawsers onto the lower deck when the first shots hit the ship. Bullets whined over the decks. Matt pulled Luciana down. The workers panicked amidst the attacking soldiers. Some jumped into the water to safety. Ivan was backing the ship away from the docks.

The Swiss, at the command of the muddied sergeant, fired over the workers' heads at the departing ferry. The shells spent themselves against her thick, rusted sides.

As they backed out toward the British ships, the commotion and gunfire attracted more and more English sailors up on deck. The men of the H.M.S. *George V* and *Jutland* were clustered at the railings, watching as the ferry backed slowly by.

The Swiss on the dock stopped shooting. It was obvious the ferry was out of range.

Ivan swung the massive ship around using the ropes and wheel in the makeshift wooden steering house, then slowed the motor and clutched it into forward. The engine began a rhythmic beat as the ferry chugged through the opening in the stone seawall of the harbor toward the blue Tyrrhenian Sea.

"We're going to make it!" Luciana cried, raising her head from the deck. "We did it!"

Matt stood and helped her up. "Not quite yet," he said.

Luciana saw that he was gazing back at the gray 306-foot British destroyer *Jutland*. Smoke, turning a serious black, was pumping from its two funnels midships. Slowly, the behemoth iron warrior wheeled and began to move out of the harbor after them.

22.

Annoyed by the open white drapes through which any ordinary tourist or wandering murderer could spy on the Holy Father, Sister Pasqualina shook her ruddy cheeks, then reached up and, with a violent tug, yanked the heavy damasks closed. Scanning the Holy Father's living quarters, she quickly checked for anything out of place. Immaculate white floor rug; royal purple walls, freshly scrubbed; desk top with red wax and Papal seal; all was spotless and in order. She wrinkled her nose at the cage on the floor that held the Holy Father's sparrows. He loved those simple birds so much. Dirty things, she thought. Probably had lice in their feathers already. Little did the Holy Father suspect that she dusted his sparrows monthly with delousing powder.

Opening the doors, she hurried out, crossing through the Borgia apartments, where the Borgia popes had once kept their families and mistresses, then down several flights of stairs, through rooms filled with Pope Pius's special bodyguards, who came to attention, finally opening a small door that led into the Sistine Chapel.

From her vantage point at the rear of the Sistine, she saw that the Papal audience was nearly finished. International scientists pressed around her white-cassocked Pope Pius XII. She stared lovingly at her Master as he stood chatting beneath the front wall that contained his throne and altar. Above and behind him was *The Last Judgment*: souls rising to heaven on the left, being dragged down by demons opposite. On the ceiling, Michelangelo's *The Creation of the World*: God stretching out his finger to touch Adam.

Sister Pasqualina felt that this room with all its history, power and sweeping vistas suited her Pope. He was a man blessed by God, an overseer to the world itself, and she was fortunate indeed to be his closest confidant.

When Pius saw Pasqualina waiting at the small side door, he mumbled something quickly to the three or four scientists around him and broke away from them, descending the dais to her.

"They love us," he said happily in German as he neared her. "They told us they are very happy that we survived the war."

"It is you they adore," she said. "Keep your hands away from your nice white soutane. They are infected."

Six Papal ushers in tuxedos from their posts in the Sistine Chapel led the way through the corridors, their medallions clinking on their chests, and threw open the doors to Pius's private study. The sparrows fluttered, batting themselves against the cage bars, as Pasqualina and Pope Pius entered. Pasqualina slammed the doors, shutting out the ushers.

"Sit, sit, Holiness," she commanded the Pontiff.

Obediently, the Pope arranged himself in the nearest chair. Pasqualina eased off the massive gold ring of St. Peter, symbol of his authority. She withdrew her bottle of alcohol from her robe and poured some into a shallow tray. Then she dipped in a white linen cloth and began to disinfect the Pontiff's hands.

"They always kiss your fingers!" she complained.

There was a hurried knock and Monsignor Helmut Kass entered. He was out of breath and almost in a state of shock. "Holiness," he announced, "I did not wish to alarm you. But now you must know. The Vatican bank has been robbed!"

"Robbed?" Pius rolled the word in his mouth. He pushed Pasqualina's hands away in alarm. "By whom?"

"The American priest! Bowles!"

"But why would he do such a thing?"

"We presume to replace the Jews' money."

The Holy Father's dark eyebrows raised very high at that news. "He must be brought to his senses!"

"Yes, Holiness. Our Swiss Guards picked up his trail. Most likely, they will capture him."

Pius gripped the arms of his chair suddenly, his face fearful. He spun to Pasqualina. "Get Alcide de Gasperi on the phone, please. Then ring up Myron Taylor."

Pasqualina slammed down the basin of alcohol and dialed the nearby ornate French telephone. She began barking orders into its mouthpiece.

There was another knock at the door and Prince Chieti Milagro asked, *"Permesso, Papa Santo?"*

The Pope waved him inside.

The Governor of the Vatican, in his long coattails, took one step into the room. He was followed by Monsignor Guido Offeri, Hans Fullmer and *Segretario* Palmo. They held their eyes sheepishly to the sparkling white rug that covered the Pontiff's private room.

"I'm afraid we have more sad news." The Prince delivered the information. "The American priest has, as of moments ago, fled Civitavecchia with a ship."

"Where has he gone?" Kass demanded quietly.

"We do not know. A British destroyer on duty there in the harbor is tracking them."

Uncharacteristically, Pope Pius showed his agitation. He slapped the palms of his hands together four or five times.

"The entire fate of Italy and our Vatican hinges on stopping Father Bowles and"—he sought the correct word—"camouflaging this whole unblessed affair!"

"Myron Taylor wishes to speak with you, Holiness," Pasqualina announced. She held out the receiver.

"And Alcide?" Pius asked her as he took the phone.

"He will be informed by your Under Secretaries Montini and Tardini. It is best not to make direct contact to the Christian Democrat from this office."

For the first time since he had taken power in 1939, Pope Pius wished he had not kept the total reins to himself. It would have been helpful for De Gasperi to hear the bad news from a full-fledged Secretary of State, not an Under Secretary. But unfortunately, one did not exist.

"You were wise, my dove," he assured Pasqualina.

He spoke into the white mouthpiece. "Mr. Taylor? *Prego*. A small problem. It concerns the 'help' from your United States. We have suffered a robbery."

Everyone in the room heard the Ambassador's voice rise in alarm.

"A priest," the Pope went on when Taylor's distressed voice stopped. "He's at sea. The British are after him, though. What? Yes, *si*, a good suggestion. It would not be good for the elections if news of this money . . ." The Pontiff listened a few moments longer, then hung up. He mulled over the words of the United States Ambassador, then turned to Monsignor Kass.

"Helmut, an American military car will be waiting outside St. Anne's Gate in ten minutes. It will take you south to Anzio Harbor. There, you will board an American cruiser to rendezvous with the British destroyer. Change your clothing. Do not appear in public or be recognized!"

Kass bowed. "I would like to take the other American priest, Father Mankowsky," he told Pius. "He was supposed to go home to New York today, but since he's still here, he might be able to reason with Bowles."

The Holy Father said, "Go, get him quickly! And anyone else you need!"

When the room had emptied, Pope Pius dropped to his knees. He clasped his hands and rested his chin on his fingertips and began to pray earnestly. Sister Pasqualina knelt beside him. She prayed also, but watched her Master closely, hoping he would not catch any sickness from those scientists, since she had not completely cleansed his hands.

Over four thousand air miles away, in Washington, D.C., the capital was iced over. Despite the foul weather and the further storm expected, President Harry S Truman was conducting one of his ambulatory news conferences as he walked rapidly past the black, spear-shaped fence in the front of the White House. The reporters, their breaths steaming in the cold, fought to keep up with him and copy down his words.

"It's a memorable occasion," Truman was chattering. "Hallmark, boys. You know what it is today?"

"Pearl Harbor Day, Mr. President?" Armstrong Brewster, from *The New York Times*, asked.

"Right, Armie. This makes six years, only six, since the Japs kicked our asses at Pearl Harbor. But look at us now. We're the most powerful nation in the world. The best! And we can beat anyone that comes along. Anyone!" He stomped his feet free of the slush that lay on the sidewalk. "My Truman Doctrine pledges to support free peoples who are resisting attempted subjugation by outside pressures. And at this very moment, we're sending aid to countries threatened by Russia!"

"Italy for openers, Mr. President?" a deep, resonant voice asked from the rear.

"That election is more important to us than our own presidential ones next November," Truman answered carefully, then added with a twinkle, "well, almost as important, anyway."

Some of the reporters laughed. Flynt Garge asked, "Will the Christian Democrats beat the Communists there, Mr. President?"

"They dang well better, Mr. Garge. Without Italy and the Mediterranean, we lose access to Greece, Turkey, and the Middle East and there goes the kit and caboodle. Like dominoes, one after the other. And you can quote me on that, Mr. Lippmann."

The reporters burst into knowing laughter. Truman had great respect for that institution in Washington known as Walter Lippmann, who, unlike a lot of reporters, never got a word wrong. It didn't matter that Lippmann was not among them that morning. He would hear about the compliment.

"Is it true, Mr. President"—the deep voice from the back again—"that we sent millions to the Vatican to help win the elections in Italy?"

The President stopped dead in his tracks. He swung around slowly, the smile that had wreathed his face fading. The reporters parted before his glare. A man in a gray trench coat stepped forward. "Edward R. Murrow," he identified himself. "CBS Radio."

"Who told you that?" the President demanded.

"Sources, Mr. President."

"Lies, Murrow! Pure and simple!" Truman spun on his heel and rushed toward the nearby guard gate and the covered portico that led up to the main door of the White House.

"Meetin's over, fellas!" Truman roared over his shoulder as the guard held open the door.

The reporters turned away, disappointed. Some grumbled at Murrow.

Then Digby from *Time* softly whistled and as one they spun to see George Marshall, Secretary of State, hurry toward the guard gate. As the President walked beneath the covered green and white portico, Marshall handed him a telegram.

Truman read the missive, squinted at Marshall. Then as the sixteen national reporters watched, puzzled, the President nearly ran up the walk with Marshall.

In Tokyo, Francis Cardinal Spellman stood at a podium in the elegant Tsuru room of the Imperial Hotel, about to address a gathering of thirteen hundred tuxedoed Japanese businessmen when General Douglas MacArthur's military attaché arrived in an obvious hurry. The colonel conferred briefly with the pipe-smoking general, who was seated at the right of the podium, then spoke to Spellman.

"Excuse me, Eminence," the colonel whispered, "but President Truman is on the hot line for you."

"What is it, man?" Spellman wondered, his blue eyes dancing.

"Italy . . ." the attaché said. "It's . . . the Vatican."

"The Vatican! What's happened? Do you know?"

"There's been a robbery," the colonel said. "It has something to do with a Father Matt Bowles you sent. It's on all the news wires, leaked, we think, by Communists there."

"Bowles!" Spellman turned red. He bent to General MacArthur, who was staring stonily forward, facing the somber faces of the Japanese.

"Mac," Spellman whispered, "I have to go. Make my apologies?"

"Of course, Eminence," the general replied, the smoke from his pipe becoming slightly furious.

Spellman dashed off the dais. MacArthur stood and began addressing the puzzled audience.

Backstage, Spellman was being accompanied by the attaché. "There's a phone in General MacArthur's car." The colonel was pointing the way.

"Good, good. Not a moment to lose." Spellman lifted his

robe up so he could hurry faster. "Have a plane ready for me to go to Rome, right? I want it when I get off the phone!"

"That may take some time to requisition. . . ."

"That's an order, Colonel!"

"Yes, sir, General!" And he saluted smartly. For in fact, honorary or not, Cardinal Spellman outranked him.

23.

When the truckload of Swiss began their search of the Tiber, Nerechenko suspected immediately that the Red Woman had failed in his attempt to stop the robbery. Sitting in the driver's seat, with a sullen and untalkative Cornos beside him, he had trailed the Swiss as they examined the waters of the river. Finally, near the Marconi Bridge, his suspicions paid off. The guards,had spotted a small, bright red car and pursued it. It was the car he had seen parked near St. Anne's Gate earlier.

Mentally, as they followed, Nerechenko made note that it was an American-produced car. A Kaiser-Frazer.

At Civitavecchia, he saw that the Swiss, as well as the carloads of *carabinieri* who had roared past them on the highway, sirens blazing, had arrived too late. The ferry was leaving. U-turning quickly, he headed back to Rome, speeding as fast as his small, badly worn-out car could handle.

Once in the center of town, near the crowded government buildings in Popolo Square, he slowed slightly, then turned left in front of an oncoming trolley and onto Babuino. He roared down that smaller street, then screeched to a halt in front of the Metro "Polizia" station.

Leaving the horned one in the car, Nerechenko sprang across the narrow avenue and went up the three steps into the police headquarters' front entrance. He strode through the receiving room where several feather-plumed *carabinieri* were questioning a man who was holding a rag to his bleeding forehead. He opened an opaque glass door that announced, BUREAU OF STREETS, and entered. Inside, a policeman in an out-of-date, too-small cotton black suit sat under a turning wooden fan. He looked up and paled noticeably.

"Igor!" he said uncertainly. "I did not expect you."

The Russian fished in his pocket and produced a slip of paper. "I want to know the owner of a red American Kaiser-Frazer. There can't be too many here in Rome."

The Inspector said, "This should only take a moment, comrade."

The Inspector left the room. The Russian sat a moment, then got up and began pacing. He was too nervous. Unusual for him. Even the liquor did not seem to calm him these days.

A calendar above the Inspector's desk caught his eye. The picture for December was of Capri, a harbor filled with fishing boats. As he stared, he remembered a tiny sea resort near his native Minsk. More and more, he thought, my mind wanders to home. It is not good. A sign of stress. Dangerous for my mind to wander like that. But he stared. He thought of his four children and how they wanted only the "good things from the West." His fat wife, Natalie. Even the boring *apparatchiks*, his fellow bureaucrats, smelling of cabbage in their small, smoky cubicles. His own vacant office.

Then he thought of his father, who had been a Deputy Commissar of Defense in 1937 when Josef Stalin, in one of his bloody purges, had had him shot. He remembered his mother stoically receiving the news and later weeping quietly in the basement of their dacha. All in all, a third of the Red Army officers were liquidated that year, including eleven Deputy Commissars of Defense and thirteen of the fifteen Generals of the Army.

Why was he doing this? He had asked himself that before. His usual reply was "Mother Russia!" But the cities he had loved were stark now. Colorless. Programmed to be without character. Who was he working for? Russia or Stalin?

He turned his eyes from the calendar and deliberately faced the door.

In a moment, the door opened and the Inspector announced,

"The car's license is NFW32. It is registered to a *Signore* Pynchon Nossi. He lives in the ghetto."

"A Jew?" Nerechenko asked, retrieving his slip of paper from him.

"More than likely. I wrote his address down."

Nerechenko nodded and strode to the door.

"Any time I can be of service," the Inspector announced proudly, "let me know. We will win our great struggle shortly, comrade! The elections will be ours!"

"Stop talking like Ferragamo!" Nerechenko roared. Then he was immediately repentant for that outburst. "Sorry, comrade. You are right, of course. We will win our great struggle." He attempted to smile as he exited.

Reentering the car, Nerechenko drove to the address in the ghetto. There, he parked out of view. The house was part of a modern Bathaus complex behind a high wall. It looked as though it had been built shortly before the war.

"Go inside now," Nerechenko told Spina. "The owner of that red American-made car lives there. Find out where the Jews expect to meet the ferry."

The horned one had not spoken to Nerechenko until now. "Maybe he will not tell," he mumbled.

Defiantly, he reached beneath his seat and withdrew an object wrapped in oiled cloth. Unwrapping the barrel quickly, he exposed the 12-gauge sawed-off shotgun. Then he filled his hand from a box of shells. Then he loaded the single-barrel, stockless weapon and slipped it up the inside of his sleeve.

All this time, Nerechenko said nothing.

Stepping from the car, Cornos buttoned his corduroy jacket and circled around the rear of the quadrate apartments. He entered the walled enclosure through a dark green wooden gate.

Crossing a small courtyard filled with drying clothes, Spina went up several steps to the back door. He knocked and noted with satisfaction that this part of the courtyard was surrounded by an additional protective low wall. The noise would not be great. He thanked the Virgin.

A short man in his fifties, hair held in place by a black hairnet, a silver smoking jacket covering his plump torso, opened the door. He had only a glimpse of the bald head before the horned one was inside the kitchen, the door closed behind him.

"Where is your car?"

"My car? Are you police?" Mr. Nossi demanded indignantly.

"Where is your car?" Spina asked him again, unbuttoning his jacket.

Mr. Nossi stared at the front of the coat. "I loaned it to someone."

"Who?" Spina asked, unhooking the leather strap that held the *lupara* beneath his arm.

Behind Nossi, some espresso he had been cooking on the stove boiled over in its steel pot. He whipped around at the sudden sizzling sounds on the fire.

"Who else is here? Anyone?" Cornos withdrew the *lupara*.

"Only my cats live with me," Nossi told the truth. "I am a bachelor!"

"Good," Cornos said, "now who has your car?"

The hissing of molasses-thick coffee as it splashed on the fire was the only noise in the kitchen. Turning briefly to look at the pot, Nossi spun back and said, "Hannah Orteglio, if you have to know. She will return it! I must turn off my coffee! Please, officer?"

"Go ahead," Spina said.

Mr. Pynchon Nossi hesitated, not understanding any of this. Yet he felt relieved at being allowed to resume control of his life. As he turned, Cornos shot him in the back of the head.

The noise was not loud at all. It sounded like a heavy door closing. Cornos turned off the fire on the single-burner stove. Then, discarding the spent shell, he reloaded. Two large cats entered the kitchen and began to sniff.

Hannah stopped the candy-apple red Kaiser-Frazer before the wrought-iron gate. The tiny street of Via Rigosa was packed with refugees in traveling coats with bundles on their shoulders. On the steps of Ruffino's house, luggage was piled high, tied sheets bulged with belongings, and some small furniture was scattered about. Rabbi Meister, clad in black Orthodox clothing, his white hair billowing from beneath his black hat, was directing the refugees, stowing their belongings.

Hannah honked the horn and Rabbi Meister came down through the gates.

"Hannah, praise God!" he beamed. "We have missed you since breakfast this morning!"

Hannah waited until he was at the car. Then she said, "There has been trouble."

A family passed behind Rabbi Meister. "Up, up there and wait for me!" he told them. "Hello, Moishe, how are you?" The smile slid from his face as he again bent close to Hannah.

"How bad?" he asked.

She took a deep breath. "Hopefully . . . things will go well now."

"Can you tell me more?" he asked.

"All you need to know," Hannah told him, "is that the meeting place has been changed. Instead of Civitavecchia, you are to go as soon as it is dark to Capo Linaro. The ferry will be waiting. Be there no later than midnight! They will need the night to load."

"How far is this Capo Linaro?" he asked, shooing away several curious children.

"Closer than Civitavecchia. The walk should take four, five hours, no more."

"And who will show us the way?"

"I will. And we must be very disciplined, very quiet and on time! That is important!"

"We will be as disciplined as trained soldiers!" Meister told her, straightening. "And there by midnight!"

Hannah put the car into gear.

"Where do you go now?"

"To return Mr. Nossi's car."

"Someone less important can take it back, Hannah. You should be here to help me organize. Why not stay?"

She hesitated, then said, "Mr. Nossi is funny about his car. It took a lot to get him to lend it to me. I should be the one to take it back."

"God be with you," Rabbi Meister said. "Hurry back!" He waved as the Kaiser-Frazer started slowly up Via Rigosa, picking its way through the families. Then he turned and went back to the front steps to organize for the long march that would begin shortly.

*   *   *

At Mr. Nossi's, Hannah got out, opened the green gates in the wall and drove the Kaiser into the garage. She padlocked the steering wheel with his chain and lock and spun the tumbler to mix up the numbers. Then she went through the small courtyard, past the low wall and up to the door and knocked. A woman, a neighbor, was gathering in her washed clothes. Hannah waved to her, then knocked again.

Now she noticed the door was standing partly open. Hannah asked, "Pynchon?"

"Here," Cornos said, hidden behind the door.

She tried to peek inside. But she could see only a little. A cat somewhere in the kitchen started to meow.

"Is something burning?"

"The coffee. Come in."

Hannah hesitated. For some reason, she did not want to enter Pynchon Nossi's kitchen. "I only came to thank you for letting me borrow your car," she said. Her voice trailed off. She had smelled something burning. It was the stink of cordite. A smell she remembered in the streets after the two Allied bombings of Rome. She eased forward around the door and then saw Mr. Nossi's hairnet on the floor. Beside it three of his Persians were meowing, nervously turning circles.

Instinctively, Hannah fled. But it was too late. Her left wrist was suddenly gripped. Before she could scream, a powerful arm encircled her neck. Her feet left the floor. The cats fled.

With a kick, the door slammed shut.

"Where do the Jews go to meet the boat?" the thick voice growled. It sounded Calabrian or Greek to her. She couldn't tell.

"Who wants to know?" she rasped back, the air catching in her strangled throat.

Several inches from her eyes, a yellow-handled screwdriver flashed. "An ice pick would be better," the voice purred sensuously.

Hannah's throat was burning but she lashed out at the screwdriver. It vanished, then entered her car.

"Where do the Jews go?"

"Civi—ta—"

"Wrong! The ferry has left there!"

"Civi—"

The screwdriver pierced the membrane. Her head exploded with a thousand flashes of light. She fell to the floor. Before she could rise, he gripped her by the hair and jammed a knee into her wide chest. She struggled. Something warm and sticky was running down the side of her neck into her bra.

"Where?" he repeated the question.

"Civi—ta—vecch—"

The screwdriver plunged inside the other ear. She heard herself scream, "Capo Linaro!" She had not meant to. The words had burst from her mouth along with the novas in her head.

The lips above her said something, but Hannah could no longer hear. She felt herself being rolled over. Again a crushing weight slammed onto her back.

"Bosco!" She heard the name of her dead husband in her mind. She knew she was speaking and joining him even before the screwdriver rammed through the base of her neck and lodged into her brain.

Outside, the afternoon had faded into evening. Cornos strode leisurely to the Fiat in which Nerechenko waited. The Russian was drinking aquavit straight from the bottle. Cornos got in, slipped the *lupara* from his coat and wrapped it in the oiled rags. Only after he had slid it beneath his seat did he say, "Capo Linaro."

"Any trouble?" Nerechenko corked the bottle and started the car. "You were gone for a long while."

"Was I?"

His voice, Nerechenko noted, sounded peaceful and melodic.

"What is our next move, comrade?" the horned one asked, yawning now.

And this made Nerechenko sure. The horned one slept only after an assassination. The rest of the time he took quick naps.

Igor Nerechenko drove toward the Russian Embassy on Via Lisbona. There, he would contact the Russian Navy and arrange the ship he needed. The last he had heard, the Third Fleet was anchored off Sardinia. It wouldn't take long.

But as he maneuvered the car through the streets, vaguely realizing that he was now driving faster than Cornos had, he could not shake a persistent image from his mind. He kept seeing himself, his wife and his children, floating peacefully in the waters of his boyhood seaside resort, their white flesh bulging over swimming costumes. And what was so strange, what bothered him most, was that never before had he liked water.

At five o'clock that night, as the sun was setting, General Raymond T. Vance's olivegreen car pulled up at the Anzio Beach guard gate. The Marine officer on duty immediately waved through the limousine without checking the occupants inside. Those were his orders.

The limo parked on the metal grating that served as a temporary dock beside the berthed cruiser. The driver hopped out and opened a side door. The interior light had been disconnected for just this occasion. Four shadowy figures in winter-length black coats quickly walked up the gangplank of the U.S.S. *Pittsburgh*, a heavy-cruiser classification vessel, which had been anchored there an hour earlier.

As soon as the four were aboard, a commander gave orders to cast off. The captain of the vessel had left earlier, since this was not to be a logged official mission. The heavy cruiser's engines pulled her out through the man-made harbor. As the U.S.S. *Pittsburgh* edged into the darker green water, each of her .50-caliber guns was tested and fired. Then, as normal procedure before a battle, her 15 six-inch cannons were swung on their huge tracks.

Inside the captain's cabin, the commander, a short man in a dazzling white uniform, welcomed each of the Vatican delegates aboard. He had been told they were to be called only Kass, Fullmer, Palmo and Mankowsky. No titles. The commander introduced himself as George Stanton, his junior officers as Martin and Zalk. Then, having provided the four with hot coffee, he went up to his command post.

In a short while, the Red Woman left the company of the other three. He went up to the bow where the wind was blowing off the water.

He thought of his flight from Germany to Rome to see his one-time classmate, Prince Chieti Milagro, now Governor of the Vatican, and of how Pope Pius, at Milagro's request, had granted the Red Woman refuge within the Vatican walls.

Now, he would repay that gift of kindness. His betrayals

would cease. He would become again the good citizen of the Vatican and continue in his job of running things there. As he stood on the bow of the U.S.S. *Pittsburgh*, aware only of a sailor near him on silent watch, the Red Woman began to formulate the ending to this unpleasant tale.

24.

The ferry was running into the wind, close to shore, so close the beaches and foaming breakers that came into view around each bend startled Matt by their proximity. The evening light made it hard to distinguish shapes. In a few minutes, it would be dark entirely and navigation no longer possible. Ivan bent over the small naked light that hung above the marine compass, then took a quick look at the maps he had gathered while working on the ship.

"We're near Capo Linaro now," he shouted over the noise of the engine below. He was standing with Matt in the windowless, unfinished wooden wheelhouse. The steel wheel that crudely rolled two stout ropes back and forth, swinging the rudder in response, seemed as outlandish as the wooden frame of the wheelhouse. But so far, the ship had obeyed Ivan's guidance.

Matt leaned out of the wheelhouse. It took a moment to find the British destroyer, *Jutland*, in the waning light. It was abreast of them still, about three miles out.

"No closer, no farther," he said, stepping back beside Ivan. The destroyer had changed position from trailing them to running beside them after Ivan had started skirting the coast, entering shallower waters.

"As close as they can get." Ivan studied the map that he

had attached by nails to the lower board of the wheelhouse. "We're flat-bottomed and don't draw much water. That destroyer'll have to keep away."

"Where are we now?" Matt scanned the dimming beachhead as it passed by.

"Two, three miles *above* Capo Linaro."

An hour ago, they had been below it. Ivan was driving in circles, biding his time until darkness fell and concealed their place of rendezvous with the refugees. Ivan seemed different to Matt. Bigger somehow now. In time of need, dipping into his own resources, he had become a new man. Matt had seen it happen before, starting with himself on Omaha.

"How will you take this ship in if it's dark?" Matt asked him.

"I was not wasting diesel oil when we passed the Capo these trips. I memorized every detail about it. By the time it is dark, I can guide us in by memory."

Matt pictured Capo Linaro. A spit. Peninsula, really, like a small crooked finger jutting out into the sea. Naked rocks facing the ocean. Beach on leeward, sheltered side. Probably the position Ivan had selected to pick up the refugees.

"Ivan, after we pick them up, we can't make it to Palestine like this! We need food, water, fuel and another engine! Have you thought about that?"

Ivan laughed. "Right now, we have fifteen hundred gallons of water, enough for about two, three days. I made sure of that. I took ten fifty-gallon drums of diesel while you were dealing with Marcheshi. Now, as for the food, we don't have any. But being good refugees, believe me, they will bring enough for a few days."

"But you can't make it to Palestine in two days."

"No, my plan is to wallow across the Tyrrhenian, put in somewhere out of the way in France that'll have us. No one in Italy will think we went in a direction *away* from Palestine. Once in a little port, we'll make repairs, fix her up, get lots of provisions. After that, I'll register her in whatever country we can, then go home to the Promised Land."

Matt's entire attention had been focused on getting the money and acquiring the ship. Now he realized that all the needed practicalities for such a long journey would require another miracle. How could Ivan be so optimistic?

"Why France?" Matt shouted at him, the noise of the creaking ferry and the oncoming breeze muffling his words.

"It's the closest, Father! And they don't give a damn about the British. They don't like to be told what to do. As long as we have money, they'll sell things to us. We do have more money, don't we?"

Now he understood. The helmsman, feeling the silence, turned but said nothing. Instead, he bent suddenly and in the shadows cast by the small light lifted up a crudely painted sign that had been resting beneath the wheel. In black on white, it read: SCHILDKROTE.

"My name for this wreck! 'The Turtle'!" Ivan planted a kiss on his hand and pressed it to the wooden sign. Then he turned and Matt could tell his face was deadly serious. "If she doesn't turn turtle and if the British don't catch us, we'll make it. Even with no more money, with God's help, we shall make it."

He turned back to steering into the fast-approaching darkness. The coastline had vanished altogether.

"What time is it?"

"Seven thirty."

"Good, in five minutes, in we go!"

Off the starboard bow, in precisely the same position it had been in for hours, the *Jutland* was lit up now.

"I'm going down to check on Luciana." Matt picked up a kerosene lantern.

The little man waved that he understood, reached into his back pocket, pulled out an oily rag and wiped the gathering sea spray off his tiny compass light. Then he began to ease blindly into shore.

Picking his way carefully across the buckled iron deck, which was seesawing under the sea's motion, Matt stepped cautiously amid the paraphernalia that had not been carried off in Civitavecchia. He descended the iron ladder into the hold, noticing again that his leg was aching.

Funny, he thought, how we forget about pain until we have time for it again.

In the lower hold, he stepped off the bottom rung of the ladder and was instantly up to his ankles in water. The ferry, Ivan had said, had never been completely drained. No time for that. He turned and shone his light down the long passageway. Behind him, he could hear the peculiar rhythm of the ferry's single, massive engine. The stench of diesel oil hung in the air.

Sloshing his way along the narrow iron corridor, he went toward the bow where the water stopped. He stamped his feet to dry them and, looking down in the halo of the light, realized that those same black clerical shoes had been in St. Anselm's parish in Porter's Quarter, Long Island. He had worn them during Mass, hearing Confessions and teaching classes. Since then, they had sat beneath the bed of a woman, had participated in a robbery of the Vatican and were currently in flight on a stolen ship.

"God help us," he begged out loud.

Winding his way several steps farther, he eased open a cabin door and saw that Luciana was awake. The floor to her room was entirely dry and a porthole above her allowed fresh air to enter. She lay on a small, iron bunk that folded out from the wall, and she was covered with Hannah's coat and several old blankets he had found. A smoking lantern, like his, that the workers had left gave off a meager light.

"How do you feel?" Matt asked, when he saw she was awake. He sat beside her.

"Better." She took his hand and kissed it, holding it to her cheek.

"You seem hot."

"I'm all right." She smiled for him. "Where are we?"

"About to anchor at Capo Linaro."

"And the British?"

"Out there, still watching."

She smiled as if at some flashing irony.

"What are you thinking, something about the British?"

"No, only that from now on, I'll have to be more careful when I toss a coin in the Trevi. It will be awhile before I can go back to Rome."

"You'll be back. We both will."

"*Matteo*, I love your confidence. I hope you're right, my beloved priest."

"I'm not a priest anymore." He bowed his head for a moment. "Not after what I've done."

"Don't think about it. Just kiss me." She raised her wan face and he did.

"Are you bleeding . . . inside?" he asked her now. He had been afraid to ask it before.

"I was a little. But it stopped."

She suppressed a cough, then lay back. "But I feel better," she said. "And I'll be all right, *Matteo,* you'll see." She reached up and swept back his thick mop of brown hair. He was still in his muddied T-shirt and black slacks, his face bearded and haggard. "You look so tired. Do you want to rest with me?"

"Later," he said, his voice thickening. "Then I'll sleep with you and afterwards we'll both *rest* a lot!"

They laughed.

"Coming down here," he said, "I stopped and looked at my shoes." He comically lifted his wet feet. "I got a crazy feeling remembering these were the same shoes I wore in a quiet little parish. I guess they have been through a lot."

"You have been through a lot," she said. "But perhaps you chose your fate. An old Italian proverb says, 'To be loved and needed always guides one's destiny.' Perhaps when all this is over you will go back to being a priest."

"Luciana, a priest doesn't do the things I've done!"

"How do you know? We have only had one type so far. Maybe in the future they will be different. Maybe the Church will be too."

The motor slowed into an idle. From above, Ivan Cohen began shouting.

"Trouble?" Luciana asked, afraid.

Matt grabbed up the light.

"I'm going with you!" she cried.

He held out his hand and together they turned down the passageway, then waded through the water. Matt went up the ladder first, lighting the way for her. On the deck above, Ivan was standing outside the wheelhouse, staring off to starboard. They looked in the same direction. There was not one but three ships.

The familiar British destroyer, recognizable by its lit-up superstructures, was very close to a new ship. The other, equally large, was off at a distance from them.

"I looked! There was one! I look again, three!" Ivan explained. "Why did the British call for more? They had enough to handle us!"

Matt turned toward the blackness at the bow. "Where's Capo Linaro? Are we there?"

"Five, six hundred meters off the beach. See? You don't feel any wind, do you? We're inside the cove of Capo Linaro!"

Matt checked his watch. "It's nearly eight. The refugees should be on their way by now."

Ivan put the engine in slow reverse so the ferry began backing out. He took the light from Matt, went up to the bow and knocked out the restraining block of wood on the anchor. The corroded chain clanked out and fed itself to the bottom.

Ivan returned, leaned into the wheelhouse and shut off the engine. Then he quickly trundled to the stern and let out that smaller anchor. The ship was safe now from being pulled in to the shore.

In the new silence, only the waves breaking on the nearby beach could be heard. Off in the distance, the three ships had not changed positions in their vigil.

"All we can do is wait." Luciana heard her voice, strange in the new quiet. "And hope Hannah gets the refugees here while it's still dark!"

Meister had the families in Ruffino's house ready. Nearly four hundred others stood in the darkened outer courtyard impatiently waiting to begin the trek to Capo Linaro, wherever that was. And there were two thousand men, women and children across Rome about to start out and rendezvous with them on the outskirts of Rome. That had been his plan, not to congregate until they were near the *campagna* area of Rome, the industrial section. There, there would be no one who would notice nearly three thousand pilgrims congregating in the night. But after that, who would take them to Capo Linaro if not Hannah?

He checked the grandmother clock in the marble entryway of the house and saw that it was forty minutes past the time of their departure now. Where was she? They could not wait much longer. In desperation, he had asked Leonardo, a resident of this ghetto, to go after her. But now Leonardo had been gone so long! What was happening? Intuitively, he feared something dreadful. Then he told himself to relax. He was used to expecting the worst.

Meister smiled encouragingly at the apprehensive children and women who were huddled amid their belongings on the floor in the passageway and went out toward the front door. He was intercepted by Leonardo.

"Where is she? Where is Hannah?" Meister asked, taking the man, who was a cobbler, by the arm and pulling him quickly out of earshot of those near him.

"There were police!" Leonardo blurted. "They brought a body out of the house!" The cobbler pulled at his black handlebar moustache. "It was *Signore* Nossi! Then they brought out Hannah!"

Meister laid a comforting hand on Leonardo's shoulder. "Say nothing," he advised him. "We need strength tonight, not grief."

The cobbler nodded that he understood. Klaus, the young boy on crutches, from Meister's rabbinical religion class, hurried up to them and tugged on Meister's sleeve.

"Later, Klaus," the Rabbi said, shaking him off.

"It is important!" the boy begged.

Meister bent impatiently to him. "What?"

"I went around the corner to the river"—he hurried to get it out, his eyes wide with terror—"I saw British soldiers!"

Meister eyed the youngster carefully. "Thank you," he said, "now run along and let me worry about those soldiers. Do you feel like you have enough strength to begin your march with us?"

"Of course, Rabbi!" Klaus said, "I am going to grow up in Palestine!" The boy crutched off and sat down with his father, who had helped him arrive here a few months ago.

"Now what?" Leonardo asked in a whisper. "If the British are there, then they are everywhere, all around you! Somehow, they know you are going to the boat tonight!"

Meister pulled at his white beard. What would his great model of virtue, Moses, have done in this situation? Nothing like this had ever occurred in the Bible!

Wracking his brain, Rabbi Meister said finally to Leonardo the cobbler, "Will you help us? There may be a way."

"We are Jews," Leonardo said. "And though we stay here and live in Rome while you go to Palestine, we are brothers!"

Rabbi Meister clasped his friend's arm. "Here's what I want you to do."

*   *   *

Major Wingate sat on the lorry's running board smoking his oval cigarette. There was no moon tonight, so it was very dark. Hard to tell who was near you until very close. But tonight was the night, he was sure. A message had been radioed from the decks of the H.M.S. *Jutland* that a *Signore* Marcheshi had been robbed of a ferry, destined, he claimed, to sail for Palestine. The Jews were going to try to migrate. And he was ready for them.

The lorry he was sitting on held twenty-three men. Two more lorries stood at opposite ends of the streets that criss-crossed this section of the ghetto, ready to spring into action at his word. But he would let the Jews march toward the sea before springing his trap. Then he would arrest them and ship them off to the places they had crawled away from. What was it that made every Jew want to go to that Godforsaken strip of desert called Palestine anyway?

The sergeant at arms stepped close, stamped his right foot and saluted. "Movement, sir. Coming this way."

This was it!

"Very good, sergeant. Tell the men at the other check-points to mount their lorries and circle around to the river here. They are to stay behind my lorry at all times, is that understood? No one is to bother the Jews until I give the order!"

"Yes, sir, Major Wingate!" the sergeant snapped. He turned and rushed off.

It was slow going, behind the refugees. The three trucks, bunched up, made numerous stops to allow them time to trudge ahead. The major kept his lead truck at a half-mile, but he could see the men, women and children, clad in their overcoats, bundles of clothing and pieces of small furniture on their shoulders, appear occasionally beneath streetlights as they marched along.

For three hours, the lorries crept along, their motors overheating. Even when the refugees had crossed the Tiber and had entered the highway toward the sea, Wingate parked and waited.

At precisely midnight, feeling the Jews had committed themselves sufficiently, he gave the orders to catch up and arrest them. Headlights snapped on, the motors growled as they roared off. In a little bit, they came upon the end of the marchers. The two lorries in the rear, by previous design, stopped to detain them. Major Wingate's truck shot past the Jews, their stunned faces illuminated in the headlights. When his lorry was at the front of the line, Wingate ordered the driver to halt and block the marchers' progress. The soldiers brought the leader to him.

"You are under arrest!" Major Wingate informed him. He grabbed a flashlight from the truck's cab and shone it in the man's face.

Leonardo rolled his handlebar moustache in his fingers. "Is there a law, Major," he asked, "against taking your family and friends out for an evening stroll?"

Meister tugged nervously at his beard as he walked. They were nearing the *campagna*, the industrial section of Rome. But that was as far as he had ever been. After the *campagna*, they would be lost! How would he lead nearly three thousand people to Capo Linaro? He kicked himself for not asking for more detailed directions from Leonardo. But in the rush to gather people to lure away the British soldiers, he had forgotten to get a map. Now he was on his own. And since they had waited for Leonardo to get a head start, they had less time than ever to find Capo Linaro!

Quickly, he checked over his shoulder. The line of refugees seemed to stretch behind him forever. But there was no sign of the British. It must mean Leonardo had succeeded!

He breathed a quick prayer to God in thanks, then begged Moses to give him vision, reminding himself that once Moses had breathed a similar prayer and led an exodus.

They passed the round, marble-pillared Temple of Vesta, then took the dirt road alongside the Circus Maximus, home of a thousand prowling cats, which led into the industrial *campagna* district. The Officine del Gas, its yard of storage tanks for the city, loomed into view.

Even though he knew the refugees were trying to walk quietly, hardly talking, he could hear them clomping like a big machine behind him. He wished his wife, Myra, had survived Buchenwald and were alive and here now. And for some crazy reason, he wished too that he had a baton or staff to lead their march openly through the night.

25.

The two ships that sat barely a half mile apart were the
U.S.S. *Pittsburgh* and H.M.S. *Jutland*. They had communi-
cated in semaphore until darkness; after that, in Morse and
radio. Captain Reginald Percy of the *Jutland* supplied the
information that the ferry had been reported stolen by a
certain Victor Marcheshi of Italian nationality, who claimed he
had been duped by Palestine-destined Jews. He also said that
a radio message had been sent to Major Wingate at Rome
HDQ to that effect and that the Jews' apprehension was
imminent.

Commander Stanton of the *Pittsburgh* thanked Percy for
"allowing them in" on the action, since this was essentially a
"Jewish immigration into Palestine issue." Stanton, however,
refused either to board the British vessel or to allow Percy on his
own ship. He was vague too as to why his United States
cruiser was there, replying only that "British law concerning
non-immigration to Palestine was not the issue, even though
we expect refugees to be involved."

Being in international waters, the British captain could do
little more than continue to be courteous to a fellow Ally,
even though he suspected that in addition to the Jewish question and the theft of this ferry there was something else afoot.
Too much attention had been paid to this limping little ferry

that had moored in the darkness off Capo Linaro. It was only when the Russian vessel, the minesweeper *K-13*, hove into view that he knew it was really something big.

On the American vessel, Commander George Stanton cooled his heels. There was nothing else to do. The orders had come from the State Department. The Vatican was running the show. At ten fifteen, he told Lieutenant Wood in his mild Georgian accent to awaken him if anything began happening. Leaving the bridge, he went below, took off his shoes, drank a glass of cranberry juice to relieve his chronic constipation and tried to sleep.

On the *K-13*, a special crew of four sailors stood on a gun parapet at forward bow. Half of them watched the British and American vessels with binoculars for any sign of movement. The other half, two young sailors who were brothers, stared through their lenses into the darkness that shrouded the shoreline three miles away. They were watching for any lights to denote movement of that vessel.

Above and behind the four sailors on a bulwark stood Igor Nerechenko. He was sipping his sixth glass of aquavit, his mind playing through this chess game for the thousandth time. Each time, he seemed satisfied at his conclusion. No matter what occurred tomorrow, there was one way to checkmate the Vatican. Make sure Matt Bowles stood trial! If that happened, if the Vatican or U.S. could not hide him away, the elections in Italy woud be theirs!

And in a cabin below the waterline, for the first time since the campaign in France, the horned one slept like a baby, snoring peacefully, dreaming dreams of death and gore and more to come on the morrow.

On the ferry, it was a quarter past midnight. Matt and Luciana were on the bow, huddled together for warmth, trying vainly to listen for any sounds or sights that would signal the arrival of the refugees.

"Fifteen minutes isn't too late," Matt said.

"But what if they're lost?"

Ivan came up behind them and squatted. "They're late," he said.

"We know." Luciana shivered. Matt put his arm around her.

They tried to listen again. But only the waves could be heard rolling in, dashing themselves on the broad beach.

The other groups of refugees who were supposed to meet them here were lost. This was the Officine del Gas, wasn't it? Rabbi Meister and his families were standing forlornly near a long ribbon of drab, paintless buildings, shadowed in dull streetlights. Not a car, not a soul was visible. The smell of spilled oil and rank chemicals filled his nostrils. He felt panic rise in his throat. Where *were* the others? *Had* something happened to them?!

He set down his rucksack, which contained a Torah, several books, clean underwear, a loaf of bread and some provolone. Motioning to his group to wait here, he went up the street toward the seven 50-foot-high gas tanks. The huge containers were silhouetted in the harsh light from their tall, specially built pylons.

Cautiously, he edged around one of the riveted and seamed monsters, circling its belly, feeling the cold metal with his fingers. As he came around, he saw that there was only another empty field. Its barrenness mocked him with its sparse growth of weeds.

"Oy vay!" he moaned.

"Arms up!" a voice commanded from behind him. "Now!"

Rabbi Meister spun, scared. A strong light found his eyes, blinding him. Then, he heard a rifle cock. He had heard that sound many times in Buchenwald. Every Saturday, the day of the Sabbath, the "expendables" were executed against the high cement wall.

"Don't shoot!" Rabbi Meister screamed. "For God's sake! Don't shoot now!"

Just before dawn, Matt awoke from a brief and much needed nap. He rubbed his aching leg and again swept the darkness in front of him. Nothing.

"What time is it?"

"Four thirty-eight," Ivan responded.

"Something terrible has happened," Luciana whispered.

"What time is sunrise?" He turned to Ivan, who was sitting behind them.

"I don't know. Five thirty, something like that."

"In a couple of minutes, it'll start to get light. Lend me the light." Ivan handed it to him. He slipped off his shoes and socks and gingerly took off his black trousers, peeling their blood-soaked material from the wound. Then he pulled his T-shirt over his head so that he wore only his shorts.

"What are you doing?" Luciana wanted to know in the darkness. "We would have heard or seen their lights."

"Maybe not." He dropped his T-shirt beside her. She caught the scent of his warmth and man-smell and pulled the shirt to her breasts. Clutching it to keep part of him there with her, she heard him ease into the water.

"I like him too," Ivan said, crouching down beside her. "In my whole life, I've never met anyone like him. It would be very hard for a woman not to fall in love with such a man."

In response, Luciana reached out and squeezed his ha acknowledging his compliment and the fact that he knew accepted.

Holding the lantern over his head, Matt swam with one arm. He could feel the tug of the undercurrent on his legs as he neared the beach. The salt water stung his wound. Then, in the roar of the surf, his feet touched bottom and he waded toward shore. He raised the light. All he could see was wet beach. He swung the light around and went up farther, his toes digging into flaky dry sand now.

God, he prayed. Let them be here. I know they're not. But, God . . .

And suddenly, his light struck little Ruth's face!

He lifted the lantern higher. A woman's, two men's. Faces, crouched on the sand, watching him quietly, catlike, apprehensive. And he began to sweep the light everywhere and there were eyes, luminous, waiting. Like the ones in his dreams! Faces from Omaha! Germans, American faces! Haunting . . .

And again he knew what it all meant. A sign of redemption! Faces that depended on him. Ones that he had saved!

In the light, the white-haired and bearded Rabbi Meister, his face strikingly set off by his black clothing, stepped forth from the crowd.

"Rabbi!" Matt cried. "The ship is out there, waiting! Why didn't you signal?"

"We only just arrived." The Rabbi seemed rattled. "We only this moment . . ."

Meister turned and babbled something to the crowd in Yiddish. As one, the beach roared in a thunder that startled Matt by its sound. He had not expected so many.

"This night," Rabbi Meister explained to Matt, "will be told in story again and again! For we were lost and God saved us." He pulled a bedraggled, bowlegged man into the reach of the light.

"Sylvester is a guard at Officine del Gas, our place of rendezvous. He arrested me, since I trespassed. Then he rounded up the others. That was his job. But his wife, who brought him his dinner, said, 'These are not thieves! They are lost, can't you see? Guide them!' And she took his rifle and his place among the tanks while Sylvester, praise God, showed us the way!"

26.

Ivan brought the ferry in so close the sand could be heard scraping its hull. When he had it reanchored, the refugees began to wade out. Lines of the strongest men stood shoulder to shoulder on the deck, pulling them up, helping settle them and stow their belongings. Matt personally set Ruth up on deck. She rewarded him with a shy, quick kiss.

The ship divided itself into camped families and friends. Sheets were strung above areas to provide tentlike shelters. Ivan had hammered the sign SCHILDKROTE lopsidedly on a wooden runner above the bow. The Turtle looked like a camp of tented nomads.

As the first light came up and the last of the refugees silently, in perfect order, had clambered aboard, Matt really saw them. Small children clinging to their mothers' hands, infants at breasts, old men and women hobbling together, and many, many cripples made Matt realize how varied were his passengers on this ferry.

There were women in scarves, clucking at their soaked children, changing them into dry clothes. Men in jackboots squatted, smoking, huddled beneath blankets, speaking in German, Austrian, Yugoslavian, Polish; northern Italians, their hair blond, features chiseled, jabbered excitedly, some telling jokes; the healthier children gamboled friskily. The mood was riotous, exuberant. All had suffered; all had been persecuted; now all were going home.

Ivan had organized what he called "the crew." These eleven able-bodied men were directing refugees to different areas, attempting to keep the rickety ferry evenly balanced as she was loaded and to keep them out of the way if the crew had to fight to keep the British from taking the ferry. Matt prayed it would not come to that.

By the time everyone was aboard, the old ferry had listed about ten degrees to port.

"What's the matter with the Turtle?" Matt asked Ivan as he stood near his wheelhouse, professorially blinking his eyes at the sight.

"We've loaded correctly. It's just that when they poured the cement inside to sink her, it settled unevenly. We were slightly lopsided before, now it's exaggerated."

"Can you steer her?"

"I'll have to compensate, especially on compass."

As the first meager gray light etched the horizon, Matt saw that the ferry had a sad, ungainly look as she wallowed against her anchors. Well, Turtle, he thought, you're all we have. And you must look beautiful to these people.

The crew announced that once underway they must all watch their footing when walking about on the decks. Since the workers at Civitavecchia had not had time to replace the guard railings, it would be easy to tumble into the sea. At that, the adults made the children sit close to them.

Luciana was at the stern, organizing a medical station, complete with pallets she had found on which the infirm might lie in some comfort. The news from Rabbi Meister about Hannah's death had driven her beyond grief. And as she had left Matt, dry-eyed, seemingly unmoved, he knew she had reached her limit and needed to be alone.

Ivan started the engine. His crew raised the anchors, hauling them up by hand. A song began somewhere at the bow and spread across the lower deck. Then it was picked up on the upper level and voices joined until they drowned out the knocks of the idling diesel altogether. The song was fast, rambunctious and joyous.

"What are they singing?" Matt asked Ivan as he joined him in his wheelhouse.

"Oh, it's sung at Passover, the time of our Exodus long ago. It's called *'Chad Gadyah,'* 'An Only Kid.' " Ivan drew in a quick breath and sang, "An only kid! An only kid! My father bought for two zuzim. An only kid! An only kid! Then came a cat and ate the kid. . . ."

"Sounds like a song I know called 'This Is the House That Jack Built.' " Matt hummed a few measures.

"That's it! Only in this song, the kid is Israel and the father is God and at the end, after even more troubles than *we* have had, there is divine justice." He shoved the gearbox into reverse.

The ferry backed up fifteen meters and hit something.

Ivan wove his way through the families to the port bow, knelt and peeked over. Matt was at his side.

"What happened?"

"We're . . . on a sandbar or something!"

"Can we get off?"

The singing was dying down now. Trouble had a strong scent.

"With one engine, I don't know," Ivan said tightly. He banged his thick, stubby fist against the gunwale in frustration. "Why now? Why!"

"Why, indeed?" Rabbi Meister commented. He pointed to sea. The third vessel, which had stood off from the other two, was bearing directly toward them, thick smoke churning from its single funnel. It was a fast ship and would be here in a few minutes.

All across the decks the singing drew to a stop. Many stood and gaped at the approaching ship. A wailing ensued among some women. Ivan leaped over an entire family and sprinted toward the wheelhouse. Revving the diesel to its full capacity, he drove the ship forward, then backwards in a violent rocking motion.

The *K-13* steamed at its full speed of twenty knots toward Capo Linaro. The order to attack had been given by Igor Nerechenko, Assistant Diplomatic Attaché from Rome. The attaché, with the strange-looking, semibald man, was standing outside just below Captain Litov, above the Russian mine-sweeper's forward four-inch gun turret. Litov pressed the alarm to send his men to battle stations. Then, looking down, he saw Nerechenko throw a bottle into the sea.

At the first burst of speed by the Russian vessel, the British captain, Reginald Percy, who had stayed on watch, picked up the ornate brass voice pipe and shouted, "Full steam ahead!"

Through the night, he had ordered the boilers of the H.M.S. *Jutland* be kept "cruise-ready," prepared at any moment to track the flight of the ferry. But the Russians getting the jump on him had come as a surprise. They must have detected some movement that his radar had not. Now, even though the Russians had a half-mile lead, he knew he would catch them. His only worry was that their minesweeper's draft was less than his destroyer's. So if the Russians went straight in, he would have to set down boats.

A lieutenant entered, allowing a surge of the cold morning air to invade the toasty glass-walled bridge house. He saluted and handed a folded paper to Percy, who glanced quickly at it. The Morse, in Allied code, was from the U.S.S. *Pittsburgh*.

> To Captain Reginald Percy, H.M.S. Jutland, we will not, as agreed to, interfere with British military operation in regard to illegal immigrants to Palestine. Would appreciate cooperation, however, in apprehension of one Matthew Bowles, criminal. Please signal by 'God Save the King' if agreed.
>
> Commander George William
> Stanton, U.S.S. Pittsburgh

"Where is the U.S. ship now?" Percy asked the helmsman who was on duty behind the big brass wheel.

"Three hundred meters off our larboard stern, sir!"

"So, they're following. Good." The captain turned to the lieutenant.

"Have teley send the first verse of 'God Save the King.' And inform Lieutenant Limbaugh to have a detachment of Royal Marines meet me at the port midships. We'll attack from there."

"Very good, sir!" The junior officer rushed out.

At the insistent sounding of the claxons on the decks below,

men scurried to their battle-ready stations, pulling on their
ear-muffler helmets, to protect themselves against the big-gun
blasts, and flak vests. Near the boarding ladder midships, a
thirty-two-foot motorized assault vehicle, complete with a
50-millimeter machine gun on its bow, swung down from a
crane and hovered fifteen feet above the water. The Royal
Marines in battle gear formed rank above and stood at the
railing in readiness. They had only pistols on their belts. But
in their hands, they held heavy leather shields and clubs
tipped with lead.

The *Schildkrote* was rocking so violently, the children
had flattened themselves on the warped decks. The grown-ups
nearest the nonexistent railings peered fearfully over the edge,
afraid at any moment they would tumble into the water. The
tall iron smokestack on the ferry quivered as the ship lurched
forward, then back, again and again. The approaching Russian ship was very close now, less than a half mile off port.
Many refugees were pointing at it and at the British ship
behind it.

In the wheelhouse, Luciana and Matt stood and watched
helplessly as Ivan revved the engine and shoved the gearbox
into forward for the hundredth time. The *Schildkrote* trembled.
Then suddenly there was a deep scraping on the bottom.

He slammed the gearbox into neutral, revved the engine
and swung the lever into reverse. The centrifugal clutch caught,
the propeller spun in the opposite direction and the ship
backed up. There was another horrible grinding sound from
Schildkrote's bowels. Then the ferry floated free.

"You did it!" Luciana screamed. Ivan slapped the throttle
in, rearranged the gears, revved the sole engine and turned
away from the beach.

It took a moment for the ferry's occupants to realize what
had happened. When they saw they were moving, their first
impulse was to resume their song. But the sight of the two
ships bearing down on them and the third one now tagging
behind strangled the music inside their throats.

"It's Russian!" Matt identified it. "A corvette or minesweeper, if it's like ours."

The Russian vessel was approaching fast, its slim prow
slicing through the salt water, hammer and sickle fluttering at

its crow's nest. A loudspeaker boomed out a strongly Slavic voice in Italian: "This is an order! Stop your engines now!"

"I thought our quarrel was with the British and Italians! Not the Russians!" Ivan groaned.

"Look above the gun in front." Matt pointed. "That man in the gray suit, the bald-headed fellow beside him?"

"What could they want?" Luciana asked.

"Whatever it is, we're not giving up to any Russians!" Ivan said.

He turned the wheel hard to port to head out to sea. The maneuver was immediately answered by a hail of machine gun bullets that splintered the wheelhouse. Refugees screamed. Matt pulled Luciana to the deck beside Ivan. Another blast of lead stitched the side of the ferry above the waterline.

"I think they mean business!" Luciana cried.

"So do we!" Ivan bellowed. He twisted the wheel harder. The ferry was now on a collision course with the Russian vessel.

"Ivan, don't be crazy!" Luciana screamed. She reached up to the wheel to change course. Matt caught her hands.

The refugees began crying out. Many flattened themselves for the impact. But the Russian ship slicing head-on broke off at a hundred meters. The Russians had declined the suicidal move.

The *K-13* swung around hard and raced up to a position off the ferry's port stern. The British destroyer steamed, also, abreast of the ferry. The third ship stayed in its wake.

"That one's American!" Luciana announced. "U.S.S. *Pittsburgh*! But why are they here?"

"Probably watching out for the Vatican's interests," Matt guessed.

"And therefore, Italy's, huh?" Ivan quipped.

A gray motorboat suddenly shot around the bow of the H.M.S. *Jutland*. Soldiers inside braced for an assault.

"Here come the Limeys," Ivan observed.

Another loudspeaker on the British destroyer announced: "You are aboard a stolen vessel and are all illegal passengers bound for the territorial waters of Palestine! Our personnel will immediately board your ship. Do not resist. I repeat: Do not resist!"

Ivan yanked the throttle stem out as far as it could go. The engine below began to labor.

The speedboat full of the British marines pulled alongside the ferry. Three of them managed to leap up on the low port gunwale.

"Smother them! Disarm them!" Ivan cried. Matt raced toward the disturbance. But Ivan's crew charged the three marines. They fell back into the sea, still thrashing their leaded clubs. Several of the crew slumped, their heads bleeding.

Matt stood ready with the crew as the assault boat again charged the ferry. But this time, as the remaining five marines scrambled up the low side of the *Schildkrote*, not only the crew but a maddened mass of refugees rushed the flailing marines. Several refugees fell as the savagely swinging clubs found their marks. A marine swung his leaded club at Matt's legs, barely missing the already injured one. Matt swiveled and escaped the blow and got in one of his own.

He stepped back from the fallen marine to see refugees swarm him and pitch him over. It was then he heard his name called in warning. Matt ducked as another Royal Marine swung his leaded club at his head. He heard the club strike someone behind him. The young marine lowered his leather shield and stood staring, his eyes filled with horror. Matt turned.

There, lying like a broken doll, was little Ruth. Her sack of belongings had opened and three bright-colored little garments lay strewn around her. She lay there, amidst ironically gay colors.

The marine, too overcome to defend himself, was pitched overboard.

Matt knelt beside Ruth. The fragile little waif opened her big brown eyes. They were full of fear. "I came to help you," she said. She was clutching her chest.

Luciana knelt quickly, gently pried the child's hands away from her dress front and looked in at the wound. The sap had struck the little child's heart. Matt saw Luciana's dismay

"You saved my life," Matt thanked Ruth. He was trying to smile. "You're very brave."

Her cheeks were pale, her eyes growing whiter.

"I don't want to die, Father. . . ."

"You're going to meet God," Matt whispered to her. "He loves you very much. He's waiting for you."

"Will . . . I go into the Promised Land?"

Matt nodded, too overcome to answer.

"Father . . ." Ruth managed, her lips ashen, "may . . . I hold your hand as I die?"

Luciana turned away and began to sob.

Matt took Ruth's slim hand and gazed into her dimming wide eyes. He began to recite the Absolution he had given a thousand times before. "*Ego te absolvo* . . ." He stopped. This child did not need absolving of anything.

"In the name of God the almighty Father who created you, in the name of Jesus Christ, Son of the living God, who suffered for you, in the name of the Holy Spirit who was poured out upon you . . . go forth, may you live in peace this day. May your home be with God in Zion. . . ."

He choked on his words as she died.

A hurt so bad inside made him feel like he was coming apart. He bent and kissed her tiny face and closed her eyes.

Two refugee women took away the body to the place they were laying others. Matt straightened. The crowd that had encircled him peeled off, sorrowful eyes downcast. The battle was over. Luciana was standing behind him, softly weeping. Near her, several women tended one of the wounded crew whose head was bleeding profusely. A woman nearby was moaning, clutching her husband's split-open jaw. Somewhere a child cried noisily, terrified.

Matt pulled Luciana away.

"We've got to stop. This can't go on!" she exploded, her voice shaking.

"No!" he shouted fiercely. "We've come too far now! It won't end like this!" He pushed past her toward the wheelhouse.

"How far out are we?" Luciana heard Matt ask Ivan as she rushed up beside him.

"A mile, maybe two!"

"Keep going! We've got to make international waters!"

Ivan nodded grimly, cramping the wheel tighter to port, aiming for the open sea. Meanwhile, the British had left the Russian ship on the port and come up on the starboard. It swung a heavily armored bow at them, aiming midships for the *Schildkrote*.

"They're going to ram us!" Luciana cried.

Ivan barked orders to his crew. Immediately, voices in Yiddish, German, Austrian, Yugoslavian and Italian passed the warning. As the refugees flattened themselves, the *Jutland* crashed heavily into the Turtle, putting a three-foot dent in her lower deck. The ferry skidded sideways, nearly hitting the Russian vessel. The wheel spun out of Ivan's hands. The destroyer swung parallel so that it now ran close beside. Sailors on its deck tossed down tear-gas bombs. But infuriated refugees began picking them up and flinging them back up at the sailors.

Running side by side with the ferry, the destroyer disgorged more Royal British Marines, who swung by ropes onto the top deck. The crew, trying desperately to stop them, managed to throw some of the marines off, but greater numbers swung onto the ferry and took up the battle. Matt scrambled up the ladder to the top deck. Many refugees followed him. They were brandishing hammers, pieces of pipe, anything heavy that had been left on the ferry's decks.

In the melee, the Russian vessel moved closer, sandwiching the ferry between itself and the destroyer.

A contingent of Russian sailors jumped onto the lower deck. Some held the refugees at bay with submachine guns, while others lashed the two vessels together with heavy hawsers. Then a man in a gray suit leaped from the minesweeper onto the cleared deck of the *Schildkrote*, followed by a man with a peculiar haircut. Two sailors with flash cameras stood with them.

Almost immediately, the four Russians split up, making their way among the seated refugees, who were held helpless by machine guns.

From the wheelhouse, Luciana had spotted them board. Instinctively, she knew they were searching for Matt. Dropping down, she crawled toward the ladder to warn him.

Outside the bridge of the American vessel, Monsignor Helmut Kass had been quietly observing the action with the commander's binoculars. But as soon as he saw the Russians board the ferry, he turned to the three men with him: Hans Fullmer, Mankowsky, and Palmo. All of them huddled against the stiff wind.

"I'm sure the Russians are after Bowles," he said. "It is imperative they do not take him!"

"Yes, Monsignor!" the albino saluted.

Mankowsky leaned down to Kass and asked, "Can I go too, Monsignor? Matthew is a friend of mine."

"That is why you were brought, Father," Kass said. "Do not wear anything priestly. Hurry!"

The gorilla opened his overcoat to reveal that he had already changed to a sweater and slacks. He swung his huge frame down the iron ladder after the albino.

On the lower deck, he followed Fullmer's example by stripping off his black wool overcoat. A contingent of U.S. Marines stood ready beside a motorized rubber boat. Commander Stanton watched them board.

As Fullmer entered the assault boat, he turned to Mankowsky and said, "I am going on the ferry first, do you understand? Wait until I give the signal, then bring these marines on board!" He was pulling on his black gloves.

On the upper deck, Luciana worked her way through heavy fighting until she reached Matt. He was grappling with a Royal Marine. He managed to wrench the English soldier's baton away by grasping his middle finger and bending it backwards.

"*Matteo!*" she cried out.

"Get out of here!" he shouted.

"No, follow me. The Russians are on board. They are looking for you!"

Matt hesitated, then noted with satisfaction that the battle up here was going against the British. They were being swarmed by refugees. He followed Luciana down the ladder and onto the main deck and saw that Nerechenko and his Russians had worked their way to the stern and were ripping apart tents, searching.

But as Matt and Luciana slipped down the ladder behind the wheelhouse and into the labyrinth of the hold, Nerechenko spotted them. He left the sailors and photographers and alone went down that ladder also.

Stepping into the sloshing water, he trailed them unseen. Reaching beneath his left armpit, he withdrew the Beretta from its holster.

The light was dim, but enough sunlight filtered through the portholes to guide him. He padded like a big cat toward the room he had seen them enter.

Pausing outside the door, he waited until he heard their voices in normal conversation, then he pushed the door open and leveled the Beretta. The woman spun at the intrusion, but the priest looked up calmly, then at the weapon.

Nerechenko tightened his grip on the snub-nosed pistol.

"My English not good," he said. "I not hurt you, you do what I say." He entered the room, his wide back flush with the doorjamb.

"What do you want?" Luciana asked him in Italian.

"Ah," the Soviet said. "I forgot you are Italian. So blond, almost White Russian in appearance. I want you both to come with me."

"What for?" Luciana demanded.

The Russian waved the gun. "We have not time." He resorted again to English. "Come!"

There was a gunshot behind the bulky man and he pitched forward. Luciana was frozen in surprise.

Matt bent quickly, picked up the Russian's weapon and peered out the open door.

The albino was standing outside, his 9-millimeter Mauser smoking in his gloved hand. Fullmer raised the gun and pointed it at Matt.

"Please drop your weapon."

Matt dropped the gun to the metal floor. The albino frowned when he saw Luciana emerge behind him. "Too bad," he said, "now there will have to be two deaths."

"Why do you want to kill us?" Luciana wondered. "The Vatican can't shoot us for a robbery!"

The albino snickered softly at her ignorance. "The Vatican has nothing to do with it. With Nerechenko gone, I am free. No one but him knew my identity. Now I end your threat to the Vatican and I shall be a hero!"

"You're the leak!" Matt guessed. "That's how the Commies knew about everything!"

"*Ja,*" Fullmer said. "And you, you are a foolish man to do all this. The joke is on you, Father Bowles! Did you think the Vatican really kept the Jews' money? I burned their money myself! The Vatican is innocent!"

"Is it?" Matt asked.

The albino's gloved finger worked nervously at the trigger.

He took a cautious step backwards. "Please walk ahead of me. The light is not good here. You wish clean shots, *ja*?"

Matt was tempted to lunge. But the chances were the albino could squeeze off one. And one would be enough for Luciana. So, he started out submissively, by Luciana's side. They went down the cabinway, and when they were near the ladder, Fullmer ordered, "*Halt!*"

Keeping them covered, he slipped past them and edged near the ladder. But as he looked up, he froze and backed away, his captives forgotten.

Brown shoes, then an outstretched sawed-off shotgun appeared. Matt pulled Luciana into the nearest cabin. He eased his head back out into the passageway.

The albino continued to back off, his gun held ready.

Cornos kept coming down, revealing himself.

"Hello, Red Woman."

"How could you . . . Nerechenko lied! He told!"

"No, little spy," Cornos nearly giggled. "I saw you leave that trattoria near the Vatican that night. Nerechenko never knew."

The horned one stepped off the ladder ir ʰe water, the shotgun inches from the albino's face.

"Where is Nerechenko?"

Matt could see the albino's hand massage thᴇ 't of his pistol.

Cornos made a clucking sound as if in pity. Then deliberately, Matt thought, he dropped his eyes, giving the albino the impression that this was the chance he had been waiting for. But the same instant that the tip of Fullmer's gun rose, the bald-headed man pulled the trigger.

The blast erased the face of the Vatican agent.

The albino's nearly headless body pitched backwards into the dirty water. Cornos reloaded. He poked Fullmer, but there was no movement. Matt ducked back inside.

The man with the horns now peered up the hallway. Then he turned left and went down the metal alley that crossed the ship laterally.

Matt listened but heard nothing. As carefully as he could, he stuck his head out. The hallway was empty. He signaled to Luciana to follow him.

"We've got to get back up that ladder!" he whispered.

"No, *Matteo!*" She grabbed his hand.

"There's no other way. Wait till I get to the ladder. Then come after me."

His sodden shoes squished sloppily on the dry floor, then quieted as he entered the water. Ahead, the albino floated near the ladder. Keeping his back against the rusted metal wall, Matt inched forward.

Fearfully, Luciana watched his movements. Suddenly, she felt eyes on her back. She turned and there was the horned one, feet planted squarely in the hallway. He had circled the passageway and come out behind them!

She turned to yell at Matt. But a heavily muscled arm twisted like a rope around her neck. She felt her feet leave the riveted steel floor. In desperation, she kicked back until she connected with his shin.

"Ow!" Cornos muttered.

Matt spun at the voice. The horned one aimed the shotgun. Matt raised his hands. Cornos released Luciana. She fell to her knees, then scrambled up and ran to Matt.

"You all right?" he asked her. She was trying to get her breath and could say nothing. The horned one advanced through the water, grunted something in thick Italian and gestured with his *lupara*.

"He wants . . . us to go up," Luciana said.

"He's the boss."

Luciana climbed the ladder first, then Cornos signaled for Matt to ascend. Pulling himself up the first few rungs, Matt felt the hard metal of the shotgun press against his back. Even as he swung out above, there was no chance for escape. The shotgun stayed steadily on him as the bald-headed assassin climbed up onto the main deck.

There, Matt saw that the Russians, with their special brand of brutality, had done what the British in their more humane methods could not. The Soviet sailors and their machine guns had subdued the entire ferry. Refugees sat sullen, unmoving. To Matt's surprise, halfway to the stern, five U.S. Marines, their weapons leveled, stood, eyeing the Russians.

Inside the wheelhouse, Ivan had stopped the engine and was glaring fiercely. The ship was dead in the water.

At Cornos's signal, a Russian sailor crept up behind Ivan and clubbed him with the butt of his Khalishnikov. As Ivan collapsed to the floor, the sailor leveled the submachine gun and fired into the controls. Metal, glass and wood exploded into the air. The compass, gearbox and helm wheel had been destroyed.

Cornos now barked a new order and pulled Luciana away. Two sailors with professional-size Hasselblads came forward and trained them on Matt. He stood there, bewildered, as a dozen flashbulbs exploded in his eyes. Then the photography stopped.

"You are no use to us anymore," Cornos said. "So now I do things my way." He cocked the hammer of his *lupara*.

Luciana screamed.

A huge form hurtled itself out of the pack of refugees into Cornos. The *lupara* flew up, discharging as it landed in the wheelhouse. Straddling the assassin, Mankowsky drove his two gargantuan fists into Cornos's face. The horned one's nose broke, his lips split in a gush of blood. He grabbed for the gorilla's throat, but the giant swatted his arms away and sent another fist to his mouth.

Recovering from the surprise attack, two Russians started for the gorilla. Matt tackled one, but the other brought the butt of his machine gun down on Mankowsky's head. The gorilla turned from his ministrations to Cornos and back-handed the sailor, who tumbled into a group of refugees. They kicked him until he blacked out.

Other Russians swarmed Mankowsky and Matt. They pinned them flat on their backs, their Khalishnikov's quarter-sized gun barrels prepared to consign them to God's mercy.

"Nyet!" a powerful voice boomed.

The sailors looked up, recognizing the familiar voice.

Igor Nerechenko, clutching a freely bleeding stomach wound, lumbered up the ladder onto the deck. Luciana rushed to Matt. The gorilla looked at his bloody hands as if he were just now realizing what he had done.

"Apologies," Nerechenko said in English, "all this unnecessary."

He uttered a few sharp phrases and the Russians lowered their weapons and retreated toward the starboard side, toward their waiting ship. Then he asked something from the photographers and when they answered affirmatively, he waved them away too. He turned wearily and stared at Cornos, who lay unconscious on the deck of the ship, his cheekbones smashed, his face pulverized.

"Is alive?" Nerechenko asked.

Matt felt for the pulse. "Barely."

"Does not matter," the Russian said. "Does not understand both our days over. A politician's ways happen now. Ferragamo's way. I go home too." He sighed, winced as a wave of pain swept through his side. The blood was seeping even through his coat. He gestured at Cornos, and two of the Soviets who were standing at the starboard gunwale ran and picked up the horned one. They lifted him under the arms and dragged him away. As they passed, the refugees spat on the assassin.

Nerechenko started toward his countrymen, walking in great pain, but striving to hide it. He was helped aboard the *K-13* by a dozen waiting hands. Then the other Soviets disembarked too and lines were cast off. The solid white minesweeper swung away to the sea.

Luciana bent and examined a prostrate but conscious Ivan. She said something to several nearby women. They stood and began to minister to his head wound.

"Thanks," Matt told the gorilla as he helped him up.

The gorilla looked at Matt. "I know why you did all this now. I understand, Matthew. We owed these people this."

Luciana was eyeing the Russian vessel as it moved off. "Is that all they wanted?" she asked Matt. "Pictures?"

"If I'm right, that's all they need."

The distant speakers of the American vessel cut across the water suddenly. "This is Commander George Stanton, U.S.S. *Pittsburgh*," they heard the twangy voice announce. "Sergeant Jessup, escort Matthew Bowles to our ship!"

The U.S. Marines, having received their command, broke from their protective circle formation and crossed toward the wheelhouse.

"What do you want him for?" Luciana shouted at them as they converged. "We all did this! Take us all!" She kicked at them.

"Luciana," Matt said, grabbing her, "maybe I can talk to them. They're Americans."

"Don't trust them!" she said, alarmed.

"What choice do we have? The ferry is without power. And Palestine is a long way off."

"Oh, *Matteo*, no!" She flung her arms around his neck. The gorilla looked away, embarrassed.

"Willie," Matt said to his friend, "will you watch over Luciana?"

She clung to him a moment longer, then dropped her arms to her sides. Tears were sliding over her cheekbones. *"Arrivederci,"* she whispered as he walked away between the marines.

Matt was transferred by pulley sling to the British destroyer. From there, he was walked a hundred feet by armed guard across that vessel and lowered into a waiting American boat. The craft chugged back to the *Pittsburgh*'s side, where he climbed up a rope ladder to that deck.

A lieutenant searched him for weapons and brought him into the captain's elevator. They rose to the third deck and entered the briefing room.

The strategy room was dark, lined with wood panels. Single spots lit up the tables and wall maps. It took Matt's eyes a moment to adjust. Then he saw that Monsignor Kass was sitting between two officers.

"Sit down, Father Bowles," Kass said. "This is Captain Reginald Percy of H.M.S. *Jutland* and Commander George Stanton of this ship, the U.S.S. *Pittsburgh*." Neither officer made any move to shake Matt's hand, so he sat down, facing the three men.

"You are now our prisoner," Kass explained. "You can come peacefully or by force, that is up to you. I have no interest in the others who participated in the robbery."

"And the boatload of refugees?"

"That also does not concern me."

"It should. Because they're going to be part of our bargain."

"Bargain, Father?" Kass seemed tired. "There is no bargain possible."

"Has to be. You see, Monsignor, the Russians took my pictures. So you can't sweep this whole thing under the rug now. I'm sure you'd like me on your side."

The short-cropped prelate's shoulders rose imperceptibly and tightened. "I see," he said. "What do you want, Father?"

"The ferry's without an engine. Not much food, fuel or water either. Let this American ship tow her across to France into a harbor where she can get repairs and supplies. It would be," Matt paused poignantly, "a most charitable act."

"And if we do this thing, you will cooperate with us . . . totally? In every way?"

"I will."

"Very well, Father." He turned to Commander Stanton. "Do you have any problems with that?"

"I'm sure it can be arranged to help that little ferry a few hundred miles," Stanton allowed in his soft southern voice. "But I cannot speak for our British allies."

Percy puffed thoughtfully on his pipe a moment, then decided, "It doesn't matter really. Our duty is to track and sink any vessel trying to land displaced persons in the restricted land of Palestine. But since we customarily do it within sight of that country's shore, we can wait." He got up, stiffly shook Stanton's hand and left.

"I hold you forever to your promise," Kass told Matt. Then he stood and went toward the door. "Oh, Father, you don't by any chance know what happened to our man, Hans Fullmer?"

"I'm afraid he is dead."

"And Father Mankowsky?"

"He's staying on the ferry."

"I see." Sourly, Kass pushed out of the door.

Matt went out to the open air and put his hands on the metal railing. Commander Stanton stood beside him. The U.S.S. *Pittsburgh* was getting underway; the British destroyer was pulling off too. The ferry was receding in the distance, alone now, wallowing, ungainly. A small island, overcrowded with people.

"Why aren't we towing the ferry?" Matt asked.

"Have to let off our honored guests first," the commander joked. "We'll come right back. Won't take but an hour to land 'em. Don't worry, the people on the ferry will be all right. I dispatched some of my men with radios."

The wind was picking up as the ship dove forward into the sea, toward shore. The ferry was growing smaller. It looked very lonely out there in the middle of the swells.

Matt could hear Luciana whisper, *"Arrivederci."*

27.

Joining the two wings of the Vatican museums was a five-story stone tower. It was called the Wind Tower and had for centuries served as the Vatican prison.

Inside, it was cold, damp and windy. Matt stood in the priest's cassock that had been given him and looked out the window with its hand-hammered steel bars in the shape of a cross. From this vantage point, he could see over and beyond the Vatican wall, down the long Via della Conciliazione with its burning gas lanterns atop their marble columns. Less than a month ago, he had guided an airplane down its striplike corridor.

On the buildings that faced Via della Conciliazione, he could see the posters, like postage stamps from this distance, glued to every wall. On each, he had been told by Amelio, his Vatican jailer, was his photo. Below each photo, it said, IMPRISONED! FATHER MATTHEW BOWLES, A ROMAN CATHOLIC PRIEST FROM AMERICA! HE TRIED TO STEAL BACK THE MONEY HE SMUGGLED IN FOR THE VATICAN'S CHRISTIAN DEMOCRATS!

L'Unità, the Communists' newspaper, had dedicated virtually its entire front page to "Bowles's criminal career," stating how he stole "millions of dollars shipped to Italy from the United States to fix Italian elections." The newspaper also ran installments that accused the Vatican and Alcide de

Gasperi of engaging in large-scale contraband of foreign currencies and stated as well that Pope Pius XII himself had knowledge of many wartime atrocities committed by the Nazis. Only yesterday, the headline in *L'Unità* had screamed, P. PIUS SLEPT WHILE 6 MILLION DIED! Amelio said that for the first time, Italians seemed to be taking *L'Unità* seriously.

Matt turned away from the window. Around him were the same stone walls, viscious with green lichen, that he had stared at for over two weeks now. The time seemed interminable. Yet he was keeping his hopes up. He had been informed that Monsignor Kass might ship him home to New York to save the Vatican from further embarrassment. Of course, he would be defrocked. But that did not matter any longer.

He was sure Luciana would be waiting for him. Somewhere . . .

Where are you now, Luciana? Have Ivan and Willie brought you and your precious cargo safely to port? Are you on your way to Palestine? With all the news of the events that were taking place here in Rome, he had been told nothing whatsoever about the ferry. Not even Cardinal Spellman, his sole outside visitor, would divulge a word.

Six hours after Matt's incarceration, Francis Cardinal Spellman had breathlessly arrived in Rome. Exhausted from the long flight from Tokyo, he was in a supremely foul mood.

"If only I could have come here sooner!" he moaned as he stood over Matt, who was sitting on his bunk. "I might have been able to talk some sense into your thick skull!"

He paced back and forth, his small frame shaking in rage beneath his black suit, red satin rabat and gold pectoral cross.

"Why didn't you call me, man?" He suddenly wheeled on Matt. "*I* would have replaced that money!"

"I tried to, Eminence," Matt told the truth. "But then there just wasn't time."

"You've upset the applecart, boyo. And no matter what happens here in Italy, win or lose, I'll see to it you never say another Mass, hear a Confession or baptize a baby for the rest of your born days! You let me down! You failed our Church! And now you're going to get your desserts! Do you have anything to say in your defense? Speak up!"

"Nothing, Eminence," Matt said, "except I followed my . . . conscience."

The word formed on the Cardinal's lips, but he couldn't speak it. "Your con . . . con . . . your . . . I don't believe it! You committed crimes, took the law into your own hands, robbed our Holy Mother Church, then proceeded to bungle everything so badly you may also have the deaths of nearly three thousand people on your hands, and you sit there and tell me you followed your con . . . CONscience?"

In total exasperation, the Cardinal swung away and stormed from the cell, muttering, "This will be the ruination of the Church!"

That had been sixteen days ago. Now, as Matt stood in his cell, his second visitor arrived.

The door opened and Sister Pasqualina came in, glanced about the room, then went back out. In a moment, a white-robed Pope Pius, bundled against the chill in a white ermine fur coat, entered. He kept his hands in the coat's pockets.

"Kneel and pay homage to your Pontiff!" Pasqualina ordered Matt.

Instead, Matt stared stubbornly at his scuffed once-black shoes. "I cannot, since I am no longer able to be the Holy Father's subject," he explained.

Pope Pius sighed, "My son, we fear we have misunderstood one another. We know you are disappointed we did not help your cause. But you must understand, our duty is to our Church. I will speak as a man momentarily. Since my birth, I was designed to be nothing except for my Church. I have a mother, I have no mother. I am Italian, yet I have no country. Like you, Father, I left everything on the floor of that church in which I prostrated myself at ordination. I have no past, no present, no future. No family except the Church. That is the way it should be for both of us. The way it *must* be. It is the most singular truth in both our lives." He paused, waiting to see if Matt would respond. "Come now. Confess and beg God's forgiveness. Know that we also forgive you. All of this has been extremely unfortunate."

Matt nodded. "Yes, it has, Holiness."

"Bowles," Pope Pius said in exasperation, his dark eyes blinking behind round gold-rimmed glasses. "We pray that some day you realize the tremendous harm you caused here.

We pray you return to our fold." Pius raised his Papal hand to bless Matt, but he was yet looking down at his shoes. He lowered his hand and left the room.

"Tsking" disapprovingly, Pasqualina picked up the hem of the Holy Father's white robe so it would not scrape along the dirty stone floor.

Almost immediately, Monsignor Kass entered. Matt looked up in anticipation. He had been waiting over two weeks to hear anything. With Kass were two men. One was tall, dignified, in a double-breasted dark blue suit, silk shirt and pin-striped tie. Matt recognized Alcide de Gasperi from the thousands of Christian Democrat posters. The other man, with shorter, thinning gray hair, looked undone. He was Myron Taylor, U.S. Ambassador to the Vatican.

"Father Bowles," Taylor began, "this is bad. You've upset our plans here. President Truman is furious at this whole mess! I don't know what to tell him. This involves the security of the United States. If we lose Italy to the Commies, we lose Europe!"

Matt stared at his shoes again.

"Bowles," Kass said, "this is *Presidente* Alcide de Gasperi. He wishes to ask you a few questions."

"*Signore*." De Gasperi spoke stiffly, his voice surprisingly squeaky for his size. He appeared not to know how to address Matt. "Sir, I wish to ask you, did you do this thing for the Communists or strictly as a favor to the Jews?"

"I'm an American, not a Commie," Matt said.

De Gasperi gave a quick look at Taylor, then asked, "Did you strike a deal with a man named Ferragamo, my opponent in the elections? Or with a Russian, Nerechenko? Were you paid to do this to us? Why are you trying to destroy my party?" His voice had risen throughout these questions.

Matt said nothing.

"Bowles," Kass explained, "this is for your own good. We need to construct a defense for you."

"Defense for what?"

"We have just received word from the Palace of Justice," Myron Taylor said, "that the crime you committed against the Vatican was also against the country of Italy. You crossed into their territory, stole a ship and shot its owner. The Communists have demanded a trial. The people are in an uproar, so . . .''

"So, I go on trial?"

"Before the entire Italian nation!" De Gasperi snorted bitterly. "Word also came that the Supreme Court will hear the trial *before* the elections! Clever work by your Communists!"

"Bowles," Kass said, "this is out of the Vatican's hands now. We will do what we can. Tomorrow, you shall meet with lawyers."

"Monsignor," Matt said quickly, "have you heard anything about the ferry?"

"I have been too busy," Kass said. "But it seems to me there was something about them arriving in France and being stranded there." He crossed to the door with De Gasperi and Taylor. "Awhile ago, I gave you some advice," he reminded Matt. "I told you Luciana Spoleto was trouble. If only you had listened, you would be a happy monsignor in the United States . . . and we would have easily won Italy."

Matt heard the door slam shut, then the keys jangled as the lock was turned. He went to the window and wrapped his hands tightly around the iron bars. Far out, he could see a bus passing. There was a drop of a hundred feet to the Courtyard of the Belvedere below. He looked down at the squat little fountain and remembered Luciana in her bishop's costume running with Ruffino toward the far wall. If he could have squeezed through the bars, he would have jumped now.

Then from far off, he heard voices singing. In the near distance, at the entrance to St. Peter's Square, there was a serpentine line of the faithful, their candles glowing in the waning evening, their line undulating toward the basilica. He listened to the melody fading in and out as the winds distorted it.

"Silent night. Holy night . . . is calm . . .''

It was the night before Christmas. He had lost track of time.

He closed his eyes and saw the faces on the ship and felt their hope. Little Ruth. Klaus. Marie Schollander. Meister, Ivan, the gorilla. Luciana. He prayed they were all right. The ferry underway on distant waters to the Promised Land. Their song of deliverance.

Bells began tolling across Rome. Melodious cacophony. Christmas Eve. Masses beginning. Solemn High Mass candles lit. Come worship the child. The child is born. We are reborn. The world will be repurchased.

And he understood then that every action or lack of one brings a reaction because everyone is connected. And all are responsible for one another, everyone a brother on this earth.

"Merry Christmas!" he congratulated himself.

Redeemed through others.

"Merry Christmas, Luciana!"

And he began to sing "Silent Night" raucously at the top of his lungs, his voice drowning out the pealing bells of the thousand churches in Rome.

28.

He automatically awoke as always at six A.M. For a moment, he lay there in his prison-striped pajamas with their black horizontal bars against gray and made himself concentrate on the work he would do in the laundry. Soaps had to be mixed, bleaches readied, drying lines prepared. It was an important job. It had taken him a long time to be appointed head of laundry. It meant first in line, first choices at meals, esteem among the thousand inmates at Regina Coeli and more freedom than most had.

The first sign of sunshine entered his six-by-ten cell in a thin ray. Regina Coeli, normally only a city jail, had been his prison home by special arrangement. He had been taken out of the world's eye, someone had remarked.

He could hear the rumbling snores of Luigi Bistari, his newest roommate, above him. How many did Luigi make? Twenty? Thirty? Eleven years was a long time. A lot of men had passed through.

But it would be nine more years before he would be released from Regina Coeli and allowed to proceed along life's journey. Nine more years with Luciana out of reach. . . . He tried not to think about it.

He heard a thrush begin to sing outside his window bars. He had pulled himself up, seen that bird. Thrushes look like little sparrows.

Pope Pius had died two weeks ago. He had read that in the tattered weekly newspaper, *Messaggero*, which was eagerly passed from hand to hand in the prison. The Pontiff had suffered a massive stroke on October 14 at Castel Gandolfo, the Papal retreat seventeen miles from Rome, used during the hot months of the year. Pius had expressed the wish to be embalmed by a new method. But the process had failed. One of the prisoners was later told by a visitor that during Pius's funeral inside St. Peter's Basilica, two Swiss Guards and an Irish diplomat fainted at the overwhelming odor emanating from his funeral bier. The traditional *Novendiali*, nine days of mourning, was cut short. Pius was buried after three.

The paper said that Monsignor Helmut Kass and Sister Pasqualina had quietly departed. Kass had returned to his homeland of Germany to await his new orders from whoever would be elected Pope; Pasqualina, to Bavaria and her order of sisters.

The "kingdom" of Pope Pius was over. And with it, Matt hoped, an epoch of power never to be seen again. Not since the days of the pope-warriors had a pontiff meddled in so many temporal areas. Pius's opposition to Communism had been extreme and finally unnecessary. An A-bomb to kill a rat, some said.

In the elections of January 1948, Alcide de Gasperi had easily won as *Presidente*, but the Communists had managed to win two seats in Parliament. So later in the year, at Pius's insistence, another special set of elections had taken place. This time, the Reds were totally trounced. But somehow this made them the official underdogs in Italy. And though the Communist Party in Italy did not manage to win a single seat in Parliament again, De Gasperi soon found he could not govern without their cooperation.

Giuseppe Ferragamo had stumbled onto a successful new career. The Communist Party candidate had been elected president of the United Trade Unions of Italy. So De Gasperi was forced to make deals with Ferragamo to keep Italy's economy stable. He never told Pius about this arrangement.

The Pope always thought he had completely obliterated the Red Menace camped at his doorstep.

Matt had heard from Mankowsky in the United States that the huge Vatican banking operation had, as planned, been converted quietly into dummy-fronted Italian banks. But before that had been accomplished, another scandal concerning money had rocked the Vatican. Monsignor Guido Offeri had been forced to resign because he had borrowed money for private speculation from a wealthy Italian industrialist. He had done so on Vatican stationery, and the industrialist, Gararpo Rossino, had thought he was lending money to the Holy Father. Offeri was hustled off to a monastery.

But again, the Communist press had got wind of it and made a heyday of it, with their bill posters. In a clipping Mankowsky had sent him, *Time* had reported: "Apparently the Communists are not the only people in Italy making votes for the Reds."

The inmates here joked that when a Roman saw a churchman coming, he should grab his genitals: "Hold on tight so the Vatican won't take them too!"

Matt was finishing shaving when he heard his name called.

Looking up from his tiny mirror, he saw that the jailer for this section was standing outside the bars with a sergeant in the Swiss Guard, wearing the traditional Michelangelo-created uniform of yellow, blue and red stripes.

"*Signore* Bowles?"

"That's me," Matt said.

"Pope John wishes to see you."

Stunned, Matt wiped the remaining cream off his face with his allotted towel. The new Pope wished to see him? Suddenly, he realized he had paid no attention to the entire election of Pope John XXIII. It had meant nothing to him. Prison gossip must have supplied the Holy Father's original name, but he could not remember hearing it. The Vatican, after the death of Pope Pius XII, somehow, had ceased to exist for him.

As the jailer slid open the cell door, Luigi, who was now awake and lounging on the upper bunk waiting for breakfast call, snorted, "Well, maybe you're free. The Pope is king. He can do anything." Luigi had been arrested the year before for stealing tires off parked cars. His sentence was nearly up.

"Put this on." The Swiss Guard ignored Luigi and handed Matt a bundle wrapped in paper. Matt opened it. Inside was a black cassock.

"I've been defrocked," he objected.

"You can't go see the Holy Father like that," the guard said, motioning to Matt's prison clothes.

"We'll wait down the hall," the jailer said. They left and Matt noticed the jailer had neglected to close the door.

He took off his much-washed striped cotton jacket, then slipped on the cassock. A Roman collar had been provided in the right front pocket.

"Well, well," Luigi said, crossing himself. "Bless me, Father, for I have sinned."

Matt finished buttoning up the long black robe, then glanced in the small shaving mirror. It was a shock. Until now, he had purposely avoided looking at himself—as if he were in a monastery. The person he remembered wearing a cassock had a different face. Forty-six now. A long time incarcerated. January 7, 1948. The day he had been sentenced for grand theft by the highest court in Italy.

He peered at his face as if seeing it in its true reality for the first time. Thinner, gaunter. Deep lines along the sides of his mouth. All traces of boyishness gone completely. A man's face. His once-brown hair speckled now with gray, the hairline receding slightly. Yet it was not an aging face. On the contrary, he looked as if he had gained a new, subtle strength.

"Hey, *Matteo.*" Luigi had rolled over on his belly and was eyeing him. "You really a priest?"

"Used to be."

"Ha, ha!" Luigi cackled. "That's a good one. I heard stories about your famous robbery, but I didn't believe them! Ha, ha! Why didn't you tell me?"

Matt fastened the top button, securing his Roman collar. The thick-edged piece of starched linen dug into his neck. He had forgotten the feel of that. Were they making them wider nowadays?

"Say, *prete,*" Luigi said, "there's a whorehouse right over that white marble line outside the Vatican. It's on Via della Conciliazione, second story above the smaller piazza. You know it?"

Matt shook his head.

"Well, they got boys, girls, you know, and priests go there all the time. You get your hands on Raphaela, you're in luck! I hear she is so tiny . . . even priests think they have big cocks!" Luigi threw back his head and laughed.

"See you at dinner." Matt grinned.

"Yeah, sure!" Luigi shouted after him. "Don't you know all priests are princes in Rome? You're free, you idiot!"

He hesitated, freezing momentarily at the cell door. Was he really?

Too often he had heard rumors that Francis Cardinal Spellman was trying to get him moved to within the Vatican walls. Mankowsky had written about that, saying he was doing what he could to help. But nothing had ever come of it. Now, as he stood outside his cell, he forced down any hope. The reality, he reminded himself, is that you have another nine years to serve.

As he followed the Swiss Guard down row after row of cement cells toward the front entrance, he did not notice the anti-clerical tauntings of the prisoners, but instead allowed himself to dwell on the one thought that had kept him alive and yet nearly driven him insane these eleven years: that of seeing Luciana again!

He had received no letters from her. Through Jews here in Rome, he had tried to reach her. But he had always encountered dead ends. The kibbutz on which she had once taught did not know her whereabouts. Her friends who had survived on the ferry said they had lost track of her altogether. Luciana, his lover, had stubbornly remained a mystery to him. Was she dead? He denied that thought vehemently.

But how could she have just disappeared? Surely *someone* knew of her whereabouts.

After Mankowsky had returned from Israel, he had written Matt from the United States. Since, after Matt's conviction, warrants for arrest had been issued for Mankowsky, Luciana and Ivan Cohen, they were effectively banned from ever returning to Italy. So the gorilla, in long letters, had told as much as he could of what had happened after Matt left the ferry: how the ferry had been towed into Port de Bouc by the U.S.S. *Pittsburgh*. Once there, it had all looked hopeless. No money. No one allowed even to venture out of the French harbor to shore. Then, when despair had gripped the vessel, money, food and fuel had mysteriously arrived. Workmen had showed up to repair the ferry, and the Governor himself had come from Montpellier with the gift of a French registry and flag for the vessel. They were never told where the largesse had come from.

They set sail for Palestine, the ferry repaired, both its engines running soundly. But as soon as they had entered the Mediterranean, the *Jutland* and two other British ships had begun tracking them. When the ferry was still more than forty miles off the coast of Palestine, the British had begun ramming the two-tiered craft to sink her. Ivan had managed to keep her afloat, had got within a hundred yards of the beach off Haifa. Many people were killed. But more than two-thirds survived. And among them, Matt knew, was Luciana. Willie Mankowsky had seen to that.

Like the others, she had been herded to a detention camp surrounded by barbed wire and high fences. For many, Matt imagined, it must have been like returning to Belsen, Auschwitz or Buchenwald. But at least they could comfort themselves with the knowledge that they were in the Promised Land.

Upon returning to the Displaced Persons camp one afternoon after shopping for "goodies" to ease the pain of the refugees' internment, Mankowsky was surprised to find that all the prisoners had been removed. The British government refused to give him any information as to their whereabouts and shuffled him onto a freighter bound for the United States with Greek olives and sisal. On the way home, Mankowsky heard the first news of Zionist victories in the Jews' war of liberation. By the time he reached Miami, in April of 1948, rumor had it that there would indeed soon be a free state of Israel.

But in his letters, the gorilla could only attest that he had seen Luciana last in the DP compound and that she was well then. Matt knew that. He clung to it.

Willie wrote often still. But being an assistant pastor (he was never rewarded with the promised rank of monsignor) and helping out in a large parish in Schenectady, New York, he had little time to pursue her whereabouts. His last letter to Matt circumspectly mentioned the fact that "he might be better off to forget her."

Outside the main gate of Regina Coeli, the Swiss got into

the back seat of a parked black Mercedes. Matt ducked inside and the driver, a red-haired priest with a balding spot, swept the car into traffic.

The chauffeur brought them across nearby St. Peter's Square. A new mobile post office had been set up beneath Bernini's right colonnade. Other than that, it was exactly the way Matt had remembered it the day his trial began: December 28, 1947.

Parking to the right of the basilica, the priest stepped out and opened the door. Matt followed the Swiss Guard up the steps toward the double Bronze Doors with their customary six Swiss Guards. They were admitted without a glance.

The guard led the way to the right up the forbidden staircase of Pius IX, the one he had been tempted to take long ago to see Pope Pius. As he climbed, he remembered meeting Archbishop Angelo Roncalli there, the prelate who had served as his guide to Pius.

Following the Swiss through the twelve rooms of bodyguards, Matt watched them come to attention and click their heels as he passed. Here he was, a former priest with a sullied reputation, and he was being given the same honor as a cardinal. He felt his palms grow sweaty as he approached the Holy Father's quarters. Why had he been summoned?

A wizened Cardinal suddenly came out of the tall gold-leafed alabaster doors ahead. ''Ah,'' the Cardinal said to the guard while eyeing Matt curiously. ''His Holiness has been anxiously waiting for him. I think you can go right in. He's just with his secretary now.''

The guard bowed to the Cardinal, who started off back through the twelve rooms, then rapped politely on one of the white doors.

''Bene!'' a hearty voice boomed. ''It's open!''

Matt followed the guard inside. The room, once a library, had been stripped. Curtains, rugs, chairs, couch, desk had all gone. Only a stuffed, high-backed chair, facing the opposite wall, sat in the middle of the room. A young Monsignor was bent over it, receiving signatures from the one seated, that one hidden from Matt's eyes.

The guard waited until the secretary finished. When the young priest came toward them, he said to the guard, ''His Holiness wants to see him alone.'' Together, they exited.

When the door closed, Matt walked across the freshly varnished wooden floor, his old shoes squeaking.

"That's right, come here!" the voice coaxed. "Let me see you, Father Bowles."

A short, fat figure in white cassock and pectoral cross sprang up energetically from the chair and wheeled around.

Matt was facing his old guide, Archbishop Angelo Roncalli.

"It's only me," the Pope said. "Took them a lot of ballots and still they couldn't decide. So they compromised on me!" He laughed his old familiar laugh.

Matt dropped to his knee and took the Pontiff's hand. He kissed the ring of St. Peter.

"All right, enough of protocol," Pope John said. "I want to take my walk. And that's good for you, since there's only one chair in this room." He laughed and led the way to the door. "Come on, come on, I've only got a few minutes." He took Matt by the arm and literally pulled him from the room.

As it had happened so long ago, Matt accompanied Angelo Roncalli through the Apostolic Palace. But now, his guide was Pontiff of five hundred million souls. Perhaps the most powerful man in the world.

"Interior decorators!" he was jabbering as he led the way toward a small glass elevator. "Wallpaper, paint, rugs, artwork from the Vatican museums. It's too much for my simple peasant head. Too much. I took a walk through the museums, like the one we took eleven years ago, and you know what?"

Matt shook his head as the Holy Father punched a button in the elevator car.

"Well, there were just too many choices. I mean, all of the great artists in the world—" He pointed through the glass panel at the U-shaped Vatican museum buildings below them as they descended. "I just couldn't decide. So, you know what I did? I'm having a new masterpiece hung in my study every month, one artist at a time, to see which I like best!" He roared with laughter.

The hydraulic elevator bounced to a stop on the bottom level and the doors opened. The Holy Father hurried off, pushed through a steel door and led Matt outside to the private Cortile del Maresciallo, courtyard of the popes.

They threaded their way through the adjoining courtyards of the Pappagalli, Borgia, and Sentinella and finally out onto the Piazza del Forno, the Square of the Oven. Then they began the familiar climb up the steps of the Salita della Zecca. The Casina of Pius IV, to the right and below, once home for the Vatican bank, nestled amidst its fir trees, surrounded by its spacious lawns. Matt saw Luciana running . . . Ruffino carrying out a smoking wastebasket. . . .

"Ah, good air, good!" the Pontiff spoke up now. "Take deep breaths, Father. I imagine that prison air was not healthy. Fill your lungs!"

Several gardeners dropped to their knees as they passed. Behind and below them, Matt spotted a half dozen Swiss watching from the rear of the basilica lest any danger present itself to the Pontiff's person. At the top of Vatican Hill, near the replica of the Grotto of Lourdes, crutches lining its cave, the Holy Father sat down heavily on a nearby marble bench. Even though the day was cool, he was perspiring.

"Sit, Father, sit. Now, tell me, or should I say, tell *us*. The Pope is plural. We have to learn that." He patted the bench beside him. "Tell us how you feel, what you want to do now."

"Do, Holiness?" Matt asked, remaining standing. "My plans, I'm afraid, are governed by Regina Coeli."

"What an irony to have named that prison after the Queen of Heaven," the Pope commented. "Ah, well. But you are speaking of serving the remainder of your term, Father?"

"Yes, Holiness."

"Your term is over. You are free to go anytime you want."

Overwhelmed, Matt was speechless. "I . . . don't have to . . . ?"

"Not unless you *wish* to stay in that wretched place." The Pontiff smiled.

"No, I certainly don't *wish* to!"

"All right, then tell us what you do want to do now."

"I have to go to Israel, Holiness. There is someone I must search for."

"Yes, yes," John rubbed his large, hooked nose. "The woman, Luciana Spoleto. Your accomplice. We've heard all about her. You and she are still the gossip around here."

"Holiness, I don't even know if she's alive."

"She is."

With those two words, Pope John XXIII erased eleven

years of tormented doubt. Night upon night of troubled sleep, days of maddening, imagined catastrophes. Now, Matt felt as though a balm of oil had been spread over the turbulent waters of his heart. But almost immediately a new fear gripped him. Why hadn't she told him herself? Had she married? Was she disfigured, ashamed?

The Pope reached into his white soutane, withdrew a small envelope and handed it to him. "This came from Father Mankowsky. He wanted you to have it only after you were released. I, we that is, agreed to pass it on to you, since we feel you must decide whether to remain a priest."

"But Holiness," Matt stared longingly at the envelope he held. "I was defrocked by Pius. I'm no longer a priest."

"Popes can do and undo," John said sternly. "And if you wish to return to us, we will reinstate you. We wish you to work here in the Vatican."

"Here? Doing what, Holiness? I'm not cut out to be an administrator or diplomat."

"We have ample proof of that." John grinned. "And we've heard from Cardinal Spellman that you're not much good at parish work, either. Nor do we think you would fit in a monastery. But we have the perfect job for you. I, we that is, need a bodyguard. We intend to go to a lot of countries no Pope has ever gone to before."

A group of sparrows flew down and alighted in the pine tree above the Holy Father. They began chattering as they fought over the seeds protruding from a ripened cone.

"Holiness," Matt said finally over their sound, "I thank you for this." He waved the envelope slightly. "But I can't promise I'll resume being a priest."

"Are you bitter against Pius, my son? Do you feel that by his omission he forced you to steal that money? That except for him, you would still be a priest and none of this would have happened?"

"I don't know, Holiness. At times, I feel very angry. Sometimes, I think it took the decision out of my hands whether to stay a priest or not."

"No matter what you do, *Matteo*," Pope John whispered, "you must forgive Pius and the Church. If you are to be whole finally, you must rid yourself of that hate. Otherwise, no growth is possible for your soul. You must see how your own deficiencies contributed to the times you have had. You committed crimes against your Church and the Italian state. And for those you deserved to be punished. But we understand why you did what you did, and we do not want to see the rest of your life ruined because you felt forced to ameliorate a situation we could not. Forget your bitterness, *Matteo*, and start thinking of your life in the future."

"I'll try, Holy Father," Matt said. "I promise I will."

"Good, like yourself, the Church is making new beginnings. Its windows are being flung open to let the stale air escape, the fresh air inside. We are going back into the *business*"—he winked at Matt—"of saving souls."

The Pontiff reached out with a chubby hand, grasped Matt's and said, "Go now. Do what you have to. We have barely five minutes before we must see more cardinals and sign more papers. And we need to pray." He squeezed Matt's hand, let him go, then closed his eyes and bowed his head.

But as Matt started down, Pope John called out, "Oh, Father? When you see Luciana, tell her we admire her greatly. She is a Judith to her people, a credit to our faith. But," he added, "I pray you'll come back to us!"

"You talk like you know Luciana, Holiness." Matt raised his voice slightly to be heard.

"Only on the phone," Pope John replied, smiling. "She managed to call me once from Port de Bouc, the place your ferry docked."

Matt wanted to ask him more about their telephone conversation, but the Holy Father had lowered his head again and was praying.

At the bottom of Vatican Hill, he approached a Swiss Guard.

"Pardon me," Matt asked him, "do you know where Pope John was stationed before he became Pontiff?"

"What?" The guard recoiled at the unusual question. "Why, Venice, of course. San Marco Cathedral."

"And before that, say 1947?"

The guard shrugged. Another came close, expertly hand-rolling a cigarette. He licked the paper to finish it and put it unlit in his mouth. "I know where Roncalli was then," he said. "He served as Apostolic Nuncio to France. He was in Paris, I think."

Matt looked up the hill. High above him the Grotto of Lourdes framed Pope John XXIII hunched over in communication with God. So, Matt thought, it was he who gave the necessary money, food and gas to send the ferry on its way. Angelo Roncalli, the newly elected peasant Pope with both feet on the earth and a heart that responded without heed of Caesar's world.

Maybe, just maybe, the Church *was* changing. Maybe it would no longer be a solitary fortress, home of the largest fortune in the world, an island floating unattached to the rest of mankind. And if times were changing, maybe he could be part of it.

Maybe . . .

He turned away. As he walked briskly toward the Arco delle Campane gate, he opened the envelope and unfolded the stiff piece of stationery that was inside. His heart began to beat wildly. In a neat hand, the note said:

> Please arrive St. Francis
> Memorial Hospital, Jerusalem,
> November 3, 1958,
> 6:00 P.M.

The note was unsigned.

29.

Travel to Medinat, Israel was limited. Even though the tiny
country had proclaimed itself independent in May of 1948, it
had since been fighting the surrounding, dominant Arabs.
Israel had finished its last war in 1956. Now, another loomed
on the horizon. But surprisingly it had been easy for Matt to
gain a visa. The return telegram from Israel's Office for
Foreign Affairs had welcomed him enthusiastically.

Now, from inside the modern TWA tri-tail Constellation,
he could see row after row of date palms line the streets of Or
Yehud, two miles distant as they landed. It looked peaceful.
But on many street corners, antiaircraft guns pointed menac-
ingly skyward. And there were soldiers atop the brown stucco
walls of the airport terminal.

He was in civilian clothing, brown-plaid thin cotton shirt,
dark brown slacks and maroon corduroy jacket, and there was
no reason for him to receive special privileges. But at customs,
instead of having the contents of his single bag unceremoniously dumped onto a metal counter, as were those of the
others, two keen-eyed Israeli officials waved him through.

Outside, in the heavy heat of the desert, he located a taxi
driver who was willing to take him the additional twenty-five
miles to Jerusalem.

By the time the wheezing and overheated taxi lumbered

into the outskirts of Jerusalem, the sun had nearly set. In the distance, the Negev Desert and the closer expanse of the Wilderness of Judah glowed brightly, their luminous sands silhouetting the holy city. The curfew, as the driver told Matt, would begin shortly, at sundown. Anyone caught on the streets would be shot.

The taxi slowed and stopped in front of a stark white three-story structure.

Matt paid him in pounds he had bought at the airport and pulled his suitcase from the car. As the taxi U-turned in the narrow street, Matt heard gunfire erupt from within the nearby elevated, walled city. Fighting was going on between Palestinians and Israelis for the control of those streets David, Elijah, Muhammad and Jesus had walked.

Following the sidewalk through the sand, he entered and set his case down in the cool, air-conditioned foyer. It was quiet here. He could not hear the gunfire now. But why was he meeting Luciana at a hospital?

"May I help you, sir?" a young nun tentatively asked from back of the receiving counter.

"I'm looking for Luciana Spoleto."

"Oh, you must be Matthew Bowles. We have been expecting you." The nun brightened. "Come with me, please." She led the way down a beige, linoleum-tiled corridor. Several nuns stared at him as he passed as though they knew him. One waved.

The young nun opened a blond-stained wooden door with PERSONNEL ONLY on it. Matt hesitated. Was Luciana inside as a sister, white-cowled, immaculately starched, crucifix at her side?

"Please go in," the nun invited.

Taking a deep breath, Matt stepped inside. The gorilla, his six-foot-nine-inch frame slouched against the desk, stood up. He was dressed in a black suit and collar.

"Hi, Matthew," he said when the door had closed. He enfolded his startled friend in his big arms.

"What . . . are you doing here?"

"You mean in the hospital, or in Israel?"

"Both!"

"Well, I've been two, three times on pilgrimages to the holy city. Luciana works here. I visit her whenever I come."

"Then all this time you knew she was here!" Matt was dumbfounded. "Why didn't you tell me?"

"She wouldn't allow me to, Matthew!"

His face clouded. "Why, Willie?"

"I'm sorry, Matthew, but this is the way she wanted it. She felt you had to make up your own mind about being a priest. She didn't want to interfere in any way."

"Interfere!" Matt shouted. He was angry now. "All these years, gorilla! She should have written me!"

For the first time, Willie Mankowsky allowed his inner strain to show. "What are you going to do, Matthew? Cardinal Strauss says Pope John has a job for you."

"I don't know yet. But it was good of His Holiness to want to hire a thief."

"I hear through the grapevine he chose you so everyone will remember what you did. He's proud of your motive, Matthew, if not of your method. He'd like you to stay with us."

"It's tempting." Then he faltered. "I'll know when I see Luciana."

"Sure you will," the gorilla said. "I sure missed you, Matthew!"

Matt smiled suddenly and pressed two fingers on his forehead. They fell into one another's arms, laughing.

"Gorilla," Matt begged, "tell me one thing."

"Anything," Mankowsky said, pulling away at the sudden seriousness.

"Is Luciana a nun?"

The gorilla smiled mysteriously and opened the door of the room. "What do you think?"

They were riding in a military jeep, compliments of the United States. Passing through the walled city filled with crowded downtown bazaars, the shopping Jews and Arabs patrolled vigorously by Israeli soldiers, Matt saw a lot of U.S. military hardware: rifles, pistols, boots, fatigues and occasional machine guns. Since the British had left Palestine, the United States' presence was very evident there.

Just outside the fabled Damascus Gate, the gorilla turned onto Suleiman Road, then Nablus Road and north toward a newly built section. The soft white light from the desert was in their eyes as they sped past the church and convent of St. Stephen, then the British Consulate. Matt's heart ached and his stomach turned over queasily into a tight knot.

If he asked the gorilla again point-blank whether she was a nun, maybe he would get an answer. But now he was afraid to know.

"Almost there," the gorilla said, as if he felt Matt's tension. They bore through the approaching darkness, the jeep's headlights bouncing crazily on the asphalt road. "I hope they're still waiting. Your plane was late, you know. I would have met you, but I was making the Stations of the Cross, the real ones, inside Jerusalem. There was a cease-fire for eight hours, and I took advantage of it. You don't get that chance often, Matthew."

Matt thought about the Via Dolorosa Willie had visited that afternoon. The Sorrowful Way where Jesus had carried His cross, met His mother, was stripped of His garments, was nailed to the cross and died. Golgotha. It was all here. Even the Garden of Gethsemane and the sepulcher in which He rested. As when he had just come to Rome, Matt felt he had come home.

Jerusalem. It would be wonderful to stay. Make a retreat, perhaps. Let the history of this holy city seep into his soul. Revive himself as a priest, then go back to Rome. It was possible! For the first time in years, he felt it so.

The gorilla braked in front of a sparkling-white L-shaped building. The sign out front advised that anyone who did not have emergency business in the American Consulate should park elsewhere. A hundred yards off, next door to the consulate, was a monstrous-sized YMCA, built for Americans. Kids were swimming in its outdoor olympic-size pool.

The gorilla swung out of the jeep and started across the salt-and-pepper gravel driveway. "We'd better hurry. Israelis are punctual. If we're too late, they might go home."

"Willie!" Matt said, stepping out of the jeep and standing his ground. "I have to know. What *is* going on?"

"Come on, Matthew," he said, trudging across the gravel.

Marine Honor Guards in polished helmets, waiting on the front portico, opened the doors and they went inside.

"Father Matthew! I'd know you anywhere!" A chubby man in a pin-striped morning suit jacked his hand. "I'm

Felworth Curtsy, our Ambassador to Israel. Follow me, please."
He spun and stepped lightly up a wide staircase.

As they gained the landing, Matt became aware of applause
starting up. It came from a double doorway. The Ambassador
and the gorilla stopped. He looked inside and saw the room
was filled with people.

"They're the refugees you helped!" Mankowsky told Matt.

A band up front struck up *"Hatikvah,"* "The Hope,"
Israel's national anthem. Everyone began singing. As Matt
walked down the aisle, men and women grabbed his hands
and kissed them.

"I was only six," a teenager shouted. "But I remember
you!"

"God bless you!" a woman wept.

"Hello, Father." Klaus, on crutches, waved.

Rabbi Meister was wheeled out in a chair. The old man raised
an arthritically deformed hand, laid it momentarily on Matt's
arm, then embraced him. Matt felt his eyes sting.

Ivan Cohen, peering tearfully through his thick lenses, stepped
forth. Two rosy-cheeked children clung to his legs, a timid
wife on his arm. He hugged Matt but could not speak, since
he was so choked up. He kept trying to say the speech he had
practiced so carefully, but, overcome by emotion, he could
only weep huge, happy tears and squeeze out his message
with his arms.

"Do you remember Marie Schollander?" a woman's voice
yelled over the continued applause. Matt received her kiss.
He remembered how old she had looked. Now, miraculously,
she had actually grown younger.

As Matt emerged at the front of the hall, the band finished.
A bald-pated man with a fringe of curly white hair that
bobbed merrily as he moved shook his hand.

"I am David Ben-Gurion," he introduced himself. He was
dressed, as a great many in the hall were, in a short-sleeved
white shirt, open at the neck, worn outside loose-fitting
trousers.

The crowd quieted in anticipation. Children were raised
onto their father's shoulders so they could see what was
happening at the front of the auditorium. The band respectfully held their instruments in readiness.

"We are gathered here," Ben-Gurion said, "to honor a

man who helped us greatly. He did so at great cost to himself. Now, we don't have a lot of time these days for ceremony. We're fighting our enemies, growing crops and doing business to establish ourselves. But for a little while, even the Knesset can wait for me. We shall dance the hora and rejoice!''

He turned and an Israeli soldier carried forward a small velvet box. Matt took that opportunity to scan the crowd for Luciana. He could not see her. But he did see more nuns from St. Francis Hospital. They were standing up front near the band.

''To you, Matthew Bowles,'' David Ben-Gurion announced, ''we humbly present our highest decoration, 'Hero of Israel.' It is normally awarded to soldiers who perform courageous acts in combat. Congratulations!''

The Prime Minister lifted a red ribbon from the box. A medallion in the form of a star hung pendulously from its bottom. A shout went up from Ivan Cohen, and the crowd burst into thunderous applause as Ben-Gurion pinned it carefully to Matt's chest. Matt stood stiffly, receiving it, his eyes wandering toward the nuns. He had identified three of them, but the fourth was standing back where he could not see her face.

Ambassador Felworth Curtsy looked toward the band. The bandleader lifted his baton to begin, but someone cried out, ''There's one more thing!''

The Ambassador spun, surprised. The bandleader looked confused. The crowd parted and out stepped Luciana Spoleto.

Her blond hair was shorter than Matt remembered, her figure in a mauve cotton dress fuller. She stood with her chin out, avoiding his eyes.

''One more honor,'' she announced, turning to the gorilla, who reached inside his clerical coat and handed her a red, white and blue leather box. Luciana opened it and inside it lay Matt's round, thick gold Medal of Honor.

''Father Mankowsky told me about this award long ago. He brought it over with him.'' She pulled the blue silk ribbon from its case. The medal gleamed as though no time had passed.

''This highest award of the United States was given to Matthew Bowles in 1945. During the war, he was a chaplain in the Army. He fought for what he believed in. He risked his

life to save the lives of many. Until now he has refused to
wear it.''

She walked past the refugees and came close to Matt.
Standing on her tiptoes, she hung the light blue silk ribbon
with the embroidered thirteen white stars around his neck.
Many began weeping openly.

"Luciana . . ." he faltered. So often he had dreamed of
this moment.

There were tears threatening at the corners of her eyes.
"*Matteo*," she said. "When the gorilla told me what you had
done . . . I knew you did what you believed in. You did it
again for me . . . for us."

The band started up. Behind Matt and Luciana, the dancers
began forming their famous circle, joining hands.

"Luciana, I . . ." he began.

"No, *caro*, let me finish. There are others out there who
need you. I realized this even on the ferry. That is the real
reason why I never wrote. I can't take you away from those
things you will do or the people who need you more than I."

The people were a blur behind her. They were wheeling in
their huge circle, the band thumping gaily.

"I love you," he said.

"I you, forever!"

Ivan Cohen grabbed hold of Matt and pulled him into the
circle. Father Mankowsky took hold of Luciana's left hand as
she reached out and grabbed Matt's free one. The circle was
complete. It began to pick up speed. The simple cement walls
rang with the joyous sounds of the hora.

Luciana was crying, squeezing his hand, looking up be-
seechingly for him to understand. And suddenly he grinned at
her that he did. They would be apart, but they would always
belong together. And the tug of the circle held strong and true
as it would for the rest of their lives.

LUCIANO'S LUCK

1943. Under cover of night, a strange group parachutes into Nazi occupied Sicily. It includes the overlord of the American Mafia, "Lucky" Luciano. The object? To convince the Sicilian Mafia king to put his power—the power of the Sicilian peasantry—behind the invading American forces. It is a dangerous gamble. If they fail, hundreds of thousands will die on Sicilian soil. If they succeed, American troops will march through Sicily toward a stunning victory on the Italian Front, forever indebted to Mafia king, Lucky Luciano.

A DELL BOOK   14321-7 $3.50

JACK HIGGINS

bestselling author of *Solo*

Dell Bestsellers

- [ ] **QUINN** by Sally Mandel **$3.50** (17176-8)
- [ ] **STILL THE MIGHTY WATERS**
  by Janice Young Brooks **$3.95** (17630-1)
- [ ] **NORTH AND SOUTH** by John Jakes **$4.95** (16204-1)
- [ ] **THE SEEDS OF SINGING**
  by Kay McGrath **$3.95** (19120-3)
- [ ] **GO SLOWLY, COME BACK QUICKLY**
  by David Niven **$3.95** (13113-8)
- [ ] **SEIZE THE DAWN** by Vanessa Royal **$3.50** (17788-X)
- [ ] **PALOMINO** by Danielle Steel **$3.50** (16753-1)
- [ ] **BETTE: THE LIFE OF BETTE DAVIS**
  by Charles Higham **$3.95** (10662-1)